The
Thunderfoot
Series

Dan Bomkamp

Lovstad Publishing
www.Lovstadpublishing.com

ISBN: 0692533281
ISBN-13: 978-0692533284

Printed in the United States of America

Cover design by Lovstad Publishing

DEDICATION

This book is dedicated to my Dad. He instilled in me at a very early age, a love of the outdoors. Our time together was much too short, but in that time, I learned more from him than many sons learn in a lifetime.

The Thunderfoot Series

The Adventures of Thunderfoot

Thunderfoot

Sometimes you know right away when you meet a person that you're going to like them. This kid was one of those who I liked as soon as he said hello. He came through the door of my sport shop as I was sitting behind the counter working on some invoices. A younger, smaller version of himself was following along behind him as he smiled and strolled up to the counter.

"Hi," he said, sticking his hand out, "My name is James, and this is my brother Caleb, like in the Bible."

"Hi James," I said, shaking hands with him, and "Hi Caleb." Caleb was a little shy but James wasn't in the least.

"My mom and Caleb and I just moved in over there," he said as he pointed down the street. "So, I guess I'm your new neighbor."

"Well, welcome to the neighborhood, what can I do for you?" I asked.

"Oh nothing. We're just going to look if that's all right."

"No problem, look all you want," I said.

He and Caleb began looking over the rods and reels, and I heard him advise Caleb not to touch stuff as they walked up and down the aisles. He was about 12 or 13, fairly tall, but pretty skinny. He was at that age where he was on the edge of a growth spurt. His hair was light brown and he had the brightest blue eyes I'd ever seen. When he smiled they seemed to sparkle. Caleb was eight or nine and quite a bit shorter, but you could tell right away that they were brothers.

After a while James came over to the counter and dug a quarter out of his pocket for a beef jerky. He tore it in half and shared it with Caleb.

"Well, we better be getting home. Thanks for letting us look around."

"You're welcome any time," I told him, and out the door they went.

The next day I heard someone shouting, "Go Rennie! Go Rennie!" I opened the door and stepped out to see James on a skateboard being pulled down the street by a huge red Doberman. I waved to him and he gave me a wave back as he lurched down the street. I went back inside and soon I heard him yelling, "Stop Rennie Stop!" A minute later he came in though the front door.

"Do you want to meet my dog?" he asked.

I had always had a little hesitancy with Dobermans. "Is he friendly?"

"Oh yeah, he's a real baby...he's not mean at all."

I walked out and met Renegade who was as mild mannered as a kitten.

"He likes to pull me on my skateboard but sometimes I have a hard time to get him to stop," James said.

He was quite a dog. James and I stood and talked a while and he told me that he had just completed the Hunter's Safety class. "I hope I can go hunting sometime," he said. "My grandpa might take me. My dad lives in another town, and I don't think he'll be able to take me."

"You know," I said, "I've got a friend who has lots of squirrels on his farm and he told me I was welcome to hunt there any time I liked. How about you and I go on Saturday?"

James thought that was a great idea, and he went to see if his mom would agree. A short time later he came back with a yes from his mom and a .22 rifle that his grandpa had given him. I outfitted him with an old hunting jacket that didn't fit me anymore and some old pants that were in the same situation. We had to roll up the cuffs on the jacket and the pants cuffs but they worked ok. I had a hat that was a little too large but it too would work. Footwear wasn't a problem since his feet were nearly as big as mine. Some of my extra hunting boots worked just fine for him.

When Saturday came, we drove to my friend's farm and parked the truck. Soon we were walking up the ridge road to the top of the hill. We had only gone a few yards when he dislodged a rock that rolled down the hill, clattering all the way. A few yards farther along he tripped and fell down. We didn't go much farther when he stepped on a dead branch that broke and made a loud crack.

I slowed up a little and watched him as he proceeded up the hill ahead of me. He was in a semi-crouch, like he was sneaking up on an enemy bunker. He was watching up the hill and not watching where his feet were going.

"Hey Thunderfoot," I said, "Maybe you should watch where you're putting your feet so you won't chase away all the squirrels."

"Thunderfoot?" he asked with a grin.

"Yeah...you make as much noise as thunder when you walk. Try to sneak and avoid all the things that make noise when you walk."

"Okay," he said grinning widely.

We continued up the hill and suddenly an apparently deaf squirrel came bounding off the bank and onto the road. The squirrel saw us just as Thunderfoot saw it and off they went down over the side of the hill. Thunderfoot was scrambling through the brush as the squirrel shinnied up a tree.

The hillside was nearly vertical, and I'm one of those guys who would rather stay on top of the hill once I've made it to the top, so I wasn't too happy about working my way down to where Thunderfoot was looking up into the treetops.

"I see him," Thunderfoot said.

He aimed his rifle and shot. I saw the squirrel as it hopped over to my side of the tree. I wanted him to shoot it, so I moved and the squirrel hopped back to his side.

Bang! The squirrel came back to my side. I moved again and back it went to his side. *Bang!* Back the squirrel came to my side. I moved again and tried to get back a little farther so I could see him better. Suddenly I slipped and started down the hillside backwards at a very rapid rate stopping only when I ran backwards into an old barbed-wire fence that was hidden in a grove of prickly ash. I hit the fence and went over it backwards. My head and shoulders smacked on the ground and my gun flew from my hands. My legs and feet were hanging on the fence.

The squirrel must have thought there had been an earthquake because he took off through the top of the trees hopping from limb to limb. Thunderfoot took off in hot pursuit shooting every so often and he and the squirrel got farther and farther away. After a while the shooting stopped and everything got very quiet.

I decided I it would be a good idea to get off the fence, but my pants were solidly hooked in the barbs and I couldn't free them. My only option was to take off my pants, so I undid my belt and slid out of them, leaving them on the fence. I was standing there in the middle of the prickly ash grove trying to retrieve my pants when Thunderfoot came huffing and puffing over the top of the hill.

He stopped short when he was me standing there in my underwear. "What'cha doin?" he asked.

"I'm trying to get my pants out of the fence," I said. I finally freed them and put them back on. Then I looked around for my gun and saw it was way down in the middle of the prickly ash so I waded in and got it, tearing many gashes in my hide. I finally hauled y battered body up the hill and onto the road.

"I'm out of bullets," Thunderfoot said. "Jeez, that must hurt."

He was looking at about a dozen punctures in my body. He stepped around behind me and his eyes got wide when he saw the hind end of my pants all ripped out.

"I think I'll live," I said, "but I think I've had enough hunting for today."

He nodded knowingly. "You know," he said, "next time I think I'll bring my .410 shotgun...my rifle doesn't shoot very straight."

We walked down the hill to the truck and when we got there I got out a first aid kit from the glove box and dabbed iodine on my cuts and scrapes. "I hope you're not disappointed that we're quitting," I said. "I'm about finished for the day."

"Oh no, that's ok. I had a lot of fun." He tried to look serious but then he burst out laughing. "That was so cool when you went over the fence...boom!"

His laughter was infectious and soon we both were laughing like crazy, tears running down our faces. "That poor squirrel must have thought it was the end of the world when I crashed through that hillside." We laughed even harder.

Soon we started back to town and Thunderfoot sat quietly in the truck for a while. Then he turned with his big blue eyes sparkling and said, "This was a real good day. I got to go hunting....saw some really funny stuff, and got a new nickname. Thunderfoot. I like it."

It had been a good day, and I had a new hunting buddy.

Thanks, Thunderfoot.

The Great Duck Excursion

We looked like a remnant of the *Lost Battalion* as our convoy of four pickups wound slowly down the sand trail to the site of our hunting camp on the high bank of the duck marsh. In addition to two adults, and two semi-adults, we had five teenagers and five golden retrievers with us on our annual pilgrimage for opening day.

Earlier that morning at 6:15 a.m. Thunderfoot had begun banging on my front door. When I got there he was standing in the middle of a mound of gear that could have sustained an excursion to the North Pole. We had made plans to leave that morning at nine a.m., so I wasn't even close to being ready to go...or to get up from bed yet.

"I thought I should get here a little early so we can load the truck," he said.

"A little early? We're not leaving until nine."

"I didn't want to oversleep so I set my alarm for five a.m.," he said smiling like it was the obvious thing to do under the circumstances.

"Yeah, it's almost 6:30. You better start loading," I said sleepily. I turned to go back to the bedroom to get dressed. "Load my stuff while you're at it," I said, since my gear was already piled on the porch. My three golden retrievers saw the guns and boots and camouflage clothes and went nuts, galloping around the house barking while Thunderfoot encouraged them.

"Yeah, that's it girls. Today is the day!" he said, and the dogs got even more excited.

Obviously my idea of taking a short nap was not going to happen, so I got ready for the day.

A few minutes later I heard the whole gang in the house. I found Thunderfoot in the kitchen looking into the refrigerator. "I thought you were going to load the truck," I said.

"I did...what's for breakfast? I hope the others aren't late."

One of my friends and his two teenaged sons, along with their golden retriever, Abby, pulled into the driveway a while later at just the appointed time. Then our two semi-adults arrived, they were former teens who hunted with us, but who had now come to the age where we could trust them alone. We could even trust them with the care of a real teenager and his golden retriever Alex.

Abby and Alex were the brother and sister of my youngest golden, Sophie. She was running excitedly back and forth to the truck with her mom Sally, and her grandma, Bea. It was kind of a family thing.

Next, Thunderfoot's two best buddies arrived. They flew in on their bikes, baskets loaded to the brim with gear and food and the group was complete.

We arrived at our campsite a short time later and began unpacking the trucks and setting up our camp. It didn't take long with so many workers. In a short time we had a fire pit dug, four tents pitched, our gear sorted out into the assigned tents, and a famished bunch of kids and dogs waiting for a pre-hunt lunch. Funny, it seemed that I had just fed Thunderfoot an hour or so ago, but he was starving as were the bottomless pits he called friends.

Soon it was an hour until the noon opening time for the season, so everyone began getting into their hunting gear. Camo clothing flew, boots were tugged on, and shells and guns were unpacked and distributed while a frenzied pack of dogs galloped around urging their masters to hurry up. Finally everyone was assigned to his blind and dog, and we took off for the swamp.

Thunderfoot and I took Bea and Sophie with us to a blind on the "Grassy Puddle", while Sally went with another group. The rest split up on other ponds in the marsh. We put our decoys on the water and got our blind in shape, then settled the dogs down while we waited for noon to come.

With fifteen minutes to go, the sky began to fill with ducks spooked by other hunters who were getting into their spots elsewhere in the marsh. "Cool, there's millions of them," Thunderfoot said, watching the flocks of birds come and go from every direction.

We waited. Ten minutes to go. Five minutes to go. Two minutes...one minute. The noon siren from town sounded and the season was officially open. One of our other groups fired a couple of shots and as we turned to look we saw a couple of teal coming our way. They were like little gray and blue missiles skimming just above the grass...coming right at us.

"Get ready...here they come," I said. I got my gun ready and when they were in range I said, "Now!" I stood and shot the lead duck. It dropped into the pond and Bea jumped into the water to fetch it. Thunderfoot just stood there looking dumbstruck.

"Why didn't you shoot?" I asked.

"Do they always go that fast? Holy cow...I didn't think they went that fast. I wasn't ready."

"You have to be quick. They aren't just going to flutter around out there and wait for you to shoot them," I said as Bea came into the blind with the teal. I put the duck away and we sat down to wait for another target. In a couple of minutes a lone wood duck started toward our decoys from the other end of the pond.

"Here he comes," I said quietly. "Get ready and take him...I'm not going to shoot."

Thunderfoot got into position, jumped to his feet, and fired one shot at the duck. His shot nailed one of the decoys about three feet behind the wood duck as it passed in front of the blind. The decoy made a large splash as the steel shot hit it, then turned on its side and began sinking in a flurry of bubbles. Bea looked over her shoulder at me and then at Thunderfoot.

"Wow, I got him!"

Thunderfoot was watching the decoy sink but then looked around as the blind began shaking. He looked up at me and saw I was laughing so hard that I was making the entire blind vibrate, so hard that it might fall down.

"Jeez, get a grip... it's not that funny," he said when he realized what he had done.

I finally came back to my senses and while we waited for some more ducks, I reminded him that shooting at a moving bird involved leading it.

We hunted the rest of the day and I got another duck but Thunderfoot failed to connect. We sat in the blind until the time had come for the days shooting to stop and then I went out and picked up the decoys. When I got back to the blind I saw Thunderfoot looking to the west at the reddish glow of the sun as it dropped below the horizon. As we watched, a flock of ducks settled into a pond a short distance away, just as the last rays of daylight disappeared.

"Wow, that was pretty," he said.

"That's what I told you about duck hunting," I said. "Or any hunting for that matter isn't about how many you kill. It's a lot more than that. It's about being in such a beautiful place with people who you enjoy being with. It's about seeing stuff like that sunset."

We hiked up the marsh toward the glow of the campfire. Some of the others were already back and were beginning supper. "I suppose you'll feel the need to tell the others that I shot a decoy," Thunderfoot said.

I grinned at him. "It would be a pretty good story, but I guess it's not necessary. Maybe it will be our little secret."

I could see his smile in the dim light as he put his arm around my neck and gave me a squeeze. "Ok buddy," he said.

"Ok buddy."

Thanks, Thunderfoot.

The Big Gun

There was just enough light from the stars for us to see where we were going. Thunderfoot and I were crunching across the frozen pasture to a goose blind near Horicon Marsh. Our little duck hunting group had arranged to rent some blinds and had left home very early to get to the farm before first light. The farmer was waiting for us when we pulled into his yard. He took us to the edge of the field and pointed us in the general direction of the blinds to which we were assigned.

The blinds were pretty crude, consisting of two sheets of 4' x 8' plywood and two sheets of 4' x 4' plywood joined in the corners by steel fence posts that were driven into the ground. A couple of holes were drilled in the corners of each plywood sheet and strung with wire that held the sheets to the posts. Inside each blind there was a wooden bench and about a thousand empty shotgun shells, a hundred empty pop cans and assorted candy bar wrappers, and other leftovers from previous hunter's lunches.

We had stopped earlier at an enterprising diner in town that catered to the goose hunting crowd by opening at 3 a.m. We filled our sleepy group with pancakes and eggs before we got to the farm, hoping that our teenagers would be able to last until at least noon on the sandwiches and snacks we had brought with us.

I was carrying two guns and the ammo bag, and Thunderfoot was carrying his gun and the lunch. As we crunched along we soon began to pick out the shapes of the blinds. Soon we came to ours which was right along the edge of the field at the fence.

"Is this it?" Thunderfoot asked.

"Yeah...I think so," I said.

"Cool, it's like a little fort."

We unwired the corner of the blind and climbed inside. After we cleared the middle of the floor of empties and trash we began to unpack our gear. I got my 12-guage pump gun out, loaded it and stood it in the corner against the side of the blind. Then I slid my 10-guage single shot out of the case and loaded it with one of the 3 ½ inch magnum shells. Thunderfoot's mouth dropped open when he saw the gun and the huge shell.

"What's that thing?"

"That's my 10-guage. I thought I'd bring it along in case the geese begin flying too high. It will give us a little more range."

"Can I shoot it?" he asked.

"Well, we'll see. Let's shoot our 12-guages for a while and then maybe later you can try it." I wasn't sure about him shooting the big gun in the first place. For one thing it weighed eleven pounds and was hard to lift and shoot even for a big guy. It also had the kick of an angry mule and I didn't know if his scrawny little shoulder would handle it.

I hoped he'd just let it go and not think about it again.

We got our lunch out and our extra shells and made everything ready for the geese to start flying. Soon we could see the eastern sky begin to turn from black to a dark blue as dawn approached. The blue turned to gray and then things began to have shape. The formerly featureless pasture came into view. We could see the other blinds where our hunting buddies were waiting like we were for the first geese to come from the marsh and begin their trip to the surrounding fields for their breakfast.

The wind was right out of the north and had a distinct bite to it. Fortunately our backs were to the wind but it didn't take long for us to get chilled. We watched and listened and in a short time we could hear the gabbling of the geese as they awoke from their night on the marsh below us. Then the gabbling became honking and the first wave of two or three thousand geese rose into the air like a swirling cloud and began drifting toward the edge of the marsh....coming our way.

Thunderfoot was gripping his gun so hard that his knuckles were white. As the geese began to drift our way his eyes got as big as saucers. "Holy cow, there's a million of them....here they come."

But, instead of coming over us, the geese drifted to our right and a blind with some of our hunting partners began shooting at them. One goose fell from the clouds and the honking became almost deafening. There was more shooting as the geese moved on and then one of

Thunderfoot's buddies raced from the blind and proudly retrieved his goose. He held it up to show us and we signaled a thumbs-up to him.

For the next hour geese came constantly from the marsh. Some flocks were just a dozen or so while others held hundreds or maybe a thousand. It was amazing to see so many geese to say the least. Every time some came near, we would shoot. Thunderfoot would spring up and empty his gun every time. He never shot once or twice, but used all three shells every time. We were finishing our third box of shells and still didn't have a goose in the blind.

"Maybe we should try the big gun," he said.

I didn't answer him.

"I bet that big gun would get one."

I pretended that I didn't hear him.

"You know…that big…"

"Ok, I heard you. Go ahead and try it, but remember it'll kick hard so be ready for it."

He had a grin from ear to ear as he hoisted the goose blaster to his shoulder. The gun was about four and a half feet long, almost as tall as he was. He looked like a crazed maniac as he scanned the sky for a victim.

"Be careful with that thing," I said. "It'll kick the snot out of you if you're not careful."

He looked at me with one of those "yeah right" looks.

A minute later a lone goose came from the marsh and was headed right for us. It was real low and honking like mad, as if it had been left behind by the flock. Thunderfoot hunkered down and waited. The goose came closer and closer.

"Get up and get ready to shoot, he's coming," I urged.

Thunderfoot struggled to his feet and raised the goose cannon to his shoulder just as the goose came into range. "Shoot!" I said.

The goose came closer. Thunderfoot raised the gun and followed it with the sight on the end of the barrel. It came closer. He raised the gun following it as it came over us. "Shoot!" I said.

The goose was right overhead when Thunderfoot touched off the shell. The blast made the whole blind shake and it seemed as if every goose in the marsh stopped honking for an instant. It even seemed like the wind stopped blowing. The recoil from the gun was directed right into the top of Thunderfoot's shoulder. He had his right hand tightly wrapped around the stock and his thumb came back and hit him right on the end of the nose causing his eyes to flood with tears. His head snapped back and his cap flew off his head and over the side of the blind. The goose flew on probably vowing never to go so close to one of those little plywood boxes again.

Smoke curled up from the end of the barrel as Thunderfoot lowered the gun and looked at me with a bewildered look in his face. Tears were running down his cheeks and he had a vacant stare in his eyes. "Holy cow...I think I broke my nose."

Well, that did it...I fell back against the side of the blind laughing so hard that I lost my footing in the piles of empty shells and slid right down to the ground. I felt kind of bad about laughing but there was nothing I could do about it. Thunderfoot rubbed his injured nose, wiped his eyes on his sleeve and then began laughing too. "Jeez, you weren't kidding about that thing kicking were you? Where's my hat?"

Remembering his hat popping off his head and flying out of the blind cracked me up again. I couldn't talk, but just pointed over the side until he finally figured out what I was trying to say. He opened the corner of the blind and retrieved his hat.

When he came back into the blind we sat and chuckled for a while about the episode and suddenly he began to grin as he saw his buddy Scott trotting across the pasture toward our blind.

"Here comes Scott. Can I let him shoot the big gun?" he asked with an evil grin on his face.

Thanks, Thunderfoot.

Ice Boating

I was snuggled in my recliner with my comforter over my lap contemplating a nap. Outside the wind was howling across the glistening snow and making little whirlwind-like swirls. I happened to look out the window across the back yard and saw a mound of clothes wading through the snow carrying an ice fishing bucket. A minute later the clothes mound flew in through the front door, letting in a blast of cold air. The clothes mound stomped its feet and soon a pile of mittens, scarves, caps, coats and sweaters began growing on my living room floor. As the pile of clothes got larger Thunderfoot emerged grinning like a mad musher from the Yukon.

"I can't believe you're not ready yet," he said.

"I am ready...ready for a nap."

"No way, we're going ice fishing. The other day you said we'd go ice fishing on Saturday and this is Saturday."

"I didn't know it would be -20 on Saturday when I said that. It's like a blizzard outside. We can't fish in that kind of wind."

"Oh piffle, it's nice out...almost balmy."

"Balmy my butt," I said.

He gave me one of those 'I can't believe that would stop you' looks. "If you dress right it's not bad at all." Then he looked at me with those sad eyes he was so good with and I shook my head.

"Once we get the shanty set up and the stove lit we'll be inside and it won't matter how cold it is," he said nodding his head up and down.

I knew it was hopeless to argue with him so I got dressed and a half hour later we were plowing through the snow drifts on the sand road that led to the lake. We pulled into an empty parking lot. Of course no one else was crazy enough to be out there like we were, so it was no surprise we were alone at the lake. We unloaded the gear from the back of the pickup and piled all of the gear onto the shanty which had a plastic sled on the bottom. Thunderfoot happily grabbed the rope from the sled and pulled it toward the bank that led down to the lake. When he got on the ice his feet kept walking but the heavy sled didn't move and soon he was marching in place. He gave me a sorrowful look and handed me the rope. "We need someone who is...um, heavier to pull. I'll run ahead and drill the holes."

I had a pair of ice cleats with me so I sat down and attached them to my boots and then started pulling the sled down the lake right into the teeth of the wind. Several minutes later I caught up to Thunderfoot at the other end. He had the auger with him and had begun to try to drill a hole. Of course with no snow on the ice, once the auger bit into the surface, Thunderfoot began spinning around as he turned the handle. He was too light to put enough pressure on the auger to make a hole. He gave me another of those sorrowful looks and handed me the auger. "I'll scoop the ice chips out after you drill."

I drilled four holes and he did manage to clean the ice chips out. We tried to light the stove but the wind was blowing so hard that it was impossible. "We'll have to light it inside when we get the shanty up," I shouted over the wind.

The shanty was attached to the sled and just unfolded when it was set up, so we unloaded all of the buckets and other gear from on top of it and positioned it over the four holes. On one end there was a zippered door. Thunderfoot lifted up the end and unzipped the door so he could arrange the aluminum frame inside. When the door was opened we heard a *Whump!* when the wind opened the tent up like a hot air balloon. It immediately began sliding over the ice with us handing on like rag dolls. I was on my knees and it only took a short way for me to fall over on my back. Thunderfoot's feet flew out from under him and he landed on his belly. Both of us were being dragged over the ice and we began going faster and faster.

Since I was wearing ice cleats on my boots, I tried to put one foot down on the ice to slow us down. As soon as the ice cleat hit the ice it came off my boot and launched into the air like a Ninja throwing star and disappeared in a shower of ice chips. By now we were going at Warp 3 so I carefully put the other boot down and applied pressure on the ice more carefully. The cleat began throwing up a rooster tail of ice chips and making a screeching sound as it was drug across the ice. But, we began slowing down and soon our rooster tail began to disappear.

We finally came to a complete stop in the cattails at the other end of the lake, where he had come from in the first place. We were both laughing like crazy. I looked over at Thunderfoot. His face was covered with ice chips and snow. Snot was running down from his nose to his chin. "Pull the tent down!"

"I can't...my nose is running," he said.

That cracked us up again and be both laughed crazily. Finally he wiped his nose on the back of his mitten and got to his knees and pulled the nylon shanty down onto the sled. The shanty deflated and I was able to release my death grip on the sled. I sat up and looked back down the lake. Our gear was strung all over creation and as I got my breath one of my poles came sliding along right to me. A little while later my cap slid up too. "I think we better retrieve our stuff and give up!" I shouted over the whine of the wind. Thunderfoot nodded in agreement.

We worked our way back upwind and gathered our gear. I found my other cleat after a long search and we headed back to the truck and loaded up. As we closed the doors and started the truck Thunderfoot looked out over the frozen lake. "I bet they would have bit today too," he said shaking his head. "But all that noise you made scraping that cleat probably spooked all the fish anyway." He looked over at me with an impish grin.

Half an hour later we were home, all the gear stowed away. I hung up our clothes to dry. I heard the refrigerator door open. Thunderfoot was looked around inside the fridge and then over at me. "Boy, fishing sure makes me hungry."

"Breathing makes you hungry."

Big grin.

Thanks, Thunderfoot.

The Great Bunny Hunt

I was backing my way through a nearly solid wall of berry briars when the sound of a shot from Thunderfoot's 20-guage came from the other side of the tangle. A couple of seconds later I heard another shot, followed by yet another. I waited for a short time and then resumed my backward bulldozing until I got to the other side.

Thunderfoot was nowhere to be seen, but he soon came stomping back over a little rise, stuffing shells into his gun. I raised my eyebrows as if to ask where the rabbit was only to be met with a "don't even ask" look.

"Well?"

"I can't believe I missed him," he said. "I had him right in my sights."

"Did you lead him?"

"No...should I have?" he asked with a puzzled look.

"Yeah...remember the ducks? Rabbits are the same. They're moving not sitting still."

Somehow he had figured that if he was shooting a shotgun he was shooting a bullet that was about three feet across because of the way the pellets spread out when they left the gun. He got an enlightened look on his face as I mentioned the ducks. We started off through the woods to the next tangle of briars.

Again, he snuck around to the far side of the berry patch and I, ever the faithful dog, plowed into the mess with the hope of driving a rabbit out in front of him. I had only gone a short way when the briars got so thick that I had to get down and crawl. I hadn't gone far when another barrage of shooting started on the other side. This time there were three fast shots followed by one lone shot long after the others.

I went a few feet farther and the shooting started again. This time he shot only three times. As I emerged from the thicket, bleeding profusely from a gash delivered to my left ear by a particularly nasty berry bush, I expected to find him with a limit of rabbits.

His hat was on sideways and he was looking pretty peeved. "I did just what you said and they still all got away."

"How far did you lead them?"

"I don't know...maybe ten feet."

"Ten feet!"

We walked over to the spot where he had shot at the second rabbit. There in the snow were rabbit tracks going up to a bare spot where his shot had hit the ground. Then the rabbit tracks made a right angle turn and went off into the distance. The bunny had taken a turn to the right when Thunderfoot blew up the snow in front of him.

"You shot a bit too far ahead," I said. "But I bet you gave him a thrill when he saw the snow blow up."

Thunderfoot reloaded and we started toward the best spot in the woods. This was the honey hole, the *Valhalla of all Rabbitdom*, the downtown gathering spot for all the rabbits in the woods.

Many years earlier the woods had been logged. After all the timber was hauled away the loggers bulldozed the limbs and branches into a big ditch, making a *Rabbit Super 8*. There were rabbit trails leading into and out of the place from all over the woods. The only problem was that the rabbits were perfectly safe unless you had a dog that could get into the tangled branches and root them out. Our dog was me. My golden retrievers were duck dogs and turned their noses up at the thought of looking for a lowly rabbit, so I got the job. The trouble was that I was way too big to crawl into the rabbit trails that led into the woodpile.

"How do we get them out?" Thunderfoot asked as we approached the *Bunny Hilton.*

"You get up on that high spot over there," I said pointing to a rise. "I'll climb up there on top of the pile and stomp. If I make enough noise maybe some of the rabbits will run out, and you can shoot them."

"Sounds like a plan," he said as he started walking toward the high spot.

I lay my shotgun on a stump, not wanting to climb through the mess carrying a gun. Then I began working my way up onto the pile of limbs and branches. I had only gone a few feet when a bunny darted out right at Thunderfoot. It nearly went right over his feet and he just stood there and watched it.

"Nice shot," I said chuckling.

He stood there with a mystified look on his face. "I wasn't ready," he said.

I climbed up farther on the pile and started jumping up and down. Rabbits popped out as if someone had yelled fire in a theater. Thunderfoot pulled up on a bunny, and then swung his gun toward another without firing at either one of them. There were rabbits running everywhere, and he was beginning to panic trying to decide which one to shoot at.

I was getting close to the middle of the pile when I stopped to catch my breath. I put one foot down on a branch and felt the pile below me settle. I carefully moved my foot to a larger branch and shifted my weight to that one. A second later the branch broke and the whole section I was standing on collapsed sending me to the basement of rabbit haven. On the way down through the branches, my jacket caught on a branch. It was pulled over my head, like skinning a bunny, and my arms were pinned upward along the side of my head. The only thing I could see was the buttons on my jacket in front of me and the sky above. My feet were hanging in mid-air as I hadn't gone all the way to the bottom of the pile. Hmm, this was not good.

I hung there for a minute trying to figure out how to get out of the mess. Suddenly I could hear a muffled choking sound. It was something like...*hrmf...hrmf.* I wasn't sure what it was, but it was getting closer. Maybe it was a rabid rabbit.

I could feel the pile of wood moving and soon I heard, "Are you ok?" It was Thunderfoot sobbing between fits of laughter. I looked up through the top of the jacket, which was actually the bottom of the jacket and there stood Thunderfoot peering down at me, tears running down his face.

"I think I'm ok as long as the rabbits don't attack me for wrecking their home," I said laughing.

He began clearing away the brush to get me out and after a bit I managed to get on top of the pile. I pulled my jacket down so I could see again. "Did you get any rabbits after all this work?"

"No...I was laughing so hard I couldn't shoot. It was like one of those magic shows...one second you were there and then poof...you were gone."

I started laughing again and we climbed down from the pile.

"Let's go home," he said. "I can't take any more of this and besides...I'm out of bullets."

That's fine with me." This old dog was ready for a nap.

Thanks, Thunderfoot.

Don't Cry Wolf

"We'll put out four tip-ups and then we can each jig with one pole," I said as Thunderfoot and I walked down over the bank and onto the ice of a frozen backwater slough. "You pick the spots for the tip-ups and drill the holes. I'll set up the tip-ups and bait them."

He took off down the ice and carefully selected the best spots for out tip-ups. I followed along behind carrying a bucket with the tip-ups in it and a bait bucket with shiners. We worked for almost half an hour before we got all the tip-ups baited and then drilled two holes for our jig poles, sat down and began fishing.

"Who gets to pull up which tip-up?" Thunderfoot asked.

"You can take them all," I said. "I want to get a good picture of a big northern coming up from the hole for a story I'm going to write, so I'll man the camera." That seemed fine with him, so we worked our jigs and kept an eye on the tip-ups. Suddenly the stillness of the day was interrupted by Thunderfoot. "FLAG!" The cry echoed down the ice as he raced toward one of the tip-ups. This was his first time pulling in a fish on a tip-up, so he was pretty excited.

"Should I pull now?" he asked.

"No....wait until the line spools stops turning. Then when the fish starts to move again, give it a good hard pull."

He carefully lifted the tip-up out of the hole in the ice, eyes glued to the nylon line which was slowly being pulled from the reel. Then it stopped. "He's turning the minnow now to swallow it," I said. "Get ready."

The spool of line began to move again and Thunderfoot jerked on the line and fell over backwards. He clambered to his feet and pulled furiously on the line.

"Take it easy," I warned. "Don't pull it out of his mouth."

He kept pressure on the line and soon a small northern popped up in the hole and he lifted it out. "Wow, that's fun."

It was his first tip-up fish. We took a quick picture and slid the fish back down the hole. Then we re-set the tip-up and walked back to our jig poles and sat down to fish some more. We had just begun when another flag popped up.

"FLAAAAG!" Thunderfoot was a blur as he took off for the tip-up. I grabbed the camera and headed down the ice. He was waiting for the appropriate time to set the hook, so I lay down on the ice so I could get a picture just as the fish cleared the hole. "Is it a big one?" I asked.

"It feels huge."

I got ready with the camera and Thunderfoot said, "Here he comes." I snapped a picture as a little "snake" northern popped out of the hole.

"I thought you said it was huge."

"Well I thought it was," he said grinning from ear to ear.

We reset the tip-up and started back to our jig poles when another flag popped up. The now familiar cry of "FLAAAAG!" echoed down the lake as Thunderfoot raced toward the fluttering orange piece of vinyl. I got there just as he set the hook. He started pulling in the line but his hands kept jerking back toward the hole, causing him to lose line for a bit, only to gain it back. "Give me time to get the camera ready," I said lying on the ice. He fought the fish back and forth bravely. Soon he said, "Get ready...he's coming up."

The camera clicked perfectly as the water in the hole began to splash and another little "snake" northern popped up. Thunderfoot fell over backwards laughing.

"You little snot!" I said starting back toward the jig poles. Thunderfoot could bait his own tip-ups.

A bit later he plopped down on his bucket. He was quiet. "Uhmmm... I said...Uhmmm."

I looked over at his big grin.

"Sorry" he said.

"Yeah I can tell. You're going to cry wolf one time to often and then we'll miss a picture of a big one because I won't trust you anymore."

"Cry wolf? I'm gonna cry NORTHERN!"

That made me laugh and just then we both noticed the farthest flag had popped up. "FLAAAAG!" He was off to the races.

I didn't feel like running all the way down the lake again so I hollered at him, "Reset the flag when you get done."

He pulled the line and soon I could see him fighting a fish. He yelled, "It's huge....I'm serious!"

I could see his arms jerking back and forth at the hole but I wasn't going to fall for that old trick again. I ignored him.

"This one is huge," he called. "Come and help me... Please, please, no wolf, no wolf."

I gave up and walked down the ice and got to the hole. I had just gotten my camera to my eye when a huge ten pound northern emerged halfway up through the hole. I snapped the picture as the fish twisted to the side....just the picture I was looking for. Thunderfoot slid the fish out onto the ice and then pushed it farther away from the hole.

"Holy cow, you weren't kidding," I said.

"Jeez I thought you'd never come," he said panting.

We unhooked the beautiful fish and took a couple more pictures of Thunderfoot grinning and holding the trophy. Then we slid her back into the water.

"That was very cool," he said. "I like this tip-up fish.... FLAAAAG!"

Thanks Thunderfoot.

Just One Last Time

"They're getting big bluegills at Postel's," Thunderfoot said as he burst through my front door. "They're congregated up where the creek runs into the lake. There're millions of them!"

We had been experiencing a warm spell and the ice was getting much too thin for my tastes and body size. "How are they getting out there?" I asked. "They must be taking boats. The ice is nearly all gone...there can't be any safe way to get to the lake by now."

Postel's "lake" as it was called, was a slough about one quarter of a mile from solid ground in the Wisconsin river bottoms. It could be reached during the dead of winter because the swamp between it and the high bank was frozen. At this time of year, the swamp became impassable. There was no other way to get to the lake.

"The path is ok...they're going out there right now. We can get there too...I'm sure of it. Just wait here, I'll be right back." Thunderfoot took off for his house across the back yard. A few minutes later he came back lugging a 5 gallon bucket that was almost full of huge bluegills. "These came from Postel's this morning," he said.

I looked at the fish and had to admit they were really nice bluegills. "Who caught those?" I asked.

"My neighbor...he went this morning and got them in about two hours. Let's go!"

Thunderfoot's neighbor was a little old guy who didn't weigh much over a hundred pounds dripping wet. Of course neither did Thunderfoot, so he had no worries. But, I was a bit more "full figured" and as agile as a cow, so

I had second thoughts about trying to get to the lake. But I had an idea. "Go out in the shed and get my hip boots," I told Thunderfoot.

He stood there with a puzzled look on his face the then his eyes brightened when he realized what I had in mind. He got my boots and in a few minutes we had our ice fishing gear loaded in the pickup and were heading to Postel's.

Thunderfoot led the way down the path to the lake. As we came to the trail that ran out across the swamp he began walking but suddenly his foot went through the frozen muck. He jumped off to the side to keep dry. I carefully stepped into the hole he had made in the ice with my hip boot and then stepped up on solid ice on the other side, quite proud of myself. We went a short way and the same thing happened again. Now I was feeling pretty clever. When we were only a few feet from the edge of the lake and good ice, we had one little area of "swamp ice" left to cover. Thunderfoot zipped right across and I took a deep breath and managed to get across too.

"See, I told you we could get out here," he said as he began drilling a hole.

He was right, the fish were there. And...they were hungry. The sun came out through the clouds and the temperature soared to almost sixty. We fished and had a glorious time sitting in our shirt sleeves, enjoying the spring weather and catching bunches of bluegill.

By mid-afternoon we both had our buckets nearly full. "We better see how many we have," I said. "We must be close to our limits." We both counted our fish and I was one short of my limit while Thunderfoot still needed three. A few minutes later we had all we could legally keep.

"Wow, I don't think I ever had such a good day of fishing," Thunderfoot said. "What a way to end the season."

We packed up and he trotted across that first area of bad ice. He was almost all the way across when he broke through. One of his feet got a little wet but he was quick and agile enough that he scampered off the ice with little trouble.

"You better go around," he said. "It's pretty thin."

"I'll be ok. I've got my hip boots on," I said. I started across the ice. I took two steps and then my left foot broke through. The water was only knee deep, so I was still ok....until I tried to step up onto the ice with my right foot. I lost my balance and went head first into the ice-cold water and mud. I came up from the mire like a whale breaching from the depths and then floundered around in the mud pit for several minutes trying to get out.

Thunderfoot stood there on solid ground and tried to look concerned for my safety, but he was having a hard time keeping a straight face. I finally got to solid ground and started picking up my gear which had been strewn all over the place with my thrashing around. I found all my stuff and then we started down the trail toward the high bank. I slogged along, my boots full of water making a sloshing sound as I walked. My clothes were saturated with an aromatic swamp scent and my mood was much less cheery than it had been earlier.

After a while Thunderfoot got far enough ahead of me that he felt safe. He looked over his shoulder and said, "You know...those hip boots proved to be a pretty good idea." I could tell he was grinning even though he kept his face straight ahead. Wise guy.

Thanks, Thunderfoot.

The Big Mushroom

Thunderfoot and I had parked alongside a gravel road in the hills near town. We were trekking through a pasture toward the hillside on our first mushroom hunt. This was Thunderfoot's first time looking for morels and he was chomping at the bit to get started.

"They look like corncobs with the corn all gone," I said as we walked toward an old dead elm that I had spotted from the road. The tree looked like a prime mushroom tree. "Once you see one you'll know what to look for and won't have any trouble find more."

At the tree I could see several morels sticking up amid the leaves and clutter on the ground. Thunderfoot stopped and began looking around about two feet from one. He was looking everyplace but at the mushroom.

"Look closer to you," I said.

He looked down and spotted the morel. Stooping down to pick it he said, "Cool...there's another over there and jeez....there's another one!" He scurried around picking the mushrooms as if they were going to grow legs and run away from him.

I bent to pick one that was poking up from some dead leaves when I saw movement in the grass as a small snake slithered away. "Jeez!" I said hot-footing it down the slope.

"What was that? Was it a snake? What's going on....are you afraid of snakes?" The little snot was having a ball teasing me.

"No it just startled me," I lied. Actually I am deathly afraid of snakes. You'd think that after spending most of my youth digging around in the river bottoms I'd be used to snakes but they just creep me out. It's so bad that when one of those guys on the animal shows on TV finds a snake, I turn to another program. They just HAVE to pick the dang things up don't they? I won't even touch the page in a magazine with a picture of a snake. I don't understand it but that's the way it is...I don't like snakes.

"Are you really afraid of snakes? You know...I bet there's some rattlers around here. What do you think?" The little monster's eyes were just twinkling.

I ignored him and picked up a substantial stick about five feet long and tested its strength. He looked at me questioningly and I explained to him that this was my mushroom stick. It was used for moving leaves and brush

26

aside when looking for mushrooms and could also be used to beat to death, any smart guy who had snake ideas.

Thunderfoot was hurt to the core to think that I might even suspect him of such notions. We decided that he'd head up the right side of the hill while I'd take the left side. We agreed to meet back at the truck in an hour or so and off we went.

I began looking at dead elms on the lower part of the hill and found several with mushrooms growing around them. In a short time I had a pretty good sack full so I decided to go back to the truck and wait for him.

I laid the tailgate down and sat up on it and soon decided to lay back and closed my eyes. I was sprawled out in the back of the pickup when movement awakened me. Thunderfoot had hopped up and was sitting on the tailgate swinging his legs over the end.

"Ah, sleeping beauty awakes," he said grinning.

"Wow, the sun was so warm and nice that I guess I dozed off. How did you do?"

"Oh not bad," he said. "How about you, did you find any?"

"I've got half a sack or so," I said.

He stood up proudly and opened his sack. It was full to the brim with nice morels. "What do you think of these babies?" he said.

I was impressed, he'd done well.

"I've got one that is so big I had to put it in my spare sack so it wouldn't crush the rest of them," he said. He picked up the second sack and opened it, turning it upside down on the ground at my feet. "Look at this baby."

A three foot blacksnake dropped almost on my feet and I jumped up and let out a shriek that probably sounded like a soprano hitting the high note in an Italian opera. I jumped about three feet in the air while automatically raising my mushroom stick to "kill mode". The snake slithered off into the grass at the roadside while Thunderfoot was staggering around doubled over with laughter. When he saw the look on my face he took off up the gravel road on a dead run with me right behind him, my mushroom stick held over my head like a war club. He was laughing so hard that I nearly caught him but it didn't take me long to figure out that running down the road was not the best thing for an old guy to do, so I stopped and tried to catch my breath.

Thunderfoot stopped a few feet away, just out of mushroom stick range and laughed with delight. "Not afraid of snakes?" He grabbed his belly and laughed so hard he nearly fell down. I finally got my breathing back to normal but my heart beat and blood pressure was probably still about as high as it could go without having "the big one."

"Come on...let's go home," I said turning toward the truck.

"No way....you're gonna hit me with that stick!" he said keeping his distance.

"I won't hit you...you know that."

"Yeah? Well prove it...lose the stick."

He knew he probably wasn't in any danger, but just in case he wanted my stick gone before he got in range. "You know, you shouldn't do something like that to an old man," I said. "What would you have done if I'd have had a heart attack?"

"I guess I'd have had to learn to drive the truck.....uh, the stick?"

I tossed the stick in the ditch and he walked up to me. "Jeez, I never saw you move so fast before or jump so high. I didn't know you could run either." He was grinning from ear to ear.

I raised my hand as if to swat him but grinned. We walked back to the truck and I carefully avoided the tall grass where the snake had gone, though I doubted he was still around after my little demonstration. We got into the truck and I pulled out onto the gravel and started for home.

Thunderfoot put his hand on my shoulder. "I am sorry...I guess I didn't think you'd be so scared. Jeez, I wouldn't want you to have a heart attack. Who would I have to pick on then?" He grinned at me and winked.

Who indeed?

Thanks, Thunderfoot.

The First Turkey Hunt

Thunderfoot was not a morning person. He was real dependable about being on time for fishing or hunting, as long as the day started at mid-morning or early afternoon. On those occasions he was usually ready to go ahead of time. But early morning trips were not his cup of tea.

I had been forced several times to go to his house and tap on his bedroom window to get him up and hated to do that. I usually ended up waking up the whole household, so the night before the first turkey hunt I suggested that he sleep in my spare bedroom. It would be easier on me and his family if he was where I could wake him up on time. By now he had left wet and muddy clothes and other gear at my house many times, so "his" room was pretty well stocked.

I turned my alarm clock off at 4 a.m. and walked down the hall to his room. I rustled him awake and then went off to dress and to get some toast and cereal ready for breakfast. He didn't seem to be making much noise so I stuck my head into his room. He was sitting on the edge of the bed scratching his head and yawning.

"Get dressed...we've got to get going," I said.

"What?"

"Get up and get dressed. We've got to get to the woods."

He started mumbling about how it was the middle of the night but he did manage to get dressed. I loaded the truck with the decoys and some camouflage netting, while he went to the bathroom. When he finally came out I was all ready to go. He grabbed a piece of toast and we headed out the door. "Jeez, it's the middle of the night," he complained.

"Just wait until you hear that first gobble. Then you'll think this is worth it," I said.

I got no answer. I turned and he was slumped down in the seat with his eyes closed.

It was only a fifteen minute drive to the farm where we were hunting so his nap didn't last long enough to suit him. He began grumbling again when I woke him and continued as we started up the ridge road to the top

29

of the hill.

"Shhh.....the turkeys roost just up the hill from here," I said. "We have to walk right below them to get to the top of the hill, so be quiet."

He was awake by now and began stepping as quietly as could, avoiding at least some of the sticks and rocks. We stopped when we got to the top of the hill. "Can you see how this field lays?" I whispered to him.

He nodded.

"The turkeys usually roost over there, I said pointing to the woods. When it gets light they'll fly down to the field and come through the gate into the pastures. The hens usually roost out on the other hill and come into this field when the sun comes up to get warmed up. I'll put the decoys out by the gate and hopefully one of the toms will come to us before he goes to the real hens."

"Sounds like a plan to me," he said grinning in the moonlight.

We unpacked the decoys and slid them onto their metal stakes. Then I stuck them into the ground about fifteen yards from two huge maples that stood as the fence-line below us. We walked over to the maples and cleared the twigs and leaves from the area and hung out camouflage material from some bushes, forming a makeshift blind. We sat down behind the blind to wait, one of us leaning back against each of the maples.

Thunderfoot was wide awake now and it didn't take long for him to get impatient. Every time there was some sound, he'd wiggle around to look where it came from.

"Sit still," I said to him.

"What?"

"Get comfortable and then sit still. You don't dare move or the turkeys will see you. They've got really good eyesight."

"Do they have flashlights?" I could see him grinning in the dim light.

The blackness was turning into a deep purple as an owl hooted from somewhere down the ridge. The sound of the hoot hadn't even faded when a turkey gobbled from his roost. He was just where I had told Thunderfoot he would be.

Thunderfoot sat upright and listened as another turkey answered the first one and then another sounded off.

"They're right where you said they'd be," he said looking surprised.

"Did you doubt the expert?"

He grinned and shook his head. In the next few minutes the woods came alive with the sounds of morning. Now there were at least a dozen turkeys gobbling up and down the ridge. There were a couple of owls hooting and dozens of songbirds chirping. Soon a group of crows began cawing for good measure and a pair of wood ducks whistled as they flew overhead. Thunderfoot was alert now, his big ten-gauge at the ready.

I slipped my favorite diaphragm call into my mouth and gave a couple of quiet yelps, which were immediately answered by at least three toms off to our right. I waited a few minutes and then made the hen yelps again. The toms answered right away but this time they were in a different place. "They're down from the tree," I whispered.

Thunderfoot nodded his head slowly to let me know he understood.

For the next hour or so I called and the toms answered, always moving our way but taking their time and not showing themselves to us. Finally they stopped answering my calls and things became quiet.

"Did they leave?" he asked.

"Some real hens probably came to them. We'll wait and see if they remember us after the real hens go to lay their egg for the day."

Another half hour passed and the toms were quiet. I called every ten minutes or so, but there was no response. Suddenly I heard a humming noise that was new to the woods. I tried to see an insect or bird that might be making the sound but there was nothing that I could see that made it. Then the noise turned from a humming noise into a fairly loud snore. I turned my head and looked over at the now-sleeping Thunderfoot. The warm morning sun was filtering down through the leaves and had taken its toll on my tired partner. I was having a hard time staying awake myself, but I kept calling for another half hour and let him have a little nap.

We had gotten permission for Thunderfoot to be a little late for school but we'd have to get going pretty soon, so I picked up a small stick and poked him a coupe of times.

He blinked his eyes and looked around, not knowing just where he was. Finally he looked at me and smiled.

"Have a nice nap?" I whispered.

"Yup....where are the turkeys?"

"You scared them away with your snoring."

"Bull...I don't snore."

"Ok but we had better be going, you have to go to school you know."

He grimaced but we gathered up our gear and started down the hill. We stopped and looked up the hill at the woods where the turkeys had been when the gobbled.

"You know, if we set up over there by the corner of that fence I think we'd have a better chance tomorrow. That is, if you can get up again."

"Just try to keep me home," he said. "But I'm going to bed a lot earlier tonight."

The next morning things went smoother as far as getting up and getting ready were concerned. Thunderfoot was a bit chattier as we drove through the dark to the farm.

We snuck up the hill and went to the left at the top and then snuck dangerously close to the place where the birds were probably roosting. When we got to the corner or the fence I put the decoys out below us. We hung the netting over some tall weeds and brush and used the corner of the fence for our backrest.

"This is a better place," Thunderfoot whispered. "Now we got them."

But the second morning was a repeat of the first, because the turkeys had roosted in a different place. Instead of being to our right, they were up the hill to the left and we were sitting with our backs to them.

"We can't move now," I whispered. "If they see the decoys they'll come right past us on the right. So, just sit real still and wait."

He nodded that he understood and we waited.

A little while later we heard a faint gobble. I couldn't quite make out where it had come from. "Did you hear that?" I whispered.

"They're right behind us," he whispered back.

"Can you see them?" I asked not daring to turn my head.

"Yup...they're right up in the corner and they're coming our way."

Things just might work out after all. The only problem was that the turkeys were to Thunderfoot's right and it would be hard to move to get the gun into position to shoot at them.

"Move really slowly," I said. "Try to turn as much to your right as you can without them seeing you...real slow."

He scooted his bottom around as much as he dared but he still wasn't in a good position to shoot.

"I can't move any farther without them seeing me," he whispered.

32

"Just get your gun up slowly to your shoulder. We'll have to wait for them to move far enough to the left for you to get a shot." I slid very slowly to the right so I could see what was going on. Two big toms were heading right for us. They didn't seem to have any idea that there was a little guy with a real big gun waiting for them.

The toms strutted for the decoys and then walked toward them a little ways and strutted again. At the rate they were coming, it would take at least five minutes for them to move far enough for Thunderfoot to get his sights on them.

"No hurry," I said. "We'll just wait for them to get here."

He nodded slightly.

The minutes seemed like hours, but the toms were finally getting close to the point where they had to be so Thunderfoot could shoot. They had about ten feet more to go when one of them stopped and raised his head as if listening to something. Then the other one raised his head too. I stopped breathing thinking they could hear me but I instantly heard the noise the turkeys were hearing.

Across the valley, the farmer was having a ridge logged off and the logger was coming down the ridge road dragging a bunch of logs behind a skidder. It was at least a quarter of a mile away, but the turkeys stopped dead in their tracks. The logger dragged the logs down to a level pasture and got off the skidder to unhook them. Our turkeys turned around and trotted back up the hill into the woods.

Thunderfoot's shoulders sagged as he lowered the gun and turned to me. "What are the odds that he'd come down there with those logs just now?

I just shook my head.

We sat a few minutes longer and then started to get our stuff together. "Well, they never said it'd be easy," I commented. "That's why only one in four hunters gets a turkey."

"That's why they call it turkey hunting instead of turkey shooting," he said grinning. "Oh well, there's always tomorrow."

That's my little trouper.

Thanks, Thunderfoot.

Saying Goodbye to Sally

Thunderfoot was walking across the back yard, but he wasn't in his usual hurry. His head was low and he seemed not to want to get to my house. I had called him earlier and asked him to come over and he knew why. He wasn't in any hurry to confront what waited for him.

He and Sally had been good buddies from the time he started hanging out with me. My older golden retriever Bea, had died shortly after I met Thunderfoot so he had not gotten to know her so well, but Sally was one of his best friends. My third golden Sophie was Sally's daughter and she was also his buddy, but he and Sal had been special friends.

Sally had been sick for quite a while. She had come down with some tumors that the Vet had removed some time ago. For a while after the surgery Sal seemed like a new dog but then we could tell that things were not right with her. Another trip to the Vet the day before had confirmed my fears.

Thunderfoot came into the living room and looked at me questioningly. "I called Dr. Pat," I said. "She's coming down later this morning for Sal."

He looked thunderstruck. "You mean today?" he said.

I nodded. "We can't wait any longer. There isn't anything more they can do for her, and I don't want to see her suffer. We can't keep her going just to make us feel better. She's not going to get better and that's it."

Thunderfoot's eyes welled up with tears and he turned and went into the spare bedroom where Sally was sleeping on her blanket on the floor. I left them alone for a while and then went to the room. Thunderfoot was sitting next to his old friend petting her on the head and talking to her. Sally's tail was wagging as they shared a last minute together.

"I'll drive you to school," I said. "We better get going or you'll be late."

He nodded and then buried his face in Sally's fur. A minute later he came out of the bedroom with red eyes and we drove in silence to the school.

I went home and helped Sally get up. We slowly walked to the door and then out into the yard. We walked and she looked over her domain one last time...her yard, the piece of ground she had guarded and protected for all these years. We walked over to the picnic table and I picked her up and laid her on a blanket on the table and then sat on the bench and stroked her silky fur. We sat there for a long time "talking" about all the fun we'd had and all the hunting trips we'd had together. It was a beautiful spring day, with a warm breeze blowing, lots of birds singing and the flowers and leaves opening up. My heart was breaking. I was saying goodbye to my friend of 12 years.

Finally I heard the sound of Dr. Pat's truck as she pulled into the driveway. I walked around to the front of the house to let her know we were waiting out back. The time had come.

I sat back down and put my arms around Sally and said goodbye and in a couple of seconds she was gone. I don't know how long I sat there after Dr. Pat left but finally I got up and wrapped Sally in her blanket and buried her in the back garden next to her mother.

It was a long day. I had no ambition to do much of anything so I just sat and thought about having a dog and the pain of seeing them grow old and then having to say goodbye to them. I looked up from my daydreaming and saw Thunderfoot walking slowly across the yard. He came into the house and sat down but neither of us said a word.

"Can I get the picture book out?" he asked.

"Yeah, that might be a good idea," I said.

He got out my photo album and we sat side by side on the couch and paged through it. The first dog pictures were of old Bea. There were lots of those. Then there were pictures of Bea with her litter of puppies. Sally had been one of a litter of nine and the puppy pictures were enough to make us laugh.

"Gosh, you could sure tell which one was Sally," Thunderfoot said pointing to a puppy with a familiar look on her face. Sally always had a look of "attitude" even when she was a few weeks old. It was why I chose her over all the others.

"She was the boss of all the puppies," I said.

There were pictures of us fishing, Sally riding in the boat. In one she was sitting on the little platform on the bow, hanging out over the water.

There were many with her swimming toward us with a tennis ball in her mouth. There was one of her eating birthday cake, and many more.

We laughed at the picture of Thunderfoot feeding Sally cake with a fork and getting frosting all over her nose.

We smiled at a picture of Thunderfoot and Sally both sleeping on the floor, his arms around her after a duck hunt. They were both still muddy from the swamp.

"She got to do a lot of stuff, didn't she?" he said.

"Yeah, she had a good life."

The more we looked the better we felt. Finally we came to the part of the book where Sophie started showing up. Sophie was asleep on the floor at our feet. "Do you think Soph knows what happened?" he asked.

"I don't think she understands death but you can tell she knows something is wrong," I said reaching down to pet Sophie.

"Hey Soph, want to go play ball?" Thunderfoot asked.

Sophie jumped to her feet and frantically began looking for a tennis ball. In a short time she ran back to us with two of them in her mouth and out they went to play ball.

I sat outside at the picnic table watching the two of them playing. After a while Sophie started getting tired. Thunderfoot walked over to the fresh ground where I had buried Sally.

He squatted down and patted the earth and said something and then took off across the yard toward his house. "I told her we won't ever forget her," he said.

We sure won't.

Goodbye Sally.

The Ice-Cream Fish

The johnboat was as silent as midnight in a cemetery. Thunderfoot, his friend Trent and I were fishing in the river bottoms for northerns. We were casting plugs and spinners to likely-looking places in hopes to be the first one in the boat to catch a fish. Normally there was a lot of conversation about everything from fishing to baseball, but right now, we were just starting out for the evening and there were no fish caught as of yet. Therefore, the ice-cream fish was still up for grabs.

I should explain. Somehow many fishing trips ago, we started a game in which the last person to catch his first fish of the trip had to buy ice-cream at the gas station on the way home. If it were just Thunderfoot and I, the first fish caught was the winner and the loser had to buy. If there were three people fishing, as there were today, the first two were eliminated and the third guy got the honors of buying.

It was serious business, not so much because of the price of the ice-cream but more for the prestige that came with being the non-loser. So, we were beating the water frothy as Thunderfoot reared back on his rod and set the hook into a mid-sized northern.

He looked to the back of the boat and got a smug look on his face. "I can't decide what flavor to have tonight," he said. Just then the northern jumped into the air and Thunderfoot's spinner-bait came flying back and hit him in the middle of the chest.

"That was close enough to count," he said quickly.

"No way, pal," Trent and I said simultaneously. "You didn't touch him, it doesn't count."

Thunderfoot looked wounded but it didn't take him long to start fishing again.

I picked up the paddle and moved us a short way down the lake so could fish some new territory. Everyone was working pretty hard for that first fish and the boys liked nothing more than to stick me with the ice-cream buying duties. We were drifting toward a spot on the lake where we always caught a northern. We called it "Ambush Point." It was a place where the weed lines from each side of the lake jutted out and almost met at mid-lake. It was a perfect ambush point for a predator fish like a northern to be lying in wait for a meal. The boys were watching it come into range but my end of the boat was closer so I had first crack at it.

I cast my spinner past the point and took about two turns on the reel when a northern smashed it and the fight was on.

"Oh, no!" Thunderfoot exclaimed. "Fall off! Fall off!"

But the fish stayed on and I worked it next to the boat, picked it up just behind the head and lifted it into the boat. "Behold," I said showing the fish to the boys. They were kind of sullen.

I removed the hook and dropped the fish over the side smiling sweetly to them. "I'll not be buying tonight," I said grinning at them.

Thunderfoot and Trent looked at each other and both cast to "Ambush Point" at the same time. Their baits landed about a foot apart and Trent's rod bent hard as a fish grabbed his spinner. He set the hook and began grinning as he fought the fish to the boat.

Thunderfoot sat there in disbelief watching as the fish got closer and closer. "Drop off, throw the hook," he urged. "Hand me something to cut the line."

Trent lifted the fish over the side of the boat and grabbed it in mid-air. Then he turned and smiled politely to Thunderfoot who was speechless.

Suddenly Trent got a funny look on his face and turned to me. "Which side of the mouth did you hook that fish you caught?"

"In the right side, right in the lip," I said.

"Look here," he said holding the fish so I could see it. Thunderfoot climbed over the seat to see also, and there in the left side of the fish's mouth was Trent's hook....and in the right side was a still bleeding hole where my bait had been just a couple of minutes earlier.

"That's the same fish I caught," I said laughing.

Trent and I laughed like crazy but Thunderfoot failed to see the humor.

"That can't be legal. He didn't catch a new fish, he caught the same one. That's not fair. We need some rule changes here I think."

Trent looked at me and said, "Chocolate or vanilla?"

Again, Thunderfoot failed to see why we thought this was so funny. We fished for another couple of hours and Thunderfoot grumbled the whole while about being cheated. Finally we loaded up and went to the local gas station for our ice-cream. We sat at a table and I ordered vanilla, Trent ordered chocolate and Thunderfoot had a twist. "Boy, this is the best ice-cream I've ever had," Trent exclaimed.

"Yeah, mine is really good too," I said.

"By the way, thanks for the ice-cream, buddy," Trent added to Thunderfoot.

"Yeah thanks..." I didn't finish. Thunderfoot was shooting death rays out of his eyes at me.

We finished up and Thunderfoot got up slowly and walked to the counter to pay for the ice-cream. He shoved his hand into his pocket and then began grinning. His hand came out of his pocket holding a nickel.

"Um, maybe I'll have to borrow about "2.95 from you," he said. "I seem to be a little short on funds."

It didn't bother me a bit. It was the principal that counted anyway.

Thanks, Thunderfoot.

The Smallmouth Caper

Thunderfoot and I were floating through the morning for on what had been planned to be a day of river fishing for smallmouth bass. He was grumbling about having to get up so early and rummaging around in my tackle box for *his* lucky lure.

"Where's my lucky pink Pop-R?" he asked.

"Did you look on the end of your pole?"

Big grin. "I didn't see it there. My eyes don't work so early in the morning."

He picked up his pole and his lucky bait and began casting toward the bank of the river. His second cast went right into the overhanging branches of one of the trees on shore. "Oh no....the Pink Lady is in the tree...Go back! Go back!"

I pulled on the starter rope and the engine roared to life. I put into gear and took us back upstream to where his lure was hanging in the tree. Thunderfoot stood up on the front seat of the boat and retrieved his lure. I cut the motor and cast behind an overhanging tree branch that looked like a good bass hideout and had a strike as soon as the bait hit the water. A nice-sized smallie jumped into the air and gave me a thrilling fight before coming alongside the boat to be lipped and released.

"Oh no, I buy again," Thunderfoot said.

"That is, if you have any money this time," I said. He grinned and cast the Pink Lady into another tree. About six trees later, Thunderfoot actually hit the water with his cast and got a good strike. He was so surprised that he jerked his bait back and missed the fish. I cast to the same spot and caught the fish as soon as my bait landed.

"Oh that's real cute," he said as I took the hook out of the fish and released it.

"You've got to be quick," I said smiling sweetly.

We fished another couple hundred yards of riverbank and I caught three more fish. I had just cast near a stump sticking out of the water and missed a fish when the Pink Lady sailed past my head and landed in the same spot. The water exploded as the fish tried to eat the Pink Lady and Thunderfoot hauled back to set the hook. He missed the fish but his lure became airborne like a little pink bullet and flew back toward the boat as supersonic speed right at me. I just had time to duck to keep from being hit in the face. The Pink Lady imbedded herself in the top of my head with a crack.

"Watch out!" Thunderfoot yelled after the lure had hit me.

"Thanks for the warning," I said. I reached up to untangle the lure from my hair but it was stuck tight. "Come here and take a look at this," I said.

"Eeee-ouch!" he said as he parted the hair. He looked carefully and the said, "I think I'll need the needle nose pliers."

"Wait! What do you mean?" I said. "I'm not sure I want you operating on my head using some pliers."

"Well, it's either that or you'll be wearing the Pink Lady for a barrette for the rest of the day."

I wasn't so sure which scared me worst, the idea of Thunderfoot operating on my head or the fact that he knew what a barrette was. But, it was too early in the day for me to think about having a fish hook stuck in my head all day so I agreed to let him work on me.

Thunderfoot took the needle nose and gripped the hook with it. "The front treble hook has two of the three stuck in your head," he said. "The back hook is free, so I'll just get hold of it and give it a jerk. Ready?"

"Ready."

He took a deep breath and jerked the hooks from my scalp. At the same time the front hook popped out of my skin, the back hook imbedded itself in the skin of my forehead about half way down between my hairline and my eyebrows.

"Whoops," Thunderfoot said. "That one's pretty shallow. It'll come out easy."

He grabbed the lure and plucked it from my forehead like picking a grape off a bunch. Then he checked his precious Pink Lacy for damage. "I hope your hard head didn't dull my hooks," he said grinning.

I was wiping blood from my forehead as the bait whizzed past my head again and right into a tree. I just shook my head and started the motor.

We fished pretty uneventfully for about three hours. I caught and released about a dozen smallies and Thunderfoot caught and released about a dozen trees. We were getting close to where he had left the truck that morning when Thunderfoot let out a whoop and the biggest smallmouth of the day jumped from the water with his Pink Lady sticking out of his mouth. He fought the fish nicely, and finally lipped it and held it up for me to see. It was a beauty, so I grabbed the camera and snapped a picture of him holding the fish and grinning.

He released the fish and said, "I don't catch a lot of them but I go for quality."

He turned toward the shore and promptly cast his Pink Lady into a tree. "Sometimes the Lady is a tree lover," he joked. "My specialty is trees, yours if fish."

I shook my head and started the motor to go back to fetch his bait. What a dull day it would have been with out him and his Pink Lady. I would have had to just fish all day long.

How boring.

Thanks, Thunderfoot.

The Mallard Hilton

"I need one of those old bus seats," Thunderfoot said as he hurried through the back door. "I'm building us a new duck blind."

"We have a duck blind," I said looking up from my newspaper.

"Yeah, I know, but I'm going to build this one for the L pond. That way we'll be able to get some of those late season mallards that are always landing in there."

The L pond was a short way from our present duck blind and named L pond because it was shaped like a backwards L. Last duck season we had watched helplessly as dozens of late season mallards and wood ducks landed in the pond every day we hunted. Unfortunately we had made the mistake of trying to get to the ducks several times....always with the same results. We came back from the L pond wet, muddy, and without ducks.

The problem was that the L pond was situated in the middle of a floating bog. The marsh grass growing there was only about two to three feet tall for about the last twenty yards on all sides of the pond. Sneaking up on the pond was as close to impossible as it could be due to the fact that the whole area was floating and there was no cover. Every step you took made the floating mass sway and rock and eventually you got to a place where there was nowhere safe to put your foot next and you ended up breaking through the floating grass and sinking into the mud underneath. Unfortunately the mud underneath was deeper than your hip boots would tolerate and you ended up with a boot, or sometimes both boots full of water and mud. Of course, the commotion of one of us dropping through the bog gave away our presence and the ducks flew away. It was a good place for ducks and a very bad place for humans. I had to admit it was a great place to put a duck blind but I was not convinced that we could accomplish such a task.

"How will we get a duck blind on the L pond?" I asked.

"Leave that to me. Now, can I have the bus seat or not?"

I relented and we went to the garage where I helped him drag a bus seat down from the rafters. I had stored them there several years earlier when I had heard that the school was replacing seats in some of the busses. I had learned that the old seats could be purchased for two dollars each, so I bought a couple of them. I really had no idea what I'd use them for but for two bucks I couldn't pass them up. As it turned out, we used one in our first duck blind and it made a great place to sit while waiting for ducks.

I offered to help him carry the seat over to his house but he told me he had everything under control. He took off carrying and dragging the seat across the back yard and I stood and watched him. I had to grin as he struggled with the seat. He did put himself into a project when he got an idea into his head.

I didn't see much of him for the next few days and kind of forgot about the duck blind. Then one day after school he came strutting in the front door and announced that the new duck blind was ready to go. I was required to follow him to his house for an inspection of his work. Off we went to his house and as I rounded the corner of the house I stopped in my tracks and gazed in amazement at the structure sitting in his yard.

The thing had the general shape of a duck blind with the front side lower than the back and a partial roof over the back side, similar to our other blind. The whole thing was covered in chicken wire and he had tied bundles of marsh grass to the wire which made the thing look like a grass covered outhouse, only a little longer than a normal outhouse would be. There was no floor in the thing but what I guessed was the floor was sitting by itself a short way away on the grass. The part that was quite amazing was the size of the thing. It was big enough to put in roosts and nests and use as a chicken coop. There was room for three hunters...possibly four if you were all good friends.

"Good Lord! How do you plan on getting that thing to the pond?" I asked.

"I've got that all figured out," Thunderfoot responded. "We'll just go out to the pond in the canoe and pound posts into the mud exactly where I measure. Then we'll take the floor out with the canoe and slide it out onto the posts and nail it down. Then we'll go back and get the blind and take it out and slide it off the canoe onto the floor. All we have to do then is put a few nails into the floor through the blind and presto...The Mallard Hilton." He acted as if I was completely dense for not seeing the simplicity of the plan on my own.

Well, I had to look this over, so I walked up and inspected the blind. I grabbed the corner and tried to lift. "Wow, that thing must weigh three hundred pounds," I said looking at him incredulously.

"Ahh, no way. Trust me. This'll work," he said gathering up the posts and tools we were going to need. "I figure we can take the bottom out tonight and then tomorrow we can take the blind and finish up, since I don't have school."

I wasn't as confident as he was but I agreed, so we loaded up all the materials and drove down to the marsh. We parked as close to the pond as we could get and then carried the canoe through the brush to the high bank and then down to the marsh. We made another trip for 4 x 4 posts, a bag of nails, a hammer, a sledgehammer and my small chain saw. One more trip was required to manhandle the floor section through the brush and onto the canoe. By the time the two of us got in, the canoe was very close to being overloaded and was very unstable.

We pushed off through the marsh grass and worked our way to the L pond. A while later Thunderfoot stood up to survey the area to choose a spot for the blind. He nearly capsized us when he stood but soon he sat down and we maneuvered to where he had decided would be the best place for the blind. Thunderfoot stood again and placed one of the 4 x 4 posts into the pond and shoved it down into the mud. Then he picked up the sledge hammer and began to pound the post down into the bottom of the pond. His first swing nearly tipped us over. He turned to me with a silly grin on his face. "I guess one of us will have to get into the water to do this. We'll tip the canoe over if we try to do it from here. I'm gonna be too short if I'm in the water, so I guess..."

Somehow I knew this was coming already. I had never been to the L pond in my duck hunting career and left it dry, so there wasn't any reason why I should expect to leave dry today either. I slid out over the side of the canoe and the water came to just about six inches over the tops of my hip boots. I nodded as the cold water filled my boots. Yeah, this was pretty much what I'd expected. I gave Thunderfoot an evil eye as I began hammering the first post into the hard packed mud at the bottom of the pond. About three thousand sledge hammer hits later I had all the posts driven into the mud in the precise places Thunderfoot directed them. I was verging on heart failure, sweating and panting. Thunderfoot was taking careful measurements from the dry canoe and marking each post with a pencil as to the right height for them to be cut off.

"Now if you can just cut on those lines, we can slide the floor over the posts and the bottom of the blind will be all done," he said cheerily.

He was very cool and calm sitting there in the canoe. I, on the other hand, was standing in muddy water, soaked to the skin from sweat and panting like a dog in August. I took the chain-saw and began cutting off the tops of the posts. It didn't take long for me to become covered in sawdust as it stuck to my sweaty body. I finished and handed the saw back to Thunderfoot who was smiling and nodding at my good work.

"Jeez, you look like a snowman," he observed. "Well, let's get the floor nailed down before the mosquitoes get bad."

We slid the floor off the canoe and onto the posts and with a little adjustment it dropped into place. Thunderfoot stepped out onto it and began nailing it down and then stood up proudly to survey his creation. "Looks good," he said. "See, I told you this wouldn't be so hard."

I managed to get myself back into the canoe and we paddled back to the shore. We left the canoe and tools there for the next phase of construction and headed home.

The next day we manhandled the chicken coop into the truck and somehow drug it through the brush to the high bank. We slid it down to the pond and got it onto the canoe. The canoe was still floating but just barely. There was very little freeboard as we paddled the monstrosity toward the floor waiting on the pond. Miraculously we made it to the floor without sinking the canoe. As we got to the platform, Thunderfoot stood up and stepped out onto the floor. When his weight was removed from the front of the canoe, the back became too heavy to keep the thing floating and within a second of him leaving, the chicken coop and I went straight to the bottom.

Of course, the blind slid back onto me and I had a heck of a time getting up and out from under it. Meanwhile Thunderfoot was shouting at me. "Watch out for the grass! Don't ruin the grass on the blind!"

This time I was wet all the way to the top of my head, something I hadn't previously experienced at the L pond. But of course, Thunderfoot was bone dry. I managed to get one end of the blind onto the platform and we manhandled the monster into place. It fit like a glove. "Not a bad piece of engineering," he said strutting. "I told you this would be a piece of cake." He took the small hammer and nailed down the blind to the floor and then put the bus seat into place.

Then he removed a newspaper covered board that he had put into the bottom of the canoe earlier. He took the paper off and nailed the pine board to the blind wall. He stood back and read what was written on the board: "The Mallard Hilton. Owned by Dan and Thunderfoot...Duck Hunting Buds."

For some reason the mud oozing around in my boots didn't seem so bad after all.

Thanks, Thunderfoot.

A Little Buck Fever?

Thunderfoot and I were cleaning up after the close of the duck season. We had brought the gear home from the duck blind and now were untangling decoy lines and sorting the decoys into piles of like ducks for storage in burlap bags in my garage. We were one week away from the deer gun season. Thunderfoot had been fretting all week about getting ready for deer hunting, so he was working extra hard to get the duck stuff put away quickly.

"I think we should be out shooting the deer guns and not fooling around with this duck stuff," he said.

"Yeah, and then the duck stuff will be in a big mess on the floor for the rest of the winter. Just get this done and we'll go shoot our guns, we've got plenty of time."

"Well, I want to be right on when that big trophy comes past me," he said.

We finally finished with the duck gear and I got the deer rifles from the gun cabinet while Thunderfoot found some paper targets. We headed down to the old lagoon to sight-in the guns. A lot of other hunters used the old lagoon too, so there was a backstop someone had built as a place to hang your target, and a wooden spool that highline wire had been on for a table to use as a shooting rest.

Thunderfoot sprinted over to the backstop and pinned up a couple of targets as I uncased the guns.

"You go first," he said.

Normally he was the first to do any shooting. He loved shooting any gun, at anything, be it targets, ducks, pigeons, whatever, but now he wanted me to go first. I figured that he might be a little afraid of the recoil of the deer guns. He didn't have a deer rifle of his own, so I lent him one of mine and he hadn't shot it before today.

I folded up my gun case for a rest, knelt behind the wire spool and sighted through the scope of my 30.06 rifle. I carefully zeroed in the crosshairs on the center of the target and squeezed the trigger. Thunderfoot almost jumped out of his shoes when the gun went off.

"Wow! That's loud. Does it kick hard?"

"No...it's no worse than a 12-gauge, it just sounds worse."

I shot a couple more times and then we walked over to the target so see how I did. All three of my shots were in a circle the size of a silver dollar so I was pretty confident I could hit a deer where I wanted.

We went back to the spool and Thunderfoot carefully slid a cartridge into the .270 I had loaned him. "Now just aim careful and squeeze," I said. "Don't worry about the recoil."

He sighted for a long time and then pulled the trigger. He jumped about a foot when the gun went off. "Holy cow! It kicks like a horse!" he said rubbing his shoulder.

"Oh come on," I said. "It's not that bad, just quit worrying about the recoil and you'll be fine."

He shot again and jumped just as badly.

"You're anticipating the kick and jumping before it even goes off," I said. "Go put up another target and try again."

He trotted out to the backstop and while he was busy, I opened the breech of the gun and removed the live shell and replaced it with an empty. He came back, picked up the gun and sighted again. He took a deep breath and squeezed the trigger. When the gun went *click* he jumped a foot.

What the...what happened?" he asked.

I held my hand out for the gun and he handed it to me. I opened the chamber and took out the empty shell. "See? You're jumping for nothing. You jumped even without a shell going off. Now put in a live one and quit being such a baby about the recoil."

He gave me a look with the baby crack but then grinned. "Ok, maybe you are right," he said.

From then on, he shot like a pro.

The next afternoon we headed out to the farm where we were going to hunt. I had obtained permission from the owner a few weeks earlier and I wanted Thunderfoot to get the lay of the land before opening morning.

That way he'd know where everything was and where I wanted him to stand opening morning.

"Ken told me he's been seeing a huge buck up here all summer," I said as we walked up the ridge road to the top of the hill. Just as I said it a nice buck and three does jumped up from a ditch and trotted up the side of the hill ahead of us.

"Wow! I don't think I can wait until next week," Thunderfoot said as he watched the deer go over the hill.

When we got to the top I took him to the place where I planned on him standing opening day and showed him around. Then we walked up to where I was going to stand. I had given him the best spot on the farm. My spot was above him on the hill where I could keep an eye on him.

The next week was a long one for Thunderfoot. He was at my house every night talking deer stories and hauling gear over. By the middle of the week he had brought over so many clothes that it looked like I was having a garage sale.

Finally Friday evening came and he showed up after school with his lunch packed for the next day. He slept in the spare room and went to bed at eight o'clock so he'd be ready for an early start in the morning.

The next morning we were at our stands on the hill about an hour before shooting time. I wanted to get to the farm early so we could get situated before other hunters on surrounding lands would begin arriving. This way they would move some deer toward us and not the other way around. We were the only ones hunting this farm, so we didn't have any competition from anyone close to us.

The darkness began to fade. Soon I was able to make out shapes. A short time later the shapes began to turn into real objects that began to take color and form. I looked down the hill and saw Thunderfoot at rigid attention as he watched a deer path below his stand.

From far away I heard the first shot of the season and soon there was another not so far away. In the next few minutes shots rang out all around us as hunters saw their first deer of the day. There was no movement in our woods for almost an hour. Finally I saw a doe working her way down the hillside toward Thunderfoot. He had told me he wasn't going to shoot a doe but was going for a trophy buck. He did have a permit for a doe, so I wondered what he'd do when he saw the deer. He slowly raised the gun and looked at the doe in the scope then lowered it again. Then he raised it, hesitated, and lowered it again as the doe walked away.

A while later I saw him raise his gun again and I looked in the direction he was aiming. There was a fork buck with two points on each side standing about eighty yards from him in the field. He held the gun up for a long time before he lowered it. The buck walked off into the woods and Thunderfoot began to pace around.

At noon he came up to my stand and sat down on the ground beside me to help me eat my lunch. "What happened to your food?" I asked.

"Oh that was gone a long time ago," he said.

"Why didn't you shoot that four –pointer?" I asked.

"I was going to but then I thought maybe I should wait for a bigger one."

"Well, don't wait too long," I said.

He went back to his stand and I settled down to wait for the afternoon action. It didn't take long until a bunch of does and a six-point buck trotted up near Thunderfoot. He again raised his gun, watched them for a while and let them go.

I noticed movement a short time later and turned to see a nice four-pointer standing below me. I knew he wasn't going up to Thunderfoot and a trophy wasn't a priority for me, so I raised my gun and fired. The buck took one step and dropped in his tracks. I laid my gun down and started walking toward the deer, but Thunderfoot passed me on the run.

"Holy cow! You got him!" he panted. "He's not a trophy but he's a nice one."

As we field dressed the deer I asked him about the six-pointer he had passed up.

"Too many does in the way," he said. "Well, I've got to get back to my stand, see you at quittin' time."

I cleaned up and settled back to wait for the end of the day. I had almost fallen asleep when I noticed something coming across the woods toward Thunderfoot. There was a huge buck and four does trotting right at him, but he wouldn't see them coming because he was too far down the hill. Finally they crested the ridge and he could see them. He raised the gun...lowered it...raised it...lowered it...and finally raised it a third time. All of the movement spooked the deer and they turned and headed back the way they had come.

Thunderfoot was stomping his feet and kicking the ground and I could see little puffs of steam coming out of his mouth as he cussed. I grinned to myself.

When quitting time finally came I dragged my deer down to his level. He walked over to me. "Get a little buck fever?" I asked.

"No!"

"That's ok, it happens to a lot of people," I said.

"I did *not* have buck fever," he said indignantly. "The does came out in the open but the buck stayed back far enough that I couldn't get a good shot at him. All I could see was his head."

"Why didn't you shoot him in the head?"

"Are you crazy? I would have ruined the trophy rack,"

Yeah right.

Thanks, Thunderfoot.

Persistence Pays

Thunderfoot had been pestering me all week to take him northern fishing. The problem was that he wanted to go to a slough we had fished the past summer that was deep in the marsh. It was fine earlier in the winter when the marsh was frozen solid but now it was early spring and the trip to the lake was over some very shaky ground.

"What do you mean we can't get there?" he asked.

"I mean that we can't get there because that marsh is full of springs and we'll get wet if we try to cross it."

"But think of all those big northerns out there just licking their lips waiting for us," he said grinning.

Against my better judgment, I gave in and about an hour later I was carefully stepping from clump of frozen swamp grass to clump of frozen swamp grass. I worked my way very carefully toward the lake while skinny little Thunderfoot abandoned me and took off across the marsh without a problem. He was waiting for me on the frozen lake.

"Hurry up with the shiners" he said as he drilled his third hole.

Somehow I made it to the lake without falling through and the lake ice was thick enough to make me feel pretty safe. I handed Thunderfoot the minnow bucket and he took off to bait up the tip-ups.

"Last one to catch a northern has to clean the fish!" he shouted over his shoulder. That was a pretty good deal for him especially since he already had his holes drilled and his tip-ups baited and was already fishing. I was still standing there with my tip-ups in my bucket, but I agreed anyway.

I was working on my second fishing-hole when he let out a whoop and took off for his far tip-up. The flag was up. He carefully lifted the tip-up from the hole, played out the line like a professional, waited for the fish to run and then jerked hard on the line. He pulled in a bare hook.

"Nuts...he got my shiner," he said. He ran back and grabbed the minnow bucket so he could re-bait his hook. He had barely gotten the tip-up back in the hole when the flag went up again. This time he waited even longer. Then he set the hook and the fish jerked him back nearly pulling him to the ice.

"He's a monster," he said as he pulled on the line. "Get over here and help..."

He never finished the sentence because the line broke. He pulled it in with a look of deep disappointment on his face. He came over to my tackle box and dug around until he found another steel leader, tied it onto his line, added a new hook and went back and baited the new rig and re-set the tip-up.

He hadn't walked fifteen feet from the tip-up when the flag went up again. This time he waited the appropriate amount of time and again hooked into a good-sized fish. He was working it toward the hole when the line went slack. He looked dejected as he pulled it from the hole.'

"He broke the leader." He began walking back toward me. "What kind of junk leaders do you buy anyway?"

I reminded him that if he didn't like the quality of my leaders he should purchase some of his own. He looked up from my tackle box in disbelief.

"You're out of leaders! Now what should I do?"

"Pull up one of your other tip-ups and use that one," I said.

"No way! I'll just tie the hook on without a leader. I don't want to give you the advantage by being one tip-up short."

He got everything set and we waited for about a half hour with no action. Suddenly Thunderfoot let out a yell and took off again for the same hole. "He's back! Bring the gaff and help me."

I doubted that it was the same fish but I thought it would be a good idea to help with a leaderless line on the tip-up. When I got to the hole he was working the fish, giving it line when it ran and carefully pulling when it gave a little. We finally got a look at it as it went past the hole. It was a big one. Thunderfoot pulled again and the fish turned and he got the head started up the hole. It looked to be at least a ten pound northern. I slipped the gaff into the fish's mouth and pulled it up onto the ice.

"All right! I got him! Look, my other lines are in his mouth."

I couldn't believe it. He was right. The first hook and leader, the second hook and broken leader, and the leaderless hook that caught the fish were all right there inside the mouth.

It was almost dark, so we packed up and started across the marsh to the truck. This time I wasn't so lucky. As I stepped onto a safe-looking spot, my foot went through up to my knee. When I tried to free my wet foot I broke through with the second foot. There I stood up to my knees in smelly swamp mud, holding my bucket and the auger.

Thunderfoot stopped and looked back at me. "Quit fooling around, "he said. "I want to get back and see if that first minnow is in this fish's stomach. Be sure you look carefully when you clean him."

Thanks, Thunderfoot.

Last Ice

It was one of those spring mornings that you dream about all winter. The sun was shining and the temperature was in the thirties by dawn. I was sitting at the kitchen table reading the morning newspaper when something caught my attention. As I looked up, I saw Thunderfoot crossing the back yard carrying his ice-fishing bucket and a sack that looked like a lunch sack. He was heading straight for my back door.

"She's a beauty today. I think we should go ice-fishing one more time," he said as he stuck his head into my refrigerator.

It's been pretty warm," I said. "Do you think the ice will still be safe?"

He looked at me with one of his "give me a break" looks. "Sure it's ok...if you're worried, I'll go first to test it."

That was real generous of him. Of course, he only weighed about a hundred pounds with his pockets full of sinkers, so he wasn't the one I was worried about. I weighed in at a higher weight bracket and was the one likely to take a drink, but it was such a beautiful day that I gave in and soon we were driving to the river bottoms.

Our first choice of lakes had about four feet of open water between the shore and the ice. We stood there looking out and I said, "Well, that's it. We can't get to the ice."

"How about Puffenrot's lake?" he said. "It's shady there where the trees are along the lake. The ice should be better there."

We drove a mile or so west and Thunderfoot had been right. The ice was solid right up to the shoreline, so he walked out to test it. When he jumped up and down the whole area shook and water splashed up in the old ice holes scattered around. "No problem," he said grinning.

I took the auger and drilled a hole. There was still about six inches of ice, but it was like packed snow, not good hard ice. The spring rains and higher angle of the sun had rotted the ice and it didn't look safe to me.

"Boy, I don't know...it's pretty soft," I said.

"Oh, come on. Don't be such a baby."

I gave in and we got the gear from the truck and started out to the main part of the lake. This particular lake is one of the few that is situated close to the high bank. The lake has a narrow arm that runs right up to the shore instead of the whole lake being in the middle of the marsh as are all the others in the area. The "arm" of water was the way to the lake since the marsh was mostly melted, so this was probably the only one we could get to.

Thunderfoot walked ahead of me with the minnows and his ice-bucket. I started walking out but stopped as the water in the old ice-holes began sloshing with each step.

I jumped up and down carefully and the whole thing was shaking. For some reason I decided to walk closer to the marsh on the shore side of the channel. I only took three steps when I went through.

At first it wasn't so terrible. The water was only about waist deep and I was standing on a sand bottom. It only took a few seconds though for the water to penetrate my clothes and run into my boots making it much more terrible very quickly.

I mistakenly tried to get back up on the ice by going closer to the marsh grass and broke through again several times before I realized my mistake and turned toward the middle where the ice was thicker. I tried several more times to climb up onto the ice but each time I broke through again. Suddenly I heard a choking sound and looked over at Thunderfoot who was lying on his back on the ice clutching his stomach and laughing hysterically, tears running down his face. "I suppose you'll want to go home now," he said sobbing with glee.

"Real funny...come here and take my buckets, so I can get out."

"No way! I'm not coming near you, I'll fall in too. Slide your buckets across the ice to me."

He sat down on his bucket to watch the show. "Try not to get the lunch wet will you?" he said laughing his fool head off.

I wallowed around back and forth like an elephant seal trying to get up on the beach and finally found some ice that I held me. I slid up on my belly and laid there completely exhausted. I was drenched from head to toe by ice cold water and smelled like a swamp, covered in grass and seaweed.

"Thanks for all the help," I said as I got to my feet.

"That was so funny. I'm sorry but I just couldn't keep from laughing," he said.

He gave me one of his impish grins and I had to smile. I suppose it had been a pretty good show at that. But I was beginning to get cold real fast, so I picked up my gear and turned to go back to the shore. It was then that I realized that the ice that connected the lake to the shore was now open water instead of ice. I also realized that Thunderfoot was now on the wrong side of the open water to be able to get to the shore. He must have read my thoughts because he stopped laughing and looked over at me. "Hey, you broke all the ice. How am I gonna get back?"

It was my turn to grin.

Thanks, Thunderfoot.

The Flying Fish

The ice went out below the dam last night," Thunderfoot said as he came through the door. "We better go and try for some walleyes from the shore." He was carrying his rod and reel and nodding his head up and down.

It didn't take much convincing to get me to go walleye fishing and not very long later we were climbing down over the bank to the sandy shore of the river, below the dam. We weren't the only ones with the idea of walleye fishing as many others had been keeping an eye on the ice, waiting for it to leave the water open.

Two old river-rats were leaving just as we walked down to the shore, so we took over their spot. Just above us were a couple of teenage boys who Thunderfoot knew and waved to and below us were a couple of other fishermen who we didn't know. The two teens were packing up and as they left, a family of African-American folks came walking down to the river bank. They took over the turf vacated by the teens. The family included a mom and dad, a young boy and an old lady that was obviously the grandma. The old lady was all decked out in a long coat and a thing on her head that looked like a turban. I thought it looked like she was on her way to church and had stopped off to fish. She was wearing a pair of knee length black rubber boots to complete her ensemble. I had to smile as she baited her hook and cast out her line. She let the bait settle and then held the pole in her hand staring intently at the tip waiting for a bite.

I put a minnow on my jig and cast out to the deeper water and let my jig sink to the bottom. When it touched bottom I lifted it and swam it back a little way toward me. As it touched again, I lifted and swam, lifted and swam. On about the fifth lift, I felt a little tic and set the hook into a nice "eating-sized" walleye. As I was putting it on the stringer Thunderfoot set the hook and reeled in a sheephead.

"Try a minnow," I said. "You'll get more walleyes. Those sheephead will pester you all day if you use worms."

59

"I don't like to reach into that cold water for a minnow. I'm going to stick with crawlers," he said.

Well within half an hour I had three more nice walleyes on the stringer and Thunderfoot had beached six sheephead. He was just reeling in his seventh one when we heard a commotion on the shore above us as the dad from the family landed a huge northern.

"Wow," Thunderfoot said. "I didn't know there were northerns in here."

"Yeah, they're here now too," I said.

He took off the six inch sheephead that was on his hook and put it in the minnow bucket. "I need a bigger hook," he said digging into my tackle box. He must have found what he was looking for because he sat down cross-legged in the sand and began re-rigging his line. A minute later he fished around in the minnow bucket and pulled out the sheephead. "I'm gonna put this sheephead on the line as bait and catch me one of those big northerns," he said. He reeled up his rig and carefully swung back toward the bank. Then he gave it a hard side-arm cast toward the river.

The hook, sinker, and bobber went about fifty yards out into the river. The sheephead came off the hook about two thirds of the way through the cast. It flew through the air up the river bank and...you guessed it...hit the old lady right in the side of the head. When it hit, the sheephead knocked her turban down over her eyes and then flopped into the water.

Thunderfoot's mouth dropped open. I looked at the old lady and she was adjusting her turban up onto her head and seemed like she hadn't been hurt, but she was plenty mad. I couldn't keep a straight face and burst out laughing. When I started laughing, Thunderfoot almost tipped over laughing so hard.

Now, I know it wasn't nice to laugh, but there was no way any human, including Thunderfoot could have done that on purpose if he'd have had a year to try. While I felt bad about laughing, it was about one of the funniest things I'd ever seen while fishing.

"I'm gonna go fish downriver," he said taking off down the bank.

"You better go over there and tell her you're sorry," I said.

"No way, her son will kill me."

Just then I had a hard hit on my minnow and set the hook into my fifth walleye. I reeled it in and squatted down to put it on the stringer. As I finished I heard footsteps on the bank behind me. I looked down at my side and there was about a size thirteen tennis shoe. The mate to it was on my other side. Above the tennis shoes were bright blue pants legs of a royal blue jump suit. I knew who was wearing it as I stood up.

The old lady's son was about six foot four and built like William-the-Refrigerator Perry, of Chicago Bears fame a few years back. He looked down at me and glowered.

"You hit my momma up side the *hay-ed* with a fish?"

"No, it wasn't me," I said trying not to let my voice quiver.

"Somebody hit my momma up side the *hay-ed* with a fish."

"Honest, it wasn't me. I saw it happen and I'm sure it was an accident."

He stood there looking down at me. With me standing almost in the water, he was nearly a foot taller than I was. He also had the distinct advantage since my choices were tangle with him or going swimming in an icy river. Neither choice was very appetizing.

He stood there thinking about it for what seemed like an eternity and then stomped off up the bank. I turned and saw Thunderfoot downriver from us with tears running down his cheeks from laughing so hard.

"Get up here!" I said as angrily as I could.

He walked back up as slowly as he could go. "You go over there and own up to your stupid move and tell that lady you're sorry."

He walked slowly up the old lady and stopped and gave her one of his famous "charm-smiles". He batted his big blue eyes at her bashfully and I could see that he was telling her hopefully that it was his fault and he was sorry. Soon she beamed and put her arm around his waist and gave him a hug. He began walking back and turned and gave her a wave.

"It's all ok," he said.

He picked up his gear and walked half way up the bank and stopped. "Oh by the way...I told her you would be happy to give her your walleyes for being so careless with your cast." He was off like a shot for the top of the riverbank.

I looked up at the old lady and she was sitting waiting for me with an empty stringer in her hand. That little...he got me again.

Thanks, Thunderfoot.

Luck Is My Middle Name

Thunderfoot and I were climbing slowly up the side of a steep hill on opening morning of his turkey season. Each spring, there are six hunting periods for which a hunter may draw a permit. Thunderfoot had drawn the second period and I had drawn a permit for the fourth season. We always hunted together so it was actually nice that we got different time periods so we could hunt more hours.

We were using the stars for light because the turkeys were roosting just a hundred yards or so up the hill. We didn't dare use a flashlight or make any noise. I bent a branch back and motioned Thunderfoot through the opening as we neared the top of the hill.

"They should be right on that point," I whispered. "Be really quiet or we'll spook them."

Thunderfoot nodded and quietly moved past me. I was amazed that he had been so quiet coming up the hill but we had spent a lot of time in the woods since I had given him his nickname and his stalking skills were much improved.

At the hilltop, I motioned toward a blown-down tree and signaled for him to sit down and wait while I put out our hen decoys. By the time I had the two fake turkeys positioned Thunderfoot had cleared all of the leaves and sticks from our hiding spot. I unfolded a piece of camouflage material and we made a blind by hanging it from the bushes and limbs in front of the treetop.

"This is a cool blind," Thunderfoot whispered. "I think..." Just then a tom turkey cobbled about sixty yards down the hill from us. Thunderfoot's eyes got as big as saucers. "I think we're in the right spot," he said smiling.

Indeed we were and soon another turkey gobbled and then a third sounded off. In a short time there were turkeys gobbling all around us. The ones we were interested in, just down the hill from us were talking up a storm. We waited for about twenty minutes and then heard the toms fly down from the trees. The first one landed very close followed by two more that landed right next to him. "Holy cow!" Thunderfoot whispered. "They're almost in range."

"Just sit still," I said. "They'll see the decoys and come right up here."

Sure enough, one of the toms looked up the hill and saw our decoys. He immediately fanned out his tail and gobbled like crazy. I called back and here he came!

Thunderfoot slid the gun up over the top of the blind and got ready. "Wait for him to get close to the decoy," I said. "It's about fifteen yards away from us, so it'll be an easy shot."

The turkey came closer. Thunderfoot quietly pulled the hammer back on the ten-gauge and took a deep breath. KABOOM!

For about three seconds, the turkey stood there like it was going to drop over. Then it high-tailed it down the side of the hill.

Thunderfoot sat there with his mouth hanging open.

"You missed!" I said. "I can't believe it. How could you miss?" I walked toward the spot where the turkey had been standing. I still could not believe he had missed a bird the size of a medium sized dog with a ten-gauge shotgun. When I turned around I could see his eyes were welling up with tears so I quickly examined a small sapling near where the turkey had been. "Wow, that's the luckiest turkey in this woods," I said. "Most of your shot hit this little tree."

He brightened up at that so I said, "We've got plenty of time. Maybe we can get another one to come into us."

I was actually pretty doubtful about calling in another turkey after we had shot the gun but I wanted to make Thunderfoot feel better. So I gathered up the decoys and we walked to the top of the hill to wait. We ate a couple of candy bars and drank some juice boxes and suddenly a long way off, maybe three hills over, we heard a turkey gobble.

"Listen," Thunderfoot said. "There's one."

We waited and he gobbled again. "Let's move that way," I said. "He's a long way off and we can get away with moving." We took off in the direction of the turkey at a fast walk and stopped partway over the hill. I called on my turkey call and the turkey gobbled right back. This time he was closer to us, so we moved very carefully and called again. When he answered he was just across the valley from us on the other hillside. I couldn't see any way to get any closer to him, so I said, "You sit next to that tree and I'll lay down by this log. We can't move any closer or he'll see us."

Thunderfoot sat down in front of a big oak tree and I lay down behind a log just a few feet from the tree. I called and the turkey gobbled on the hillside right below us. We waited and all of a sudden the turkey materialized out of the brush. He was about fifty yards away....too far for a shot. He was working his way toward us looking for that sweet sounding hen that had been talking to him.

When he disappeared behind a treetop, Thunderfoot raised the gun and got ready. Soon the turkey jumped onto a log about forty yards away. Thunderfoot waited. The turkey hopped down from the log and started up the hill. Thirty-five yards....thirty yards...now he was in range. Twenty-five yards.....on the bird came. Then time stood still for a second.

Thunderfoot touched off the three-and-a-half inch shell and the turkey tipped over like he had been hit by a truck. In the same instant, Thunderfoot was up and on his feet racing down the hill. The turkey flopped around for a couple of seconds, then got to his feet and took off running with Thunderfoot in hot pursuit.

Thunderfoot caught up in a matter of seconds. Since the gun was a single-shot, he grabbed it by the barrel and swung it like a baseball bat, knocking the bird down. Feathers flew as he tossed the gun onto the ground and tackled the turkey.

I sat there dumbfounded watching the whole thing. "Get down here and help me with this thing!" he yelled. Leaves, brush and feathers were flying as the turkey flapped his wings. Thunderfoot was getting a beating from the critter's wings and sharp toenails.

I ran down the hill and picked up a strong stick and cracked the bird over the head. That was the end of that. I sat down and began laughing. "Boy you weren't taking any chances on that one were you?" I said.

"No way! I wasn't going to lose two birds in one day," he said grinning through the dirt and debris that was stuck to the sweat on his face.

We smoothed out the feathers on the turkey and took a couple of pictures. Then we picked up the gun and found Thunderfoot's cap hanging from a tree branch. As we started down the hill I said, "Boy, you've got some luck. Most people get one chance in a whole season for a turkey. Some don't even get that....and you got two chances in one day."

Thunderfoot grinned as he proudly carried his turkey over his shoulder. "Some guys got skill, some got luck...I guess luck is my middle name. Plus, I have the advantage of a pretty good hunting guide."

Maybe so.

Thanks, Thunderfoot.

The Mother Lode

I was sitting on the front patio sipping a soda when Thunderfoot came around the corner of the house carrying a grocery bag. He gave me a grin and held out the bag in front of him. "It looks like a good day to go mushroom hunting," he said.

It was one of those early spring days when the humidity was almost unbearable. There were rain clouds building in the west and I wasn't too excited about tromping up and down the hills looking for mushrooms. With the clouds building up it was a pretty good bet that we'd get caught in a storm anyway. "It's going to rain, and I'm pretty comfortable right here," I said.

"Just think of those big morels popping out of the ground, waiting for us to pick them. Just think of a nice walk in the woods in the spring, communing with nature. Just think..."

"Ok, ok. I give up" I said. There was no use arguing with him and he'd keep pestering me until I gave in, so I decided to just get it over with. I grabbed a plastic bag from the house and off we went for the hills. Thunderfoot wanted to go to one of the farms where we had hunted squirrels last fall. We stopped and ask for permission to hunt and then started off through the woods. We casually walked up the valley and I strolled along the creek and tried to see some brook trout. Thunderfoot, meanwhile, was loping up every hillside along the way, checking out dead trees.

"Any up there?" I asked when he stopped below a tree.

"Just a few, don't bother coming up, I'll get them." He was on his knees picking mushrooms and he didn't have to tell me twice not to climb up the steep hill. Soon he came down and rejoined me. "I got a few," he said opening his mushroom bag and holding it out to me. I looked over the edge of the bag cautiously not knowing what to expect and saw about a dozen nice morels.

"Those aren't bad," I said.

He grinned. "What were you expecting, a snake?"

"I don't trust you after that first time," I said grinning.

He looked offended. "What? Would I do something like that?"

"Yes you would and I'm not going to fall for it twice."

"I'm going way up on top. I remember a big tree up there that was dead from when we were squirrel hunting last fall," he said. "Want to come?"

"Go ahead," I said. "I'll stay down here and look for valley mushrooms."

I sat down next to a shade tree and stretched out. It was nice and cool and the sounds of the stream in the valley soon put me to sleep. I woke about half-an-hour later when something began tickling my nose. I looked up and it was Thunderfoot with a weed in his hand grinning at me.

"Jeez, I could hear you snoring clear up on top of the hill," he said. I was still groggy from sleep but woke fast when he dropped his mushroom sack in my lap. It was full to the top with mushrooms.

"Wow, where did you get those?" I asked.

"Up by that tree I told you about," he said. "And this is only a start. There are about a million more up there."

I was on my feet quickly when he said that and started off to where he had just been when he stopped me. "We need more bags," he said. "These two won't hold all of them."

Now I was really excited. "Honest?" I asked.

"No foolin...we need at least ten bags."

Just then I remembered some shoe bags that were in back of the truck. I had been an usher in a friend's wedding a few weeks earlier and all of the bags and boxes from the other usher's shoes and rented tuxes ended up in a garbage box in the truck. "There are a bunch of those shoe bags in the truck from Jon's wedding," I said. "We can use them."

Thunderfoot was off toward the truck like a shot. I sat down to wait for him even though I could hardly wait for him to get back so I could see this huge mushroom find. I figured I'd better wait since it was his spot, but it didn't take long for him to come huffing and puffing down the valley with an armful of bags.

We headed up the hill, Thunderfoot galloping along at a breakneck pace and me panting along behind him. We got to the top and started down the other side when I saw the tree. It was an enormous elm, probably twenty feet around. The bark was hanging on it just beginning to drop off, a prefect age for a mushroom tree. Thunderfoot stopped in front of the tree, turned and spread his arms like Moses parting the Red Sea. "Behold...the mother lode," he said.

I stood there with my mouth hanging open. I had heard many times of miracle trees where you could find hundreds of mushrooms, but had never found one. This tree was one of those miracle trees. There were mushrooms for thirty feet or forty feet in each direction around the tree. They were so thick in places that you couldn't walk without stepping on them. I stood there taking in the once-in-a-lifetime sight...and then it began to rain.

Thunderfoot and I didn't care if it rained, snowed, or hailed. We both got down on our hands and knees and began crawling around the tree picking mushrooms and filling plastic bags. We picked for over two hours and ran out of bags so Thunderfoot took off his shirt, tied the sleeves and head hole shut and we put the last of the mushrooms in the shirt. We were soaked to the skin, covered in dirt and leaves and we had eleven bags and a t-shirt full of mushrooms. We couldn't have been happier.

We picked up the bags and started back to the truck. "Wow, I've never seen so many mushrooms in one place in my life," I said grinning.

"Just think...you could be still sitting on the porch, nice and dry, and you'd have missed this day," he said.

I looked at my shirtless, wet little buddy and smiled. "I wouldn't have missed this for anything," I said. "And it's even better because I got to share it with you."

He grinned back at me. "This will be one mushroom trip we'll remember for a long time."

No kidding, a long time for sure.

Thanks, Thunderfoot.

Night Fishing

I was just finishing the dishes when I happened to look out my window and saw Thunderfoot coming across the back yard with his arms full of fishing gear. A minute later he came through the front door with a big grin.

"It sure would be a nice night to do some night fishing for catfish," he said with an expectant look on his face. "One of my friends at school went last night and he caught a whole bunch of catfish."

"Fishing at night?" I asked. "You get into enough trouble fishing in the daytime. Don't you think that throwing darkness into the mix will make things a little hazardous?"

He scoffed at me. "I've got a lantern and I already dug worms. All you have to do is grab your pole and we're ready." He nodded his head up and down like a bobble-dead doll.

"Well, I guess it might be fun," I said. "And since you've got everything ready to go, I'll go along."

"Good, I'll load everything up while you make the lunch."

"Lunch?" I had just finished my dinner ten minutes earlier and he was talking about having lunch already? I threw together a few sandwiches and some chips and tossed them into a small cooler with some pop and joined him at the truck.

A little later we walked down the bank of a stream that fed into the river known for a good catfish population. He picked a spot just above a treetop that had fallen into the water. We set up our camp. I got the gear ready while Thunderfoot cut a couple of forked sticks to use as "pole holders."

We had just baited up and tossed out lines out when Thunderfoot opened the cooler saying, "Boy, this fishing makes me faminished, what's in here?" He began inhaling sandwiches and chips as if he'd been without a

68

meal for a week. Suddenly he dropped his food and grabbed his rod and set the hook into a fish. "All right," he said. "That's the first fish of the day, you have to buy ice-cream." He worked the fish close to the bank and slid it up onto the grass. It was a nice sized catfish and he unhooked it, put it on the stringer and re-baited his hook.

Meanwhile I salvaged half of a sandwich from the lunch cooler and settled back in my fishing chair to relax. Actually my fishing chair was really a turkey hunting chair. It was like an aluminum lawn chair but the legs on it were only about six inches long instead of a couple of feet. It was great for turkey hunting because you could sit low where the turkeys wouldn't see you but still have a backrest to lean against. It worked real nice on the river bank for fishing too.

We caught a few more fish and soon darkness began to creep up on us. It was getting hard to see our lines so Thunderfoot lit the lantern and sat it between us on the ground. I was pretty comfortable and getting kind of drowsy when Thunderfoot grabbed his pole and hauled back on it to set the hook. His reel began screaming as the drag was pulled out and his pole was bent nearly double.

"Holy cow! It's a monster!" he yelled. While he fought his fish I was contentedly watching from my chair. I could see that his line was caught in the treetop as the fish had pulled it downriver while fighting him.

"Your fish is under the tree," I said.

"Oh yeah? I've got strong line on here, I'll winch him right out of there," he said as he hauled back on his pole. I started to sit up to get a better look just as his line came clear of the tree. His "fish" came out of the water and flew through the air right at me. Now, it was pretty dark and it all happened pretty fast, but what I saw flying through the air was a long snake-like critter coming right at me. It landed in my lap and began writhing around as I tipped my chair over backwards. I was skidding backwards and got turned toward the river and in less than a second I rolled off the bank into the water with the snake-thing in my lap.

I may have set a world record for the backstroke from a sitting position because it only took a couple of seconds to get out into the middle of the river. Meanwhile, Thunderfoot had reeled up the slack in his line. He began to pull the snake-thing and me toward the bank. The critter was wrapped around one of my chair arms. After a couple of pulls it came free.

He pulled it up onto the bank while I floundered around in the water.

"Hey, it's an eel!" he said cheerfully. "Come here and look at it...it's cool."

I was standing in chest deep water, my fishing chair floating around next to me and he wanted me to look at his eel. I stood there and let my heart rate slow down to less than three hundred beats per minute and then slogged my way to the riverbank dragging my chair behind me. The eel was writhing around on the ground and Thunderfoot was standing there looking at it with the lantern in his hand.

He looked up at me. "Will you take it off? It's kind of creepy and I don't want to touch it."

When he saw the look on my face he said, "Oh never mind, I'll just cut the line."

He clipped the line a little way from the critter and it slithered down over the bank and back into the river. It was probably going to look for a new place to call home.

I was standing there dripping wet, covered in stinky mud and still panting when Thunderfoot said, "Boy, you sure can move fast when you want to. I never saw anybody jump so high from a sitting position." He was smirking as he looked me up and down.

"Thanks for noticing. And, by the way, no I'm not hurt."

"I knew you weren't hurt, you moved too fast to be hurt," he said. "I suppose you want to go home now. We might as well. You probably scared all the fish away when you went swimming anyway."

Sometimes he was such a compassionate boy.

Thanks, Thunderfoot.

The Fish Fry

Thunderfoot came through my front door carrying his fishing pole and a sleeping bag. "What'cha doin' tonight?" he asked.

"I don't have anything planned. What do you have in mind?"

"It's such a nice evening. I think we should go set up the tent on a sandbar and fish late, and then sleep overnight on the sandbar. Sounds good huh?"

I didn't really have anything better to do so I agreed. We began gathering gear that we would need for the evening. We put the small tent, our sleeping bags, a couple of rods and reels and a lantern in the boat plus a cooler and some pop.

"We'll have to stop at the grocery store and get some hot dogs or brats for supper," I said.

"No way...we'll eat fish. Let's just take some potatoes and beans and bread. We'll catch some fish, clean them and fry them up. It'll be great."

"Maybe we should take some hot dogs, just in case," I said.

"Are you in doubt of my ability to procure food for myself and my fellow explorer? No way. No hot dogs and no brats will be taken. We will eat fish." His mind was made up.

A short time later we were cruising down the river. My dog Sophie stood in the bow as we drove along looking for a good sandbar to set up our camp. We hadn't gone too far when Thunderfoot began pointing to the right and declared that we had found the perfect spot.

It did look like a good fishing spot, with a nice current break just below the bar and a high, dry sandbar for camping. We pulled the boat up on the dry sand and began setting up our little camp. I was working on the tent when I heard a splash and looked to see Thunderfoot and Sophie in the river goofing around as only kids and dogs can. In a few minutes I had everything ready and Thunderfoot ran back dripping wet with Sophie right on his heels.

"Just remember, when we go to bed, Sophie is sleeping on your side of the tent," I said at which he grinned from ear to ear. He and Sophie were good buddies and he didn't care if she smelled a little like wet dog.

"Let's fish," he said. "I'm getting hungry."

We baited up and cast out our lines and sat back on the edge of the sandbar with our feet in the water to wait for a bite. Sophie watched expectantly. We waited. And we waited. And we waited some more. Finally Thunderfoot got a bite and when he set the hook he missed the fish.

"Nice going," I said. "Looks like I'll have to catch enough for both of us."

A minute later I got a bite and set the hook into a good-sized fish. I fought it to the sandbar and when it got close I could see it was a carp.

"Let's see you eat that," Thunderfoot said chuckling.

I let the carp go and we continued fishing for another hour. "Wow, it's getting pretty late and we still don't have any supper," he said looking pitiful. "Maybe you should take the boat back and get some hot dogs after all."

"Oh year, sure," I said. "I wanted to bring some just in case but oh no, you wouldn't hear of it. Now its pitch dark out and you want me to go up the river and get some weenies. Well, I hope you like fried potatoes and beans because that's what we're going to have for supper."

"Well, you don't have to be nasty about it," he said acting hurt. Then he grinned. "Beans are my favorite fruit anyway."

After another forty-five minutes of fishing we could see that our fish fry was going to be fishless, so I set my pole down and began lighting the stove. I peeled potatoes and chopped them up with some onions and put them on the fire in a frying pan. Thunderfoot kept fishing while the food cooked. I put the beans into a pot, set them on the stove and when everything was ready he reluctantly came over and sat down in the sand to eat. He scooped a big spoonful of beans onto a slice of bread and made a bean sandwich.

"I'll just pretend it's a walleye fillet," he said as he chomped down on his food.

We ate the whole pan of potatoes and beans except for the portion we gave Sophie and mopped up all of the bread with the other food.

"Boy, I'm stuffed," Thunderfoot said. "That wasn't so bad after all."

I had begun cleaning up the supper mess and Sophie was busy licking every molecule of food from her dish when Thunderfoot sprang to his feet and ran to his pole. He grabbed it and began fighting a fish that seemed to be a good size. Finally he lifted a nice walleye from the water. "Wow, look at this," he said.

Just then my pole began jumping with a bite and I too had a good walleye. I took it off the hook and put it back into the river.

"What did you do that for?" he asked.

"We already ate. We might as well put them back. We don't have enough ice to keep them until morning."

He grudgingly released his fish and we both re-baited and cast back out. Within a minute we each were fighting another fish. This time I had a bass and he had a nice catfish. We released them. A few minutes later we were fighting more fish and the action continued until we ran out of worms.

"Wow, I don't think we've ever caught fish that fast before," he said as he reeled in for the last time. We put our poles away and crawled into the tent. We wiped off our feet and crawled in with Sophie coming in right behind us. Sophie snuggled down by Thunderfoot and things began to quiet down. I was lying there listening to the night sounds and the sound of Sophie snoring when Thunderfoot whispered. "You asleep yet?"

"No."

"This is cool, huh?"

"Yeah, it's good."

After a few minutes of silence he said, "I think supper was good even without fish."

"It was ok," I said sleepily.

"It was good. But next time you shouldn't listen to a kid. You're the grown-up, you should be the one to decide to bring hot dogs or not."

"I'll remember that."

Thanks, Thunderfoot.

Just Call Me Humphrey Bogart

"We really need a blind on the grassy puddle," Thunderfoot said as he searched my refrigerator for something to snack on. "That's the best pond in the swamp. If we had a blind there we would get more ducks and be a lot more comfortable."

I was in agreement but the grassy puddle, as we called it, was a long way from the high bank where we parked the truck. That meant it was a long way to carry all the materials that it took to build a duck blind. The distance was close to half-a-mile each way, and the trail was through head tall grass. "We'd be better off to wait until winter and then slide everything out there on some sleds," I said. I was hoping to escape the torture of hauling lumber and chicken wire to the pond in extremely hot weather that we were now experiencing. I might as well have saved my breath because Thunderfoot was already making work details for our first night of labor.

"If we build the floor here and then haul it down there and carry it out in one trip it will save a lot of walking," he said. Then we go back to the truck for the posts for the corners and it only takes two trips. We'll have the worst part done. I've got some lumber and posts. Should we go now, or wait until after supper. By the way, what's for supper?"

An hour and a half and a dozen brats later we were nailing the boards together for the floor. Of course by the time we finished, it had become a lot bigger and heavier than we had anticipated. It was all Thunderfoot and I could do to get it into the back of the pickup, let alone carry it across the swamp.

"I'll call Scot," he said. "He'll help us, and he's pretty strong." In a few minutes Scot, one of Thunderfoot's friends from school, arrived in a great cloud of dust sliding his bike to a halt in the driveway. Since he often hunted with us he was more than willing to help. "Let's go," Thunderfoot said, and we headed toward the duck marsh.

We hauled the floor down over the high bank and started out across the swamp. It was tough going and of course, they let me lead, breaking the trail. The grass was shoulder high and the footing was mushy at best and soupy at worst. Much of the tall grass was cut-grass and it soon slashed my arms and face into a bloody pulp. After about two hundred yards of work I called for a breather. I was about to have a coronary and Thunderfoot and Scot were barely breathing hard.

"You know, we should get this thing out there before duck season opens, and it's only a month away," Thunderfoot said. I glared at him, wiped the sweat from my eyes and picked up my end of the floor.

After two more stops we were at the edge of the pond. I was gasping for breath so I sat down on the blind floor to rest while the boys ran back to the truck for the posts and the sledge hammer. They returned much too soon. When I started to get up I got a cramp in my left calf. As I tried to straighten it out the right one cramped up too. I let out a yell and keeled over into the grass, thrashing around like I had some kind of voodoo curse.

Thunderfoot just stood there with his mouth open looking at me. Scot looked like he was ready to run for the hills, not wanting to be around when I expired. I was in agony, wallowing around in the mud, cramped up like a pretzel.

The cramps finally relaxed and I straightened out my legs. I struggled to my feet and the boys still hadn't said a word. They both just stood there with amazed looks on their faces.

"Are you going to die or what?" Thunderfoot finally asked.

"If I have to go through a double cramp like that again, I'd rather die," I said.

"Well, let's get this done before you do," he said. He handed me the mall and a post. I waded out to waist-deep water and began pounding the post into the mud. It went easily for about two feet. Then it hit hard bottom and it took a lot more energy to get it any deeper. After a few minutes, the post was solid. We measured the position for the second post and the third and forth and I pounded them into the mud.

"They're not the same height," Thunderfoot said looking critically at my work.

"The small chain saw is in the truck," I said. "Go back and get it and we'll have to even them up with that." They both took off sprinting for the truck and I had a breather standing in the cool water.

When they arrived with the chain saw I measured and marked each of the posts and then began cutting them off. Thunderfoot was impressed with my work when I finished and had a satisfied look on his face. "Not bad," he said.

He and Scot went back for the floor which would sit right on top of the posts if we had everything measured correctly. Soon I saw them struggling through the marsh toward me. When they were just a short way away from me, I saw Thunderfoot look down into the water and a look of horror came over his face. Scot's eyes followed his and he let out a yell and released his end of the floor and ran for high ground.

I didn't want to look down but I had to. I saw about two hundred leeches swimming around my legs in the water. "Hurry up with that floor," I said. "Get it over here, so I can get it up on the posts and get out of the water."

Thunderfoot slid the floor over to me and took off for the bank. I man-handled it up onto the posts and it fit perfectly. Then I crawled up onto it and turned down my hip boots that were full of water since the water was deeper than the boots were tall. A gush of water and leeches poured out onto the floor.

"Are any stuck on you?" Thunderfoot asked.

"I don't think so," I said inspecting my legs and feet. Then I got a funny feeling just inside the leg of my shorts. I lifted up the material to find a leech hooked onto my thigh very close to my parts that seldom see sunlight.

"Oh no! He's hooked on you. Oh, yuck!" Thunderfoot grimaced. He was about as fond of leeches as I was of snakes.

I took hold of the leech and pulled steadily until it let loose of my leg and then tossed it into the water. There was a small spot that bled but he apparently hadn't been hooked onto me long enough to do much damage.

Thunderfoot threw me a hammer and bag of nails and I nailed down the floor. Then I waded back to the higher ground.

"That was *gross,*" he said. "You know what were gonna build out here next?"

"No, what are we going to build?"

"A bridge."

Thanks, Thunderfoot.

The Opener

"Well, what did he say?" Thunderfoot asked as he burst through my front door on a dead run.

"What did who say?" I answered trying to act dumb.

He gave me one of his exasperated looks. "Ken! What did Ken say?"

"Oh Ken. I didn't know what you were talking about. Well, I called him and we talked a while about you and I hunting on the old farm. We talked about the price of milk and...."

"If you're trying to make me crazy, you're doing a good job," he interrupted. "What did he say about us hunting there?"

I grinned. "He said yes. We can hunt on the old farm and we'll have it all to ourselves."

Thunderfoot jumped into the air and let out a yell. "All-righty-then!"

The previous spring we had hunted on this farm for turkeys and we loved the place. It was a small farm but had a lot of good hunting ground on it and we had gotten to know our way around pretty well. The best part was that we'd be the only ones hunting there, so we would be safe and not have to worry about others getting in our way. During the turkey season we'd seen a lot of deer on the farm, so we decided to ask permission to hunt deer there in the upcoming season. Now we had permission to do just that.

"Wow, this is so cool," Thunderfoot said. "We need to go up there and scout it out, so we can find a good place to sit. And we need to get some stuff up there to sit on and some stuff for shelter if it rains and some food together and..."

"Whoa," I said. "Deer season is a month off. We don't need to start making sandwiches just yet."

He looked up and grinned. "Yeah, I guess we can wait a while to make the lunch."

Over the next coupe of weeks we went up to the farm several times. We just sat and watched the deer, turkeys, squirrels, and foxes that made the place their home. We watched where the deer came from and where they went. Soon we had a pretty good idea of where to sit on opening day.

Thunderfoot dragged more and more gear over to my house each day and soon my porch began to look like a garage sale was in progress. We had two of almost everything that had ever been invented for deer hunting and three of some of the essential items that Thunderfoot felt were more important. He wasn't leaving anything to chance.

Thunderfoot and I each carried gear up the hill three times the day before the season opened. We had stools to sit on, plastic for rain protection, binoculars, cushions, hand warmers, knives, ropes, and an assortment of candy bars and snacks. I had chosen a corner in a field that looked over the entire hilltop. Thunderfoot was going to sit at the top of an old road that came up the hill just across the field from where I was sitting.

Thunderfoot nearly ran up the hill with each load while I struggled along, sweating and panting, waiting for my heart to explode in my chest. When we finally got everything up the hill we were ready for anything Mother Nature could throw at us.

That night Thunderfoot slept at my house. Well he mostly paced around in the dark most of the night. I got a good night's sleep until 4:30 a.m. when Thunderfoot turned my bedroom light on and reminded me that it was time to get ready. I made bacon and eggs but he was too nervous to eat. So I cleaned up the dishes and we took off into the dark morning. We had about a ten minute drive and it was over an hour and a half until shooting time.

Thunderfoot was ready to go when we got to the farm. "Why don't we wait a half hour or so?" I asked. "Otherwise we'll be cold by daylight."

He would have nothing to do with that suggestion and took off up to his stand. I slid back in the seat, closed my eyes and woke back up about a half hour before opening time. I walked leisurely up the hill to my stand just as the black sky was turning into a deep blue. Stumps and clumps of grass that had looked like deer or other critters standing along the way soon became what they really were as the light increased. I sat in my chair and nestled down and got comfortable. A short time later, I heard shooting in the distance. The season was open.

I noticed some movement off to my right and watched as two hen turkeys came into the field and began to feed. I was enjoying them when one of the hens suddenly looked up and clucked. I looked across the field in the direction she was looking and saw three does moving across the pasture. They were headed right for Thunderfoot, so I didn't move. Soon they were gone and no sound came from his stand. I figured he didn't see them or let them go.

The sun came up over the hill and I got real relaxed, closing my eyes for just a second. Suddenly I felt something on my nose and awoke with a jolt to find Thunderfoot standing there with a weed in his hand that he had been tickling my nose with.

"Have a nice nap?" he asked grinning.

"I wasn't sleeping. I was just resting my eyes."

"It's ten o'clock...that was a long blink."

Ten o'clock! I had been sleeping for three hours.

"I could hear you snoring all the way down the hill. By the way, do you have anything left to eat?"

"I have all of my lunch left. What happened to yours?"

"It's been gone for a long time," he said as he dug through my food pack.

"Did you see those does?" I asked.

"Yeah, but I'm shooting a buck," he said helping himself to one of my ham sandwiches. He took a huge bite and said mumbling, "Boy, I was starting to get cold." His eyes suddenly got as big as silver dollars. He tried to swallow the big chunk of ham but he began gasping for air. He pointed frantically across the field. I looked where he was pointing and saw two bucks and a doe heading right for us.

"Get down on one knee," I said quietly. "Let them keep coming."

He knelt down chewing furiously trying to get the ham swallowed. The buck on the left was much larger than the one on the right. The doe was right between them and they were still coming right at us with no idea we were there. "When they get close, you shoot the one on the left and I'll take the one on the right. Ok?"

Thunderfoot nodded and gripped his gun so tightly his knuckles were white. "Just stay calm and shoot when you're ready," I advised. "It's just like target shooting."

The deer came on, unhurried and suddenly Thunderfoot touched off a shot. The deer all jumped up and began running in different directions and soon everything was mass confusion. I'll never know who shot what, but when the smoke cleared the smaller buck lay in the field and the doe and larger buck had disappeared into the woods. Thunderfoot was up and running toward the downed deer. I picked up my knife and followed him.

When I got there I could see how excited he was. He put his hand on the deer's side and petted it a little and had a sad look in his eyes. "We got him."

I nodded.

"Did you shoot him, or did I?" he asked.

"You got this one. I was shooting at the other one."

His response was a grin.

"He sure is pretty," he said quietly.

"Are you ok?" I asked.

"Yeah, I'm ok. It's kind of funny though isn't it? I'm glad I got him but I'm kinda sad I killed him too. Is that stupid?"

I squatted down and put my arm around his shoulder. "That's not stupid at all. In fact I'm glad you feel that way. It shows you have respect for his life. Hunting is mostly getting ready and waiting. The killing part is the smallest part of it, but it's necessary. It's just life."

He nodded thoughtfully.

"Well, now the fun starts. Do you think you can field dress him?"

"No problem," he said. He took the knife out of the sheath and we turned the deer over. He put the knife to the belly, just below the ribs and paused. He looked up at me. "Maybe you could show me."

I smiled and thought back to the first time I'd dressed a deer and how scared I was of messing up. "No problem," I said.

Thanks, Thunderfoot.

One Will Do Nicely

I had called one of my friends who lives near the Mississippi River and he assured me that the ice was thick enough on the river for ice-fishing. Thunderfoot and I didn't have to think twice about that and we were now heading for our fist trip of the year on the ice. We usually stuck closer to home since we had a lot of good fishing spots within a mile of the house, but Thunderfoot had been wanting to try the "Big River" for a quite a while so here we were on our way.

"I didn't see any lunch in the pails," he said looking worried. "Are we going to stop for groceries?"

I smiled. "Nope, we're going to take a break at lunch time and go in for a burger."

He looked at me. "One burger? You know how hungry fishing makes me don't you?"

I just grinned at him. "One will be enough...trust me."

The conversation was soon over because I was pulling alongside a bunch of cars parked near a makeshift parking area along the railroad tracks that ran along the riverbank. Thunderfoot leaped out and began unloading fishing gear and piling it onto our sled. "Oh boy, let's get going. This looks really good."

He started down the steep bank and I followed along at a slower, safer pace. He was already on the ice when I got to the edge and he stopped and looked back at me. "Look at this! There are hundreds of fish down there!"

I caught up to him and as we walked we could see hundreds of bluegills swimming away from us. Every time one of us took a step they swam off in schools like flocks of birds. "Holy cow! Let's get some holes drilled!" he said over his shoulder as he approached a group of fishermen. I had been watching the fishermen on the way out and not one of them had pulled a fish up, so I moved off a little way away from them and set up my fishing area. As I walked I could see fish moving ahead of me in amazing numbers. Any time someone on the ice walked around, the fish scattered. I began to have a feeling that things weren't going to be as good as we hoped they would be.

After about an hour of fishing I walked over to Thunderfoot and he looked up glumly. "They're not going to bite, are they?"

I shook my head. "They're too spooked by the clear ice. I'm afraid we're wasting our time." He looked miserable. "Let's go get a burger and decide what to do next."

He brightened up when he heard that. After hunting and fishing, eating was his favorite pastime. We drove downriver to the next small town and went into a bar and grill. We sat at a table and a waitress came over to take our order. "I'm pretty hungry," Thunderfoot said. "Maybe I'll have a couple burgers."

She looked him up and down and then looked at me and grinned. "First time here?" she asked and I nodded. Then to Thunderfoot she said, "You better start with one. If you finish that one, we'll make you another." Then she walked away.

Thunderfoot looked at me with an amazed look. "Boy, she's got a lot of nerve. Apparently she doesn't have any idea of the capacity I have for burgers." I just shrugged my shoulders.

About twenty minutes later, just as Thunderfoot was about to collapse from hunger, the waitress came with our food. She set the little plastic baskets holding our burgers and fries in front of us and watched as Thunderfoot's eyes bugged out. "Stricken" was about the only way you could describe his slack-jawed expression as he stared at the biggest burger he'd ever seen. "Holy smokes, how many cows do you go through in a week?" She walked off chuckling.

This particular bar was known far and wide for these huge burgers. Each burger starts out in the neighborhood of three quarters of a pound of meat. Then cheese and onions are added and the thing is way more than most people can eat. Thunderfoot looked the monster burger over for a while and then decided to attack it. He gnawed away at the thing and shoveled fries into his mouth and had just about conquered the thing when he looked up. "I don't know if I can finish this. Hey look...it's snowing."

I looked out the window and it was snowing like crazy. It was a typical late spring snow storm that would cover the ground and then be melted in a few hours. Suddenly both Thunderfoot and I looked at each other with the same thought. The ice was now covered with snow. The spooky bluegills wouldn't be able to see us. We finished up as fast as we could and headed back up to the fishing spot.

As we walked down toward the other fishermen I could see them all catching fish one after the other. There were fish flopping all over the ice and we sat down at a couple of holes that were not being used and began fishing.

For the next hour, we caught fish so fast that we didn't have time to keep track of them. Finally as much as I hated to do it, I stopped and counted up the fish we had on the ice. "We've got to see how many we have," I said. "I don't want to go over the limit."

"You count...I'll fish," Thunderfoot said. This was his usual solution to the number-of-fish problem. I began counting and putting the fish into a bucket as I counted them. In no time one bucket was filled and the other soon was also full. "We've got enough," I said. I slid six flopping fish back into the water since they were over our limit.

"No way. You want to quit when they're biting like this?"

"I don't want to quit but we can't take any more."

He looked crushed. We gathered up our gear and loaded up the sled. "I've never caught fish in the ice so fast," he said. "This is the best fishing day I've ever had."

When we got back to the truck we loaded up and started down the road. We were just coming into the town with the big burgers and I looked over at Thunderfoot. "Ready for another burger yet?"

"I think I'll wait a week or so before I eat again. One of those will do quite nicely," he said.

I couldn't believe it...Thunderfoot was filled up.

Not quite.

"I probably could force down an ice-cream cone if we happened to go past an ice-cream store," he said. "You know, ice-cream melts down in all the little cracks where there's room in your stomach, so there's always room for ice-cream."

That's my boy.

Thanks, Thunderfoot.

It'll be Cheaper, and Better

"I think we need one of these," Thunderfoot proclaimed pointing to a new ice shanty that was displayed in a big-box store we were browsing through. "This is really nice, and that thing we're fishing in is about done for."

I had to admit he was right. My old ice shanty had seen better days. There were patches on the patches on the old one and it was pretty well ready for the dump. But the price on these new ones was a little more than I felt like spending right then, so I said, "That would be nice, but look at the price."

He looked at the tag and nodded his head. "Yea it is pretty pricey...hey, why don't I build us a new one? I've got wood and all we need is some pipes and some cloth and bingo, we've got a new shanty. It'll be cheaper and better than this thing."

For some reason I wasn't quite as enthusiastic as he was. I remembered back to his duck blind project that turned out the size of a garage and nearly drowned me when we tried to get it to the marsh. "I don't know, you usually get carried away on these projects."

He gave me one of those looks. "Trust me," he said.

We went home and I kind of forgot about the whole thing when three days later the phone rang. It was Thunderfoot. "Is it ok if I charge a few things at the hardware store on your account?"

"Charge what?" I asked. "What are you building now?"

"The shanty...I need some stuff like connectors and a few nails and staples and stuff," he said.

"Oh," I said. "I didn't know you were actually doing that project. I guess its ok for you to get some stuff, just tell them I said it was all right."

Big mistake.

The weekend was at hand and Thunderfoot came stomping up my front steps early on Saturday morning. "Well are you ready to give the shanty a try?" he asked.

"You actually finished it?"

He gave me a disgusted look. "Of course I finished it...and it's a beauty."

I was skeptical, but I got my boots on and we walked over to his garage to see the new shanty. When he opened the garage door I just stood there with my mouth hanging open. This thing wasn't an ice-shanty it was the size of a small shed. It must have measured nearly eight feet on a side and was at least seven feet tall. It was made out of plywood, conduit and orange sailcloth.

"We'll have a lot more room in this one," he said nodding his head up and down.

"How are we going to get it onto the ice?"

He strode over to the shanty and tugged at one corner. A seam that was held together with Velcro opened up. We crawled through the opening and inside the frame consisted of conduit pipes and connectors. These connectors were screwed down to a plywood floor with a one-by-seven-foot-wide hole cut in one half. This was obviously the place we'd fish through. There was a seam in the middle of the floor that was hinged so it could be folded in half.

"It's simple," Thunderfoot said. "You just take these little connectors out of these little holes and they all come apart. The pipes go on the floor and the cloth comes down and the whole thing folds in the middle with all the parts inside. Then we just latch it together and pull it with this handy rope I've attached to the end."

He took the thing down and it all packed nicely into the floor, which when folded up looked like a very thin casket. "For easy maneuvering, I've installed skis on the half that will stay on the ice."

I had to admit I was pretty impressed. "I've got to admit, you did a good job on it," I said. "How heavy is it?"

He got a worried look on his face. "Well, it got a little out of hand in the weight department. I think we can pull it pretty easy, especially when we get it on slick ice."

I went home and got the truck so we could take the shanty for a "test drive" as Thunderfoot said. I backed up to the door and we grabbed the shanty to lift it into the truck. We could hardly budge the thing. "A little heavy? This weighs a ton!" I said.

"Oh quit acting like a wuss and lift," he grumbled.

We finally managed to get the shanty into the truck and took off for the lake. I backed as close to the ice as I could get and we slid the shanty off onto the ground. It slid along pretty well as long as we were on a packed trail but when we set out across the lake in the deep snow we could barely move it.

"Oh yeah, this is lots better than one of those other shanties," I said grunting.

"Oh dry up and pull!" he said glaring at me.

We finally made it to a good fishing area and Thunderfoot began his assembly while I drilled holes. After much clattering and cussing the shanty was finally up and looked pretty good. I opened the corner where the door was and stepped inside. It was pretty cozy in there and there was a lot of room for gear and people.

"See? I told you this was going to be good," he said proudly surveying his creation. We got our poles out and fished for a couple of hours. The shanty was really comfortable and roomy. As the sun began to set we took the shanty down and began dragging it back to the truck. I nearly had the *Big One* pulling the thing up the high bank to the parking lot.

As we got into town I said, "I'll stop and pay the bill at the hardware store as long as we're going past it."

"Oh, why don't you wait...they're in no hurry. I'm sure they trust you."

"Well, I might as well get it over with," I said as I pulled into the front of the store and parked.

"You coming in?" I asked.

"No I'm pretty tired I think I'll just wait here."

I went in and talked to my friend who owned the store and then asked for the bill. He picked up a pile of receipts and totaled them up on the adding machine. "It comes to "$237.56," he said.

I almost fainted. "Are you sure those are all mine" I asked.

"Yeah, they're from some project your neighbor kid said you were doing."

When I got back to the truck Thunderfoot was pretending to sleep.

"Do you know how much you spent for this shanty that would save me a lot of money? I asked.

He didn't move. "I said," I repeated.

"I heard you the first time," he said opening one eye. "I'm not sure but I think I went a bit over budget."

"A bit over budget? We could have bought the one in the store and had money left over to buy bait all winter."

"Well, I might have overdone it a bit but look at how nice this shanty is. Other than being a bit heavy, it'll be a great place for us to fish all winter. And think of the bonding we can do."

I laughed. "Yeah we'll bond all right. Maybe we can have a barn dance in it to help pay for it."

We backed out and started down the street. Thunderfoot hemmed and hawed and finally said, "I hesitate to bring this up, but there is one teeny little other bill that needs to be paid.'

"What bill?"

"Well I couldn't sew the cloth myself, so I took it to that upholsterer guy on the corner. He did all the sewing for only $25. Good deal huh?"

Good deal for you maybe.

Thanks, Thunderfoot.

The Polar Expedition

"I just got a call from my buddy on the Mississippi," I said as Thunderfoot answered the phone. "The ice is breaking up today and should be gone by morning."

"What time are we leaving?" he asked without hesitation.

"I'll pick you up at six...be ready."

It was early spring and this would be our first trip to the Mississippi for walleyes. The ice below the dams didn't get as thick as the rest of the river and consequently it went out much earlier in the spring. My friend lived just a short way from the dam and kept an eye on it for me and had called when the ice began breaking up.

Ice-out-day is often one of those once-in-a-season days. The fish have been congregating below the ice at the dams all winter waiting for spawning time to arrive. They are hungry and have seen few fishermen for quite a long time, so when the ice goes out, the first fishermen at the dam can usually have some amazingly good fishing. Thunderfoot and I were going to be some of those chosen ones this spring.

The next morning he started loading his gear into the truck before I was even ready. Soon he was waiting and trying to hurry me. "All you gotta do is back up to the boat and I'll hook it on," he said. In no time we were coming down the river side of the Mississippi bluffs and pulling into the boat landing. "The ice isn't all gone yet, but the other boats have made a pretty good channel through it," I said surveying the river. The landing was about a mile downriver from the dam and much of the broken up ice was being held in place by an island that plugged the channel in the spring. The earlier boats had maneuvered their way through the floating chunks and we were going to do the same thing.

Thunderfoot was in the bow directing me. "Whoa...go right.

Whoa...more right. OK, now straight...whoa more right again." It took us about ten minutes to get through the ice and then we headed up to the dam. As we coasted to a stop Thunderfoot had his rod ready and as soon as we stopped he dropped his jig to the bottom. He only lifted it twice when he set the hook into a walleye.

"Yahoo! This is just like in the movies," he said grinning as he reeled the fish up. "By the way, you have the honor of buying me an ice cream on the way home." He was grinning.

I got my rod out and soon was fighting a walleye too. "Boy this is the way it should be all the time," I said. I released the small fish and said, "Let's not keep too many right away. If we get greedy we'll have to quit too soon."

We had an absolute ball for the next two hours. We caught walleyes and sauger about as fast as we could reel tem up. "This is the best fish...wow, look at the ice," Thunderfoot said.

I turned around and looked. The channel we had used to come upriver was now gone. Boat traffic and wind had plugged it up tight with huge blocks of ice.

"Oh-oh. We're gonna have some fun getting back," Thunderfoot said. Then as if it were a sign from above it started snowing. Well, snowing isn't probably the best word... blizzard, or maybe white-out would be better. In a matter of minutes the boat was inches deep with heavy snow. We couldn't see for more than a few feet in any direction.

"I think we better start back," I said.

"What? Are you serious? The fish are biting like mad, and you want to leave?"

"I don't want to leave, but if it keeps snowing like this we're going to have a hard time getting home with the boat behind us. A few more minutes and then we better start back."

In ten minutes it was snowing even harder and things were going from bad to worse. We put our rods away and Thunderfoot got in the bow of the boat. We began working our way downriver through the ice blocks. There were about a dozen other boats with us so we weren't alone. It was slow going and often we had to stop and look over the side to see which way the current was going so we knew which way to go. The snow was so thick that we couldn't see the bank so we had no idea where we were.

Finally we got the idea of running the bow of the boat up on the chunks and then we both walked to the bow and the boat broke through. Then we'd repeat that action. It worked pretty well and soon all the other boats were following us like little ducks through the blizzard.

"I'm going to work us to the left so we can see the bank," I said. "Otherwise we'll miss the boat landing."

We angled to our left and many icebergs later the boat landing came into view. We beached the boat and I walked up to the parking lot and got the truck. I backed the truck down and we managed to get the boat loaded. We were strapping the boat down and Thunderfoot said, "Boy this is one fishing trip we'll remember for a while."

I was sure he was right. A short time later we were creeping down the highway toward home. "At this rate it'll take s two hours to get home," I said.

"Yeah but the fishing was worth it. And the ice jam and all the snow, that was a good adventure," he said grinning. "It was like a polar expedition...but you know..."

I looked at my fishing buddy. He had dropped off to sleep in mid-sentence. I sighed and gripped the steering wheel trying to keep the truck on the road. It would be a long drive with no one to talk to but I didn't have the heart to wake him.

A while later we came to the river town with the hamburger joint that served the huge burgers. His eyes popped open like he had radar. "You are planning to stop," he said. "You know how hungry catching all those fish made me, don't you? And besides, we have to stop anyway...you owe me an ice-cream."

There's only one thing that Thunderfoot likes better than walleye fishing, and that's eating on the road to and from walleye fishing.

Thanks, Thunderfoot.

A Bit Early for a Dip

"I just rode my bike down to the river and the water temperature is over fifty degrees," Thunderfoot said as he slid to a stop in my driveway. "Do you think the smallmouths will be biting?"

"How far over fifty?" I asked.

"It was only fifty-two but the sun's out and they should be up in shallow water where it's warmer."

I was impressed. After the time we'd spent fishing together he was actually learning a lot about fishing. It seemed that fifty degrees was the magic temperature in the Wisconsin River. In the fall as soon as the water temperature dropped below fifty, the smallmouths seemed to disappear. Then in the spring the reverse happened. As soon as the water temperatures get in the fifty degree range, the smallmouths begin to bite again, just like clockwork. And, Thunderfoot and I loved fishing for smallmouths.

"Don't you think we should go and try for some?" he asked.

"Sure, I think it would be our duty to go," I said. "Unfortunately I have to finish this raking."

He looked like a cat caught in a live-trap. He shook his head and walked to the shed and grabbed a rake. "They *better* be biting," he said.

A couple of hours later we slid the boat into the river and motored upstream. We stopped at some rocky shorelines that were usually good smallmouth haunts. Thunderfoot was sitting in the front seat grinning. "There's nothing better than catching that first smallmouth of the season," he said. He tied a small spinner on his line and cast toward the rocks. I tied a small bait on my line and tossed it toward the shore. I had only turned the reel handle twice when I had a jarring strike. A nice smallie leaped into the air and then made a swift run up against the current. The fish came up again and jumped and then I led it to the boat, lipped it and held it up for Thunderfoot to see. He glared at me.

"Jeez, you didn't hardly give me time to fish."

I grinned and he cast right to the same place my fish had come from and caught the twin brother of my fish. "All righty then," he said.

We moved a little way downriver and began casting again.

Thunderfoot's spinner had no more than hit the water when he reared back and set the hook. "I think I've died and gone to heaven," he said.

It was an amazing start to an amazing day of fishing. We cast the entire rocky shore and then went back upriver and did it again. We caught a total of eleven bass and one walleye on that shoreline and then went to look for a similar spot. As we motored up the river Thunderfoot sat in his seat with a smile on his face as we looked for another hot-spot. There wasn't much more you could have given him just then that would have made him happier than he was right now.

"Let's try over there," he said pointing to some rocks sticking up along the shore. I pulled the boat to a stop above the rocks and cast back to them, hooking a fish right away. "That's pretty greedy of you," he said.

"That's the advantage of being the boat driver," I said grinning.

Like the previous spot, this one was full of fish. About halfway through our first drift Thunderfoot hauled back and set the hook into a much bigger fish than we had been catching. This fish stripped off line and took off for the middle of the river. "This is a world record smallmouth," he said as he struggled with the fish. He did a really good job of fighting the fish and soon a huge northern was lying on the surface beside the boat. Thunderfoot lifted it up by the gill plate and held it up for me to see. "I'm a multi-species angler," he said proudly. Then he removed the lure from the fish and slid it back into the river. "This is going to be one of those days to remember," he said.

We fished the new shoreline for about an hour and then decided to move again. "Why don't you let me drive?" he said. "You can relax and enjoy the scenery."

I knew he wasn't concerned about me enjoying the scenery as much as he wanted to control the boat on the next spot, but I agreed and let him drive. Soon we saw another likely looking spot and in addition to the rocks, this spot had tree tops that had fallen into the water. This was going to be a good spot for sure.

Thunderfoot pulled in on the spot and managed to position the boat so he was nearer the shore and I was out in the middle of the river.

"How do you expect me to cast?" I asked. "You've got the boat sitting so I don't have anywhere to fish but the middle of the river."

He looked at me innocently. "Oh, can't you cast? I'm real sorry." Then he cast to a nearby log and hooked a bass. He turned around with an evil grin as he reeled in the fish.

I wasn't going to sit and watch him catch all the fish so I stood up and climbed up onto the deck on the front of the boat so I could cast over him. "You'd better be careful...you might fall in," he said.

It wasn't ten seconds later, that the boat hit an underwater log. We were traveling along with the current at a pretty good rate, so when we hit the log I did a back flip off the front of the boat in less time than it took to type this sentence. I landed on m back and as I hit, my rod and reel came loose from my grip and was gone. The water felt like ice. I was under water and not sure which way was up because it all happened to fast. I wasn't afraid so I just let myself drop down until I hit bottom. I had spent my entire youth in the river and knew that all I had to do was go with the current and I'd be ok. Once I hit bottom, I knew which way was up. I pushed off and swam to the surface.

When I popped up at the surface Thunderfoot was in a panic. "Holy cow...are you ok?"

"Yeah, I'm alright, I lost my rod and reel though. I'll swim down to that sandbar, you come and pick me up," I said.

He started the motor and I waded into the shallow water at the sandbar. He stopped and I climbed into the boat. "Holy cow, I thought you were caught under a snag or something and had drowned," he said. "You were under the water for hours."

"I don't think it was hours. I didn't know which way was up, so I had to wait till I got to the bottom. Let's go back and see if we can find my rod and reel."

We motored up the shoreline and lo and behold, my lure was hanging from a branch in a treetop. Thunderfoot motored up so I cold grab the lure and then I began pulling up the line and soon my rod and reel came up from the bottom of the river. "It's good you can't cast very well," he said laughing. "If you'd hit your target your rod would still be on the bottom."

By now I was getting pretty chilly. It was late in the afternoon and the sun was low on the horizon. "I hate to say this but I'm freezing and we've got along way to go to get home. I think we should call it quits for today," I said.

He looked a little disappointed the then smiled. "I told you we'd remember this day, and now that you did that nice back flip I'm sure of it."

My teeth were chattering by the time we got the boat loaded. When we got home I jumped in the shower and warmed up. Thunderfoot came into the house as I finished dressing. He had put away the gear and had a grin on his face.

"So, when are you leaving for training camp?"

"What do you mean?" I asked smiling.

"I mean to try out for the Olympic diving team. I'd give you at least a nine point five on that back flip."

Wasn't that nice of him?

Thanks, Thunderfoot.

Who's Smarter Now?

I was driving as fast as you dare to drive in the darkness in deer country toward our turkey hunting woods. Thunderfoot was stuffing shells and other gear into our fanny packs.

"We should have gotten up about half an hour earlier," I said. "I don't know if we can make it to the top of the hill before the birds wake up." Thunderfoot gave me a worried look.

We had been out the two previous mornings and had heard turkeys gobbling from their roost trees so we knew where to go. But we had miscalculated on our time this morning and we were probably going to be late. We pulled into the driveway of the abandoned farm where we hunted and quietly got out of the pickup. We were careful not to slam the doors and wake up the whole neighborhood. Thunderfoot got his gun out of the case and slid a big three-and-a-half inch shell into the chamber of the ten-gauge. He carefully closed the breech and made sure the hammer was down in the safe position. Then we picked up the decoys and the rest of the gear and started across the field toward the hill.

It was still pretty dark but the sky was beginning to turn into a dark blue in the east as we climbed the hill. We had to be very quiet because we had to pass within about fifty yards of the roost trees to get to the top of the hill. We were hoping that the birds would go up the hill when they left their roosts later.

Thunderfoot knew where we were going and was leading the way. He kept looking up at the sky that was getting brighter and brighter by the minute. I was right behind him when he let a branch go that slapped me right across the left ear.

"Jeez!" I whispered. "Take it easy. You almost took my ear off." I was rubbing my smarting ear and saw his grin in the darkness.

"Sorry," he said. "It slipped."

By the time we got to the top of the hill it was fully light. We heard the noise as the turkeys flew down from their roosts. We crept up behind a little knoll and peeked over. The turkeys were standing right next to the brush pile we had planned on sitting behind. "Oh great," I whispered. "Lie down and get the gun ready. I'll try to call them." I was panting from the climb and excited at being so close to the birds.

Thunderfoot lay down next to a big oak and I pulled my favorite diaphragm call out of my call box. I gave a seductive yelp. The turkeys stopped walking and craned their necks listening. I waited a few minutes and they began moving away. I called again and they completely ignored me.

We lay there for a quite a while and finally I rolled over and looked at Thunderfoot. "Well we blew that one. Tomorrow we'll be here at least half an hour earlier."

He nodded in agreement. We sat and called and listened for three hours but there were no interested turkeys in our woods. "We might as well go home," I said. "We'll leave the decoys and camouflage netting here so we don't have to carry it all back up here tomorrow. I put the decoys in the brush pile and covered them with the camo netting and we left for the day.

The next morning we were on top of the hill almost an hour earlier than the previous day. We had the decoys out and our blind built long before any turkey would even think of gobbling and beginning his day.

"Today we score," Thunderfoot said. "They don't have a clue that we're here."

I felt pretty smug also. We both leaned back against a log and waited for light to come. The sky brightened and suddenly a turkey gobbled on the next hill over from the one we were on. Then another gobbled from the same area. I expected "our" turkeys to answer them from just below us, but there wasn't a peep from our hill.

Thunderfoot looked at me. "You don't suppose those are our birds do you?"

I shrugged my shoulders and motioned to just wait for a while. After another ten minutes of listening to turkeys gobble all around us, I decided to try a call on my diaphragm. I called. No response. I called again. No response.

The birds on the other hill were carrying on like crazy. We sat there looking kind of glum. "They moved to the other hill," Thunderfoot said dejectedly.

I nodded. "We might was well sit here for now," I said. "If we try to get over there they'll see us anyway."

The next morning we hauled all the gear up the side of the hill next to the one we had been on the day before. This hill was nearly vertical. We were following a path that had been made many years earlier when the gas company buried its pipeline. There wasn't much brush and there were a lot of loose rocks to work around as we climbed. We were trying not to launch any rocks down the hill which would scare the turkeys we were stalking.

I was sweating and huffing and puffing and thought I'd keel over at any minute. Finally we got to the top and I sat down to get my breath.

"Those birds better be there today after all of this," I panted.

We found a spot to hide and got ready for daylight. After about ten minutes we heard a turkey calling from the next hill down the line. "I can't believe it," I said.

Our birds had moved again. For some reason they had roosted on another hill rather than on the one they had used the day before. We were not having very good luck and were running out of time and hills. There was only one more hill in that valley that was still on the land we were hunting. If they moved off onto other land we'd be out of luck.

The next morning we decided to try the next hill though it was foreign to us. We'd never been this far south on the farm, so we were kind of hunting blind. This new hill turned out to be the steepest of the bunch. Even Thunderfoot was panting when we got to the top. We didn't know exactly where to go so we naturally picked the wrong spot. We settled down in a little corner of a field and placed our decoys at about twenty yards. I began calling and got little response.

"I guess we'll just stay put and try to call one over from one of the other hills," I said. Thunderfoot was less than enthusiastic, but we didn't have much choice.

I called every ten minutes or so and heard a gobble after about half an hour. I kept calling and suddenly Thunderfoot whispered. "There he is!"

I looked and saw a tom standing on top of the hill about a hundred yards away. He was looking at our decoys, but he didn't seem convinced that they were real. Try as I might I couldn't get him to come any closer. I tried every trick I knew but he finally just walked slowly back into the woods.

Thunderfoot breathed a long sigh. "Now what?"

"Let's leave the gear here. Tomorrow instead of setting up here we'll set up right on top of the hill where he was today. Then we'll see who's smarter."

Thunderfoot looked like he was going to say something but decided not to. We took off for home.

The next morning was our last chance. We got to the top of the hill right on schedule. I must have been getting into shape because the hill seemed less difficult to climb each day. If the season was 6 months long, I'd be an Olympian. We picked up our gear and placed the decoys in the field where the tom had been the previous day. I turned to see where Thunderfoot was sitting and couldn't see him. I looked and looked and then I saw him wave from the brush pile. I crawled into the pile and sat down just behind him.

Thunderfoot was resting the ten-gauge on a log that was in just the right place in our little blind. The brush pile had been pushed there by a bulldozer some years back and was a combination of branches and logs all piled up.

"This is a good spot," he whispered. "Just let him show his face and he's mine."

When it got light we heard gobbling all around us, but none that was really close. I began to call every few minutes without much response from any of the toms. This went on for about an hour.

"Where the heck did they all go?" Thunderfoot asked.

I was going to lean forward to answer him when something caught my eye from the right. I turned my head just a fraction of an inch and saw a tom standing to the right of us, about fifty yards away.

"Don't move," I whispered. "There's a tom on the right about fifty yards out."

The bird stood there for a while and then took a couple of steps toward the decoys. He stayed on the edge of the field just out of range. I saw

Thunderfoot turn his head a bit so he cold se the bird. The tom would take a few steps and then stop and eat some alfalfa or pick at something on the ground. Then it would move a little closer to the decoys, always just out of range.

Thunderfoot moved the gun around very slowly so it was pointed at the bird. I saw the barrel begin to waver as he tried to hold the big gun up and keep it on the turkey.

Finally the tom looked right at us and then stood as tall as he could and then looked some more. He brought his neck back down and took a step backwards.

"Uh oh," I said. "He saw something he didn't like."

"What should I do?" Thunderfoot whispered.

"I don't know. I don't think he's gong to come any closer. I'm guessing he's about forty-five yards out. That gun can reach him. If he looks like he's going to run, blast him."

The turkey stood rock still for several minutes then turned and took a step to the right. Thunderfoot touched off the big gun just as he raised his other leg to take a step. The turkey's next step was a leap straight up into the air. He took off for the woods with Thunderfoot in hot pursuit. He jumped up and ran after the turkey the instant after he fired the gun. I was trying to get up from my nest in the brush pile. My legs had fallen asleep from sitting so long.

Soon Thunderfoot came back over the top of the hill shaking his head. "Not a feather," he said.

I decided to pace off the distance. Thunderfoot followed counting steps. When we got to where the turkey had been standing we found it had been almost sixty yards. "No wonder," I said. "He was a lot farther out that we thought."

"It was pretty exciting when he came in silent like that," he said. "At least I got to shoot the gun."

He handed me a juice box that he had taken from his pack. "Here can you open this?" His hands were shaking.

I grinned. "No bird but we had a little excitement huh?"

"Yeah, and we sure found out who's smarter didn't we?"

I never claimed to be a genius.

Thanks, Thunderfoot.

The Rabbit

I was puttering around in the yard on one of the first really warm days of spring when Thunderfoot came up my driveway on his new riding lawnmower.

"I thought maybe I'd mow your grass for you," he said looking over the yard.

I looked around at the new grass which was barely two inches tall. "Don't you think it's a little short yet?

"Nope, I think I better cut it. It's kind of uneven, I'll just shape it up for you. This way if we want to go fishing later in the week, we won't have to worry about the grass getting too long," he said as he lowered the cutting head and started across the yard.

Now if the truth be known, Thunderfoot wasn't all that worried about the quality of my lawn, or future fishing trips. His mom had just bought the new rider after years of him pestering her for one, and he was trying to keep the machine running day and night. He had mowed their grass so many times that his mom forbade him to do it again. He loved driving the new toy and my lawn was a good excuse to get it moving again. He was like most teenage boys. He was at that age where he thought he just had to have something to drive, and if it was a lawnmower, so be it.

He was merrily riding back and forth across my lawn, so I went back to my puttering. Occasionally he'd yell at me to watch and he's stop, rev up the engine and try to pop-a-wheelie. I just shook my head, so obvious was his derangement.

He finished an hour later and we went into the house for some lunch. It started to rain while we were eating so he hurried up so he could get his "wheels" home and into the garage so it wouldn't get wet.

I cleaned up from lunch and settled down with a book. It was a perfect afternoon to do nothing and I was doing just that. The windows were open and the smell of a spring rain drifted into the living room making it very peaceful and relaxing. It must have been very relaxing because in no time I was sleeping quite soundly with my book in my lap.

Suddenly I woke with a start as someone pounded on my front door. I got up and walked to the door and it was Thunderfoot, who was standing on the front porch. I opened the door and looked at him. "Why didn't you just come in?" I asked.

He had a terrified look on his face. "You better come out here, I'm kind of muddy."

I looked down at his feet and his shoes and pant legs were covered with mud. He was soaking wet the rest of the way up and he was sweating and panting like he had just run a marathon.

"I buried the Rabbit," he panted.

"You what? What rabbit?"

"Mom's Rabbit. I buried it down by the lake."

I was still trying to figure out what he was talking about.

"Mom's gone for the day, so I kind of borrowed her Rabbit and took it for a spin. You know where the road is kind of low and there's usually a big mud puddle there? Well, I went ramming into that puddle and half way through the Rabbit died."

Now I knew what he was talking about. His mom had an old VW Rabbit which she had used before she bought her new car. The Rabbit was just sitting in the driveway not being used and Thunderfoot had taken it for a joyride.

"What the heck were you doing driving the Rabbit? Are you crazy?"

He hung his head.

"How did you get back here from the lake?"

"I ran."

"You ran? That's three miles."

He looked at me pleadingly. "Please, don't start. I know I shouldn't have taken it but I did, so that part is done. I need you to help me get it out of the mud puddle and back home so mom doesn't find out. She'll never let me get my driver's license until I'm like eighty years old if she does."

I was hesitant to become part of this little conspiracy but I could see the terror in his eyes. I was kind of touched that he came to me for help too, so I said I'd help him. "Under one condition," I said.

"Anything."

"Promise me you'll never take that car again or any car, until you're old enough to get your license and drive."

"I won't even walk close to it," he said.

I went to the phone and called a friend of mine who had a long chain and he agreed to meet me down by the lake. Thunderfoot and I got into the pickup and drove down through the river bottoms road to the lake. We came to the low spot in the road and sure enough, there was a huge mud puddle. The spring thaw had filled the low spot that was about fifty yards long with water and mud. Sitting almost exactly in the middle of the puddle was the drowned Rabbit. It was quite a sight. The poor Rabbit was covered with mud from top to bottom. If the puddle had been an inch or two deeper the car would have had mud running in through the doors also.

"Boy, you did a good job of it," I said.

Thunderfoot shook his head mournfully.

I stopped near the puddle and put on my hip boots as did my friend who had just arrived. Then I drove slowly toward the Rabbit with my 4-wheel drive engaged. My friend waded along with the chain and attached it to the bumper of the Rabbit. I tightened up the chain and began towing the Rabbit back to dry ground.

Once it was out of the puddle, my friend got in and started the Rabbit. Then he drove it back to Thunderfoot's house and parked it exactly where Thunderfoot directed him. We went back to get his truck while Thunderfoot set out to clean up the Rabbit so his mom wouldn't notice.

I dropped my friend off as his truck, thanked him for his help and went home.

A while later I saw Thunderfoot's mom go past on her way home. I felt a little guilty for helping him deceive her but hoped it would be a good lesson for him.

A while later Thunderfoot came walking glumly into m living room. "Busted!" he said.

"Busted? I thought you cleaned it all up."

He sat down and shook his head. "I did...well I thought I did. I had my brother help and he was doing the top parts while I did the bottom. He missed a big stripe right down the middle of the roof. It looked like a brown racing stripe. Mom saw it as soon as she pulled into the driveway."

I couldn't help but laugh. "Well, we tried," I said. "Was she mad?"

"Oh she was plenty mad. But when she found out that you had helped me she really got mad."

Oh boy.

Thanks, Thunderfoot.

Great America

"Mom's taking me and my brother to Great America for my birthday. Do you want to come along?" Thunderfoot asked as he walked into the house.

"Great America...isn't that some kind of amusement park?"

"Yeah, it's really a cool place. They have all kind of neat rides and roller coasters and stuff."

I wasn't too sure about roller coasters. I had made it to this point in my life without feeling a necessity to ride a roller coaster and wasn't sure I wanted to change that. "Why do you want me to go?"

"Well, my brother is too short to get on some of the rides, so I want someone to go so I have someone to ride with. Mom won't go on them, so I was hoping you'd go along."

"Why won't your mom ride on them?

He hesitated. "Well, she doesn't want Caleb to have to wait by himself while we ride. She's scared somebody might steal him or something."

Well I guess that made sense.

"Please say you'll go. We'll have a lot of fun, I promise."

It was his birthday and I did enjoy spending time with him and his family so I agreed to go along. We left bright and early the following Saturday. "We want to get there early so we get our money's worth," he said.

As soon as we left town Thunderfoot and Caleb were fast asleep in the back seat. His mom and I talked about the usual stuff on the road and sometime later the subject of roller coasters came up. She seemed pretty surprised that I had agreed to ride them with Thunderfoot.

"You've never seen them have you?" she asked.

"I've seen the ads on TV, but no, I've never seen an actual roller coaster," I admitted.

She just grinned.

A while later you could see the tops of the roller coaster tracks from the highway several miles away from the park. My stomach began to quiver as I watched little colorful cars full of screaming people hurtle up and down the tracks. When we got to the park Thunderfoot and Caleb were off and running for the entrance as soon as we had parked the car.

We all got our tickets and walked into the park which was teeming with people of all ages, sizes and colors, going one way or the other in a seemingly huge hurry. There was a giant merry-go-round just inside the entrance that was playing loud circus music and screams filled the air from the direction of the first roller coaster.

"Let's try the Shock Wave first....it's right over that way," Thunderfoot said motioning for me to follow him. His mom smiled and said she and Caleb were going on some of the smaller rides and they'd catch up with us later.

As we approached the line of people waiting to get on the Shock Wave, my stomach began to feel like it had a couple of bowling balls rolling around in it. The line followed back and forth in some stanchion-like walkways. Once you got in line and more people filled in behind you, it was pretty hard to change your mind and leave without making a lot of people move out of the way.

Thunderfoot was merrily chattering with a couple of kids ahead of us in line. I began looking around and saw that not only were there kids, but also there were lots of adults and even a grandma or two. Hmm, maybe this wouldn't be so bad after all.

We went through the first enclosure and up some steps. Suddenly a roar came from overhead as one of the little cars hurtled past filled with screaming people. The car shot past us, spun in a loop and then turned upside-down in a series of spirals before continuing on down the track. I stood there with my mouth hanging open watching the car disappear into the distance when I felt someone tugging on my sleeve. It was Thunderfoot.

"You're holding up the line," he said gesturing at the people behind me that looked impatiently at me. I looked ahead and there was a big gap in the line caused by me standing there like a dimwit. I wasn't sure I wanted to move up but I sure didn't want to wade back through a few hundred people in the stanchions to get out of there either, so I followed Thunderfoot.

We kept moving forward until we got to the "loading station" where half a dozen college kids clad in bright blue jumpsuits merrily loaded passengers into the waiting "trains". They made sure each passenger was locked in and then all gave a cheery "thumbs-up" and off we went.

Thunderfoot's eyes were sparkling as we got close to the front of the line. "Don't worry, this is really fun," he said. I could only nod. My mouth was as dry as dust and I didn't think I could speak.

Finally we were first in line and our train came in. The survivors from the previous ride climbed out of their seats and it was our turn. I sat in the seat next to Thunderfoot and we pulled down the restraining bar that was suppose to keep us from being hurled out into the parking lot as the train rocketed down the tracks. A cheery girl checked our bar and gave us a hearty thumbs-up and off we went.

The train started with a jerk and then we moved from the station and turned a corner right away. After the corner we began climbing the first hill. It was very steep and we clattered along up and up and up toward the top of the track. I peeked over the side and could see the parking lot a long, long way down.

"This is real cool," Thunderfoot exclaimed. I just nodded.

We climbed and climbed and finally reached the top. For a couple of seconds we just hung there. Then we started down the other side, our speed increasing each second. Half way down the hill we tipped on our side and increased speed even more. We were headed toward the earth on our side when I gripped the restraining bar and began screaming like a ten-year-old girl. My stomach seemed to rise up and I expected it to pop out of my mouth at any second. We got to the bottom of the first hill, and immediately headed into a series of loops that took us upside down three or four times, and then into a series of corkscrew spins. I think there were more loops after that but my memory is kind of fuzzy from there on. I think I was holding my breath and had a small brain meltdown due to lack of oxygen. My body was preparing for shut-down and eternity.

Then, just as suddenly as the whole thing had started, the car jerked to a stop and we were back at the station. The smiling college girl came over to release our restraint bar but I was gripping it so tightly she couldn't budge it. My fingers were frozen to the bar.

"You gotta let go," Thunderfoot said. I nodded and pried my fingers loose. I couldn't talk because my throat was cramped up from the way I had tightened it during the ride in an effort to keep my stomach from flying out into space.

I finally staggered to my feet and followed Thunderfoot down the exit ramp. He was babbling excitedly about the next rids and how it was even better than the Shock Wave. When we got to the exit there were lines of people looking at TV monitors that showed people on the ride as they went over the first hill in stop-motion.

"Come and see this," Thunderfoot said laughing.

"What's this?" I asked.

"They've got a camera on the first drop. It takes your picture as you go by."

Soon we saw our car come into view and then slowly each pair of riders went past. Thunderfoot was laughing with his hands in the air and I was looking like I was about to expire, my hands gripped on the bar, my hair flying, and a look of terror on my face. My mouth was wide open making me look quite mad.

"We can buy that for only five dollars," Thunderfoot said.

"I think I'll pass. I'd never hear the end of it if you have proof of how bad I looked."

I walked over to a bench and sat down, still a little wobbly.

"What did you think of it?" Thunderfoot asked.

"Well, it was pretty bad, but I guess it was kind of fun too. I guess that if those little kids and grannies can do it, I can too."

"Cool, the next one's even better."

"Even better? What does that mean...even better?"

"Well there're seven coasters in the park. We started at the least scary one. So they get better all day long."

Oh boy, I could hardly wait.

Thanks, Thunderfoot.

The Fishing Was Hot

It was one of those hot summer days where you could work up a sweat just sitting still. I had worked all day in the heat and humidity and was now relaxing after a shower. My recliner was tipped back and I was soaking up the air-conditioning, when Thunderfoot came through the front door. He was carrying his fishing pole and his hair was wet and matted against his head with sweat.

"Whew…it's hot out there," he said. "You know this is one of those days when the northerns will just about jump into the boat don't you?"

I shook my head. "It's way too hot to go fishing."

He looked at me in disbelief. "I didn't mean go now…I meant a little while later when the sun starts to go down. Then it'll be a lot cooler."

"It's going to have to cool down a whole lot to get me outside again today," I said as I flipped on the TV to watch the evening news.

Thunderfoot went to the refrigerator and rummaged around until he found something he liked. Then he sat down on the couch and tried to look interested in the television. The weather-lady came on and told us of an impending storm front that would be passing through at any time and that it would cool off as the front passed. Thunderfoot heard that and looked at me nodding his head up and down.

I sighed. I knew he would bug me until I went fishing so I told him to get the gear ready and I'd be out in a minute. He took off like a shot to the garage to get the fishing gear ready. I turned off the TV and grudgingly got up from my recliner. When I walked outside it was like walking into a wet blanket of hot, moist air.

We loaded the johnboat into the back of the pickup and started off for our favorite river bottom slough. Ten minutes later we were sliding the boat down a sandy bank and into the water.

Sweat ran into my eyes as I paddled toward the main part of the lake. Thunderfoot was in the front casting to logs and lily pads along the way trying to be the first to catch a fish. On about his fourth cast he let out a whoop and hooked into a nice northern. The battle was on and after a good fight the fish was soon lying quietly at the side of the boat. Thunderfoot led the fish back to where I could reach it and I took it off the hook and released it.

"I told you," he said grinning.

As much as I hated to admit it I knew he was right. For some unknown reason the fish seemed to bite like crazy on hot humid days like this one. Something about the heat and humidity turned them on and if you could stand the fishing conditions, you would usually have a great day of fishing. This was definitely going to be one of those days.

We paddled into the main part of the lake and a slight breeze came up. We paddled to the end where the breeze was coming from and let it take us back down the lake slowly. As we drifted along we started catching fish after fish. One of us was fighting a fish almost all the time. We often both had one on at once. It was really lots of fun, so when we got to the end of the lake we paddled back upwind and did it again.

This went on for about an hour and a half at which time we began to hear thunder off in the west. I looked and there were some pretty big ugly black storm clouds coming our way. They were still quite a way off so we kind of ignored them.

When we got to the downwind end of the lake again we started back to the other end. "Those storm clouds are getting pretty close," I said. "Maybe we should start back to the shore."

"We've got time for another drift," Thunderfoot said. "It won't take long to get to shore."

We started another drift but the thunder was getting louder and louder. The clouds were getting blacker and uglier by the minute. Suddenly a huge bolt of lightning cracked and it was very close. It was followed by a deafening clap of thunder.

"That's it," I said, "Roll up your line, we're out of here."

Thunderfoot didn't argue and looked uneasily at the sky as he reeled in his line. About half way back, a fish struck his lure. He looked over his shoulder at me and shrugged. "I didn't do that on purpose," he said.

I picked up my paddle and began moving us toward the shore. The wind picked up and now it was blowing hard right in our faces. We had to go into the wind for quite a long way before we could turn and go into the bank. Lightning began snapping all around us and the thunder was booming. "Get that fish off your line and lay your pole down in the boat," I yelled. "Holding that rod up in the air like that is just like holding a lightning rod."

For once, Thunderfoot didn't argue with me. He horsed the fish in and laid his rod in the boat after quickly releasing the fish. He was looking kind of worried as he picked up his paddle and helped me move us toward the bank. We reached the shore just as it started raining. I say raining because I don't know a word for what it was doing. It was actually like being under a waterfall. The rain was coming down so hard that there weren't individual drops, just large sheets of it hammering us. And, of course, for good measure, the wind picked up to gale force at the same time.

We each grabbed an end of the boat and carried it up the embankment through the maelstrom. We slid the boat into the back of the truck and ran for the cab just as the hail began to beat down on us.

We were panting while we waited for the windows to clear up from the fog and Thunderfoot said, "Maybe one less drift would have been more prudent."

I laughed. "No kidding, that's the understatement of the year."

I could finally see well enough to drive so I started down the dirt road through the woods that led back to the highway. Thunderfoot was wiping the fog off the back window when he suddenly yelled out. "Holy smokes! A big tree just fell across the road right behind the truck!"

I looked out at the mirror and sure enough a large old oak tree was lying in the road where we had been just seconds earlier. "Wow, that was close," I said. "A minute or two earlier and we'd have been trapped in here or crushed."

"If it had trapped us, we could have just stayed all night and fished for our supper," Thunderfoot said grinning. He loved the thought of any adventure like that.

We slowly made our way home and when we got to the driveway we made a run for the house. "We'll put the boat away after the storm passes,"

I said as I ran inside. Thunderfoot was right behind me. Of course there wasn't any reason to hurry because we were soaked to the skin already anyway.

"Jeez, it's like a freezer in here," he said wrapping his arms around his wet chest.

I went to the bathroom and grabbed a couple of towels and some dry clothes from my closet and "his" room. We dried off and changed into dry clothes and felt much better.

"That was pretty cool," he said. "Boy, we sure got the fish didn't we? And we almost got blown away by the storm. And we got really wet too. And now I don't even have to take a shower."

That boy could find good in almost any situation.

Thanks, Thunderfoot.

Goodbye to Sophie

Anyone who has ever loved a dog be it a hunting companion or a lap dog, knows how hard it is to watch them get old and sick. Dogs are much more than pets. They are much more than a helper that fetches game for you. They are a friend, and are loved very much. When the time comes at the end of their life, when you have to make the decision to have them put to sleep, it just about tears your heart out. That was the dilemma I was facing with my dear old Sophie. She had cancer and was failing badly. Her time was near and I was dreading it more than anything.

Thunderfoot also knew that his old friend was sick. Try as he might he couldn't coax her for more than one fetch of the tennis ball anymore. He came over and we talked about what needed to be done and I told him I had called my vet and she was coming in the morning. Thunderfoot sat quietly for a while and then said he was going home. He stopped and petted Sophie a few minutes and then hurried out with his eyes brimming with tears.

The next morning he came over with a small plastic bag in his hand. He sat down by Sophie and gave her a chew-bone. Her tail thumped on the floor as he hugged her and petted her for the last time. His eyes were full of tears and he came and hugged me and then left for school. My heart was nearly breaking as I watched him saying goodbye to his old pal.

Later that morning Dr. Pat arrived and my dear sweet Sophie's suffering was over very gently and quickly. My heart was aching as I dug a grave in the back yard near Sophie's mom and grandma. I wrapped her in a blanket and put the chew bone Thunderfoot had given her inside with her. When I was done, I pretty much just let the rest of the day go by without doing much of anything.

After school Thunderfoot came walking across the back yard from his house. I saw him glance over in the yard at the fresh earth of Sophie's grave. He sat down next to me on the couch and sighed. He turned to look at me and his eyes were brimming full of tears.

"It was really peaceful," I said. "Dr. Pat just put the shot in and Sophie was looking at me and then she just closed her eyes and she was gone."

He smiled and put his arms around me and we hugged for a long time. "Well, now what?" he asked.

"I guess we better start looking for a dog," I said.

"Are you sure?"

"It's going to be way to quiet and you know how used to dog hair I've become."

He smiled, and headed home.

The next morning I heard the refrigerator door open just after dawn. I got out of bed to see what was going on and there was Thunderfoot sitting at the table eating cereal with the newspaper opened to the Want Ads. "The paperboy just left the newspaper a while ago and I saw an ad for golden retriever pups," he said as he shoveled cereal into his face. He had circled the ad and I read it while I got the waffle maker out and began whipping up some batter.

It was Saturday and he didn't have school so we decided to go look at the puppies after breakfast. He was really excited about it but then he stopped and looked seriously at me. "This isn't too soon is it? I mean, I don't want you to think I'm forgetting Sophie already. I'll never forget her."

I put my arm around his shoulder and hugged him. "We won't ever forget Sophie. This puppy, if we get one, will be another new adventure for us to share. We had a great time with Sophie and we made memories we'll always keep in our hearts. She'll always be with us." He smiled and hugged me back.

After breakfast we loaded up in the pickup and drove to the address where the puppies were located. I told him we were just going to look and not to get too excited about bringing a puppy home with us. We might want to think about it a while before we made a decision.

When we pulled into the driveway of the address from the paper we saw a kennel in the back yard and a pile of sleeping puppies. A huge grin spread over Thunderfoot's face as we approached the pen. The sleeping puppies began waking up and climbing over each other all vying for the attention of these strangers. I knocked on the door and a teenaged boy came out of the house and offered to let the puppies out so we could look at them. When he unlocked the door of the kennel it was like a rain barrel had tipped over and a flood of puppies rolled out of the pen. There were nine of them and they were all over us in an instant. They were tugging at shoe laces and Thunderfoot had knelt down so he had three puppies pulling on his shirttail. He was already picking them up checking for girls but as soon as he put one down, it mixed with the others and it was impossible to figure out who was who. The boy from the house started putting male puppies back in the pen much to their dismay. They whined and barked at being left out of the fun. One of the females had a little blue collar and was spoken for already. We were left with four females to choose from. Thunderfoot played with the "girls" and soon one stood out from the others. She was determined to get Thunderfoot's shoe laces untied and as quickly as he took her away from them she went right back for more. I could tell he was falling in love.

"That's the one my little sister likes best too," the boy said.

Thunderfoot picked up the little blond fur ball and hugged her. "This one's a sweetie," he said kissing the puppy on the nose.

I sighed. I should have known that if we saw puppies we'd be going home with one. It's not that I didn't want one but I felt just a little guilty with Sophie so recently gone. On the other hand I knew there was no way we were leaving that pup behind, so I told the teenager we'd take her and he went to get the papers. Thunderfoot took the pup to the pen so she could say goodbye to her family and we headed out down the road toward home.

The puppy wasn't real happy about her first ride in a truck. She was obviously frightened so Thunderfoot picked her up and held her in his arms like a baby. She settled down and went right to sleep. "She's just so beautiful," he said beaming. "And she looks really smart too." I just smiled.

After we got home Thunderfoot and the puppy took off for the back yard to play. I watched them romping and playing fetch and knew we had done the right thing

"What are we going to call her?" I said.

A serious look came over his face. "Gosh, I don't know. It has to be something just right."

He looked at the puppy. She was jumping up and down waiting for him to start playing again. "I just love her, that's for sure."

"What about Lucy?" I said.

"Lucy?"

"Yeah, like you said...you love her. Kind of like 'I Love Lucy'."

He broke into a huge grin. "Lucy...I love Lucy. Cool."

Soon the puppy was tired out and she laid down under the picnic table for a nap. We sat down at the table and watched her sleep.

After a while Thunderfoot got up and walked over to Sophie's grave and squatted down. He sat there for a while and I could see he was talking to Sophie. Then he patted the ground gently and walked back. "I told Soph about the puppy and I told her we really miss her. I told her we'll never forget her.'

He looked down at the puppy sleeping and grinned. "She looks like a little angel."

Finally he got up and started for home. He stopped and turned back to me. "You know, when you get to heaven I bet you'll find a lot of dogs there. That would be about the best thing I could think of...to be able to spend all eternity with your dogs. That's what heaven is...a whole lot of dogs."

I hope he's right.

Thanks, Thunderfoot.

Goodbye, Sophie.

#

The longest duck season in many years had given Thunderfoot and me a chance to do some late season duck hunting on the Mississippi River. Our local duck ponds had long ago frozen over but the big river was still open and there were lots of migrating ducks using it. An old friend of mine owned a cottage on the riverbank just north of Lynxville and he and I had been talking the previous evening. The subject of the cottage came up and he informed me that there was no one using it next weekend, and I was welcome to it. It was perfect for a place to stay while we hunted late season ducks. I got the key to the cottage and called Thunderfoot.

"Are you crazy? What do you mean, do I want to go? How soon are we leaving?" I guess he thought it was a good idea. Ten minutes later he came running across the back yard with a duffel bag and his shotgun.

"Gus said we can use the boat at the cottage," I said, "and he has three dozen decoys in the shed. So all we need to take is our clothes and guns."

"And lunch," Thunderfoot corrected. "You know how hungry this late fall air makes me." Cold air, hot air, late fall air, any air made him hungry.

We got to the cottage as dusk and began getting the gear ready. "Check out the boat and make sure the plug is in it," I said. I went to the shed and found the decoys, oars, and life jackets and piled everything on the porch of the cottage. Thunderfoot was rummaging around in the boat, but soon he came over and helped me transfer the decoys from the porch to the boat.

We stood there on the bank of the big river and looked out across the black water. It was almost three miles to the Iowa side and as the light faded we watched several flocks of ducks settling onto the cold water.

"How are we gonna find the boat blind in the dark?" he asked.

I pointed across the water. "See those two yellow lights over there? Those are in Iowa and are right in line with the boat blind. We just steer for them and we should run right into it." Thunderfoot nodded that he understood.

That evening we made a sack of sandwiches and got the rest of our gear ready. We set the alarm for 4:15. I wanted to give us plenty of time to get across the river before it got light in the morning.

By about 4:30 the next morning we were setting out across the dark water toward the two little yellow lights. The small duck boat was loaded to the gills. We had three dozen decoys, our guns, eight boxes of shotgun shells in a waterproof box, lunch, hot chocolate, a gas heater, extra gloves and Lucy my golden retriever puppy. We were all packed into a small fiberglass boat pushed by a nine horsepower motor.

I watched the yellow lights and kept aiming for them. We slid through the water at a good rate and our beacons were getting closer and closer when we suddenly slammed to a halt.

Thunderfoot tipped over backwards off his seat. "Holy cow! What the heck happened?" he asked.

I grabbed the flashlight and pointed it over the side of the boat. We were sitting on top of a tree stump that was the size of a card table. It was about six inches under the water.

"Wow, I forgot, this is a stump field. I guess we found one of them," I said. "Take the oar and see if you can push us off."

Thunderfoot pushed and grunted but we were stuck fast. Finally I got up and carefully stepped over the side onto the stump and when the boat lightened, it slid back off the stump. I carefully got back to my seat and pulled the cord on the motor.

"Wow...that was thrilling. It's a good thing we're wearing hip boots or you would have gotten wet," he said.

We were getting close to the blind when Lucy suddenly climbed up onto Thunderfoot's lap.

"Lucy, get down," he said. "Hey, Lucy's all wet!"

"How did she get wet?" I asked.

Thunderfoot grabbed the flashlight and turned it on. He aimed it toward the bottom of the boat. It was three quarters full of water!

"Whoa! We're sinking, we're sinking!" he yelled.

I shut off the motor and grabbed an ice cream pail that was in the boat for bailing if needed, and we needed it right now. I began throwing water over the side as fast as I could.

"We must have punched a hole in the boat," I said. "We've got to get it bailed out and head for the nearest shore."

Thunderfoot sat there with the flashlight aimed at the floor of the boat. All of a sudden he let out a gasp and grabbed a piece of driftwood that was floating around in the water. He held it out to me. "Here, shove this back in the hole where the boat plug goes! This is the plug."

I grabbed the stick and pulled up my sleeve feeling around in the icy water for the hole for the plug. I finally found it and jammed the stick into the hole stopping the flood. Meanwhile Thunderfoot was bailing like mad. After a few minutes we were again floating safely.

"What pray tell, was that stick doing in the plug hole?" I asked.

"Well, I couldn't find the plug so I whittled that plug out of some driftwood on the shore while you were doing the other stuff. If you hadn't smacked into that stump at warp speed it would have been ok."

Now that the situation was at hand I had to laugh. It had been quite an exciting few minutes.

We continued on and a few yards later I could make out the form of the boat blind. My friend had built the blind so you could open one end and just drive the boat inside and hunt from the boat. It was on the edge of a big weed bed and a perfect place for hunting. We put out the decoys and positioned the boat in the blind just as the sky started to lighten. Soon after, the ducks began to fly.

Despite how badly the day had begun, it turned out to be an absolutely glorious morning. The sun came up and the ducks flew. Since it was so late in the season, we saw ducks that we'd never had a chance to hunt before. Many of these ducks were big-water ducks. They seldom used small ponds like we usually hunted, so we'd never had a chance at a shot at many kinds of them. Also these were the very late ducks that often came down from the north after the season had closed. We saw canvasbacks, redheads, golden eyes, blue bills, buffleheads, and hundreds of huge late mallards. Ducks flew up and down the river all day long. We had some of the greatest shooting we'd ever seen. By mid-afternoon we were one duck short of our limit. So, instead of shooting that last duck, we just sat in the boat and watched the ducks fly by and enjoyed the scene.

Finally I told Thunderfoot to pick one more duck and take it because it was getting late in the afternoon. "Let's get that last shot of the season and start back," I said. "I want to be past that stump field before it gets dark."

Thunderfoot shot the lead duck in a flock of blue bills and the day was over. We picked up the decoys and started back.

As we got to the area where we had hit the stump, he turned and looked at me. "Try not to slam into another stump...ok?"

I started to say something about we wouldn't have had any trouble if he'd found the real plug, but didn't bother. It had been a perfect day and I didn't want to spoil it with an argument. Besides, I usually lost those arguments anyway.

Thanks, Thunderfoot.

Let Them Get Close

"I really don't think it takes two of us to listen," Thunderfoot grumbled as he pulled his collar up over his head and slid down in the tall grass like a turtle withdrawing into his shell.

I had forced him to get up with me to "turkey listen", as he called it. Today was the morning before his turkey season would start. I wanted to hear the turkeys gobble when they woke up so we would know where to go the next morning. Turkeys usually roosted in nearly the same place each night, so knowing where they were this morning would give us a pretty good idea where they'd be tomorrow morning. Thunderfoot, on the other hand, thought this should be a one man operation and he should be home in his warm bed instead of out in the darkness.

I could just begin to make out the tops of the hills as the black sky turned to a dark blue when the first turkey gobbled. Thunderfoot sat up with a snap and looked at me, grinning from ear to ear.

"They're up by the corner of the field," he said nodding.

I nodded in agreement and soon we heard another gobble and then another. There seemed to be at least half a dozen turkeys in the area, so our chances seemed pretty good for the following morning.

Than night Thunderfoot stayed over at my house in "his room" which used to be my spare bedroom. We got up in plenty of time so we could be on top of the hill before light. We walked as cautiously and quietly as possible, so as not to disturb any roosting turkeys and climbed the hill.

When we reached the corner of the field I took our three decoys and placed them about twenty yards from the brush pile we were going to use for a blind. Thunderfoot cleared out the dead branches and was already sitting down when I got to the blind. I sat down in the only spot available and when it got light I found that I couldn't see the decoys. I mentioned that to Thunderfoot and he whispered, "That's ok, I can see them and I'm the shooter anyway."

I took out my calls and we soon heard a gobbler not far off. I waited a short time and then made a soft, very sexy hen yelp. Thunderfoot looked over and winked his approval. A short time later the gobbler called again and I responded. This went on for about twenty minutes but then all was quiet.

We sat very still for quite a while and then Thunderfoot very slowly began raising the gun. I couldn't see a thing. He got the gun up to his shoulder and I heard him cock the hammer. I still couldn't see anything. He waited. I waited. Nothing happened. After what seemed like hours, he quietly lowered the gun and looked back at me. "Why didn't you tell me whether or not to shoot?"

"I didn't see him."

"Well, I didn't know if he was close enough."

"Where was he?"

"He was just to the left of the farthest decoy."

I leaned up far enough to see the decoy and knew the bird had been plenty close enough to shoot. "He was close enough," I said.

"Great, now you tell me," he said sarcastically.

"Next time, when they're by the decoys, you know they're close enough. But, if they're coming toward us, let them come. Each step they get closer to us is another step they have farther to go to get away from us." He nodded that he understood.

We waited a while longer and then decided to move up the ridge a little farther. There were turkeys calling all around us, so we thought a little move might help. As we moved the turkeys began gobbling all around us one after another. "Boy, we better sit down and get ready, we're surrounded," I said.

My heart was just about popping out of my chest by the time we got to the top of the ridge. We sat down in a little clearing. There were only two trees that were big enough to sit next to, so Thunderfoot took one and I the other which was a little way behind him. I was afraid to put out the decoys so we just sat down to wait.

"Remember, if he's coming closer, let him come," I whispered.

He nodded and laid the gun across his knees. It wasn't only a couple of minutes later when I saw a tom sneaking up to the side of us behind a brush pile. "There," I whispered. "Look behind the brush to your left."

The turkey was standing behind a downed tree and looking out over the top of the ridge. Nobody moved a muscle for many seconds and then the turkey suddenly ducked down and snuck off through the brush.

Thunderfoot slowly moved the gun back to the original place he had rested it and I slipped a turkey call into my mouth. I made a short yelp and almost swallowed the call when several toms answered immediately from just over the knoll. I didn't dare move and I could hardly breathe. Then I saw the head of a gobbler coming over the knoll right in front of us. He was only fifteen yards away. Right behind him was another gobbler and then another. There were three of them and they were all headed right at us. Although we were covered in camouflage from head to toe including our faces, I felt naked sitting against the tree with nothing between me and the turkeys but air.

The turkeys stretched their necks looking for the hen that had called to them. I sat there trying not to breathe fearful that they'd hear my heart pounding in my chest. They were in a little group with their heads almost together when I had a panicked thought. What if Thunderfoot shot them all in one shot?

Then they started moving toward us again. They were ten yards away. Then they were eight yards away. Now they were six yards away. I could see their eyes blinking. Why wasn't Thunderfoot shooting? "Shoot!!!!!" I whispered.

Thunderfoot touched off the ten-gauge and all hell broke loose. One turkey went straight up in the air through the trees knocking branches and leaves down like rain. Another took off down the ridge on a full run and the third one, the unfortunate one, lay flapping his wings in the leaves on the ground. Thunderfoot jumped up and dived on the bird so we wouldn't get away. There was no need for that but he wasn't taking any chances.

I sat there realizing that I was shaking like a leaf. I couldn't ever remember having a turkey that close to me before and it was pretty unnerving.

"What took you so long to shoot?" I asked as Thunderfoot picked up his trophy and grinned.

"What do you mean?"

"They were in range from the first minute we saw them. Why did you wait so long?"

"If I remember right, an old turkey hunter, an expert I think, once told me...not so long ago, mind you...that I should wait for my shot as long as they were heading my way. Do you recall something like that?"

Dang, I hated it when he did that.

Thanks, Thunderfoot.

The New Boat

"Wow, is that it?" Thunderfoot asked as he came bursting through the front door. "When are we going fishing? Can I drive it? How fast will it go?"

"Whoa, take it easy. We've got a lot of work to do on it before we take it out for a test run," I said. I hardly had finished my response when he ran to the shop for tools.

I had been fishing in some walleye tournaments for a few years and as it happens in any sport, the more you get involved in something, the more equipment you think that you need. In this case the equipment was a new boat that was much fancier and bigger than my old one. When I had begun fishing tournaments most of the other fishermen had similar rigs to mine. The standard outfit was a fifteen or sixteen foot boat with about a fifty horse motor on it. Over the years the boats had grown to eighteen feet and the motors to one hundred and fifty horses. I had an opportunity to get this rig and jumped at the chance. After all, I had to keep up to the Joneses.

Thunderfoot and I began installing all the gear. We mounted the trolling motor and two fish finders, a radio, compass and GPS unit. Fishing had become high-tech and this boat had it all. There were a lot of holes to drill and what seemed like miles of wires to feed and we spent most of the day doing it. By evening we had it pretty well finished.

"Let's take her for a test drive tomorrow," Thunderfoot said enthusiastically.

"Well, the walleyes have been biting pretty well. I want to make sure everything works before I go to a tournament, so I guess it'd be a good idea to take her for a spin." I was talking to the back of Thunderfoot's head as he was running for home to get his fishing gear.

The next day after we parked at the boat landing, I showed Thunderfoot what to do to drive the boat off the trailer. He got in and I backed the boat down the landing and into the edge of the water. When the motor was in the water he started it and grinned like a madman as he backed the boat off the trailer. I parked the truck and trailer and walked down to the river where he had pulled up to the shore. I climbed into the boat and took over the steering wheel much to his dismay. "I'm driving it first," I said.

Soon we were flying upriver. At first I was a little hesitant but soon I felt more confident and gave the motor more gas. We flew like the wind in the new boat and both of us had wide grins on our faces. Thunderfoot was hanging onto his cap to keep it from blowing off.

"This is so cool," he said over the noise of the engine. Cool was an understatement for this boat.

We got to a good fishing area and I stopped the boat. I shut off the big motor and moved up to the front pedestal seat and lowered the foot-controlled trolling motor. We began drifting and jigging for walleyes. The first drift was more or less a test run for the trolling motor so I could get used to using it. When we got downriver a little way, I pulled up the trolling motor, started the big motor and took us back upriver. This time I got a small walleye right after we stopped to fish. Thunderfoot got a fish a short time later and then got another. When we got to the lower part of the drift again I turned and said, "Why don't you drive us back up? I'll lift the trolling motor and stay up front here. Just take it slow and easy."

He had a smile a mile wide as he drove us upriver. He did a good job and soon we reached the starting point, and began another drift. This time we got two more fish. When we got to the lower end again, he drove us back upriver. After several more drifts, the fishing began to slow down so we pulled onto shore for some lunch.

We were out on the shore stretching our legs and Thunderfoot just stood there looking at the boat. "That's the most beautiful boat I've ever seen," he said. I think the boy was in love.

After lunch we made two more drifts without getting any more fish so we decided to move downriver to another area. I stowed away the trolling motor and moved back to the driver's seat. Thunderfoot looked at me questioningly before he grudgingly got up so I could sit down.

"I better drive out in the river traffic," I said. "I've had more experience." He wasn't real happy about it but I had paid a lot of money for this boat and if someone was going to put the first scratch in it, I wanted it to be me.

We went downriver to another spot and again I worked the electric, and he drove us back upriver at the end of each drift. As the day wore on we accumulated a fair number of fish so we decided to call it quits. I strapped down the trolling motor and put away all the gear. When I moved back to the driver's seat Thunderfoot sat there looking at me pleading with his eyes.

"If I let you drive will you be really careful?" I asked.

He nodded his head up and down and started the motor.

We took off and he did pretty well. After a time he nudged the throttle ahead a bit and we were moving at a pretty fast clip. I had showed him how to trim the motor and raise the front of the boat, and that increased our speed also. Soon we were going real fast and I shot him a warning glance. He looked back with a look of supreme confidence. I hung on and gritted my teeth.

We were going up the channel and ahead of us was a pontoon boat that was cruising along much slower than we were. Thunderfoot looked over at me questioningly and I yelled over the noise of the motor to pass him just like you do in a car, on the left. He nodded that he understood. Instead of swinging out to the left, he kept going right at the back of the now increasingly close pontoon. In a couple more seconds we were right behind it and began wallowing in the wake of the big flat boat. The man driving the pontoon saw us overtaking him and began waving with his arms to get us to turn off. Thunderfoot tried to turn to the left but the wake of the pontoon was very large and kept pushing us back behind it. I yelled at Thunderfoot to give the motor throttle so we could jump the pontoon's wake and he finally understood and turned hard to the left as he punched the throttle. We managed to jump the wake and went around the pontoon.

As soon as we got past, I signaled to Thunderfoot to cut the motor. The man on the pontoon slumped down in his seat and shook his head as he went past us. I let out a long breath and looked over at Thunderfoot who was looking like a swim might be safer than waiting to hear what I was going to say.

"I thought you understood to pass him on the left," I said. "I don't recall telling you to drive up on his transom."

"You said to pass him like in a car. I thought you meant get right behind him and then pass. I didn't know he'd be making such a big wave. You're just lucky I'm such a good driver of we might have had a terrible accident."

Despite my near heart attack, I had to laugh. I signaled him with my thumb that he was "out" of the driver's seat. "I'll drive the rest of the way," I said. "I can't stand another close call like that today."

When we got back to the landing I backed the trailer into the water and he did a good job of driving the boat up onto it. We tied everything down and took off down the road for home.

"Boy, that's a cool boat," he said. "I sure would've felt bad if I would've crashed it. But I had it under control... really."

Even though I had been terrified, I had to grin.

"You know that guy on the pontoon?" he said. "He kind of distracted me when he was waving at me." Then he laughed. "I bet he had to go home and put on some new shorts.'

Me too.

Thanks, Thunderfoot.

Almost Too Hot to Fish

I was dozing in my recliner which I had moved to the center of the room positioning it directly under the ceiling fan. The air conditioning was running full tilt and the ceiling fan was on high and it was still warm in the house. The front door burst open and Thunderfoot came running into the house.

"Jeez, I almost melted coming from my house to here," he said. He opened the refrigerator and fanned himself with the cool air coming from it, while grabbing a cold pop. "It's nice in here. Oh, were you sleeping?"

"Well, I was but I'm not now," I said stretching to get the kinks out of my back.

We were into our third week of 100-degree weather. It was one of the longest hot spells we had ever had. I had become a hermit, content to read and sit in the air-conditioning during the day. I did some work in the evening when it cooled down to the mid-eighties. Thunderfoot who wasn't much into reading, had watched all the fishing and hunting videos I owned at least three times and was getting restless. He pestered me to go fishing every day and the longer the heat wave went on, the worse it got.

"There's a nice breeze today," he said.

"More like a blast furnace," I replied.

"Oh come on, it's not that bad. I'm going nuts sitting around here. I need to fish or I might forget how. Then what would we do?"

"What do you mean forget how?" I said. "You never knew much in the first place."

"Oh ha ha, you really crack me up! Let's go down to the river. If we get hot we can go swimming. I can't stand this anymore, please, please, please."

I almost suggested that he go home and pester his family but I had to admit that I too was getting cabin fever. "Ok, we'll try it," I said.

Of course we had to get some lunch ready. Thunderfoot never did anything without taking lunch along. We filled a cooler with cold pop and some fruit and then I opened the front door to go outside. When the hot humid air hit me I almost turned right around and went back into the house, but Thunderfoot was ahead of me chattering like a squirrel about how much fun we would have.

We backed the truck into the yard and loaded the johnboat into the back. Then we got out the volleyball net and poles, a couple of old sheets and some clothespins, and headed for the river.

The truck was like a furnace and we were sweating like construction workers. Lucy, my golden was panting up a storm as we got to the boat landing. Soon we were paddling the boat across the river to a sandbar.

When we got to the sandbar we beached the boat and stood up the volleyball net. Then we cut a couple of long branches from a tree and stuck them in near the volleyball net. We then pinned the sheets between the net and sticks making a kind of canopy from them, giving us some shade.

"Wow, this is as cool as air-conditioning," Thunderfoot gushed as we sat beneath the awning. "I'm such a smart guy to think of stuff like this. Sometimes I amaze myself."

I had to laugh. It had been a pretty good idea. We moved the boat over to the shady spot and got our poles out and began fishing. We were just fishing on the bottom with night crawlers and it didn't take long for Thunderfoot to get a bite and catch a small catfish. He quickly swung it over for me to take off for him, since he was shy about handling cats with their stingers.

Before long I had a bite and caught another catfish, then I caught another. We started catching catfish and sheephead about as fast as we could reel them in.

"This is more like it," Thunderfoot said, laughing as he set the hook into yet another fish. "I just hope our night crawlers last. It would be a shame to run out of bait when the fish are biting so good."

I didn't like the sound of that because it would entail someone, meaning me, going to the hot truck to get more bait. "Use them sparingly," I said. "Maybe we'll have enough."

After a couple of hours we took a break and walked a little way away from our fishing-hole and took a swim. Lucy had a great time frolicking in the water with Thunderfoot and we spent an hour in the water before returning to fish.

"Wow, the sun is shining right into our fishing spot," Thunderfoot said when we got back. Indeed, the sun had moved enough that our shade was now too far away for us to take advantage of it and we'd be fishing right in the sun. We adjusted the canopy so we could squeeze another hour or so from it and then began fishing again. I reached for the crawlers and dug through the bedding but found only bedding.

"The worms are gone," I said.

"You should've been more careful about using so many. Now you'll have to go get more I suppose. I'd be glad to do it but, of course, I can't drive," he said with a satisfied look.

I wasn't too keen on walking back up the sand to the boat landing and then driving for more worms but Thunderfoot kept pestering me to go so I gave up and started for the truck.

I was almost cooked when I got to the truck and by the time I drove to the bait shop and back I *was* cooked. I waded back out to the sandbar and walked toward our fishing spot. Soon I began to get worried as I couldn't see Thunderfoot or Lucy sitting under the canopy. I looked up and down the sandbar and they weren't anywhere to be found. Now I was getting worried because the river has a fast current and can be dangerous if you get careless.

I began to trot and then run toward the fishing spot. As I neared it I finally figured out why I hadn't seen them. Thunderfoot was sitting in the water with just his head and one hand showing, holding his pole. Lucy was sitting right beside him with just her head showing.

"It's about time, I was almost out of bait," he said grinning from the water.

"Jeez, you guys gave me a scare, I thought you must have drowned or something."

"Me drown? Me, part man part fish?" he said as he hooked another fish.

I sat down and laid the worm container in the sand when a thought struck me. "Hey, how is it that you're still fishing when we were out of bait?"

"Oh, that's a funny story," he said. "It seems that I had put a few worms into another can and forgot about them. Right after you left I happened to find them but you were already gone...but there were only a few anyway, not enough for both of us." He put on his most innocent face and sat there actually expecting me to buy this line of baloney.

"Yeah right," I said. I opened the cooler for a pop. It was empty. "What happened to all the pop and food?"

"Well, Lucy and I were pretty hungry. I guess we must have eaten it all. Maybe you should go and...oh never mind."

"Never mind is right, at least until I check and see what else you've stashed away around here."

He gave me an innocent look and then a big grin.

Thanks, Thunderfoot.

The Safari North

Thunderfoot was standing beside the pile of gear in his front yard and began picking up bags as I drove onto the driveway. We were taking a fishing trip "up north" and he was ready and waiting.

"Jeez! Where have you been?" he asked. "I've been ready for hours." He struggled to get the two duffel bags into the back of the truck.

"I'm three minutes late," I answered. "And by the way, what *is* all this stuff?"

He shot me a look of amazement. "This is all necessary stuff. The big bag is my sleeping bag, an extra blanket, pillow, air mattress and my heavy coat. The smaller bag is clothes, shoes, raingear, and mosquito stuff. The little bag is beautifying stuff, like my shampoo, soap, stink-me-pretty, and my shaving machine. The rest is fishing stuff."

"Your shaving machine? Since when do you shave?" I asked.

"My grandpa gave me his old shaving machine a couple of years ago and I shaved with it then."

"And you think you might just have to shave again while we're on vacation? What are you going to use for electricity?"

He looked at me questioningly. "What do you mean? No electricity? What am I going to use to play my Discman?"

We loaded the gear and headed up the road to the north woods. As we passed through countless towns, he announced the name and population of each. It was if I couldn't see the sign I guess. Somehow the conversation ended up being about whether the American flag decals on a Harvester silo meant it was paid for or not.

"See that one? It's got a flag so that's a rich farmer," he said every time we spotted a silo with a flag. I didn't know if it was true so I didn't argue about it.

On we went with only a couple of pit stops and soon the countryside began to look more "northern".

"Are there any bears up here?" he asked.

"Yeah, from here on up this is bear country, but we most likely won't see one."

The words had hardly left my lips when he yelled, "Stop! Look, a bear!"

I looked to the left where he was pointing and sure enough there was a huge black bear lying along the road dead as a doornail.

"Stop, let's look at it," he said, digging for his camera.

I pulled over on the shoulder and he ran back to the bear. As he got closer he slowed to a walk and then to a stealthy walk. He stopped and watched for it to breathe and then carefully walked up to it.

It was a really big black bear and had probably been hit by a car. "I'll sit on its back and you take my picture," he said handing me the camera.

He stepped across the bear and sat down on his back, grabbed his ears and lifted up the head grinning like a madman and I snapped a picture.

"Boy, just wait till the guys at school see that," he said grinning from ear to ear.

We started off down the road again and soon crossed the border into Michigan. We came to a town a short while later and he didn't read the name and population. Instead he had a puzzled look on his face. Down the road a few miles the same thing happened.

"Where do the people go when the limit is filled?" he asked.

"What limit? What do you mean?" I replied.

"Well, both of those last towns said the name and city limit. I guess that means they have all the people they want. They must have a limit. What do the people who want to live here do? Wait till somebody moves out?"

I started laughing and he looked even more confused. "City limit is the edge of the city's jurisdiction," I explained. "It's the edge of the city, not the population limit. They don't population figures on signs in Michigan I guess."

"Oh." He looked kind of embarrassed.

Before long we arrived at the town on the edge of the national forest campground that was our destination. We stopped at a bait shop and got licenses and some information from an old-timer who was sitting behind the counter.

"Any bears in this campground?" Thunderfoot asked.

"Bears? You betcha! They's thick around here. Why just last week they carried off a couple of college kids."

Thunderfoot's eyes got real big.

"The state-record bear was shot up the road a piece," the old-timer continued. "He was so big it took a log skidder to get him out of the woods.

But usually they don't bother campers too much. Once in a while they might chomp somebody but not too often. Just be sure to keep your food in the truck and you'll most likely come back alive."

The old guy winked at me while Thunderfoot was deep in thought.

"Which lake you boys goin to?"

"White Goose Lake," I said.

"Uh-oh. That's the one nearest where that giant bear was killed. He probably has some giant kids that are all grown up by now, I'd be plenty careful up there."

Thunderfoot was very quiet taking it all in. "You want to take a few candy bars with us?" I asked.

He shook his head no. "It's your last chance for snacks," I warned.

He declined again, so we packed into the truck and started down the highway until we came to a forest road that led to the lake. The road was a rocky track that snaked through the trees and in some places it was so narrow that we couldn't have opened the truck doors if we had wanted to get out. We drove for what seemed like many miles and then suddenly we came over a little rise and there was the lake. It was very pretty with a tree-lined shoreline and a pit toilet with a hand pumped well. There wasn't another tent or camper to be seen.

"The bears probably ate all the other people who were here," Thunderfoot concluded matter-of-factly.

"Oh don't worry," I said. "That old guy was just having fun with you. Chances are that neither of us will get eaten."

It was pretty late in the afternoon so we decided to get the tent set up and the camp ready rather than go fishing. It took the better part of a couple of hours but when we were done we had a dandy little campsite. I lit a fire in our fire pit and after it died down a little we grilled some hamburgers, ate some chips and drank a couple of pops. Soon it was time for bed. Thunderfoot searched the campsite for any scrap of food and made sure all the coolers were locked in the truck. Then he came into the tent.

"There's nothing edible in here but us," he said.

"Quit worrying. We'll be fine."

We rolled out our sleeping bags onto our cots and climbed in. I lay on my back and listened to the sounds of the night. I loved the sounds near a lake. There were frogs croaking, some cicadas singing and an occasional owl hooting. It was very peaceful and soon the sounds were joined by the gently deep breathing of my young friend. I rolled over on my side and was just about to sleep when I heard the sound of a loon echoing across the lake.

To those who have never heard a loon, it's a pretty scary sound. Their call starts out with a low wailing sound that increases in volume and pitch as it goes on. The moaning sound ends up with a high pitched whistling sound that is quite un-nerving if you don't know what it is.

Thunderfoot had never heard a loon before.

"What the heck was that?" I heard him ask from deep in his sleeping bag. He had pulled the bag up over his head and he was crunched down inside. The loon call came again and he peeked out of the opening. "Did you hear that? Hey, are you awake?"

I began to laugh. "It's only a loon," I said.

'A what?"

"A loon...you know...those big black and white birds that cruise on the water up here."

"Are you sure?"

"Yup."

Out came his head. "Jeez, I almost had the big one. I thought it was a bear screaming at me and coming to eat me. You're sure that's a bird?"

The sound came again. "Yeah, it's a loon. If we go down by the lake I bet we'll see him in the moonlight."

"As interesting as that sounds, I think I'll just stay here in my sleeping bag," he said.

"Suit yourself. I'm going to go see if I can spot him."

"Are you nuts? You'd leave me here alone? I'll make a deal with you. You stay here and I'll do all the chores all week. All you have to do is relax."

"Well, I'd really like to see that loon."

"I'll clean all the fish too."

"Ok, I'll stay," I said.

"Good, now go to sleep."

This was looking like a real good vacation.

Thanks Thunderfoot.

Right Place, Wrong Time

The north wind bit into our faces as we hunkered down in our duck blind, straining to see any moving ducks through the morning darkness. It was late in the season and Thunderfoot and I had gotten to the blind early so we could replace some of the teal and wood duck decoys with large mallards and goose decoys. This would be one of our last hunts of the season.

"Jeez, I'm just about froze," he grumbled from somewhere inside his hunting coat. He had the thing zipped up so far that only the top of his head was showing. "How long is it until we can shoot?"

I checked my watch. Shooting time has just started but with the cloudy skies and cold wind it was hard to see anything that might be close enough to shoot at.

"It's time right now," I said.

Thunderfoot's head poked out of his collar and he got ready for some shooting. Before long we saw a flock of mallards flying up the river and I called to them. They kept right on going, showing no interest in us.

Suddenly Thunderfoot grabbed my arm and whispered, "Listen...geese."

I strained my ears and soon heard the unmistakable barking call of Canada geese coming from our right. We looked and looked but couldn't see them even though their calls were obviously getting closer. Finally Thunderfoot whispered, "Look, they're real low over the lake."

Sure enough, the geese were just above the water of the lake just east of us. We hunted on a small beaver pond west of the lake which was about a quarter of a mile away. The lake took a dog-leg at the west end and the flock followed that dog-leg and settled into the narrow arm of water. Soon another flock followed the same route and settled down with the first bunch.

"We should have been over there," Thunderfoot said.

"Yeah, and if we were they would have landed here," I answered.

"Maybe we should pick up our decoys and go over there."

We had one dozen Canada goose decoys sitting on the pond but I wasn't real enthused about picking them all up and then carrying everything over to the lake. Thunderfoot kept pestering me and then another flock of geese landed in the same dog-leg and that sealed it. We began the big move.

I took the canoe out to the pond and wrapped the cords around the necks of the decoys while Thunderfoot carried the guns, ammo, and seat cushions back to high ground. Then we carried the decoys up the high bank and walked through the woods a short was and started toward the lake. Of course when we got close to the lake the geese got up and flew away, but we expected that. There was some reason geese were landing in the dog-leg and we figured if we put our decoys there we might just get some shooting.

The whole process took almost two hours and during that time four more flocks of geese came down the marsh and followed pretty much the same course.

This is going to be great," Thunderfoot said as we finished putting out the decoys. "It's lucky the lake is shallow here or you'd have had to get wet to put out the decoys." How thoughtful of him.

While I had been placing the decoys Thunderfoot constructed a makeshift blind out of cattails and buttonball brush ad the edge of the lake.

We settled in and felt sure we were now in the right place for some action. We waited. We waited some more. An hour later we were still waiting. Not one goose had shown his face on the marsh since we had moved. Another hour passed. The clouds began to dissipate and the sun came out. It turned into a bluebird day and not one goose came near us.

"I can't believe it," Thunderfoot said. "Now it's a nice day and the ducks and geese will be flying way too high and we're gonna sit here all day and shoot nothing." He lay back in the tall grass and folded his arms across his chest.

"Well, at least it warmed up," I said trying to cheer him up. I dug into our lunch bag and offered him a sandwich, which seemed to boost his moral a little. In the hours that followed we sat there and enjoyed a beautiful afternoon but saw no ducks or geese.

By mid-afternoon we were getting pretty bored and still hoped that the evening flight would be better. We had seen a lot of birds in the morning, so hopefully some of them would come past again towards evening.

"I think I'll go over there and cut some of that tall grass to make us a better blind," he said. He stood up and began walking toward the marsh. "That way if they do come back we'll be hidden better."

I was ready for as stretch too, so I went along with him. We cut some grass with our hunting knives and carried it back to the lake. We needed a bit more so we walked back and were cutting it when I heard the first honk. Thunderfoot stopped in mid-cut and gave me a panicked look.

"Did you hear that?" he whispered. I nodded and we turned slowly toward the lake. Hovering above our decoys about ten feet off the water were fifteen geese. A couple of seconds later they landed in among our decoys.

"Our guns! We left our guns over there!" Thunderfoot was having a meltdown.

I knew it was futile but I said. "Let's get down and belly-crawl over and see if we can get to the guns before the geese see us."

We low-crawled as fast as we could go, and got within ten feet of the guns when the geese began honking and lifted off the water. By the time we grabbed our guns they were safely out of range.

"Sure, go!" he yelled at the geese. "I can't believe we did that. I can't believe we left our guns behind!"

As exasperated as I was I had to laugh. Soon Thunderfoot was laughing too. "Can you believe we did that?" he said shaking his head. "I thought you taught me better than that."

We settled back down in our now much improved blind and didn't see a waterfowl of any kind the rest of the afternoon. The time ticked by and soon it was time go home.

"Not one goose came by here all afternoon except those that came while we were over there," he said. "What are the odds of that happening?"

"With us? Pretty good," I said.

We picked up the decoys and began hauling all the stuff back toward the high bank and about half way back we heard geese honking. We stopped and watched as a flock of about twenty landed right in the dog-leg where our blind was built. "Well that's about it," he said shaking his head.

I grinned. "Look at it this way. We got to spend a beautiful day in the outdoors and now we don't have to spend an hour picking geese."

He nodded. "So, what's the plan for tomorrow?"

At least the boy wasn't a quitter.

Thanks, Thunderfoot.

The Great Coyote Hunt

"I'm just about to climb the walls," Thunderfoot said, pacing back and forth across the living room. "We've been cooped up like this for weeks. There's got to be something we can do outside."

It had been one of those winters. January had been as bitter cold as Siberia. The thermometer hadn't been higher than ten degrees above zero for almost three weeks. It was beginning to drive everyone crazy.....especially Thunderfoot. The fishing had been at an all time low due to the cold and the high pressure fronts that came through every other day. The last few times we had gone we'd caught nothing.

I was trying to read a magazine but he kept pacing around like a caged animal.

"Here," I said tossing him the magazine. "This is a new magazine...look through it and see if you can entertain yourself while I get us something to eat.

He grabbed the magazine and I went into the kitchen to see what there was to eat. It seemed like food usually improved his mood. When I came back to the living room he was intently reading an article in the magazine. I put his food down next to him but he kept reading and ignored the food. That *must* have been a good article.

"We have a lot of coyotes around here don't we?" he asked.

"Yeah, I guess so. They say there are a lot of them but you don't see them very often because they're so stealthy."

"This story tells about calling them in so you can shoot them. It tells how to camouflage yourself and call and how to get them to come to you. It sounds like fun. I think we should try it."

I read the article and while he devoured both his snack and mine. When I finished he looked at me and grinned. "Well, what do you think? Let's try hunting for them we've done stupider things than this."

I laughed and couldn't argue with that. And so we began our preparations for the great coyote hunt.

First we needed sheets to use as camouflage. We found some old ones in the closet that were about worn out so we cut holes in them so we could wear them over our clothes like a poncho. Then we got some plastic sheeting to lay on the ground and an old sleeping bag to lay over the sheeting to keep the cold from seeping into us. Finally we found some old pillow cases that we could wear over our hats and faces. We cut eyeholes in them and tried them on.

"Yikes, we look like Ku Kluxers," Thunderfoot said. "We better wait until we get where we're going before we put them on."

Next we went to buy a coyote call. Of course there aren't just a couple of calls for coyotes. There are dozens of different models that make many different sounds. Some sound like a mouse squeaking and others sound like a dying rabbit. One mimicked a coyote bark. We finally decided on a dying rabbit and when we got outside Thunderfoot gave it a try.

The wailing sound was as spooky as heck. "Wow," he said, "I'd hate to hear that on a dark and stormy night."

It was getting late in the day, so we decided to start our hunt first thing the next morning. As is usually the case when we're going hunting, Thunderfoot stayed over in "his" room. It saved me waking him up and the rest of his family at the same time.

At dawn we got up and had a big breakfast and then drove down to the river bottoms looking for a good coyote spot. We found a place that looked just right. It was near the marsh and a little higher than the surrounding terrain so it had a good view of the prairie near a pine woods. There was a lot of cover but many open areas so we'd be able to see a coyote if he came close.

We unloaded the gear and I drove the truck about a quarter of a mile down the road and parked it. I walked back and we carried the gear to the little knoll. It was pretty brushy but looked like a really good spot.

First we cleared off a small area and laid the plastic down. Then we put down the sleeping bag and spread a sheet over it. Next we got out our sheets and hoods and covered up. Finally we lay down on the sleeping bag and Thunderfoot loaded the gun. We had lunch, of course, and we covered it with another pillow case. We blended in and looked like a little bump in the snow.

"We're camouflaged so good that nothing can see us," he said as he dug into his pocket for the dying-rabbit call. He put it in his mouth and produced a horrifying call that would have given shivers to an undertaker. We scanned the area, expecting a coyote to come bounding up at any second, but none came. After a while Thunderfoot wailed on the call again and then again. We waited and waited but we saw no coyotes.

"That article said they should come on the run," Thunderfoot said.

"Well, those articles sometimes tell it like we want it to be, not like it is," I said. "We've got all day, so just be patient."

But it was cold and it wasn't getting any warmer. At first we were pretty comfortable but as we lay there the cold began to creep in.

"We should have brought a blanket or sleeping bag to put on top of us too," Thunderfoot said. I nodded in agreement. Then he put the call in his mouth and blew. "Ummmffe".

When I looked over he had the call in his mouth but it was frozen shut. Now it was also frozen to his lips. He had a panicked look on his face.

"Nice calling," I said laughing. "That should bring them in running."

He didn't think I was very funny. "Put your hands around the call and blow on it, so it'll thaw out," I said.

He cupped his hands around the call and huffed and puffed and before long the call slipped from his lips.

"Holy cow, I never thought it was *that* cold. Here, you call from now on."

I slipped the call inside my coat and it quickly thawed out. Then I blew a long mournful note on it.

It was getting colder and colder and I looked at my watch. We had been there two hours already without seeing a thing.

"What do you think?" I asked. "Maybe we should try it another time. There don't seem to be any coyotes around here."

Thunderfoot looked at me with chattering teeth. "Yeah, I think...Wait! Look!"

I turned and way off at the edge of the trees was a coyote standing there looking out over the prairie.

I dug furiously for the call and gave it a short blow, trying to let the coyote know where the dying rabbit was located. Sure enough he began trotting toward us.

"Jeez, he's coming," Thunderfoot said, slowly moving his gun into shooting position. The coyote was still coming our way slowly but surely.

I called again. He stopped and looked right at us. We froze and didn't move a muscle.

There was a little dip in the terrain and the coyote dropped into it and out of our sight for a minute.

"Where did he go?" Thunderfoot whispered.

"I think he's still coming. Just be real still and quiet."

Time seemed to stand still. We lay there shivering waiting for the coyote to reappear. Suddenly like a ghost there he was. He stood only twenty yards from us.

"There he is," I whispered. Thunderfoot nodded and thumbed off the safety.

The coyote stood looking our way staring hard, looking for the rabbit. I didn't dare move or try to call again.

Suddenly he acted like he got a whiff of our scent and he whirled and disappeared back into the swale. Then we saw him trotting back into the woods.

I looked at Thunderfoot who took off his hood and gave ma an amazed look.

"I didn't know how much they look like dogs," he said. "I just couldn't shoot it."

I patted him on the back. "No problem pal," I said. "We did what we set out to do. We called him in and fooled him...whether or not we killed him doesn't matter. We had the fun of fooling a wild critter into thinking we were dinner."

He looked at me and grinned. "I thought you might be mad that I didn't shoot."

"You should know by now that something like that wouldn't bother me," I said. "Did you wonder why I gave you the gun? I didn't want to shoot a coyote in the first place."

We stood up and stretched the kinks out of our backs. "I think I've had enough fresh air for one day," I said.

"Me too," he answered. "Boy this cold air makes me hungry."

Somehow I knew he was going to say that.

Thanks, Thunderfoot.

How About a Little Help Here?

I was sitting in the back yard enjoying the shade on one of those hot, humid days when even the thought of movement made me start to sweat. The western sky was filling with big high fluffy white clouds that would soon begin to turn black and threatening. There would be a storm before the day was out.

I knew it wouldn't be long before Thunderfoot would run over from his house and want to go fishing. It never failed. On the hottest days of the year he always thought we should go fishing. Of course, he was right. Northerns and bass become very active right before a storm hits and many times in the past we had seen fabulous fishing on days just like this one.

Right on cue, I saw Thunderfoot heading across the yard. He was marching along...a man on a mission.

"You're not going to catch any fish sitting here in the shade," he said as he plopped down in the lawn chair next to me.

"Yeah, but I'm also not going to die of heat-stroke by going out in the sun either," I replied.

"Yeah, I know you old guys can't take the heat. When you begin to get feeble, it's hard on you. That's ok. I just thought it looked like a nice evening to go fishing, but never mind.....I'll just stay home, or I could ride my bike down to the river and fish off the bank. You know down by the boat landing...it's not good fishing but it's better than nothing at all." He sat there looking miserable, kind of like Oliver Twist asking for more porridge...the poor pathetic little thing.

"Get the stuff," I said. I was so easy.

We loaded the johnboat and the gear into the back of the pickup. When we arrived at the lake we slid the boat into the water and I drove the pickup to the parking area. By the time I had walked back to the boat landing Thunderfoot had distributed the gear to the proper ends of the boat and was sharpening the hook of a new lure he had bought.

"This is going to be a killer," he said proudly showing off a plastic frog.

"That looks good," I said. "I'm surprised that you knew where to *buy* lures. I thought you figured they all came free from my tackle box." He looked up innocently and kept sharpening.

"I'll have you know…" he began.

"Just get in the boat," I said as I began pushing off.

As we moved away from the shore, Thunderfoot cast his new frog lure into the lily pads and then began making it crawl slowly across the tops of the plants. The plastic frog hadn't gone two feet when the lily pads exploded and a nice bass engulfed his lure. He fought it expertly and soon had it alongside the boat. As he lifted the fish he grinned like a maniac. He didn't say a word, but unhooked the fish and released it, grinning slyly all the while. He reeled up and cast to another spot in the weeds. This time he reeled the lure back without a strike but got another bass on the next cast.

Meanwhile I paddled the boat and cast to the weeds with different baits that I thought might produce a fish for me. But I had no bites. Thunderfoot sat in the front of the boat, casting and catching fish like a machine.

"What do you think of my frog now?" he asked.

"I think you should have bought two…one for me too," I said glumly with sweat running into my eyes.

"Well, it just so happens that I have another just like this one…here in my pocket," he said reaching into his shorts pocket and producing another frog lure. "If someone would like to use it I might be able to let them if they ask real nice."

I wiped the sweat from my eyes and gave him a hard look. "If you'd like to swim back to shore, keep that frog, otherwise toss it over here."

"Sounds like a plan to me," he said grinning as he tossed the precious lure back to me.

"How many fish were you going to catch before you let me have this extra bait?" I asked.

"I completely forgot I had it in my pocket until you asked," he said innocently.

Well, it didn't really make much difference because now I had a frog and soon we both began catching fish, one after another. We caught northerns, bass, dogfish and Thunderfoot even caught a huge crappie that was 16 inches long. As much as I hated to admit it, the fishing had turned out as good as he had predicted it would be just before a storm.

We were near a little island with a couple of trees on it when Thunderfoot cast toward the spot and his frog ended up in one of the trees. He pulled and pulled and suddenly his line snapped. "Holy cow, I lost my frog. I might need that one I lent to you back."

"I'll take you over to the island. You can climb that tree and get yours back," I said.

He seemed ok with that so I paddled over and he climbed out and walked to the tree. Up he went and soon he was shimmying out onto the branch that held his frog. He broke off the branch holding the frog and then climbed back down from the tree. He tossed the bait into the boat and began walking back towards me when he suddenly stopped and grabbed something in the grass. I watched as he tugged and pulled on something that was hidden by the tall grass.

"Come here and help me," he said.

"What are you doing?"

"I need help. Come here."

I wasn't real sure I wanted to get too close to whatever he was doing but I stepped out onto the island and carefully made my way to where he was crouching in the grass. When I got to him I stepped back quickly as soon as I saw what he was doing. He was holding onto the tail of a huge snake that was partly in a hole in the ground. He was tugging on the tail trying to pull the dang thing out of the hole.

"Are you crazy?" I said retreating back to the boat as fast as I could go. "Let that thing go and get back into the boat or I'm leaving you here." My patience with snakes was zero.

"I thought you might like to see this nice snake," he said laughing. Suddenly he fell over backward holding onto about six inches of the snake's tail.

"Goodbye," I said backing the boat away.

"Oops, I didn't mean to do that."

As he spoke, a huge water snake came to the surface right by the boat. The snake was obviously not in a good mood. It swam by my end of the boat and I could see that its rear end was kind of blunt. It didn't even slow down as it passed, heading for the other side of the lake.

"Come back and get me...please," Thunderfoot begged.

"Not until you get rid of that snake tail." I knew that if he got in the boat with it, it would somehow end up in my lap.

He grinned and tossed the tail, so I picked him up.

"You're pretty sensitive about snakes," he said grinning.

"You're darn right and the sooner you learn that the better off you'll be," I said.

"Sorry, I was just having fun."

We fished in silence for a while and soon began catching fish again. We worked our way back to the landing because the thunderstorm was getting close. We wanted to be off the water before the lightning began to strike.

"What did you think of my frog baits?" Thunderfoot asked as we loaded the boat.

"Not bad," I replied.

"I think I'll get a couple more just in case we lose one next time. Then we won't have to go up on the bank and risk a venomous encounter with a killer grass snake." He grinned at me. "I wouldn't want my best boat-rower to have a heart attack."

He was such a considerate boy.

Thanks, Thunderfoot.

You Chase...I'll Shoot

Thunderfoot and I drove up past the barn and parked the pickup at the edge of the field. We were at the end of a long valley with hay fields along the edges and picked corn up the middle. The valley was guarded by steep hills on both sides, and our host had given us directions the previous evening as to where the best spot would be to get a deer.

We had not had too successful a season so far, and Thunderfoot was a bit on the grumpy side. During opening day and Sunday of the first weekend, we had sat on stands along the river bottoms and had seen absolutely nothing to shoot at. School forced Thunderfoot to give it a rest for the next three days and now we were back at it on Thanksgiving morning.

"We'll see some deer here," I said. "Ken said there are lots of does and some nice bucks still roaming around." The owner and his family had filled all of their buck tags on the previous weekend and wanted some does taken off the farm, so things looked good for us.

Thunderfoot was still down. He wasn't the patient type. He liked a lot of action and the previous two days of fruitless hunting were about enough to make him have a fit.

"Well, we can't do any worse than that last 'hot spot' you took me to," he said gloomily.

I didn't answer him, but opened my door quietly and reached back into the pickup for my gun and my other gear. He also got out of the truck and we got prepared to move up the valley in the darkness.

"Ken said to go up the side valley by the old windmill," I whispered as we walked slowly along the fence.

We soon saw the windmill and crossed the fence a short way from it. I saw a nice stump up on the side of the nearby hill and told Thunderfoot to sit there. I would go back and climb up the hill on the other side of the point, where I could hopefully chase some deer to him.

"I'll start up the hill in about an hour," I said. "You just watch from here. If I move any, they should come right through here."

He nodded, and I walked back toward the point of the hill so I could go up the next valley and ascend the hill from the other side.

When I got to the back side of the hill, it was still way too dark for an old man with bad knees to start climbing, so I sat down on a log and rested for a while.

Blackness turned to gray, and my eyes and ears were soon imagining critters all around me in the woods. Stumps seemed to make small movements, like a deer standing and watching you might make. A stick or an acorn falling to the ground sounded like a footstep on the dry leaves. But as the light got stronger, the stumps became what they really were and the footsteps became acorns and sticks that fell naturally all day long. It's funny how your eyes and ears can play mind tricks on you when you're in a dark woods.

As it got light I looked up at the hillside I planned to climb. It was much steeper than I expected. In fact it was real steep, and the top was a long, long way from me. "Oh boy, what have I gotten myself into?" I thought.

I started up the hill and at first I followed a deer path. Soon the deer path became too steep for me to follow and I had to abandon it. Then I worked my way from tree to tree and rock to rock trying not to make too much noise and trying not to slip and slide all the way to the bottom of the hill. I hated the idea of having to re-conquer land that I had already once trod over.

It didn't take long for me to work up a sweat. Soon I was huffing and puffing like a steam engine. I would move up a few feet and then hang onto a tree for a few minutes to let my heart rate go down again. Then I'd move up another few feet. It was slow going and suddenly I looked up and saw a small bunch of deer up the hill from me. They were casually waking away from Thunderfoot's direction.

I would gain ten or fifteen feet, rest, and then climb some more. The top of the hill seemed to stay the same distance away. Just as I was beginning to think I would never reach the top I heard a shot, followed about ten seconds later by another shot.

I stood there panting and listened. No more shots, no shouts, nothing came from the other side of the hill. Now I had to make a decision. Should I keep going up or should I go back to see if Thunderfoot was the shooter and had he shot a deer? Since I was already halfway up the hill, I decided I should go the rest of the way and finish out my drive. I waited another ten minutes and didn't hear a thing.

So, I started on up to the top of the hill. Once on high ground, I always hate to go back down unless I have to. High ground is gained at too high a price for a "seasoned hunter", as Thunderfoot called me. Of course I knew he was saying "Old Man."

I kept working my way to the top and finally made it. It was a beautiful spot. The ridge top was flat and dozens of deer trails crisscrossed it. I found a dandy stump and sat on it with my back against a nice flat tree trunk, resting.

"I think I'll sit here for half and hour or so and see what comes by," I thought to myself.

I was very comfortable and then I heard a "hey" coming from the bottom of the hill. I listened and heard it again. Thunderfoot.

I didn't really want to yell back, because I had just settled into my comfortable seat, but thought I'd better answer him in case he had trouble. "What?" I yelled back.

"Come down."

"Did you get one?"

"Come down."

"Do you have a deer?"

"Just come down."

I grudgingly picked up my gear and started down the face of the hill. I tried to go slow and pick my way down but soon I had to almost run to stay upright. The front of the hill was as steep as the back had been. Soon I was panting and sweating again from my "controlled fall" down the hill.

I finally saw Thunderfoot sitting on a stump at the bottom of the hill, so I stopped.

"Did you get one?"

"Two."

"What?"

"Two."

That was great news. He had a Hunter's Choice tag and I had a buck tag, so he had filled both of them.

He was all grins and swagger as I got to him.

"How big is he? Where is he?" I asked.

"He who? I got two does."

I looked at him. "Two does? We don't have two doe permits, just one."

His mouth dropped open. "I thought you had a Hunter's Choice too."

"No, I've just got my regular buck tag. Why did you shoot two?"

"Well, three came over that little knoll over there and I shot and they all ran away. But pretty soon two of them came back over the little knoll again. I shot again and they ran away again, and when I walked over there, two of them were lying there."

We walked across the valley and sure enough, there were two nice does lying side by side.

Thunderfoot was getting worried, so I told him that Ken had mentioned that they had several doe tags left and if we got an extra one, they'd take it. He brightened up when he heard that.

"It's not exactly the way it should be done, but we won't leave a deer go to waste over some little rule infraction. It'll all work out fine," I said.

"Well, it makes me feel better about climbing that mountain since you got these deer for all my effort," I said.

He gave me a funny look. "Those deer came from the other side of the valley. I don't think you chased them, but it was a nice idea anyway."

I had climbed that monster hill for nothing.

"I'd like to try field dressing them, but I think I want to watch you one or two more times, just to see how an expert does it," Thunderfoot said.

Why not? I might as well do something right.

Thanks, Thunderfoot.

Go Toward the Light

It was a clear cold January day and I was nice and cozy in my recliner when Thunderfoot came through the front door. He stomped the snow from his boots and stood grinning at me. He was dressed for hunting so I knew what to expect.

"My grandpa wants me to take his beagle out and hunt him for a while. What do you think?"

"Your grandpa asked you to take his dog hunting?"

"Yeah...well, I was talking to him on the phone and it kind of came up. He said the dog was restless and could use some exercise so I told him we would be glad to help out."

I couldn't argue with logic like that, so I dressed in my hunting clothes and grabbed a shotgun and some shells. Meanwhile Thunderfoot rummaged through the refrigerator looking for some 'pocket food' to take along.

We drove to grandpa's farm and picked up Pat, the three-year old beagle who needed to be taken hunting. Grandpa was content to let us crawl through the snow by ourselves. He gave us some ideas as to where to go, we headed to the woods.

We started up a long valley and it wasn't too long before Pat picked up the track of a rabbit and took off, howling like a fire siren. We separated and waited. In just a little while a bunny came hopping through the brush. He was just out of my range but plenty close to Thunderfoot who stopped him in his tracks.

"Nice shooting," I said.

"Nothing to it."

We resumed walking and soon Pat took off again. This time the bunny came close to me and picked him off. It was turning out to be a pretty good day, despite the biting cold and the foot-deep snow.

We walked to the end of the long valley and then decided to go up the hill and hunt on top, and then back toward the farm. Pat picked up another track halfway up the hill but this bunny was luckier than his partners. He came out behind me and just out of Thunderfoot's range, and got into a hole. Poor Pat was beside himself trying to worry the rabbit from the hole but we finally convinced him to forget it by offering him some of

Thunderfoot's lunch.

We got to the top of the hill and started through some really thick brush. Suddenly Pat began singing again. This time Thunderfoot's 20-gauge barked and the bunny was in the bag.

I was getting pretty tuckered out from the hill climbing so we decided to take a little break. We found a nice log and sat down. Thunderfoot shared the lunch he had brought with him.

"See, you always yell about me bringing food, but here you are eating most of it," he said.

"I don't yell," I said. "Sometimes I get a little perturbed when you clean out all my food, but I don't yell."

He grinned knowing my griping was all in fun...at least most of the time.

"Well, let's finish going out this ridge and then go back of the barn on that hill out there," Thunderfoot suggested. "Grandpa says there are a lot of rabbits on that hill."

It sounded like a lot of walking to me, but I decided to give it a try. We hunted the rest of the hill we were on and didn't see another bunny. Then we went back behind the barn and climbed the hill. Suddenly it was rabbit heaven. There were tracks and rabbit pellets everywhere. Poor Pat almost went crazy with so much rabbit smell in the air. The woods echoed with his howling and the shots from our shotguns rang out in the cold air. We hunted for another two hours and ended up a long, long way from the farm.

"We better start back," I said. "It's going to be dark in about half an hour."

"I want to try that one last brush pile," Thunderfoot said pointing up the hill to a large pile of limbs from a long-ago logging operation.

"Not me," I said. "I'm going to work my way down the hill. I'll meet you by the barn."

He and Pat took off up the hill. I sat for a minute or two and let my legs rest. Then I started to move down the side of the hill.

This hillside was very steep and I was trying to be very careful to keep from sliding all the way to the bottom in an uncontrolled descent. I was getting pretty winded and stopped next to a tall thin dead elm. I leaned back against the tree to rest.

As I leaned on the tree, I heard a cracking sound. Then all was quiet.

The next thing I knew, I wasn't tired any more. I wasn't breathing hard and I was cold. It was also very dark. Suddenly I realized I didn't know for sure where I was. I sat in the snow and then I could hear my name being called from quite a long way away. I wasn't sure if I was awake or dreaming. Soon the sound got louder and I could see a light moving through the trees. "Holy cow," I thought to myself. "Maybe I'm dead."

Then the light got real bright and I could hear Thunderfoot's voice. "Hey, are you ok? Hey, can you hear me?"

I shook my head and suddenly my face got all wet. Pat was lapping my face with his large wet tongue. I realized I was sitting in the snow on the side of the hill. Thunderfoot was holding a flashlight in my face looking at me with a strange look on his face.

"Get that light out of my eyes," I said somewhat impatiently. I pushed Pat back. "Jeez, Pat needs a breath mint." I tried to stand up but my head started to throb and I got dizzy.

"What happened?" Thunderfoot asked. "I waited for an hour, and I thought you were lost, so I got grandpa's flashlight and found you sitting here in the snow."

I looked around and the top five or six feet of the elm tree that I had been leaning against was now lying in the snow on either side of me...split in two. "It looks like the top of this tree broke off when I leaned against it and hit me on the head," I said. "It must have knocked me out."

"No way!" Thunderfoot said. "That's really cool. I never saw anybody who was knocked out before."

When I struggled to my feet, everything seemed to be working but I had a terrible headache. "I guess I'm ok, let's get out of here."

We started down the hillside, got to the valley and then back to the farm. We thanked grandpa and loaded up the pickup for the drive home.

"Are you sure you're ok?" Thunderfoot asked.

"Yeah, I guess so."

"Then you'll be able to help clean the rabbits probably."

"I suppose I will."

"That was kind of scary. You could have been hurt real bad." He paused for a long time and then I could see his grin in the light from the dashboard. "It's a good thing you have such a hard head," he said.

Thanks, Thunderfoot.

Hail, Hail, the Gang's All Here

Spring and walleye fishing had become almost synonymous around my house. Each year, as the ice began to melt and the river began to open up, Thunderfoot and I spent a day getting the boat ready for our first spring walleye fishing trip.

One day we had the boat in the back yard and had run an extension cord to the batteries. We were puttering around, putting the gear back into the compartments.

"I didn't think we had this much stuff," Thunderfoot said as he lugged the fourth load from the storage closet to the boat. On his three previous trips he had carried rods and reels and tackle boxes. This time he was bringing the net and the toolbox that held extra spark plugs and the ever-popular roll of black tape that could fix almost anything.

"What's left in there?" I asked.

"Just the raingear and boots and life jackets," he said as he opened one of the tackle boxes and began sorting plugs and hooks and other items into piles. "It looks like somebody just threw all of this stuff in here last time and didn't put things where they're supposed to be."

"I wonder who that could have been?" I asked. No reply. Soon he had the tackle box empty, and we began putting

things back where they belonged. It took nearly half an hour, and we had three more tackle boxes left to do. Thunderfoot began working on number two while I fired up the grill and cooked half a dozen hot dogs.

"Corne and have some lunch," I said. "We can finish up when we're done eating."

I didn't have to call twice. Thunderfoot came on a run, then inhaled four of the hot dogs and the majority of a large bag of chips in just a few minutes. He washed it all down with a couple of pops.

"Ahhh. That hit the spot," he said.

"Can you tell me what you ate?" I asked, finishing my second dog.

"A hungry boy must eat," he replied, grinning.

We cleaned up the lunch plates and went back to work on the tackle boxes. In a couple of hours, we had the boat all ready to be launched the next morning.

Thunderfoot stayed over that evening, and we were up at first light, heading for the Mississippi River. We stopped for a good breakfast, and a short time later we were backing the boat into the water. I parked the truck, and after a little smoking and choking, the motor roared to life. We headed off for the darn where, hopefully, we'd meet some hungry walleyes.

The boat ride to the darn was brisk. Thunderfoot soon slid off his chair into the bottom of the boat, where he curled up like a turtle. I had to continue staring into the cold wind. Tears ran back on the side of my head as I slowed and carne to a stop near some other boats that were drifting and jigging for walleyes.

Thunderfoot crawled out of his nice warm nest and stretched. "You look cold," he said, grinning. "It's nice and warm down there out of the wind."

"If you think I'm going to let you drive the boat just so I can stay warm, think again," I said.

He shrugged. It was a nice try.

We soon joined the pack of boats jigging for walleyes. It didn't take long for Thunderfoot to jerk back and start reeling up the first fish of the day. He boated a respectable fish, then turned to show me. "This is what we're after," he said, chuckling.

The sun rose and the day turned into one that was almost too nice to be true. The temperature rose to the mid-fifties, the wind was nice and calm, and the fish were biting. We made drift after drift and caught lots of fish. Once in awhile, we put one in the live well, but most were released. The limit was six per person, and we didn't want to reach that number too soon.

By mid-day the sky had begun to cloud up, but the temperature stayed nice and the fishing was still great. I noticed that some of the other fishermen were putting on raingear, so I looked to the west. Some very ugly black clouds were coming our way. The temperature was also beginning to drop. It looked as though our dream day was going to turn on us.

"We'd better get our raingear out," I said. "It looks like we're going to get wet."

Thunderfoot reached down and opened the compartment that held the life jackets and raingear. He gave me a worried look. "It seems that I might have forgotten to put them in the boat yesterday," he said.

"What? No life jackets or raingear?"

"Well, you remember how good of a job I did on rearranging the tackle boxes? I kind of got caught up in that and forgot to go back to the closet for the last load."

"Oh, boy. What are we going to do now? We're illegal without life jackets, and we're going to get wet without raingear. "

The storm was getting close real fast. We decided to ride it out and then go to shore and buy a couple of cheap life jackets. That way we would be legal for the rest of the day.

"A little rain never hurt anybody," Thunderfoot said bravely as the first drops began to splatter into the bottom of the boat.

The little sprinkle soon became a downpour, and in a minute or two it changed to hail. In another minute, it became lots and lots of hail. We both hunkered down in the bottom of the boat as the hailstones pelted us and began filling the boat. Thankfully, they were fairly small, but they were plenty large enough to hurt real bad as they smashed into our bodies.

As quickly as it had begun, the storm was over. The bottom of the boat was about two inches deep in hailstones. Thunderfoot sat up and looked around, kind of dazed.

"Holy cow. That was pretty cool," he commented. "Yeah," I said. "That was lots of fun."

All around us, fishermen in other boats were coming back to life. However, we were the only ones who weren't in raingear, the only ones soaked to the skin.

"It's not going to take long for me to be real cold," I predicted.

"No kidding. I'm soaked, too," Thunderfoot said. He checked the live well, counting the fish we had in it.

"We're three short of a limit," he said.

We decided to try to get the last three and then head in, but before long we were both shivering and decided to call it quits. "We've got enough fish. A limit isn't that important," I said. He agreed with a shivering nod.

The ride back was torture. The wind felt like it came from a freezer now that I was wet, but we finally got there and I walked stiffly up to get the truck. Thankfully, we got the boat loaded without any of the usual first-time-of-the-year problems and pulled it up into the parking lot to stow the gear and tie it down.

"I guess this isn't so bad after all," Thunderfoot said as we worked on the boat. "We got some nice fish and had a pretty good adventure." He scooped up a few handfuls of hail and put them into the live well. "We don't even have to buy ice to keep the fish fresh." He gave me a huge grin.

Thanks, Thunderfoot.

The Best Laid Plans

Thunderfoot and I had been up for four mornings in a row. We were "turkey listening," as he liked to call it, and we thought we had everything figured out. Every morning, a group of hens came down a little draw and through a gate in the fence, then headed into the corner of a hay field to eat and preen. Half an hour later, two to five toms came down the same path and joined the hens, showing off their huge tails and strutting in front of them, hoping to impress them with their superior beauty and size.

We had been across the field each morning, watching this little parade, and tomorrow morning we were going to be waiting for the show with our gun ready. It was Thunderfoot's season. I was going along as caller, so he could concentrate on shooting. Actually, he wasn't too bad a caller himself at home, but he kind of got stage fright when we got into the woods, so he always felt better if I did the calling.

"We're going to spoil their morning tomorrow," he said, grinning at me through his head net.

"Yeah. They've been here every day, so we should be in great shape if we can get in without spooking them."

We slipped back down the hill and took off for home, feeling pretty smug.

The next morning, we snuck up to the corner of the field and put four hen decoys and one jake out just in range of the gun. Then we slipped through the fence and got into comfortable positions to await the coming dawn. I was beginning to get a bit drowsy when an owl hooted up the valley and was answered by a gobble. Thunderfoot looked over his shoulder at me and grinned. Soon we heard another gobble, followed by another and another. There were turkeys all around us.

In about twenty minutes, we saw a hen fly down off the hill and land in the field about a hundred yards from us. Then several more hens came flying down. They began feeding and going about their business, slowly moving our way toward what they thought were more hens.

Meanwhile the toms kept up their gobbling, some coming closer, some going the other way. I called every few minutes, and we soon spotted one that seemed interested in my calling. He would gobble furiously every time I called, so I began calling more urgently. He got hotter and hotter.

"He's coming right down the trail to the gate," Thunderfoot whispered. I nodded quietly.

"Turn a little to the right," I said. "Then you'll be able to shoot if he decides to go toward the real hens instead of coming to the decoys."

He nodded and very slowly and quietly slipped to the right, giving himself a wider shooting range. He did the move with almost no noise or motion, and I was impressed by how good a woodsman he had become in the past few years. He had made a lot of progress since I had dubbed him Thunderfoot.

The real hens began feeding toward us and were soon positioned just below our fakes. I looked out of the corner of my eye and saw the bluish-white head of a tom coming down the field, right alongside the fence we were sitting by.

"He's coming right by the fence, to the right," I whispered. Thunderfoot moved his head in a very slow nod and repositioned the gun a bit.

As the hens came closer, they began clucking and talking among themselves and looked up toward the tom. He stopped and displayed for them, but they seemed unimpressed and went on feeding. He stood there for a few minutes, turning from side to side so the hens could get a good look, then laid his feathers back down and started walking along the fence again.

I heard the faint click as Thunderfoot slipped the safety off and slowly moved the gun up to his cheek. The tom came closer and closer. Thunderfoot followed him with the gun until he was just a few feet away from our decoys. I had always told him that if a tom was coming toward you, you should let him come. The closer he is when you fire, the longer it takes him to run away if you miss.

I had the urge to whisper "shoot," but I figured he knew what he was doing. He held the gun on the tom, and I could see his index finger moving when I noticed that he was raising his head. Suddenly he fired. The tom stood there for about two seconds with no idea what had just happened, then ran into the field a short distance away and stood there, looking around.

"Shoot him again," I whispered loudly.

Thunderfoot was just sitting there with his mouth hanging open. He heard me and brought the gun up to shoot again, but he hadn't ejected the used shell. He had to bring it down again to eject it and feed another into the chamber. Of course, all of this commotion gave our position away to the tom, which by now was hightailing off down the field toward friendlier places.

I pulled my head net off and stuffed it into my pocket.

Thunderfoot never moved.

Finally, after several minutes, he turned around and looked at me. There was a look of utter disbelief on his face.

"He was only ten yards away," Thunderfoot said. "I can't believe it!"

I grinned. "What do you think happened?"

"Must be bad bullets."

"I think the bullets are okay. Think about it."

He pondered for a minute or so and then shook his head.

"I raised my head up to see what happened when I shot," he began. "I brought the front of the gun up and shot over him."

"Yup. I saw you raise your head," I said. "At least you know what you did wrong, so hopefully you won't do it again."

"Boy, you can be sure of that. What now?"

I looked at my watch. It was getting close to time for us to head back to town. He was allowed to miss his first class of the day, but he had to be at school by about nine.

"I guess we'll call it quits for today," 1 said. "Maybe we'll get another chance tomorrow."

We gathered our gear and picked up the decoys, leaving everything in a pile just inside the fence, where we could find it the next morning.

I dropped Thunderfoot off at home. While he was getting ready for school, I drove to the local sporting goods store and bought a set of fiber-optic sights for the shotgun. Then I drove back to his house and picked him up.

"I bought you a little present while you were showering," I said, tossing the package to him.

"Cool! These should make me keep my head where it's supposed to be."

"They can't hurt," I said.

When we got to the school, he jumped out and started up the walk. Then he stopped and came back to the truck.

"I hope you're not mad at me for missing."

I grinned at him. "Nope. What would we do tomorrow at four o'clock if you hadn't missed? Besides, this will give me some ammo the next time you start telling stories about me."

"You won't tell anybody, will you?" Who, me?

Thanks, Thunderfoot.

Thunderfoot Speaks

Now that I've seen all the stuff Dan wrote about our times hunting and fishing together, I can hardly believe we did so much crazy stuff. But we really did.

Sometimes I think he makes things sound a little worse than what really happened, but all of the stuff he wrote about is true, and actually happened. A lot of the time, he blames me for stuff that I don't think was my fault. But you know how old guys can be.

We've done some cool stuff and had a lot of fun. But really, when you think about it, we didn't do anything out of the ordinary. It was regular outdoor stuff, but we seemed to always have fun doing it, even when it didn't turn out like we planned.

I guess we don't take things too seriously. Don't get me wrong-we try hard to catch fish and get game, but if we don't it's not the end of the world. Some of our best times fishing or hunting have been fishless or gameless, but we still had a good time trying.

One thing we both agree on all the time is that being out in nature is the best part of any trip. Coming home with lots of fish or game isn't as important as being outdoors and enjoying the cool stuff you see in a marsh or woods.

I've sure enjoyed doing all the things you've read about, and I hope you've enjoyed reading about them. It has been a good time, and I'm looking forward to lots more adventures in the future. Thanks for reading this book, and watch for us on the water or in the marsh. I'll be the one with the big grin on my face.

Your Buddy, Thunderfoot.

More Adventures of Thunderfoot

It Seems Like Yesterday

I had put a little too much force into my cast, and before my popping bug had even hit the water, I knew it was going to be much too close to the brush pile. I was right, the bug landed too close to the log jam, and the current whisked it toward the logs very quickly. It took me a couple of precious seconds to strip the loop of line off the water so I could get the bug moving, and in that short time the swift current quickly caught the popper. I tried to strip the line a second time, but it was already in the log pile. With a quick snap of the rod, I tried to lift it to safety, but the hook snagged a log and my bug was hooked solidly. I snapped the rod up and down a couple more times, trying to get the hook free, but finally I resigned myself to the fact that my bug was a goner. Taking hold of the line and pulling, my leader soon snapped just a few inches up from the popper. There sat my little Bumble Bee imitation on the log, like a real insect, that had just landed and was taking a rest and watching the world go by.

I turned and began to wade back to the sandbar where the canoe was beached, and as I did, Thunderfoot stepped into the water and began wading toward me.

"Get a little close?" he said, with a twinkle in his eyes and a big grin on his face.

"Yeah, just a bit. I suppose you'll go and catch all of the fish while I tie on another bug."

"I'd consider it my duty," he said mischievously, and began wading toward the bank.

I sat down on the canoe and opened the tackle box, trying to decide which popper to try next. As I sat there, I watched Thunderfoot wade out to the drop off which was about twenty feet from the riverbank. There the water dropped into a channel that ran right along the bank. We had pulled up on the sandbar farther out in the river, so we could fish the brush piles along the bank for smallmouth bass.

It was the middle of the summer and the water was warm, so we were both wearing shorts and tee shirts, and wading barefoot, in the sandy-bottomed river. He waded to the edge of the deep water and then stripped off several loops of line and snapped his fly rod up, made one false cast, to feed some line out, and then expertly dropped the bug within a few inches of the bank and about three feet above the log pile ... He stripped in the excess line and twitched his bug across the upper side of the logs, just a few inches from the uppermost branches, and a nice smallmouth smashed it just as it got about half way past the brush pile. He raised his rod up quickly to set the hook and pulled the smallie from the dangerous, log infested waters, and then took his time and fought the fish in dose. His fly rod almost doubled over when the fish made a hard run and then jumped high out of the water, shaking his head, trying to get rid of the hook. Finally the fish tired, so he dipped his hand into the water, and grabbed the bass by the lip and held it up for me to admire.

"A beauty," I said, looking at the bronze fish, with drops of water dripping off its sides, like little diamonds shining in the sunlight.

He just grinned and took the hook from the fish's lip and slid it back into the water, and began fishing again.

It seemed like only yesterday when I had met Thunderfoot, and now three years later, here we were, best friends. I sat there watching him fish and thought back to the first time I'd seen him.

I owned a sport shop, and like most sport shops, it was a magnet for kids. There were always a few kids hanging around, looking at the rods and reels, or talking fish stories with me. On this particular day, a couple of new kids came through the front door. The older one was about 12 or 13 and introduced himself as James, or "Jamie" as his mom called him. His younger brother was Caleb, "like in the Bible." They looked around for a while and then Jamie mentioned that they had just moved to town and were living just down the street, so we were new neighbors.

Well, it didn't take long, and we became friends. His parents had recently split up, so his hunting and fishing trips were few and far between, because his dad lived in another city.

A short while later, I suggested we go and do some squirrel hunting, and that trip was the first of many adventures we had together over the next years. It was also on that squirrel-hunting trip that I had nicknamed him Thunderfoot.

I had lent him some hunting clothes and boots, which were all a bit too big for him. We had to roll up the pants cuffs and the shirtsleeves, and the boots fit just fine with a couple of extra pairs of socks. As we started walking up the ridge road to the woods, he kept stumbling and dislodging rocks and stepping on sticks, and making such a racket that I told him he had feet that made noise like thunder. And, somehow that got changed into Thunderfoot, and stuck.

When I first met him, he was fairly tall and skinny, with a shock of light brown hair and the bluest blue eyes I'd ever seen. He was a real likable kid with a smile a mile wide. Now, he had matured into a handsome young man. He hadn't grown much taller, but he had filled out nicely. Instead of a tall skinny kid, he was now a tall young man ... He still wore his hair fairly short, and in the summer time, it turned to a dishwater blonde color from all the time we spent in the sun. He had grown into the hand-me-down hunting clothing I had given him, and his feet had caught up to me, so now my shoes and boots were always being borrowed by him for one activity or another.

He still had those incredible, sparkling blue eyes and combined with his perpetual grin, he was a good-looking kid, who was as likable as they came. Except for an occasional very early morning "wake up," he never complained about anything and always could find something good in everyone and everything. Along with maturing physically, he had matured a lot in his adeptness in the outdoors. He was a safe, compassionate hunter, and a very skillful fisherman. All in all, he was a delight to spend time with, hunting, fishing, or just hanging around together.

I was sitting there in the canoe watching him fish, and kind of forgot about tying a new bug on my line.

He pulled another smallmouth out of the log pile and then moved down the bank a short way and began working another brush pile.

"Are you taking the afternoon off" he said, as he looked back and saw me just sitting there.

"No, I was just sitting here thinking."

"Oh, I see. I thought I could see smoke coming out of your left ear. Solving the world's problems or trying to figure out which popper to try."

I ignored him and tied a new bug on my line and then waded down beside him. We fished the brush pile a while longer and then decided to get the canoe and continue on down the river.

We had started just after daylight, and had conned his mom into leaving her car for us at the boat landing, while we drove upriver about 20 miles to another landing in my pickup truck. There we launched the canoe and the plan was to fish the whole day and end up back at the lower boat landing. Then we could pick up his mom's car and drive back up river to get the pickup. Finally, we'd go back to the lower landing and load the canoe in the pickup and the day would be done. It was kind of complicated, but the only way to fish the river from a canoe without paddling upstream.

A mile or so downriver, we beached the canoe again, and began wading toward the bank to fish, when we heard a honk. Instinctively we both looked up toward the sky, looking for the goose that was honking. We looked and looked but couldn't pick out any geese, when we heard the honk again. This time it was close, and not up, but down. We looked down and there was a Canada goose standing about ten feet away, looking at us.

"Holy cow, look at that," Thunderfoot said.

"He must be lost," I said, "or, maybe he's hurt and can't fly."

We crouched down and the goose waddled over to us. He wouldn't let us touch him, but he seemed to be happy to have some company. We waded into the water again and began fishing, and soon the goose was swimming around us while we fished.

"This is pretty cool," Thunderfoot said, as the goose swam and preened himself.

We fished for a while, caught several fish, and then decided to move on again. We got into the canoe, and began paddling, and the goose swam alongside the canoe with us.

"Come on Gordon," Thunderfoot said.

"Gordon?"

"Yeah, I think he looks like a Gordon. Don't you?" he said.

"I thought maybe Gloria, but probably Gordon is fine," I said.

"I wonder if he can fly. Let's paddle fast and see if he tries to fly to keep up."

We began paddling as fast as we could and soon the goose was falling behind. When we got about 50 yards ahead, he honked a couple of times and then he took off and flew up to join us.

"Well, I guess that answers that question," I said.

We pulled up on the next sandbar and decided to have some lunch. Soon, the goose was honking and waddling around begging for food. Thunderfoot shared his sandwich with him and then threw him some corn chips, which he seemed to like very much. He was making a grunting sound as he ate them and kept begging for more like a pet dog.

The rest of the afternoon slipped by too quickly. We caught quite a few fish, took a swim with Gordon, enjoyed the warm sun, the sparkling white sand, and the swift current as it carried us downriver, and all in all had a pretty fine day.

As we got to the boat landing, the goose swam to a sandbar a short way away, and watched as we pulled the canoe up onto the landing. Then he began walking back upriver across the sandbar toward where we had met him.

"Gosh," Thunderfoot said, "I hope he's gonna be OK."

"Oh, I think he'll manage all right without us. He must have just thought it would be fun to see how humans are for company."

"I wonder if he's going way back up river?" Thunderfoot said. He was obviously sad that the goose was leaving.

"I haven't got a clue, but I guess we should think that we were pretty lucky to have such a neat experience of sharing that time with him," I said.

Thunderfoot nodded. "Bye, Gordon." Gordon honked.

We got into his mom's car and took off up the road to the upriver landing to get the pickup. He was driving since he had just gotten his driver's license and would have no part of me doing the driving. I held my foot to the floor, helping brake on every turn, and there were permanent indentations in the armrest where I held on for dear life. The road ran along the river for a while, and then followed along beneath the bluffs. The river bottoms were on the right side of the road as we drove along, and suddenly, as we came around a curve, there were two emus standing by the side of the road. As we got closer, they trotted down over the bank and into the river bottoms.

We drove for another mile and neither of us said a word. Finally, Thunderfoot looked over at me and said, "Did you see those ostriches?"

"Emus."

"What?"

"Emus, they were emus. Yeah, I saw them, but I wasn't sure if I was going nuts or what."

"If you're nuts, so am I," he said. "What were those things doing there?"

"I have no idea. I know there are some farmers who raise them, but there isn't a farm for miles along here."

"Whew," he said, "I thought I might have gotten too much sun and baked my brain when I first saw them." We both were quiet for the rest of the trip. The shock of seeing the emus after our encounter with Gordon, made us wonder what was next.

We got to the boat landing and I got into the truck and Thunderfoot stayed in his mom's car. Since he had gotten his driver's license he was always pestering to do the driving, and I didn't expect him to wait for me, but instead to take off right away. But, he waited for me to get the truck started and then motioned for me to go first.

"You lead," he said.

"Why? You usually say I drive like a granny. Why don't you go first?"

"Mom's car is smaller than your pickup, and the way today has been going with strange critters, we'll probably see an elephant or rhino on the way home and it's better if you go first to clear the road."

We both laughed at the joke, but I think he was serious. It had been quite a strange day, but that's what you get sometimes when you get to spend a lot of time outdoors. You see things that you just wouldn't see any place else, and sometimes the rules just don't count. Just in case, I planned on driving really carefully all the way.

Thanks, Thunderfoot.

Charlie Brown

"Did you call the marina yet?" Thunderfoot asked as he came through the front door.

"Yup, and I didn't get the answer I wanted."

"Oh, no! What are we gonna do now?" he said, slumping down into a chair.

The fuel pump on the outboard motor had died, and I had taken it to the marina for a new one, and, of course, they didn't have the right part, so they had to order it. They had guaranteed me that it would be ready by the weekend, but the weekend started tomorrow, and the part wasn't in yet, so we were without a boat.

"You know," I said, "we could go over to the Barge."

"Where?" Thunderfoot asked.

"The fishing barge, the raft below the dam. I used to fish there all the time before I got my boat," I said.

"Is the fishing good there?"

"Yeah, great. It's right below the dam and there's lots of room to fish. It's a big raft that's anchored there. It's about twenty feet wide, and about three hundred feet long, and shaped like a backwards capital L. There's a bait shop and restaurant on the shore. The people who run it are old friends of mine," I said. "I haven't seen them in a long time. It would be nice to go over and spend the day visiting with them and fishing."

"Well, let's go for it then," he said, much enthused.

We packed a couple of rods each and some tackle and decided to leave early in the morning, so we could have a full day of fishing.

"How about lunch?" he said.

"Adeline has real good hamburgers on the fishing barge," I said.

"We can eat out there."

"Adeline?"

"Yeah, the people who own it, Chris and Adeline. Chris runs the boat and takes care of the fishermen and Adeline runs the restaurant and feeds the fishermen. They're real nice folks, you'll like them," I said.

The barge was anchored at the dam, and the boat landing was about a mile downriver, so Chris drove his boat down to the landing every hour to pick up fishermen who were waiting to go out to fish. He also hauled back those fishermen who were done for the day at the same time. Chris and Adeline charged a few bucks per person for the boat ride and your day of fishing. The boat was about twenty feet long and had a large open deck for tackle, and then a cabin for the customers to sit in, to keep warm and dry. He could haul twenty people at a time, and it was a pretty neat set up. The bait shop/restaurant was run by his wife who served up lots of good burgers and fries, gallons of soup, and some chili that would take the chrome off your car bumper.

I had known Chris and Adeline for many years and had become friends with them. They were both in their sixties, but you'd never know it, as spry as they were.

Thunderfoot and I left the next morning and somehow got to the boat landing about ten minutes after the hour, so we had missed the boat. Now we had a fifty-minute wait.

"Well, let's go up to the bar and have a pop and a snack while we wait," I said, motioning to the roadside tavern up on the highway above the landing.

Of course, Thunderfoot, who was always hungry, was in favor of that, so we walked up, went in, and ordered a pop each and some chips.

I was visiting with the bartender and noticed an old friend coming toward us. I turned to Thunderfoot and said. "I'd like you to meet my friend, Charlie Brown."

Thunderfoot turned and looked and then looked one way and then the other way and saw no one. I motioned down with my finger and there was Charlie Brown, a full figured beagle, sitting on his haunches with his paw up waiting to shake.

Thunderfoot broke out in a big grin and grabbed the dog's paw.

"Hello, Charlie Brown," he said as he shook with him. Charlie Brown then raised his paw to me and we shook also.

I gave him a couple of chips, and he looked at Thunderfoot expectantly.

"He would appreciate a taste of your food," I said.

Thunderfoot gave him a chip and he got back down on all four legs and walked back to his rug behind the bar.

"He's cool," Thunderfoot said.

"Yeah, he's been here forever. You can see that he's a bit chunky from all the mooching, but everybody likes him," I said. "He goes out on the barge every day to visit, too."

We finished our pops and went back to the landing to wait for the boat. We could see it pull away from the barge and start down to us about five minutes before the hour.

Just as the boat was almost to the landing, I looked up the road and saw Charlie Brown sauntering along toward us. I poked Thunderfoot. "Here comes Charlie Brown. It looks like he's going over with us."

Thunderfoot began grinning and knelt down to pet him as we waited for the boat to dock. There were four other fishermen this trip, and we all put our gear on the deck of the boat and then filed down the steps to the cabin. I introduced Thunderfoot to Chris and then we took off for the barge. Charlie Brown sat in the middle of the floor, keeping an eye out for anyone who might have something to eat for him.

When we got to the barge, Chris slid the boat along side the railing and then cut the motor and jumped off onto the barge with the bow rope, and secured the boat. Charlie Brown waited until we were tied up, and then jumped off the boat onto the barge and began his appointed rounds.

He would start at one end and work his way to the other end.

The barge had a wooden railing all around it, to keep people from falling off, and it also made a good place to prop up your fishing pole, while waiting for a bite. There were little wooden benches all over the place to sit on, and many of them were occupied with fishermen of every size and shape and age.

Charlie Brown would walk up and sit down next to one of the benches and watch the person fish that was sitting there. Most people knew him and talked to him like he was a person. Of course, most also gave him a part of a sandwich or cookie, and that was his real motive. He would then get up and move to the next fisherman and work his way all around the barge until he had visited everyone.

We picked out a couple of benches and I walked up to the bait shop and said hi to Adeline and got some minnows. Then we fished for a couple of hours and had some pretty good luck catching quite a few walleyes and saugers.

"I'm beginning to get a bit gant," Thunderfoot said.

Gant was his word for starved, hungry, famished, whatever. It meant he needed food, and he used it a lot. Gant was getting hungry, faminished was really hungry, and he was one or the other all the time.

"Well, reel up and we'll go up and have something to eat," I said. Adeline made each of us a burger and we both tried the chili.

Thunderfoot almost tipped off his stool as he put a big spoonful of the red hot stuff in his mouth, but managed to get it down.

"Wow, that's hot," he said, but added quickly, with a big smile to Adeline, "but really good, too."

Adeline smiled.

We finished our lunch and Thunderfoot took a bite of hamburger with him for Charlie Brown, who by now, was almost done with his daily rounds.

A while later, he walked over and sat by the boat, waiting for a ride back to the landing.

"When he was younger, he would swim back sometimes," I said.

"No kidding?" Thunderfoot said.

"Yeah, he would just jump off and swim across the river and go home. But he got hit by a car a few years ago and has a bad hip now, so he waits for a ride."

Pretty soon, Chris came walking down the barge toward the boat, to make his hourly run, and Charlie Brown jumped on and disappeared down into the cabin.

We fished a couple of hours longer and then decided to call it a day. We went up to say goodbye to Adeline and then loaded our gear and fish onto the boat. Chris took us back and Thunderfoot thanked him for such a good fishing trip.

Chris smiled as he pulled away from the bank and gave us a wave.

"They sure are nice people," Thunderfoot said.

We loaded the gear up and started down the road from the landing. "This has been a really good fishing trip," Thunderfoot said.

"Yeah," I said. "I kind of forgot how pleasant it was to go out there fishing."

As we got to the highway, Thunderfoot looked over at the bar where Charlie Brown lived and grinned. "Gosh, he's a cool dog."

Just then Charlie Brown walked out through the open front door and looked our way.

Thunderfoot looked at me and grinned. "I think he's got ESP, too."

Could be.

Thanks, Thunderfoot.

Bogus Bluff

I was just finishing breakfast when Thunderfoot came through the front door.

"Have you ever heard of Bogus Blum" he said.

"Yeah."

"How come you never told me about it?"

"I don't know, I guess it never came up. Why the sudden interest in Bogus Bluff?"

"The gold," he said. "The buried gold is there someplace and maybe we can find it."

I began laughing, and he looked a bit peeved at me. "There's no gold there; that's just an old story that's been handed down for a hundred years."

"One of the guys at school said that his grandpa had told him about a shipment of gold that was being hauled down the river on rafts in like 1832 or something like that, and the Indians attacked them at Lone Rock and they went ashore at Bogus Bluff and hid the gold in a cave, and it's still there because nobody's ever found it so far," he said.

"And where did this grandpa get all of this intimate knowledge?" "I don't know. Jeez how am I supposed to know," he said. "I just thought it might be a fun thing to do, to go and look for it."

Right away I felt bad throwing cold water on his idea, but I'm just not the kind of a guy who sees crawling around in a cave as some kind of exciting recreation. I've never felt real comfortable in tight places, and being a bit "full figured" never felt the need to squeeze into some hole in the ground, just for fun.

"I really think that gold story is mostly fiction," I said. "Besides, if the gold was there, somebody would have found it by now. The counterfeiters were there for months and never found it." Right then I knew I had said too much.

"Counterfeiters? What counterfeiters?" he said, his eyes wide and excited.

"Oh, there's an old story about some counterfeiters who held up in the cave back in the early 1920's, about 1922 I think. They were counterfeiting 1913 liberty head nickels up in the cave."

"Oh, that sounds like a money-making enterprise," Thunderfoot said. "1 know a nickel bought a lot back then, but I don't think you'd get rich by making nickels."

"Well," I said, "this nickel was worth a lot more than a nickel. You see, in 1913 the mint changed the design of the nickel to the buffalo head, but a few nickels were struck in the old liberty head design with the date 1913 on them, before the change order got to the mint, so there were a few liberty head nickels made. These counterfeiters made some plates to forge fake nickels and then were planning on selling them to collectors for about a thousand dollars apiece, which was big money back then. All they had to do was sell one here and there, and they would make a lot of money.

"Well, supposedly, the Treasury Department found out somehow, and surrounded the cave, but the counterfeiters snuck out a back entrance and snuck down the hill to the river, where they had a boat hidden, and took off down the river to get away. The Feds chased them and started shooting at them and finally caught up with them, and the counterfeiters threw the plates that made the nickels into the river to get rid of the evidence.

"Of course, the Feds had evidence anyway, because they caught the guys with a whole sack full of bogus nickels. And, that's where Bogus Bluff got its name, from the bogus nickels that were made there."

"Wow, that's a cool story. Did they ever find the counterfeit plates?" Thunderfoot asked.

"Nope, they sunk into the sand and are probably still out there someplace."

"Cool. Now I know we should go up there and see it. Do you know who owns it?"

"Yeah, I know whose land it's on."

"Do you suppose he'd let us go see it?"

I knew I should say that the owner didn't let people into the cave, but that was a lie, so, against my better judgment, I said I'd look into it and see if we could go and explore it. I was hoping that some other hot topic would come up in the next few days and he would forget about it.

That weekend, Thunderfoot came over early Saturday morning, dressed in what looked to be caving gear. He had on long pants, boots and a sweatshirt, even though the weather was warm and humid. He also had a flashlight in each pocket of his pants.

"Are you wearing that?" he said, looking at my shorts and tee shirt.

"It depends on where we're going."

"We're going spelunking, doncha know?"

He hadn't forgotten. I was trapped, so I went into the house and changed into some bib overalls and a sweatshirt and some old hunting boots.

We drove across the river and up the north side, to the hill where Bogus Bluff overlooked the river valley. I parked the truck and we got out.

"See up there, on the face of the hill?" I said, pointing to the opening of the cave. "That's it."

"Wow, I've seen that before, from the river, but never thought it was anything but a dent in the rocks," he said. "That's pretty steep and high up. Do you think you can get up there?"

"Of course. I'm old, not dead. I'll be right behind you."

Boy, was that the wrong thing to say.

He took off up the hillside, and we followed a cow path for the first fifty feet. Then the hill became real steep, I mean almost vertical. There was a narrow path that ran right along the rock wall of the hillside. fu we continued on up, the hill became steeper and the path became narrower. Soon, we had to hang onto cracks in the rocks and grab hold of brush and roots to pull ourselves up along the narrow track.

"Are you OK?" Thunderfoot asked, looking back down the hill at me.

"Yeah, I'm coming. What's this, a race?"

"Sorry, I'll wait for you to catch up."

I slowly worked my way up to where he was standing on a little wide spot, and stopped to catch my breath.

"Wow, this sure is steep," he said. "How come the front side of these hills are so steep?"

"The river did this," I said. "Back when the glaciers melted, there was some kind of huge flood that came down through here and formed this whole river valley."

"Wow, you mean there was water way up here?"

"Yup, from one side of the valley to the other, the water was all the way up these hills. That's what scoured all of the dirt and rock away from the fronts, and made these cliffs. It's probably what made the caves, too."

We stood looking out across the river valley. It was at least four or five miles to the hills on the other side. In between, on the valley floor, the farm fields were laid out in squares. The dry flat ground gave way to the river bottom sloughs that extended for several hundred feet on each side of the river. The river bottoms were made up of ponds, marshes, and swamps that bordered the river itself. Now, the river was only a trickle of what it once had been. While it still was several hundred feet across, thinking of the time when it reached from bluff to bluff was a sobering thought. The sun sparkled off the water and the sandbars looked like little patches of gold on the blue water as it meandered through the valley for as far as we could see.

"Awesome," Thunderfoot said.

"Yeah, it sure is," I said, leaning back against the rock.

"Well, are you ready to go on?" he said, "or are you going to give me some more geology lessons, to stall for more time?"

"Let's go, smart guy."

We climbed another twenty-five feet, and the track leveled out, and we were at the entrance to the cave.

It was larger than it looked from the road, and there were names carved into the sandstone at the entrance and as far as you could see back into the depths, before it got too dark to see.

"Well, it looks like somebody's been here before us," Thunderfoot said. "I guess the gold's probably been found by now."

"You didn't actually think you'd find gold here, did you?"

"Well, you never know," he said, grinning. "Let's go inside."

"You want to go in there?" I said.

"Well, that's where the cave is, so I guess we'll have to if we're going cave exploring."

He handed me one of the flashlights and we started in. I switched my light on and it didn't work. "This light is dead," I said. "Looks like we'll have to go back down."

"You have to hold it straight up and down and shake it and it'll come on," he said.

I held the flashlight like a candle and shook it and it came on, but as soon as I turned it horizontal, it went out.

"Oh, this is nice," I said. "I'll trade lights with you."

"No way," he said. "That one works fine, just be careful with it." So off I went, into the darkness, with my light held so it shined on the ground in front of my feet.

The entrance went back for about 30 feet and then began to narrow and the ceiling started to get lower. The walls were black, and slick with moisture. Soon, we were stooping and then the opening became larger and we came to an area where the cave split into three tunnels.

"Now what?" I said.

"Well, let's take the left one and see where it goes, and then come back and try the other two," he said.

We started down the left tunnel and it stayed about the same size all the way to the end. It was about twenty-five feet long and came out to another entrance on the side of the hill.

"I bet this is where the counterfeiters came out," Thunderfoot said, looking down the hill.

We turned back and got back to the starting point of the first tunnel, and tried the middle one. It went back about twenty feet and then the ceiling got low enough that we had to get down and crawl for another ten feet. Then we came to a hole that opened into a large room. The room was about ten feet wide and twenty feet long with a ceiling that was at least ten feet high. The ceiling was black with soot, and the walls had names carved into them from people who had been there before us. Some of the names were back into the 1800's. Brad and Becky, June 1896. Dave was here, 8/23/51, and on and on. "Wow, this is probably where they counterfeited the nickels," Thunderfoot said. "Look at the ceiling, their candles and torches probably made all that soot."

"Imagine working in here, though," I said, as a shudder went up my back. "And sleeping in here. Not me."

I was starting to get a closed-in feeling and wasn't at all comfortable in this dark, cold place.

"Let's go try the last tunnel," Thunderfoot said.

"Oh, let's leave it go. It's probably just another short side tunnel."

"Aw, come on, let's look," he said. "As long as we climbed all the way up here, we might as well get our money's worth."

We crawled back out to the entrance to the middle tunnel and looked down the third one. Thunderfoot shined his light down it and it went for a long way, as far as we could see.

"Wow, this one goes a lot farther," he said. "You go first."

"Why me? You're the one with the thirst for knowledge and the good flashlight."

"Yeah, but think of this. We get back there and say, you get stuck, and I'm ahead of you, and I can't get out because you're blocking the way, so we both starve. This way if you get stuck, I can get out and go for help," he said, shaking his head yes.

I shook my flashlight to life and started down the tunnel. We went for a long, long way, and the end was still a long way off. The floor of the tunnel was damp clay, and soon our shoes were covered with it. After a while, the tunnel became lower, and we had to crawl. We crawled for what seemed like hundreds of feet, and then it became smaller yet. Now, the sides were about thirty inches apart, and the roof was only about two feet high. We now had clay smeared over our clothes from head to toe, and our hands and faces were covered in it also. "Boy, this is sure fun," I said, sarcastically.

"Just keep going and quit griping," came Thunderfoot's reply. "This is getting smaller and smaller. I think we should turn around and go back," I said.

"How are we gonna turn around? There's no way to turn around. Do you want to crawl backwards all the way out?"

"What if there's animals or snakes in here?"

"What would a snake or animal be doing in here?" he said.

"There's nothing here but rock and mud."

Just then my flashlight went out for about the fiftieth time. With the light off, it was as black as black could be. I shook it back on and began thinking about the millions of pounds of rock and dirt that was above me and how dark and cold it was in the cave, and decided that I was not particularly happy about being in there. But, the only way to fix the situation was to keep going.

I began crawling on my belly, and by pushing with my elbows and toes, could move forward about a foot at a time. Soon, I could see that the tunnel turned to the right a short way ahead. As we got closer to the corner, my light fell on something just at the side of the wall to the right. I looked in horror at the rattles of a rattlesnake's tail!

"Oh my God, go back, go back!" I shouted, and began backing up as fast as I could go. Thunderfoot wasn't moving as fast as I was and I quickly overtook him and began crawling right over the top of him.

He couldn't go fast enough to stay ahead of me so we piled up about ten feet from the snake. We were wedged in tight between the mud floor and the rock ceiling.

"Whoa, whoa, what the heck is wrong with you?" he shouted.

"A rattlesnake is up there. Get back out of here! Get back! Get back!"

"Wait, wait, are you sure?" His voice was muffled because I was halfway on top of him. "What would a snake be doing in here? Think about it."

I took a couple of deep breaths. "Give me your light," I said as I slid my hand back between the wall and my side. His hand came up from under my legs and handed me the light.

I was afraid to shine the light up the tunnel to see if the snake was after us, but I had to before we could keep on going, so I finally shined the light ahead and cautiously pointed it up the tunnel. The snake hadn't come around the corner. I shined it up to the corner and the snake tail was still there. I looked closer, closer. Now I wasn't sure it was a snake tail after all. Now it looked more like a corncob. I crawled a couple of feet closer, and now it really looked like a corncob.

"Well," Thunderfoot whispered, "is it a snake?"

"Uh, no, I think it's a corncob."

Silence.

Then, a snicker, then a laugh, then all heck broke loose. "Good Lord, you almost had a heart attack over a corncob?" His laughter echoed down the tunnel walls.

I felt a bit stupid, but now I had the good light and was keeping it, so I crawled a little closer to the corner and could see the corncob and some oak leaves lying on the floor of the cave.

"I think we're near the end. There are some leaves laying here too," I said.

"You better make sure there aren't any poisonous scorpions or something lurking under them."

More laughter.

We turned the corner and then you could begin to see a little light up ahead, and the air became warmer and fresher. We were at the other end of the tunnel. We crawled out of the hole and were amazed to find ourselves on top of the hill.

"Wow, we came out clear on top," Thunderfoot said, squinting in the bright light. His face was covered with clay from being pushed down into the floor when I tried to climb over him.

"I had no idea we were going uphill all that time," I said, sitting in the grass, so very glad to be out of the darkness.

We sat there breathing the fresh air and enjoying the view of the river and the valley far below us for a long while. We were both covered with mud and clay and it felt good to just sit in the sunshine and soak up the warmth after the chilly dampness of the cave.

"You know, it's hard to believe that so many people have come and gone here. All those names in the cave, and this valley, just think how much it's changed in the years. It kind of makes you feel that you're just passing through during your time in history," Thunderfoot said.

"Wow, that's pretty philosophical for you," I said.

"That's me, a pretty philosophical kind of guy," he said, grinning and wiping the mud and clay from his hands onto his pants. "Well, shall we hike down hill or go back through the cave?"

"It's a real nice day for a hike."

"I thought you might say that," he grinned and slapped me on the back."Come on, old man, let's go."

Thanks, Thunderfoot

Katy

I was just finishing my breakfast when Thunderfoot came bounding into the kitchen.

"Did you call about the puppies?" he asked.

"Yup, they've got four girls left. I told them we'd be up this morning to look at them."

"Oh boy, oh boy," he said, as he grabbed a bowl from the cupboard and poured himself some cereal.

He wolfed the cereal down and we put things away and took off for the farm where our next little friend waited for us. As we pulled into the driveway and our mouths dropped open. There were about a dozen golden retrievers galloping around the place and another five or six in a pen, plus puppies that were tumbling around in a fenced-in part of the yard.

"Holy cow, these people like goldens," Thunderfoot said.

We got out and were surrounded by big friendly slobbering golden retrievers, all trying to get as much attention as they could from these strangers. We walked up toward the house, followed by our new friends, and the lady in charge came out.

"You the guys looking for a puppy?" she asked.

"That's us," Thunderfoot answered. "Looks like you like golden retrievers pretty good."

She laughed and explained to us that the six dogs in the pens were their males and all of the loose ones were females of various ages that they had as either pets or used for breeding purposes to raise litters.

We walked to a shaded part of the yard where the puppies were fenced in and climbed over the low fenced-in enclosure. The puppies were all excited to see us and began vying for our attention.

I told the lady that we wanted a female, so she picked up the males and held them in her arms, amid much protesting. We got down on the grass with the girls and began looking them over. One was from a litter that was born two weeks ahead of the others. The other three were sisters. We watched them and began picking them up and playing with them. The three sisters were pretty feisty and wild, but the older pup was really laid back and real snuggly. Thunderfoot picked her up and she nestled right down in the crook of his arm and began going to sleep.

He looked at me with a smile. "A little angel," he said.

The lady walked over and said, "That one is the last one from the other litter, and I want to tell you why."

She took the puppy from Thunderfoot and laid her on her back.

She had a little hernia on her belly where the umbilical cord had been.

"I've had this before, and they aren't any problem," she said.

"Most times they grow shut on their own, but sometimes they need a little surgery to close them. The other families were afraid of having problems, so no one took this puppy, but I'll guarantee her and if she needs surgery, I'll pay for half of it."

I took the pup in my arms and she was so sweet and gentle acting that I decided right then and there that I wanted her. I didn't care about the hernia and I guess I felt a little sorry for her for being the last of the litter.

Just then one of the lady's daughters came out of the house and the lady told her to go and get the mother of the puppy and bring her out so we could meet her.

The daughter came out with an older dog, and as soon as we saw her, Thunderfoot and I looked at each other, wide eyed. She was an exact copy of my old dog Bea, same color, same head shape, same white on her face from old age, and same mannerisms.

The old dog came up and we petted her and talked to her, and soon, she was leaning up against my leg, just like old Bea did many years ago.

"Well, that settles it," I said. "This is the one."

I paid the lady and got the papers for the puppy, while Thunderfoot held her in his arms and nuzzled her.

We got into the truck and took off, and within a mile, the puppy was sleeping in the crook of his arm.

"Gosh, she's a sweetie," he whispered.

When we got home, we put the puppy in the yard and let her run around and look over her new home. After a while, she became tired and needed a nap, so we went into the house and Thunderfoot sat in the rocker and rocked her to sleep.

"What are we gonna call her?" he asked.

I hadn't decided on a name yet, so we both thought for a while trying to find a good name for her.

"It can't be something goofy like Queenie, or Lady. It's got to be a good name for a girl. Something short and tough," he said.

I tried to think of a tough sounding girl's name but couldn't come up with any. Suddenly I thought of a tough woman from a play I once saw.

"How about Kate?" I said. "Like in The Taming of the Shrew."

She was a tough gal.

"Kate, Katy. Yeah, that sounds good," he said.

He rocked the puppy and whispered her name in her ear. "Hi, Katy." I got out the registration papers, began filling them out and filled in the name: Ka Ka Ka Katy.

"What's all the Ka's for?"

"There's an old song that I used listen to at my grandma's house," I said. "It went, Ka Ka Ka Katy, beautiful Katy, you're the only ga ga ga girl that I adore, and when the ma ma moon shines, over the cow shed, I'll be waiting at the ki ki ki kitchen door."

"Ok, just don't sing that around any other people," he said, shaking his head like I had lost my mind.

That night, Thunderfoot decided to stay over and sleep in his room, so Katy would have a place to sleep that would be warm and so she wouldn't be lonesome for the other puppies.

They went to bed, and a while later, I peeked in to see him laying on his side with Katy snuggled up against his chest, her head laying on his arm, sleeping like an angel. They were two pretty satisfied youngsters.

The next morning, Thunderfoot hustled Katy outside to go potty and she did an admirable job. Then we had breakfast and decided to take her for a little fishing trip down to the river bottoms sloughs.

We loaded the john boat into the back of the truck and threw in some rods and reels and a few baits, and took off for our favorite lake.

When we got there, Katy was fascinated with all the new things to look at and chew on and she had a great time exploring while we launched the boat and transferred the gear. She wandered off through the tall grass and we had a hard time finding her until we saw her little blonde tail sticking up out of the grass a short way away.

Thunderfoot picked her up and put her in the middle of the boat, and he went to the front end, and we began paddling out into the lake. Katy could just barely see over the side of the boat, so we didn't have to worry about her falling in, and we began casting plugs in and around the lily pads trying to catch a bass or northern.

It didn't take Katy long to figure out how to climb up on the middle seat, so she could see better, and soon she was scampering back and forth across the seat, looking at all the wonderful new things. We drifted into the lily pads and she quickly was reaching over the side of the boat, trying to touch one of the big flat leaved pads.

"Look at her," Thunderfoot said. "She thinks she can walk on the lily pads."

He had just finished the sentence when Katy stepped out over the side of the boat onto a lily pad, and disappeared with a little splash under the water.

"Oh my gosh," Thunderfoot gasped and threw his pole into the bottom of the boat and jumped to the middle seat. He looked over the side and then stuck his arm down into the water and came up with what looked like a blond drowned rat.

Katy didn't seem a bit fazed by her dunking. She shook a little and climbed up onto the front seat where Thunderfoot had been.

"She's a brave little thing. She was on the bottom, and just kind of walking around," he said. "I don't think she had any idea what was going on."

It was funny, but we decided to keep a better eye on her for the rest of the fishing trip.

He sat back down in his seat, and soon Katy climbed up in his lap and curled up for a nap.

"Try not to make a lot of noise. Kate's tired," he whispered.

We fished for a while and then went home. Thunderfoot held Katy in his lap, so she could look out the window while we drove.

"You know," I said, "you're gonna spoil her. Pretty soon she'll be a big dog and she'll think she has to be in your lap all the time."

"I could think of worse things," he said, grinning.

That evening, he hem-hawed around for quite a while, and finally I asked him if he wanted to stay again.

"Maybe just one more night, so Katy will feel secure," he said. She was one lucky dog. He was one happy boy.

Welcome home Katy.

Thanks, Thunderfoot.

The Grass Is Always Greener

The water level in the river was at an all time low and consequently, our favorite duck pond was almost dry. Thunderfoot and 1 had been scouting a couple of weeks before the season and had found that the little lake we hunted on was now a mud hole with a tiny puddle of water right in the middle that was hardly big enough to hold even a few ducks. All of the other ponds in the river bottoms were in the same shape, and the numbers of ducks were just as dismal as the water levels.

"There aren't any ducks around and I don't blame them for not stopping by here," 1 said. "There's hardly enough water here for them to find a place to land."

"I know, but what are we gonna do for opening day?" Thunderfoot asked.

"You know, I used to hunt up on the Mill Pond bottoms, and they aren't affected by the river level, because they're fed by the Mill Creek. It's almost always the same level, so there should be good water there."

We would have preferred to hunt our regular ponds, but we had no choice, so off we went to scout the Mill Pond bottoms. Sure enough, there was water, and lots of ducks. We walked to the high bank of the creek and sat on a log and watched until dusk as dozens of flocks of ducks came from the nearby fields and streams. The sky was glowing orange with a slate blue border creeping in as the flights of ducks settled quietly onto the pond for the night.

"This is where all of our ducks are," Thunderfoot said, smiling, as the light faded to dusk.

"Well, now we know where to go on opening day."

We prepared to hunt unfamiliar territory on the first day of the season, so instead of having a canoe, decoys, blind, and all the comforts of our regular spot, we had to rough it with a portable blind and a couple of folding stools. We each took two decoys, and with them added to our guns, ammo and other gear, we were pretty well loaded down as we trekked off toward the marsh.

The Mill Pond was formed many years before, when a dam was built at the end of the valley and a hydroelectric generator was installed, providing the area with electricity. The dam had served the area for many years, until the appetite for electricity outgrew the capacity of the generator. Now, it was used occasionally to generate extra electricity in peak usage times, but it was not economically feasible to keep it going all the time. The pond that was formed when the project was begun was still a great place for fishing and hunting for waterfowl.

It was fed by a creek that was a trout stream much farther upstream. It meandered for many miles through two counties before it emptied into the pond. The creek ran through a pasture and was bordered by a high bank on each side that was good solid ground and easy walking. As you got closer to the pond, the hard bank turned into a marsh and walking was much harder if not impossible.

"We have to decide which side of the pond we want to hunt on," I said. "We'll have to cross the creek here where it's running across the pasture or otherwise we'll be in too much mud to get to one side or the other."

"Which side do you think?" he said. "Either is all right with me."

"OK, let's go on the other side," he said.

We walked to the creek and began following it toward the pond.

A short way from where we joined it, the creek turned to the right, and there was a tree laying across it.

"This is the bridge," I said.

Thunderfoot looked at me. "Did you cut this tree across the creek?"

"No, a friend of mine did, a long time ago. Go ahead, it's safe." He stepped out onto the tree and began tight rope walking to the other side. It was a snap for him, and he stepped off onto the far bank in a few seconds.

"Your turn."

I stepped onto the tree trunk and since I was a lot heavier than Thunderfoot, it began to swing and sway. I inched my way forward and looked down at the swift water running under me. It was about five feet deep, and probably ice cold, since it was the end of a trout stream. I worked my way along and almost went over the side a couple of times, but managed to get to the other side, much to Thunderfoot's chagrin.

"You hoped I'd fall in, didn't you?" I asked.

"Of course not, then you would have whined all day about how cold and wet you were. Let's get to the duck pond."

We took off toward the pond, found a good-looking spot to set up our little blind and deployed our gear. We each took our two decoys and waded out into the pond a short way and set them out.

The mud was sucking at our boots as we waded back.

"Boy, this stuff's really sticky," Thunderfoot said.

"Yeah, it's a good thing we have our chest waders, and not our hip boots. This stuff would pull your boots right off."

We settled in to wait for noon which was the opening of the season, and right on schedule a few minutes after noon, a little flock of ducks came flying down the pond, and flew along the shoreline on the other side and kept on going. Soon, another flock came by and they too went along the other shore.

"Jeez, what's wrong with some coming over here," Thunderfoot said. A while later a flock of ducks came from the other way, and they too skirted the other side of the pond.

"Well, this is just about enough to make me a tad bit mad," he said.

"Be patient, they'll come on this side, just wait and see."

Famous last words. We sat and watched ducks fly along the other side of the pond for the next two hours and not a duck came by on our side.

"What are we doing wrong?" he asked.

"I don't know, maybe they just like that side better." "Let's pack up and go over there," he said.

"Oh, man, we have to go all the way back up to the creek and cross and then all the way back, it will take an hour and a half. We've only got a couple of hours of hunting left anyway. I don't think it's worth it."

"Let's just wade across. It's only a foot deep all the way," he said. "Oh, I don't know. What about the mud?"

"How bad can it be? If it gets too bad, we can turn around and wade back."

Well, that seemed to be the best plan, so I rolled up the blind, Thunderfoot folded up the stools and we each carried our guns out to the decoys. We each picked up the lead weights of the two decoys we had placed, rinsed the mud off them, and stuck the weights into our back pockets. The decoys swam along behind us like a couple of trained ducks.

"Come along, Daisy and Donald," Thunderfoot chuckled as we waded out across the pond.

It was about a hundred yards across to the other side, and all was going well, until we got to the middle. The mud was only about a foot deep, until we came to the old creek channel and then we stepped into the channel and the mud became deeper real quick. In about two steps, I was up to my waist and Thunderfoot was up to the middle of his belly.

"Uh oh, I think we're in trouble," he said. "I don't think, I know!" I said.

I tried to back up, but I was stuck and sinking. I began wallowing around, like a beached hippo and soon was in mud up to about the middle of my belly, too. With the foot of water on top of the mud, I was at the maximum depth that my waders would allow before I got wet.

Thunderfoot was struggling trying to get free and suddenly managed to pull himself back up onto the shallower mud.

"I'm out,"he panted.

"I'm happy for you. I'm stuck for good here," I said.

Other than the fact that I was holding my gun over my head to keep it dry, I wasn't in any pain or discomfort. I did, of course, feel like one of the stupidest people probably in the entire state at the moment.

"Go back and get rid of your gun and the other stuff, and then come back and get mine, and maybe I can get out if I'm not holding all this stuff," I said.

He nodded and waded back to the shore with his two ducklings swimming along behind him. Soon, he returned and took my gun and the blind and my ducklings back to the shore with the rest of the gear.

I tried to get loose, but couldn't budge. I had no leverage and there was just no way that I could get out.

"Find a log or something that I can use to push on to try to push up out of this stuff," I yelled over to him.

He took off for the woods.

I stood there with my fingers laced together and placed on top of my head. I couldn't put my arms down because if I did, they'd get wet. As I stood there, a bullhead swam up to me and acted like it was trying to figure out what the big thing standing in the middle of the pond was, and probably wondering if it was edible.

"Hurry up!" I shouted. "The bullheads are starting to think about feeding on my carcass."

Soon, Thunderfoot came panting down the bank with a long log dragging behind him, and then he waded into the pond and brought the log out to me.

"Here, try this," he said, sliding the log through the water to me. I pushed the log in front of me and had to put my arms down into the water to push down on it, and began trying to pry myself from the muck. It wasn't working, so Thunderfoot grabbed down into the water around my waist and began lifting as hard as he could. Between the two of us, I moved a few inches. We tried again, and this time I moved a little more. Again, and again we lifted and pulled and pried, and finally, I came loose from the mud.

We were both panting and sweating when I finally got my feet free, and just laid there in the water for a few minutes catching our breath. I was so exhausted, that I couldn't get to my feet, and crawled the fifty yards back to the bank. When I got there, I just collapsed onto the dry ground.

"I thought I was a goner," I said.

"Wow, I don't think anyone has ever been stuck so bad as that," Thunderfoot said, gasping for breath.

By now, it was almost quitting time, and it really didn't matter.

We both were completely exhausted and wet and covered with mud from head to toe, inside and outside our waders. Both of us had mud all over our faces and Thunderfoot's hat was even covered in it. We tried to wipe as much mud off as we could, so we could pick up our guns, then loaded up our gear and started back to the truck.

When we got to the pasture and the bridge, we stopped and looked back toward the pond. The water was like chocolate milk from all the mud we had stirred up, and just as we started to turn away, a flock of mallards landed right in the spot we had put our blind originally.

"Well, that just does it," he said. "I don't think I like this new duck spot very much."

He walked across the log and stopped on the other side.

I started across, and the log began to wobble and, of course, to complete a perfect day, I fell in, right in the deepest part of the creek. The water was just as cold as I thought it would be, and after I got to my feet and found my gun on the bottom, I handed it up to Thunderfoot who was standing on the bank looking concerned.

"Here, take this and shoot me," I said as I handed the gun to him. He broke out laughing and held a branch out for me to hang onto while I climbed out of the creek. I laid on my back and Thunderfoot held my legs up as high as he could get them so some of the water drained out of my waders.

The cold water was running out of the waders and soaking into my back. "Well, I guess that pretty much ends a perfect day," I said as I struggled to my feet. "Yup," he said, grinning. "I think tomorrow we'll try fishing or squirrel hunting, or maybe yard work, anything but duck hunting here again."

"Yard work?"

"Sorry, my mind must have been damaged by all the mud." Thanks, Thunderfoot.

The Great Goose Hunt

The fall goose hunting season was upon us, and Thunderfoot and I were getting ready for a trip to the Horicon Marsh. I had just purchased some new goose decoys and we were getting them ready for the trip.

"Wow, these are really cool," Thunderfoot said as he slid the head and neck into the shell body of one of the geese.

"Yeah, with those two dozen full body shells and fifty silhouettes, we should be in good shape."

He opened the box with the silhouette decoys in it and took one out. "Jeez, they look like a road killed goose," he said, examining the flat piece of rubber.

The silhouettes were shaped like the outline of a goose as seen looking from above, with a little paint on the sides to simulate the gray color and a curving piece of material on one end representing the head and neck.

The idea was to place the silhouettes in among the full bodied decoys and make it look like a larger flock of geese to any flock that was passing by that might be looking for company. The silhouettes were about one third the cost of the regular ones, so economy was a major factor in my choosing them.

"We'll have seventy-five birds out, so that should be plenty to attract some real ones," I said. Thunderfoot agreed.

We packed up our gear, which included the decoys, a piece of camouflage material for a blind, lunch, stools, guns, and shells and decided to go to bed early so we could get an early start in the morning.

What seemed like only a couple of hours later, we were driving through the darkness toward the Horicon Marsh. I had called an acquaintance that had a farm outside the intensive zone of the marsh and asked him if we could hunt in one of his fields that day, and he had given us permission. When you hunt outside the intensive zone, you hunt in an area where you are not required to be in a blind. Inside the intensive zone, you must hunt from a blind that is rented out by the landowner. Not that renting a blind is any problem, but we wanted to use decoys and they weren't very effective so close to the marsh. The geese usually wanted to land in the fields outside the marsh area to feed, and that is where we planned on hunting.

We got to the farm while it was still dark and decided on a field that was mostly alfalfa with some picked corn rows still standing in it. We erected our blind just inside the rows of corn and then began placing our decoys in little family groups in the field. This took quite a while and by the time we were done, the sky was turning dark blue. The sounds of honking geese began coming from the vicinity of the marsh, which was a couple of miles away.

"We better get hid," Thunderfoot said, and we sprinted to the blind and got settled.

Soon, flocks of geese began appearing in the sky from the marsh and some drifted toward us. They looked like shoe laces drifting on the wind as they flew through the gray morning sky.

"Here comes some," Thunderfoot said.

The geese came over us and looked at our decoys but kept going across the road and circled once and then began to drop into a plowed field.

"Well, that's nice," Thunderfoot said.

In a few minutes another flock came our way, and they circled our decoys once and on their second trip around, they set their wings and glided into the plowed field across the road with their cousins.

"Uh oh," I said. "This doesn't look good. Pretty soon there'll be more real geese over there than we have decoys and we'll be out of luck."

Sure enough, the next two small flocks landed in the plowed field and then the rest of the morning, we watched as hundreds, no, probably a thousand or more geese landed just out of our reach. There we sat with our measly little flock and us sitting in our blind, feeling pretty glum.

"There's no way we can sneak up on them, and if we spook them, they'll all just go someplace else," Thunderfoot said.

I just shook my head. "Let's go ask the farmer if we can hunt there this afternoon, and then go spook them and set up and hope some of them will come back."

That suited Thunderfoot, so we drove over to the farm and the farmer was OK with our plan. We went back to our field and packed all of our gear up, including all the decoys and moved camp to the plowed field. As we drove up to the edge of the field, the thousand or so geese got up amid much honking and confusion, and began flying away. The noise was deafening, and the sky was full of geese but in less than a minute, things quieted down and we watched the geese heading off toward the marsh for a mid-day siesta.

"They should come back since we didn't shoot at them," I said. "At least, I hope so."

We made two trips each and managed to get all the gear out into the field. Our problem was that there was no place to set the blind up. The field was an old cornfield that had been picked, and then chisel plowed, so there wasn't anyplace that the blind wouldn't look out of place. The geese would see it and know it meant danger and would probably avoid us. There were lots of corn stalks and stubble in the field, which was why the geese were there in the first place.

"Why don't we gather up some of these corn stalks and make a place to lie down, and then cover up with the stalks, and when the geese come, we'll sit up and shoot them?" Thunderfoot said.

It sounded about as good a plan as we could come up with, so we deployed our decoys and got our little beds ready in the middle of them.

There weren't any geese to be seen anywhere, so we went back to the truck and had lunch and took it easy for an hour. Then we began seeing small flocks of geese drifting back out from the marsh to feed for the afternoon.

"Time to get back to the field," I said, and we headed back and laid down in our cornstalk beds and covered ourselves up. We were both wearing waterproof camouflage coats and pants and had hunting boots on our feet, so we were pretty well camouflaged when we added a few cornstalks. We had also painted our faces with camouflage make-up, to keep our white faces from showing up and scaring the geese. All in all, we felt pretty secure there, waiting for the geese to begin showing up.

We laid there about a half hour when we saw a little flock of geese coming our way. "Lay still, they're coming," I said.

The geese circled us once and then set their wings and began settling into the field. "Now!" I said, and Thunderfoot and I sat up and began shooting at the descending geese. We both emptied our guns and the geese flew away.

"Wow, it's kind of hard shooting like this," he said.

"No kidding," I said. "It's hard to turn to shoot to the side. Oh well, if all of those geese come back that were here this morning, we'll do lots of shooting and figure out how to do it."

We laid back down and waited for more geese. A few minutes later, I heard the sound of thunder, a long way off in the west. "Sounds like a storm is coming."

Thunderfoot raised up and looked to the west. "It's pretty black, but it's a long way away."

We waited and soon the thunder came again, and it was louder and closer. I looked over my shoulder, and the storm had moved a lot closer and it was getting black and ugly looking, real fast.

"That storm is going to be here in a few minutes. Maybe we should head back to the truck."

"Are you gonna melt? We're dressed in waterproof clothes. What can a little rain do to us?" he said.

Against my better judgment, I decided that we probably would be OK.

"Besides, if we get up and move, you know some geese will land right here where we're laying," he said. He was probably right about that, too.

So we stayed.

The rain started as a sprinkle a few minutes later. A big drop splattered onto the ground, here and there. It sprinkled for a minute or two and then the light sprinkle became a steady shower. A minute later it began to rain hard, then it turned to a downpour, then a cloudburst, and then an all out monsoon. It was raining so hard that I could barely see Thunderfoot only ten feet from me. He had pulled the hood of his coat up over his face and all I could see was steam coming up from the collar of the coat. The nice dry field turned to a black gooey mess, and soon little rivulets of muddy water began running down between where the rows of corn had stood. One of those little rivulets began running right up the back of my jacket.

"Oh, this is real nice," I said.

"Quit complaining. This can't last long, as hard as it's raining." I could barely hear him over the noise of the rain splattering on my coat and into the corn stalks.

It rained as hard as I've ever seen it rain for the next half hour, and we were still laying face up in the middle of the field. I wondered what the farmer, nice and warm and dry in his house, was thinking about the two idiots laying in his cornfield.

"OK, maybe you're right, this isn't gonna quit," Thunderfoot said finally. "Besides, I haven't seen a goose in the air for a long time."

"Geese have more sense than to fly in this weather," I said.

We both sat up and sloughed to our feet. The field was pure mud, sticky and black and deep enough that we sunk up to mid-calf when we began picking up the decoys.

"This is about enough to make me give up hunting for geese," Thunderfoot said as his feet went out from under him when he bent to pick up a silhouette.

It took us about an hour to make about four trips each to the truck to get all the gear out of the mud. By the time we were done, we both were covered with the black stuff from head to toe, and were sweating up a storm inside our heavy clothing.

Just about the time we finished, the rain let up and the sun began to show beneath the clouds in the west.

"Isn't that lovely," Thunderfoot said, as he pulled his muddy boots off and threw them into the back of the truck. His socks, that had been white earlier, were now hanging off the end of his feet and were completely black.

We took off our outer clothes and boots and socks and ended up wearing soaked tee shirts and our underwear as we drove out of the farmyard toward home. Everything we had was covered with mud and laying in the back of the truck. I turned on the heater to warm us up and soon the cab was warm and toasty, making us feel a little better.

"You know, I think maybe geese are a bit too difficult for us.

Maybe we better stick to something easier to hunt, like clay pigeons," Thunderfoot said.

I looked over at him, and he grinned at me through a mud covered face.

"I just hope we get home without any trouble, seeing as how we're in our underwear," I said.

"We'll be fine. If you want, I can drive."

I declined. "I guess we probably better go through the drive-through for some lunch. We probably would create a bit of an uproar if we walked into a cafe like this," he said, laughing.

"I don't know which would scare them worse, our muddy faces or our lack of clothing," I said.

"Let's not find out."

Thanks, Thunderfoot.

They Shoot Horses Don't They?

"Why don't we go up to my grandpa's and do some rabbit hunting tomorrow?" Thunderfoot asked.

"Yeah, I guess we can do that," I replied. "We usually have pretty good luck up there, and there isn't much else that we have to do. Let's do it."

The next morning, we drove up to his grandpa's farm and stopped by the house to visit with his grandparents for a while. Of course, like any grandma, we had to have some fresh cinnamon rolls and hot chocolate before we went to the woods to hunt. With our bellies full, we promised we would stop back after we had hunted, and began walking back toward the woods.

Grandpa's land had a huge ditch that had been filled with trees and brush over the years as land was cleared, and the ditch was a great place to hunt rabbits. It was way back on the backside of the farm and we had to walk back across several pastures to get to it. As we came up to the fence that enclosed the pasture, I noticed a horse down near the other end.

"When did your grandpa get that horse?" I said.

"Oh, a while ago," Thunderfoot said. "He got him from a neighbor who didn't want him anymore."

I watched the horse, and as we approached the fence, he came to attention and his ears pricked up while he watched us. Then he began walking our way, looking kind of menacing.

"He looks mean," I said.

"Oh, cripes, he's not mean. He's just curious."

I wasn't so sure. The horse came closer but then stopped and watched us from a fair distance.

"Come on, we've got to cross this pasture to get to the rabbit place," he said.

"Maybe we should hunt someplace else. That horse looks like he doesn't want us in his pasture."

"Are you scared of a horse?"

"I don't like horses," I answered. "When I was just a kid like you, we had a family reunion at one of my uncle's farm, and after we ate, all of us kids were going to ride the horse. Well, the other kids got on and the horse went around the barn and back and they got off and the next one got on. When it was my turn, the horse got behind the barn and then stopped. So, I kicked him in the belly like I was told to do, and he laid down and rolled on his back. He almost crushed me. I think he was trying to kill me."

Thunderfoot was standing there with his mouth agape and then burst out laughing. "What a sissy. Tried to crush you."

"Yeah, well a few years later, some of my friends and I went to one of the guy's farms to ride their horses one day, and we all got on and rode up to the top of the hill, and then my horse decided to go back to the barn and took off like a bat out of hell and ran under an apple tree and almost took my head off," I said. "That was the last time I got on a horse."

"Yeah, there's a horse conspiracy out there and they're planning on assassinating you," he chuckled.

"Laugh all you want. That horse doesn't like me," I said, indicating the horse standing at the other end of the pasture.

"Watch," he said. "I'll go across and you'll see that he isn't mean." He climbed up and over the barbed wire fence and started walking across the pasture. It was about a hundred yards across, and the horse watched him but didn't move. He got to the other side and turned around and spread his hands and shrugged his shoulders. "See, no mad horse."

As much as I hated to, I slid my gun under the fence and climbed up and over. Once I was on the other side, the horse began watching me and his ears came forward, like he was listening for me to say something wrong so he could charge. I began walking toward the other side and he took a few steps toward me. I stopped and the horse stopped.

"Come on, just keep walking and he'll leave you alone," Thunderfoot said from the safety of the other side of the fence.

I began walking again and the horse began walking toward me. I was getting pretty nervous now, and didn't know whether to stop or keep going. I was coming to the middle of the field and had to decide soon. I looked at the horse and now his ears were flattened back and he really looked mad. I began walking faster and the horse began trotting toward me.

"Uh, maybe you better get moving," Thunderfoot said. "He looks like he may come after you."

Oh, great, here I was at the point of no return, and I had an angry horse coming at me at a much faster rate than I could run. But, heedless of the fact that I was much slower than my pursuer, I took off at a dead run for the safety of the fence. The horse began to trot and then to gallop after me.

"Hurry up, he's gaining on you!" Thunderfoot shouted.

I was going as fast as I could go but the horse was getting closer and closer. "Shoot him, shoot him!" I yelled at Thunderfoot.

Now I only had about ten feet to go, and the horse was right behind me with his teeth bared and he was snapping his jaws at me, trying to bite me. I got to the fence and my right foot hit the middle wire while I hurled my body over the top wire in one motion, and I landed on my back on the other side. My gun went flying through the air and landed in the brush.

The horse came to the wire and stood there, staring at me.

"See, I told you he was mean. Horses don't like me. I told you."

I was stammering like a fool.

Thunderfoot was bent over double with laughter. "Jeez, you vaulted the fence. I didn't think you could do that in a hundred years. Where did you get that burst of speed? Shoot him! Shoot him!" More stupid laughter.

When death at the hooves of a horse stares at you, even a full figured guy can move pretty fast.

I was still laying on the ground panting as the horse trotted off and stood in the middle of the field, like he was telling me that he'd be waiting for me if I wanted to take another try at it.

I got to my feet, picked up my gun and walked over to the fence.

The horse stiffened up, thinking that I may be coming back over for another confrontation.

"That's the meanest horse I've ever seen," I said. "No wonder the neighbor didn't want it."

Thunderfoot was still laughing as we walked back to the rabbit ditch. We hunted for a couple of hours and had lots of shooting but connected on very few bunnies.

"Well, grandma wants us to stop for something to eat on the way back," he said, "and I'm getting pretty faminished."

"We're going to have to go around the horse this time," I said. "I'm not good for two record sprints and high jumps in one day."

We hiked up to the end of the valley and then climbed up the hill and around the pasture. We put our hunting gear in the truck and walked up to the house and were greeted with some wonderful smells coming from the kitchen.

"Any luck?" grandpa said.

"Not much with the bunnies," Thunderfoot said, "but, a new world record was set for fifty yard dash and high jump."

Grandpa looked at me, not getting the joke.

"The horse chased me and your grandson thought it was hilarious," I said.

"Oh, yeah, he's a bit spirited, but I don't think he'd hurt you."

"Who, the horse or the grandson?"

Thanks, Thunderfoot.

Thunderfoot had come over about lunch time and was sitting complaining about not being able to go fishing because of the minus 20 degree temperatures outside. It was mid-January and one of the coldest days of the year. I believed that his mom had suggested that he come over to see what I was up to, because he had just about driven her crazy with his pacing around the house.

"I can't understand why all of these cold days have to come on the weekend when I don't have to go to school!" he lamented.

"Yeah, that's a real tragedy," I said, mockingly.

"No, really, we should be out doing something and here we sit," he whined.

I wasn't going to let him talk me into anything that would require me to go out in the subzero temperatures and driving wind, so I just stuck my nose into a book and ignored him.

He watched a couple of fishing shows on TV and then began to pace, trying to think of something to do. As he walked past the living room window, he stopped and looked out.

"Hey, look, there's a dog out there."

"So what, there are lots of dogs around here," I said.

"Yeah, but look at this poor guy; he looks like he's starving to death."

I got up and walked over to the window. There was a stray dog watering my flagpole, and he was indeed skinny. In fact, as I looked closer, I could see all of his ribs and his backbone sticking up through his skin. He looked to be part golden retriever and part collie, but he had been on his own for a long time. His tail was covered with burrs, and he had lots of dirt and grime covering his coat. We watched as he sniffed around and then began sniffing his way across the yard toward the neighbors.

Thunderfoot looked at me. "We should help him; he's gonna freeze to death if he doesn't get some food and some place to sleep where it's warm."

As much as I agreed with him, I didn't need another dog to look after, but I couldn't turn my back on him. It was supposed to be in the minus 30s that night, and as skinny and poor looking as this poor fella was, I doubted if he would survive.

"Let's go see if he'll come to us," I said.

We pulled on our boots and coats and hats and walked out into the yard. We began looking for the dog, but he was gone.

"There he is," Thunderfoot said, pointing across the road to the neighbor's yard.

We walked over and found the dog had walked through a gate in the backyard and was inside a little pen that the neighbor had to keep her kids from straying all over the neighborhood. The dog was standing in the other end of the pen.

I walked in and closed the door. "You stay here and if he turns out to be mean, let me out quick," I said to Thunderfoot.

I walked toward the dog and he began to shiver and whine and cower. I squatted down and talked real low and mellow to him, but he wouldn't come to me. He was afraid of me.

"Run over home and get some of that sliced ham that's in the fridge," I said to Thunderfoot. He hooked the gate and sprinted across the street and returned in a couple of minutes. He handed me the ham, and I walked back toward the dog.

I took a piece of ham and tossed it to him. He sniffed it and gobbled it up like it was his first meal in a long time. I talked to him a bit more and he shuffled toward me a bit. I tossed him another piece of ham, but this time I tossed it half way between us. He snuck forward and picked it up, and stayed there. I took a couple of steps toward him and held out my hand with a piece of ham in it. He stretched out his neck and took it from me. The next piece was hardly out of my pocket when he greedily snapped it up.

We were buddies now.

I petted him and fed him the rest of the ham. His tail was wagging so fiercely that his whole body moved back and forth. "He's a real friendly guy," I said.

"Here, I brought Katy's slip collar and leash. See what he'll do if you put it on him," Thunderfoot said.

I slipped the collar over the dog's head and he fell into step right beside me. "He's been on a leash before," I said, as I led the dog over to Thunderfoot. He was on his knees and petting the dog, and they were fast becoming buddies.

"Let's take him home and we'll feed and water him and put him in Katy's kennel. Then I'll call the radio station and sheriff's department and see if anyone's looking for him. We can fix him up a nice warm bed in the kennel for the night, and then we'll see tomorrow if anyone claims him or not."

Thunderfoot thought that it was a good idea, and we took the dog home and gave him a huge bowl of dry dog food with a full can of canned food on top of it. He eyes almost popped out when he saw it and he wolfed it down in no time. Then he had a good drink and immediately crawled into the bed in the kennel and went to sleep. The poor guy was exhausted.

That evening, I took him another big bowl of food and some more water and he woke up just long enough to eat again and then went right back to sleep.

"He's been out, trying to survive for a long time and he's pretty tired," Thunderfoot said, as he looked in on the dog. "What are we going to do if nobody claims him?"

"Let's wait and see," I said.

By the next day, we had no information on the dog and nobody called despite several mentions on the radio station of a found dog, so we needed to make a decision as to what to do with our new friend.

"Let's see what Katy thinks of him," I said. "If she likes him, maybe I'll just keep him, but if she doesn't like him, I'll have to find a home for him. I'm not going to turn him out again." Thunderfoot grinned from ear to ear.

We brought the dog into the workshop and I went into the house to get Katy. Both of the dogs were real excited to see each other, and they went into a frenzy of sniffing and posturing, and seemed to get along. We let them be together for a while and just sat and watched. Soon, they were both satisfied that they were friends and laid down side by side to take a nap.

"Well, the princess seems to like him," Thunderfoot said. "Yeah, she seems to like him just fine," I agreed.

The next battle was going to be a bath and cleaning of our new friend. He was filthy and his tail was stiff with burrs, to the point that I didn't think we could even brush them out. We took the brush and began brushing him and finally got out the scissors and began cutting clumps of hair from his tail. When we finished, his tail looked kind of ragged, but it was free of burrs. Once we had him de-burred, we decided to try to give him a bath.

Katy was real interested in what we were doing until we began running water in the bath tub, and then she took off for the living room, not being fond of baths. The new dog was glad for all the attention and didn't know what was happening until we lifted him into the tub and the warm water. He wasn't exactly thrilled at the idea of a bath but didn't fight it, and soon we had him covered in suds and were scrubbing the grime from him. Once we got him wet we could see just how skinny he was. The poor devil was just a skeleton with skin on it. We washed and rinsed him and then toweled him off and turned him loose. He galloped into the living room and played with Katy for a minute, and then took a tour of the house and came back to the living room. He did a couple of circles on the living room floor and flopped down and stretched out and said, "Hmmmmmmm." He was home.

"Looks like he likes it here," Thunderfoot said, smiling.

We watched the two dogs sleeping side by side on the floor and I began to assess what the new guy was. He looked exactly like a golden retriever from the neck to the butt. His head was narrower, like a collie, and he had a white stripe in the middle of his forehead. His tail was more like a collie also, standing up more than a golden's. The rest of him was golden retriever.

"If we keep him, we'll have to think of a name," I said.

"How about Skunk?" Thunderfoot said.

"Skunk?"

"Yeah, he's got that stripe on his head like a skunk."

"No. We need something that goes with Katy.

Katy and ..... "

He was deep in thought. "Katy and... How about Kirby?"

"Kirby," I said. "Yeah, I like that."

Just then Kirby looked up at me. "How do you like that name?"

I asked. Kirby thumped his tail in agreement and went back to sleep.

I waited a week just to be sure nobody would come to claim him and then made an appointment with the vet to get Kirby checked over. He seemed to be fine and got his full dose of vaccinations and de-wormed, just in case he was missing anything from wherever he lived before.

He and Katy became great friends and have gotten along great ever since. Thunderfoot has taken a shine to him since he was the one that found him in the yard.

A few weeks later, we were sitting and watching the two dogs frolicking in the snow and Thunderfoot looked at me and said. "I wonder where Kirby would be right now if we hadn't gone after him?"

"He'd probably be dead," I said. "He wouldn't have made it much longer without food and shelter."

"We did good, huh?" he said, grinning.

"Yeah, we did good."

"Whoever abandoned him must not have taken much interest in him or they would have seen what a nice guy he is," he said, as Kirby came running toward us looking for a little petting. He grabbed Kirby and wrestled him into the snow and soon Katy joined the fun. I watched as the three of them rolled and played in the snow.

"Their loss, our gain," I said.

Thanks, Thunderfoot.

Take Me Out to the Ball Game

"Take a look at what's on my desk," I said to Thunderfoot as he walked into the house after a spring day at school.

"It better be good," he said. "I've just been imprisoned in school on a day that would have been perfect for fishing."

He walked into my office and suddenly I heard him say. "No way, box seats behind the home plate."

He came running back into the living room holding four tickets to a doubleheader at County Stadium for the following Saturday. "Where did you get these?" he asked.

"One of the companies that I buy merchandise from had a drawing and I won. I don't suppose you'd like to go with me?"

"Suppose, you better suppose I will," he said, jumping up and down. "Why don't you ask a couple of your buddies to come, too," I said. "Who should I ask?"

"I don't care. Whoever you want."

He thought a while and then decided on Scott and Trent. They were both kids that came hunting and fishing with us often and I liked both of them, so I said that they were fine with me and off he went to tell them the news.

Saturday came and we got the group together at about 7 a.m. so we could get a good start on the three-hour trip. Of course I figured at least an hour to stop for breakfast and another hour or so for pit stops, and that would put us at the stadium at about noon, which was plenty early for the first game of the doubleheader which started at one o'clock.

We had hardly gone a mile from town when I could hear the two in the back seat whispering something to Thunderfoot. "Just wait a few minutes, I'm sure he's planned for it," he said.

"Planned for what?" I asked.

"Well, Scott is kind of faminished, and he was wondering if we were gonna stop for breakfast soon?"

"We just left town," I said. "Scott, can you last a while if I stop and get some donuts?"

Scott thought that a few donuts would keep him alive for a while, so I stopped at a convenience store and got a half dozen donuts and some cartons of milk to hold them over until we could get to where I was planning to stop for breakfast.

On we went, and soon we were about half way to Milwaukee and I took an exit to a little shopping area that had a breakfast buffet restaurant. "OK guys, this is breakfast."

They were all sacked out and began stretching and yawning and one by one came to life and shuffled into the restaurant.

As we walked through the door, they all looked wide-eyed.

There, laid out in front of them, was every kind of conceivable food that could be eaten for breakfast in the entire country. There were eggs, pancakes, waffles, sausages, bacon, ham, grits, fruit, rolls, cereal, and a few things that I wasn't too sure of what they actually were.

"Anyone who leaves hungry has no one to blame but themselves," I said as they attacked the buffet.

We spent about an hour in the restaurant and the boys sampled practically everything on the menu. They were all sitting back in the booth groaning and moaning about how stuffed they were, as I got up to pay the check. Soon, I was driving on toward the stadium and they were sleeping again.

An hour later, we were coming into Milwaukee and they woke up and began playing some game about license plates that I didn't get the gist of, and it wasn't long until we took the exit to the stadium. We parked and the boys piled out and began excitedly hurrying toward the gate marked on the tickets. I had to hustle to keep up, and when we got to the gate, I gave each of them a ticket and we went inside.

The stadium was filling up, and we got to our seats, which were the best I had ever had. We were right behind home plate and about ten rows up from the field.

"These are awesome seats," Thunderfoot exclaimed, and the other two chimed in with a couple of more "awesomes."

There was a lot of hustle and bustle, and before long the vendors started hawking their overpriced snacks and souvenirs. The boys each had to buy a baseball cap, and soon they were digging into peanuts and popcorn and big glasses of pop.

"How can you guys eat already?" I said.

"We're just lucky." Thunderfoot grinned as he popped a salted in the shell peanut into his mouth. "We're young; we burn up food like a furnace."

A little later, they sang the Star Spangled Banner and the game was on. The boys cheered and booed and were having a great time. About halfway through the fifth inning, Thunderfoot announced that he had to go up and get a Polish sausage.

"The Polish sausage guy hasn't come by here for three innings," he said. "I'm gonna go up and get one. Anybody else want one?"

By then I was beginning to get a bit hungry, so I told him to get me one, too. "No problem," he said and off he went up the steps.

By the seventh inning, he wasn't back yet, and I was beginning to get a little worried. I was getting more worried when game number one ended, and he still wasn't back.

"When the second game starts, all the people will go back to their seats, and I'll go up and see if I can find him by the Polish sausage stand," Scott said.

We waited for the crowd to get back to their seats and the second game was underway. Scott went up the steps and was gone for about fifteen minutes when he returned without Thunderfoot. "I can't see him anywhere," he said. "I looked all over the place."

I was getting pretty worried but didn't know what to do about it. I thought about going up and seeing if they could page him over the PA system but didn't know if that was possible. He had to be someplace in the stadium, but where?

The fourth inning was just over, and I was now beginning to panic. Scott and Trent both assured me that Thunderfoot could take care of himself and not to worry, but I could tell that they, too, were beginning to wonder what had happened to him.

I decided that if he wasn't back by the end of the fifth inning, I was going to see what I could do about having him paged when, all of a sudden, there he was, walking down the aisle to our seats with a big grin on his face.

"Where have you been?" I asked.

"What, why?"

"You left two hours ago for a Polish sausage. Where did you go to get it, Poland?"

"Oh, well, I kinda got turned around a bit, and took a wrong turn," he said nonchalantly.

"So, where were you all that time?"

"Well, when I came back out from all the tunnels, see that scoreboard out there in center field? Well, I was right there."

"Center field?"

"Yup, I could see you guys. I waved but nobody waved back."

"You've got a real sense of direction."

"Yup, that's why I'm such a good guide," he said, grinning.

"Weren't you scared?"

"Why should I be scared? I wasn't lost, just in the wrong part of the stadium. I met a lot of nice people that I visited with. No problem."

"Well," I said, "if you need to go for anything else, take one of these guys with you so you don't get lost. By the way, where's my Polish sausage?"

"Oh, I ate that in center field. I thought it would be cold by the time I got back here. I can go for another for you."

"No thanks. You just stay here where I can keep an eye on you." Look of indignation, then a big grin.

Thanks, Thunderfoot.

Fly In

Thunderfoot and I were just finishing the dishes when the phone rang. Since I was up to my elbows in soap suds, he answered the phone.

"Oh, hi Lump, yeah, he's here. He's washing the dishes; I'll get him." He held the phone out to me as I dried my hands off

I took the phone and it was Rick, one of my fishing buddies, who was nicknamed Lumpy. We talked a bit and I found that he was looking for two people to go to Canada on a fly-in fishing trip with him and his son the following month.

"Yeah, uh huh, six nights, yeah, oh, that's not bad, uh huh, OK, yeah. Oh yeah, I think I can find a partner," I said, looking at Thunderfoot questioningly. "OK, let's figure on it, the 16th, OK, yeah. I'll call you next week and we can get together and do some planning."

I hung up the phone and went back to the kitchen sink. "Well, what did Lump want?"

"Who? Oh, Lumpy, I forgot you call him that. Oh, he had a fishing trip proposition for me."

Thunderfoot was just about to explode. "OK, what trip did he have to ask you about?"

I acted like I didn't hear him. It was kind of fun to make him sweat, since he always had such great sport making fun of me when he got the chance.

Finally, he came to the sink and took the dishrag from my hand.

"What trip!"

"A fly-in trip to Canada," I said.

His mouth dropped open. "Fly-in, like with a plane?"

"No, like we'll flap our arms real fast. Of course with a plane," I said.

"I hope you were talking about me when you said you had a partner," he said.

"Well, actually, I guess, well, yeah, who else would I take?" I said. He let out a whoop and began pacing back and forth across the floor. "When are we going?"

"The third week of June. We drive to a little town in Ontario and then take the plane to Marshall Lake and they leave us there for six days and then come back and pick us up."

"That's only a few weeks away; I gotta go pack," he said and started for the door.

"Whoa, we have lots of time to pack. We're going up to Lumpy's this weekend and have a meeting to make a list of gear and food. We have a weight limit, so we have to be careful on what we take."

Saturday afternoon we drove to my friend's house, which was a few miles away, and met up with him and his son Chris. Chris was a couple of years older than Thunderfoot, but they had known each other for many years from fishing and hunting trips they had taken together with us.

We grilled out and then sat down to make a list of items for the trip. We figured out the food needed for each meal, with a meal of fish each day, and then made a list of clothes and fishing equipment for each of us to take.

The cabin came with a boat, motor and gas, for every two fishermen and we had to furnish our fishing gear and food, plus our clothing and a few extra items for good measure. We each had a sixty pound limit on our gear, so we had to pack light.

Thunderfoot was beside himself, worrying about having enough stuff along. He reveled in lots of gear and if it were up to him, he'd take everything he owned.

During the next few weeks we managed to collect everything that was on our lists, and it all got deposited on my front porch. Finally the big day came, and we loaded up and took off for the North Country. Thunderfoot and Chris were so excited that they were babbling like a couple of geese in the back seat as we left town. Twelve hours later, they were sacked out as we pulled into the parking lot of the outfitter that was going to fly us into the lake.

"Wake up, you two sleeping beauties," I said. "We're here." They woke up slowly and finally realized where they were and bounded out of the van and took off for the dock and the floatplane.

"Whoa, you guys, come back here and carry something down there with you," I said, and they each came back and picked up some of the gear.

We met the outfitter, and he introduced us to our pilot, who looked to be just a kid, too. He looked like he was maybe 21, if that, and had shaggy blond hair and an easy attitude. It didn't take him long to start goofing around with the kids, and Lumpy and I looked at each other with a misgiving look.

"How old do you think he is?" I asked.

"I don't know, but if I was a bartender, I'd check him for an ID," he said.

Well, obviously, he knew how to fly the plane or the outfitter wouldn't have hired him. At least we hoped so.

We packed the plane and climbed inside. It was pretty tight, but we were ready and no matter how tight, we were on our way.

The pilot untied the ropes that held the plane, stepped onto the float and climbed in and started the engine. "One of you can come sit up here, eh," he said, looking at me. I climbed up through the little opening in the fuselage and sat in the co-pilot seat. "Buckle up, eh."

He revved the engine up, and we began taxiing down the lake. It was a little choppy on the water and the ride was pretty bumpy. We went a long way down the lake, and then he pushed his feet on some pedals and we turned around and were looking back at where we had come from.

"OK then, here we go," he said, and he pushed in the throttle and off we went down the lake. It was noisy and really bumpy and we kept going and going and going, toward some orange milk jugs that were anchored down the lake a short way. As we began to pick up speed, we lifted off the water a little and then banged down again, only to lift again. The milk jugs were getting closer and closer, and I was beginning to think we weren't going to leave the lake before we got to them, when suddenly, we lifted up and cruised right up over the end of the lake.

I looked over my shoulder, and Thunderfoot's face was white.

He grinned and blew out his breath, like he had been holding it for a long time.

Once we were up, it was nice, and we could see down into the trees and swamps below. I leaned over to the pilot and asked him if he ever saw bears or moose or any other wildlife, and he shook his head yes.

On we flew, and everyone was getting pretty comfortable when suddenly the plane dropped like a rock over onto its left side and fell toward the woods below.

"A couple of moose, eh." The pilot pointed and grinned. I looked around in the cockpit for my breakfast, because I was sure it had slipped out when we dropped so fast. The rest of the group was hanging on with white knuckles in the back.

"Jeez, you don't have to show us any more wildlife if that's OK with you," I shouted.

The pilot smiled and took us back up to regular flying altitude. On we went for another twenty minutes until suddenly he put the plane over on its side again and began dropping onto a fairly large lake. "This is it," he said, motioning toward the lake with his head.

We dropped like a headshot duck and leveled off just as we got to the water, and then made a nice landing about a football field away from the dock. The pilot taxied up to the dock and shut down the engine and jumped out and tied up the plane.

"Here we are, eh."

Thunderfoot looked a little green around the gills as he climbed out of the back of the plane. "Was that fun or what?" he said, clutching his stomach.

When everyone was out on the dock, we began unloading all the gear. Soon we were unloaded, and we walked up to the cabin. The pilot showed us how to turn on the gas tanks that were outside behind the building and light the gas stove and gas refrigerator inside. He got a couple of outboard motors out of a little shed and showed us where the gas and oars and other gear were. Then he took us down a path that led back into the woods to the privy.

"So, when you get some fish, clean them and then take the guts out in the boat and dump them in the lake," he said.

"Why not bury them?" Thunderfoot asked.

"The bears will come and dig them up," he said. "The last guys here had a bear right up by the cabin, eh."

Thunderfoot shook his head yes, his mouth hanging open.

"If something happens that you need help, lay a white tee shirt on the dock, and someone will come and help you. I'll fly by in a couple days and check on you, and any other plane that sees a white shirt on the dock will stop. So don't dry your laundry on the dock, eh?"

We thanked him and soon he was taking off for home, leaving us in the middle of nowhere with tee shirt communications.

Thunderfoot watched the plane as it disappeared over the trees.

"How far are we from other people, do you think?"

"Oh, it's a long way to a town, probably a hundred miles or so, but there could be some other fishermen on another lake near here."

He nodded and picked up some of the gear and walked up the dock to the cabin.

We all pitched in and soon we had everything that needed to be inside the cabin carried up. We went inside and found that it was pretty primitive. There were two sets of cots stacked up on top of each other like bunk beds and a stove that was built out of a 55-gallon barrel in the middle of the room for heat. Then there was a gas range and a gas refrigerator and a kitchen table and half a dozen chairs, two of which matched. There were some open cupboards on the wall and a sink that had no plumbing attached to it. Underneath the sink was a bucket that caught the water, which was then hauled outside and dumped. The water for washing and drinking came from the lake.

"It looks like we have roommates," Thunderfoot said, looking at the mattress.

Obviously, there were several mice that lived in the cabin when it wasn't occupied by people because there were mouse pellets all over the place.

"Well, let's carry the mattresses outside and shake them off and then we can start cleaning up the place before we bring our stuff in," I said.

We all pitched in and soon had the cabin ship-shape.

"We've got plenty of time to go fishing, don't we?" Thunderfoot asked.

"Yeah, I guess. It probably doesn't get dark till 10 or 11 o'clock up here, so I guess we can go and try to catch some fish for supper."

Off we went, to the dock. We chose a couple of boats from the pile stacked on the dock and put two motors on them and put a gas tank, life jackets and oars in each one. Then we loaded our tackle boxes and poles and shoved off.

Since it was our first time on the lake, we stayed together, making each of us feel a little safer. I had a map of the lake provided by the outfitter, and we took off for a place where a small stream ran in. When we got there, we found a little rapids where the stream entered the lake and began casting into the pool below the rapids. It didn't take but a minute for

Thunderfoot to rear back on his rod and boat a nice walleye. He held it up, grinning from ear to ear.

"Look at that beauty," he said.

Just then Lumpy and Chris both set their hooks into identical fish and a second later I felt a tick on my line and soon was boating another identical walleye.

"Jeez, they're all twins," Thunderfoot said.

We fished for another hour and had more than enough fish for supper, so we motored back to the dock and tied up the boats. There was a fish-cleaning bench on the shore by the dock and the boys ran ahead and got their fillet knives and a pail for fillets and met us on their way back as Lumpy and I went to the cabin to begin preparing the rest of the supper. Soon, Chris came up to the cabin with the fillets and asked, "Should we take the guts out in the boat?" I looked at Lumpy, and he shrugged like he didn't see anything wrong with the two boys going out alone.

"Yeah, but don't goof around. That water's really cold and if you fall in, you'll freeze up."

We watched out the front window as they jumped into the boat and took off to dump the guts. They looked like Tom and Huck, only dressed a little warmer. Thunderfoot was driving the boat and they went about a half mile from shore and then stopped and dumped the fish guts. Then, of course, instead of turning around and coming back, they had to do a few circles and jump their wakes before they returned. We watched them in the diminishing light, two kids, having the time of their lives.

That evening, we ate fresh walleye fillets, fried potatoes and beans, and if I had ever had a meal that was better, I couldn't remember it.

"Holy cow, I'm gonna explode," Thunderfoot said, patting his belly. We heated some water for dishes and before Lumpy and I had them done, both of the boys were dozing in their chairs.

It was getting chilly, so I went outside and carried in an arm full of firewood that the last group of fishermen had left for us. I filled the barrel stove up and soon the fire was crackling and popping. We all got ready and climbed into our sleeping bags and were asleep in no time. The last thing I remembered was that the stove was so hot that it was glowing red and it lit the cabin with an eerie glow.

Blam! Blam! Blam!

I woke with a start. Blam! I couldn't figure out at first where I was and finally I realized that I was in the cabin when, Blam!, the sound came again. I looked up from the warmth of my sleeping bag and could see Thunderfoot in his underwear and tee shirt, barefoot, with a frying pan held over his head. There was some light coming in through the windows from the stars and moon. Blam! He hit something on the kitchen counter.

"What in the Sam Hill are you doing?" I said.

"Those mice are all over the place. They were eating our popcorn and I heard them, so I'm smacking them when they come back for more. Shhhh, here comes one." Blam!

By now everyone was awake and watching the show. Thunderfoot would stand real still, and soon a mouse would sneak out onto the counter toward the bag of unpopped popcorn. He would let them get out in the open and then slam them with the pan, and lift the lifeless carcass up by the tail and drop it into the stove.

"How many have you got so far?" Chris said.

"I think that makes 18 or 19," Thunderfoot said. "I kinda lost count."

You could see him grinning in the low light, as he turned to look at us. "I'll quit when I get an even two dozen."

The action slowed up a while later. Either he had killed all the mice, or they were getting wise to him and staying out of sight.

"Well, that'll be enough for tonight," he said, and climbed back into his sleeping bag. "Night all."

The next morning, it was freezing in the cabin. The stove was out and so I hurriedly got into my clothes and went out to get some kindling and wood to get things warmed up. It didn't take long for the stove to heat up, and I began making breakfast, which aroused the rest of the crew.

"Hmmmm, I smell food," Thunderfoot said from down inside his sleeping bag.

"I thought you'd never be able to eat again," I said.

"Actually, all that mouse slamming made me pretty hungry," he said, as his head poked up from the sleeping bag with a big grin. "What a mouse killer I am, huh?"

"I found a whole bunch of traps in the drawer over there," I said.

"Let's set some of them with some peanut butter and maybe we can get rid of the rest of them."

He jumped up and dressed and began preparing the trap line, while I finished getting breakfast ready.

After breakfast, we hauled up some water from the lake and cleaned up the dishes. Then we heated up some more for washing, and in an hour or so, we were at the dock ready to go fishing for the day. We had made up a box with a couple of frying pans and a kettle and some cooking oil and plates and utensils for a shore lunch. The night before I had boiled some potatoes which I put in the refrigerator overnight, and they were in the box, too.

"Each boat saves six fish for lunch," I said as we took off "And we'll meet on this rock at about noon," I said, pointing to a spot on the map.

Off we went in different directions to explore the lake. It wasn't that we didn't want to fish with Chris and Lumpy, but this way we had a better chance of finding some good spots to fish by searching more of the lake.

Thunderfoot and I headed up to the end of the lake that was shallow. We wanted to find some places to fish for northerns. Now, in Canada, the locals think that a northern is a junk fish and hate them. Where we come from, we love to fish for them. They're good fighters, and just about always willing to bite, and good eating if you take them home. We began to see more and more weeds and soon could see that we were coming into a bay that was filled with a huge weed bed, probably the home of lots of northerns. We shut off the motor and began casting spoons into the weed pockets and in a short time were battling a northern each. Once we found the spoon that they liked best, we got a fish on almost every cast. We were having a great time as we drifted deeper and deeper into the bay.

Suddenly, Thunderfoot whispered, "Look, there's a moose."

I looked the way he was looking and, sure enough, there was a huge bull moose standing in the water about two hundred yards away from us.

The moose was standing knee deep in the water and didn't seem to be bothered by us. He stood there looking at us, and then suddenly stuck his head into the water and a while later came up with a mouthful of aquatic weeds that he proceeded to munch on. Soon he went down again and picked up another mouthful of weeds. He was huge, with broad antlers and looked like a big black Buick. His antlers had weeds and lily pads hanging from them.

"Let's try to work our way over closer, and I'll get some pictures,"

Thunderfoot whispered.

I put the oars into the oarlocks quietly and began rowing slowly toward the moose. I kept the front of the boat toward the moose so Thunderfoot would have a clear view for his pictures. We kept going closer and closer, and Thunderfoot was kneeling on the front seat taking a picture every so often. The moose didn't seem to mind a bit.

We were only about twenty yards away, and I stopped rowing, thinking that it was about as close as we should get.

"Go closer," Thunderfoot urged.

Against my better judgment, I pushed on the oars a few more times and we slid closer yet. Now we were only about ten yards away, and the moose had his head under water. When he came up, he looked at us and he didn't look friendly. He let out a bellow and shook his head, causing water and plants to fly through the air.

Suddenly, he began walking our way.

"Go back, quick," Thunderfoot said, looking over his shoulder at me.

I reached back and pulled the cord on the motor and it didn't take. I pulled out the choke and pulled the cord again, and this time it took but I still had it choked, so it sputtered. I pushed the choke in and revved the handle and it roared to life. I reached around the side and slid the gear shift lever into reverse and when I looked around again, the moose was only a few feet from the boat and was coming on a dead run. The water was flying from his hooves as he rushed toward the boat.

"Go back, go back, fast!" Thunderfoot said. He was still kneeling on the front seat of the boat.

I gunned the motor and we began moving backwards, but not fast enough to get ahead of the moose.

Thunderfoot was now leaning backwards away from the moose, who looked like he was ten feet tall. "Go fast, go fast!"

The weeds were fouling the prop, and I couldn't get the boat to move any faster without turning it around, and I thought the moose would surely catch up to us if I tried to turn it.

Thunderfoot now crawled down off the seat backwards and was on his hands and knees, crawling backwards toward the back of the boat. The moose's head was towering over the front seat. He let out an enraged bellow as he bumped the front of the boat with his hooves.

"We gotta go fast, we gotta go now!" he said as he tumbled over backwards and landed at my feet.

Then, just as suddenly as he charged us, the moose stopped and stood there shaking his head at us as we motored backward through the weeds. We were about thirty feet away when I thought it was safe to turn the boat around. As soon as we got turned around, we made tracks for a safer distance. Once we were about a hundred yards away, I stopped the boat.

Thunderfoot was sitting on the floor of the boat at my feet. He looked up over his shoulder at me. "Holy cow, I almost peed myself." I began laughing. He just sat there with his mouth hanging open. "I thought we were goners," he said. "Did you do that on purpose?" "No way, the weeds were getting stuck in the prop. These boats aren't made to go backwards. That's why they have a point on the front."

"Wow, I didn't know those things could go so fast and were that big. That thing was twenty feet tall."

"Well, probably more like eight or nine feet tall," I said.

"You weren't looking up at him from where I was sitting," he said.

Just then I noticed that he had bits of weed from the bull's antlers hanging from his hair.

"Maybe that's enough weed bed fishing for a while. What do you say we go and catch some walleyes for lunch?" I said.

"Yeah, someplace away from the weed beds would be fine with me." We stopped at a little island and began catching walleyes off a reef that stuck out into the water. In a short time, we had our share of "lunch fish" and headed up the lake to the meeting place with Lumpy and Chris. They were already there and had a fire going.

"How was your morning?" Lumpy asked.

"Oh, just ducky," Thunderfoot exclaimed. "My illustrious partner here tried to get me trampled by a huge enraged moose."

Lumpy looked at me questioningly.

"We got a little too close to a moose and he didn't like us, but I wasn't the one who kept saying 'get a little closer' if I remember right," I said, looking accusingly at Thunderfoot.

"I was looking through the viewfinder of the camera and he looked pretty small until he charged and then I looked at him for real and he was mega big," he said.

That got a good laugh from our friends, but Thunderfoot still kept accusing me of some kind of plot to get him murdered by a moose.

We had a fabulous lunch. Actually, it was the exact same thing we had last evening for dinner, and then all laid back on the rock for a siesta in the mid-day sun. About an hour later, Thunderfoot woke up and began waking everybody so we could go and do some fishing during the afternoon.

We spent the rest of the day on the water and that evening, the boys cut some firewood while Lumpy and I prepared supper. We were just finishing up when the boys came in with an armload each of firewood, and dropped it on the floor near the stove. It was beginning to cool off, so we lit a fire and ate supper as the cabin began to warm up and feel real cozy.

After supper we had a rousing game of Monopoly and it was getting to be bedtime when Thunderfoot and Chris decided to go out and bring in some more firewood. They were barely out the door when they came crashing back in screaming like banshees.

"There's a skunk right outside the door!" Thunderfoot yelled as he nearly tore the screen door off the hinges.

We snuck over to the door and sure enough, there was a big skunk scratching through some of our garbage that we had bagged up to put in the garbage can.

We closed the door and decided to get along with what firewood we had for now.

That night it began to blow and rain, and by morning, it was really cold inside the cabin. The skunk was gone and we carried in some firewood, but it was sopping wet, and wouldn't burn. We finally decided to pour a little gas on some kindling and got that going and that dried out the wood enough to get it going, too, and soon had the cabin toasty warm again.

We had breakfast and tidied up the place a bit but took our time because the weather looked pretty threatening. In another half hour, it began raining really hard and the wind whipped up and the lake began to look less and less inviting. Soon big waves were crashing in on the dock, so we all donned our rain gear and went down to lash the boats down and take everything that we wanted to keep dry up to the cabin. When we got back inside the nice warm cabin, we all decided that we could stand a day inside instead of out on the angry lake.

"Let's play some cards," Thunderfoot suggested. "Chris and I will take on you two old guys, twenty-five cents a game and ten cents a bump." I looked at Lumpy, and he smiled and nodded yes. He and I had been partners many times in Euchre games, and were pretty good partners.

We cut cards to see who would deal and soon the game was going along at a good pace. Lumpy and I took the lead, but then Thunderfoot got a lone hand, which scored four points and he and Chris moved ahead of us. Soon, he got another loner and the game was over. "It looks like you experts owe us fifty-five cents," he said smugly.

Lumpy and I paid up and then I said, "How about fifty cents a game and a quarter a bump?" The boys grinned and agreed.

We began pretty even and soon Thunderfoot got another lone hand and the boys took a lead. The Chris got a loner two hands later and we were behind by eight points. I tried .to push a poor hand and we got bumped, and the next hand Lumpy got us into trouble with a shaky hand also and we got another bump. It was Thunderfoot's deal and he managed to dump the cards on the floor for the fourth or fifth time while he shuffled, and when the cards were dealt, he had another lone hand. Wham, we were beaten again, and this time it cost us a dollar each.

"Care to try to get your money back?" Thunderfoot asked, grinning like the cat that had just eaten the canary.

"OK, wise guy, buck a game and fifty cents a bump?" I said.

"You're on."

Well, it wasn't pretty. Lumpy and I got bumped the first two times we tried to make trump, Thunderfoot dealt himself two loners and Chris got one loner, and soon we were at the point where we were almost beaten again. We were playing a hand that I had made trump, and I took a trick and led an ace. Thunderfoot trumped it and that beat us. As we threw the cards in, I noticed that Thunderfoot was trying to slide his last card under the rest of the cards lying on the table. I grabbed his hand and took the card from him. He was holding the suit that he had trumped. "You little cheater, you reneged."

"What? Was that suit played?" He was trying hard to look innocent.

"You know darn well it was played, you cheater."

It was Thunderfoot's deal and he dumped the cards onto the floor again.

"For someone with such good luck, you sure can't shuffle the cards worth a darn," I said. But, suddenly, I got a thought. Every time he got the cards, he managed to drop them on the floor, and every time he did that, he got a lone hand. I watched as he picked up the cards and put them into a pile, with his hands under the table, and then shuffled. But his shuffle was not exactly a shuffle. It was more like just a shuffle of the top few cards. He dealt the cards out and naturally turned over an ace. I had nothing, so I passed. Chris passed, and Lumpy passed. Thunderfoot picked up the ace and passed the rest of the cards over to Chris. "I'll play it alone," he announced.

I looked at Lumpy and he realized the same thing just as I had.

Thunderfoot was stacking the deck and getting lone hands almost every time he dealt. "You little cheater!" I said.

Thunderfoot looked at me with that choirboy look of innocence.

"What are you talking about?" You could almost see the halo above his head.

"I'm talking about you getting a lone hand every time you deal," I said.

"I'm just lucky," he said, keeping up the innocent act.

"Yeah, well, let's see your cards," I said, grabbing the cards from his hand. He had the four highest cards and an ace. He looked over at me indignantly. "That's it, I quit. If you're gonna look at my cards, I don't want to play any more." He tried hard to make Lumpy and I believe that he was just lucky, but we weren't buying it. That was the end of our card game.

Later, we decided to play Monopoly, and Lumpy and I didn't fare any better. Chris and Thunderfoot ganged up on us and soon they both had properties with lots of houses and hotels, and Lumpy and I had mismatched pieces of property that were worthless. We were both being whittled down dollar by dollar, when I landed on one of Thunderfoot's green properties with three houses on it. "That will be $950," he said.

It was about enough to break me, but I began counting money and after I had mortgaged almost everything, I came up with the money. A couple of turns later, Chris landed on the same property, and Thunderfoot said to him, "That's $600."

"Whoa, wait a minute. How come I paid $950 and Chris only has to pay $600?"

Thunderfoot looked puzzled, then scratched his head, and you could tell he was cooking up some story in his head. "Oh, my gosh, I must have read the wrong line on this card. I thought I had four houses on it but only had three. I guess I owe you a refund of $250."

He counted out the money and I took it, smiling to myself that I had caught him cheating again. I picked up the dice, and then it hit me. The little rat owed me $350, not $250!

"That's it, I quit, you little cheater," I said.

Thunderfoot put on his most innocent face but he knew we were onto him, so that was the end of our game day in the cabin. It had cost Lumpy and me a little cash but in the long run it had passed the time, and even though we were playing with a couple of cheaters, we did have fun. We ate supper, sat and talked a while and went to bed, glad to get the rainy day over with.

The next morning it was sunny and beautiful, and we all went out and had a great day of fishing. Thunderfoot and I caught dozens of northerns while fishing with spoons along a string of islands and then we all met for shore lunch.

That afternoon we went to an area that was supposed to have lake trout and fished for them without much success.

On the way back to camp, Thunderfoot and I came around an island and got a glimpse of a black bear running from the shoreline just ahead of us. We stopped on the lake by where we had seen the bear but couldn't find him, so we went on home. "I wonder if that's the bear that came into the camp when the last guys were here?" Thunderfoot asked.

That night, I woke up with Nature calling me in a most urgent manner. Now, the privy was behind the cabin, about fifty yards back into the woods. There was a little path through the trees back to it. It was built of logs and not exactly the place you wanted to go to in the middle of the night. Why they had chosen to build it so far away from the cabin escaped me, but I supposed the obvious aromatic scents that wafted from it were less noticeable if it was farther away. That did me no good in the middle of the night. As hard as I tried, I couldn't go back to sleep and the longer I waited, the more urgent I needed to get up and get going.

Finally, I couldn't wait any longer and got up and slipped on my sweatpants and a jacket and some shoes over my bare feet. There was still a glow of light from the stove, and I looked on top of the refrigerator for the flashlight that was suppose to be sitting there. We had designated one flashlight as the privy light, and it was supposed to be there at all times, just for this kind of emergency, but it was gone. I searched and searched but couldn't find it and the longer I searched, the more urgent my need to go became. There was no more waiting, so I decided to go without it.

I walked out of the cabin and it was dark. It was as dark as I have ever seen it. No stars, no streetlights, no moon, just complete darkness. There was a breeze blowing through the tops of the trees making a spooky howling sound. I stood on the porch for a couple of seconds to let my eyes adjust, but still couldn't make out anything that looked like a path. I started toward where I thought the path was, and began walking slowly, with my hand out in front of me trying to feel my way back to the privy. This was insanity! Not only could I not find my way back there, but if I did, the odds of me finding my way back to the cabin were slim. And then I remembered the bear. We had seen that bear just down the lake from the cabin earlier in the evening. Suppose he had come up to check out our garbage. I imagined my hand out in front of me, coming in contact with a wet, cold nose, and then feeling up higher to a hairy forehead, and the bear opening his mouth and snapping my hand off, and I became utterly terrified.

I couldn't take another step. The hair on the back of my neck was standing straight up, but I couldn't go back until I did my job, so civility be damned, I dropped my sweatpants and let her go right on the path to the privy. I had a roll of toilet paper with me and hastily finished up and sprinted back to the cabin, knowing that at any second I would hear a roar and a giant bear would spring on me and eat me. By the time I got on the porch, I was shaking like a leaf and could barely open the screen door. Now that I was so close to safety, I became even more terrified as I groped for the handle of the door. I finally found the door handle and flung the door open, jumped inside and slammed the door shut.

Once I made it inside, I felt pretty foolish, but I was still shaking from the cold and the fright. I slipped back into bed and went right to sleep.

"Oh, my gosh! Who did this?" I heard Thunderfoot bellow outside the back door.

I groggily rolled over and lay there, wondering what he was hollering about as he came through the back door.

"Who pooped on the back path?" he asked.

The other two of our party, the innocent ones just looked stupefied, wondering what the heck he was talking about. I tried to look innocent and asked him what he was yelling about.

"Somebody pooped on the path." "Maybe it was a bear," I suggested. "A bear that used Charmin?" Everybody looked at me.

"Where was the flashlight that was supposed to be for the privy?" "Oh, I had that in my bed, in case I needed to go out during the night," Thunderfoot said.

"Well, had the flashlight been where it was supposed to be, there might not be poop on the path," I said.

"Oh, well, in that case, I guess we can forgive you," he said magnanimously.

"In that case, take the shovel out and get rid of it," I said. "And put the flashlight back up on the refrigerator where it's supposed to be."

He didn't argue for a change.

Later that day, we were out fishing, when Thunderfoot took a can of chewing tobacco out of his pocket and tapped it against his hand, and took a pinch of the nasty stuff and put it in his lip, spilling it all over the bottom of the boat.

He put the can away and went on fishing as if this was a normal happening.

I just looked at him and kept looking until he said, "What?" "What did you just do? Did you put some chew in your mouth?" "Yeah, Chris gave it to me. He chews, you know."

No, I didn't know.

"Just because Chris chews doesn't mean you're going to," I said.

"Do you suppose your mom would appreciate seeing you with a big wad of that stuff in your face?"

He just looked at me and shrugged.

By now he had had the stuff in his mouth for about five minutes, and I could see he was swallowing the juice, so I thought I'd give him a little more time and see what happened.

He sat in the front of the boat and began to look a little pale.

Soon, he kind of laid his head back on the edge of the boat and slid down on the seat, so he could partially lie down.

"What's the matter, big shot?"

"I'm feeling a little dizzy, kinda woozy in my stomach," he mumbled.

He kept getting paler and paler, and suddenly, he threw his fishing pole into the bottom of the boat and hung his head over the side and "fed the ducks."

"Oh, I think I'm gonna die," he murmured.

"Good, I hope you feel terrible. Remember that the next time you think about putting that junk in your mouth," I said, without any pity.

He laid there for quite a while and finally felt well enough to fish again. That evening, I saw him go over to Chris and give him back the can of snuff. I think he learned his lesson.

We spent our last day on the lake and that evening after supper, Thunderfoot was suddenly missing, so I walked out on the porch to look for him. I could see him down on the dock by the starlight and walked down and sat by him on the bench.

"What a week," I said.

"Gosh, I can't believe we've been here a week already. What a great time this has been. I can't believe I'm in a place like this. I never thought I'd do something like this in my whole life," he said. We sat silently for a while, listening to the sounds of the water lapping at the sides of the boats.

"Just look at all those stars," he said. "Pretty awesome," I said.

"They look clearer and closer than they do at home," he said. "The air is clearer, and there isn't any other light to hide them up here."

Just then the Northern Lights began dancing across the north horizon. We watched as they climbed into the sky and began swirling and sparkling and making vivid patterns in the night sky. Bright shafts of gold and red climbed and then fell back, like waves on a pond.

He put his arm on my shoulder. "You know how much I appreciate you bringing me on this trip, and all the other trips and other stuff that you do for me. I don't know how to thank you enough," he said.

"You just did. Nothing else required," I said as I gave him a squeeze around the shoulders.

Soon Lumpy and Chris came down to the boat dock and joined us. The four of us sat and watched Mother Nature's light show. It was the perfect ending to a perfect week.

Thanks, Thunderfoot.

State Fair Fun

"Our State Fair is a great State Fair, don't miss it, don't even be late." Thunderfoot was singing as he came across the backyard toward me. I was on my hands and knees pulling weeds from the garden.

"My, gosh, what did you do with the money?" I asked.

"What money?"

"The money your mom gave you for singing lessons," I said.

"Oh, real funny, I'll have you know that I'm an excellent singer," he said indignantly.

Actually he wasn't half bad, but I always took the opportunity to poke a little fun at him whenever I could. I was usually way behind in the practical joke category because he was always on the lookout for a way to make fun of me.

"Have you ever gone to the State Fair?" he asked.

"Yeah, a long time ago. Why?"

"Oh, I just thought it might be a fun thing to do, and it's starting this weekend, you know."

I hadn't been to the State Fair for many years, and actually it did seem like it would be a good time, so I agreed that we should go. We made plans to go on the following Saturday. Thunderfoot asked if he could take his pal Dillon along and I said that was OK.

Saturday morning, we left early since it was almost a three-hour drive to the fairgrounds. We didn't go far until we had to stop for a breakfast break, and as soon as we were back on the road, the two boys both snuggled down in their seats and napped until we were at the fairgrounds parking lot. We parked and went to the entrance and got our tickets and began looking at all the fun stuff that the fair had to offer.

We had to go to the rides first, and I mostly watched as the boys climbed onto the rides and flew through the air on various contraptions that went round and round and up and down. I was content to watch from the sidelines on most of the rides, but the boys got me to get onto a few, most of which were not exactly my type of entertainment.

After a couple of hours, we had to stop for lunch and had brats, corn on the cob and cream puffs for dessert. The boys were ready for some timeout, so we decided to go through the exhibits in the barns and see some of the animals and things that the fair was really about.

First we went into the sheep barn and looked at the many kinds of sheep and lambs that were all finely groomed and being shown. Then we went to the pig barn, but didn't linger too long there because of the aromatic nature of the place. Next came the rabbits and other pet-type critters, including the fancy poultry exhibits.

As we were walking down the aisles, Thunderfoot and Dillon stopped at a cage that held some fancy chickens, and Thunderfoot lifted up the little door and stuck his hand into the cage and took an egg that one of the hens had laid that day.

"What are you doing?" I asked.

"What, nothing."

"What are you going to do with that egg?"

"Egg, what egg?" he said, giving me his most innocent look.

"The egg you took from that cage."

"Oh, that egg. I'm just gonna take it and find someplace to put it." I looked at him with a disapproving look, but he ignored me and kept walking away, so I just gave up and joined him and Dillon as they left the building.

"Let's see the cows next," he said, as he led the way into the dairy barn exhibit.

As we walked in, we came 'to the bulls first, and they were truly impressive. I had never seen a bovine of any nature that was as huge as some of the big bulls that were tethered to the stalls. Some of them were so huge that they were standing halfway out into the walkway and we had to get uncomfortably close to the rear ends of them to get by.

Thunderfoot and Dillon were goofing around and making wisecracks about the bull's anatomy and I gave them a disapproving look. I tried to hurry them past that part of the barn before they made one of the huge animals mad.

We started down the next aisle, and soon the two boys were making eyes at a young girl who was brushing one of the cows. She was a young farm girl with blond hair and was as cute as they come. She apparently was spending a lot of time in the barn because there was a lawn chair and a trunk with lots of clothes and things in it. Her blond hair was tied up in a ponytail, and she smiled at the boys as they came by. Thunderfoot was making eyes at her, flashing his baby blues, trying to impress her. She was trying to act unimpressed, but you could see that she was enjoying the show, too.

As they walked by, Thunderfoot slipped the egg that he had pilfered earlier from his pocket and showed it to her and then slipped it into the pocket of Dillon's shorts when he wasn't looking.

The cow that the girl was brushing, raised her tail just then and began peeing into the gutter of the barn. The cow's tail had been carefully shaved and just a little powder puff of hair was left on the very tip. As she let go her stream, the powder puff was just at the right angle and got soaked with the pee. Just then, Thunderfoot smacked Dillon in the pocket where the egg was and took off running down the aisle, laughing like a fool, thinking he had impressed the girl by breaking the egg in Dillon's pocket.

He had only taken about half a step when the cow raised her tail and began to whip it up over her back to swat a fly. The tail flew into the path of Thunderfoot who was running past her backside, trying to get away from Dillon. The little muff of hair on the end of the dripping cow's tail hit him in the open mouth at about mid-swing, and made a kind of "Splooosh" sound as it hit. He stopped, dead in his tracks, as the cow pee splattered allover his face and shirt, and over his shoulder onto Dillon, who was chasing him.

There he stood for a second or two, like in stop motion, with his hands spread out to the sides like he had been crucified. Then he turned around, cow pee dripping from his mouth and nose.

"Oh, my God, I got hit by cow pee!" he stammered.

Dillon fell over backwards onto the floor and doubled up with laughter. The cute little girl fell back onto a couple of hay bales laughing, and fortunately, there was a lawn chair right behind me. I sat down in it, laughing until I thought I'd have a coronary.

Poor Thunderfoot just stood there, dripping.

Pretty soon, everyone in the barn was laughing and pointing at the boy covered with fresh cow pee. Thunderfoot just stood there with his arms out to the side, waiting for somebody to come to his rescue.

Finally, an older man, possibly the girl's father, came over and pointed Thunderfoot to a water hose on the floor. He walked stiff legged over to it and the man hosed him off.

Thunderfoot's mouth was still wide open and the man squirted water into it to rinse out the cow pee. Dillon went over and washed off the over-splash that had hit him and turned his pocket inside out and rinsed out the egg that had started the whole episode.

Thunderfoot came back and I was still having a hard time catching my breath. 1 had tears running down my face and was panting from laughing so hard.

"I suppose you think this is funny," he said.

"I think this is hilarious," I said, starting to laugh again.

"Let's go. I've seen enough cows for a long time," he said and stomped out of the barn.

Dillon and I followed him outside. "Well, anyone want anything to drink or eat?" I asked.

Thunderfoot glared at me. Dillon said, "Yeah, I'm a little thirsty. I think I could drink something. How about you?" he said, looking at Thunderfoot.

"Oh, you two are a real riot. Just a laugh a minute," he said. "Let's go to the tee shirt stand, and I'll buy you a new shirt."

He perked up at that. "So, you do feel sorry for me?"

"No, I just don't want you sitting in my car with that cow pee shirt all the way home."

"Gee thanks, you're such a swell pal," he said, trying to pout. Then he began to grin. "I guess it was pretty funny, probably. But I don't think I made a very good impression on that cute little blonde girl."

Probably not, but I'll bet she'll never forget him.

Thanks, Thunderfoot.

Fore No More

"Are you sure you know what you're doing?" I asked.

Thunderfoot just looked at me with one of his exasperated looks.

"Of course, I know what I'm doing," he said.

"Well, I better be able to watch my TV when we're done, and it better be the same as before," I said.

He had taken the cable and wires off the back of my new TV and was attaching some kind of electronic game to it so we could play with his new game machine. I hadn't been in favor of the idea in the first place, and now that I could see what he was doing with all the wires and gadgets that he was attaching, it made me pretty nervous.

Finally, he had everything working to his satisfaction and told me to sit on the couch, so he could show me how to play.

"You see, this thing is the joystick. It controls right, left, up, down, and this thing makes the guy jump. Now, you start here, and see, he jumps and now you go right ... "

I watched as some little cartoon character climbed over blocks and obstructions in some kind of race to someplace important. It seemed easy enough, so I took the joystick and began maneuvering the thing that made the little man jump and run, and apparently I did something wrong, because the machine went, woo, woo, woo, and my turn was over.

Thunderfoot took the joystick and began running and jumping and seemed to be having a great time for the next ten minutes or so, until he finally had racked up several hundred thousand points to my couple of dozen, and the machine went woo, woo, woo, and he handed the joystick back to me.

"Your turn."

I moved the little man over one block and began to go over another, when the machine went woo, woo, woo, and I was again finished with my turn.

"Too bad, gotta move faster," he said, maneuvering the little man through the maze of obstructions. Fifteen minutes later, I was reading a magazine, when he finished his turn and handed me the joystick.

"You gotta pay attention. You'll never learn this if you don't watch," he said.

"I'll never learn if I get to play for ten seconds and then have to watch you for half an hour. Isn't there some game that we can play that I get to play for a while, too?"

"This is the easiest one," he said, shrugging his shoulders. "Well, this is lots of fun," I said, unenthusiastically.

I took my turn, which lasted about a full minute and then gave the joystick back to him and went into the kitchen to fix us a snack. When I came back he was still playing, so I went back to my magazine.

"I guess you don't wanna play?"

"Is it that obvious?"

"OK, what should we do then?"

I couldn't think of anything right off the bat, so he began taking the game apart and restoring my TV: When we turned it back on, miraculously it worked and just happened to be tuned to a channel that had a golf game on.

"I used to play that silly game," I said.

"No foolin'? I didn't know that. Why did you quit?"

"Well, I wasn't very good at it, and it's a frustrating game," I said.

"I've always wanted to try it," he said.

"I've still got my clubs somewhere here," I said.

"No kidding. Let's get them out and see them."

We went out to the garage and dug the clubs out of an old cabinet.

They were dusty and dirty but still in good condition, considering that I hadn't played with them for almost twenty years.

Thunderfoot took an iron out and began chopping holes in my backyard, trying to hit a ball across the street.

"Take it easy on the grass," I said.

"Let's go play," he said, shaking his head yes.

I wasn't too enthused about the idea, but I guessed that he probably would never let up on me about it, so I agreed. We dusted off the dubs and drove about 15 miles to a public golf course.

I showed him how to grip the dub and how to tee it up and then drove my first ball straight into the rough on the right side of the fairway.

"Good shot," he said, enthusiastically. "That's down there a long ways."

He teed up a ball, lined up his shot and made a perfect drive straight down the middle of the fairway half way to the green.

"Are you sure you never played this before?"

"Nope, just watched it on TV a couple of times."

We played to the green and I three putted for a double bogey while Thunderfoot took a par.

"That's good, huh, a par?"

"Yes, that's good."

The next couple of holes were the same. He played like Tiger Woods and I played like, well, like me.

"This is fun. How come you quit playing?" he asked.

"Well, I played in high school, and then in college I had a friend who was on the golf team and he taught me a lot of good stuff, and I got pretty good at it. Then I began to get worse. I don't know what happened, but my game got worse and worse, so I decided to quit rather than play like crap."

He shook his head like a psychiatrist. "Uh huh, uh huh."

On we went and a few holes later, I was playing my ball to the green, which was just about 40 yards ahead. The only problem was that there were two big pine trees right in line with it, so rather than chip around them, I decided to make a high shot over them, so my ball would land right on the middle of the green.

I lined it up and made sure to get under the ball, gave it a mighty whack, and it went up and up and hit the left pine tree dead center. It hit about five feet down from the top, made a "whop" sound and bounced back right over my head and landed on the fairway behind me.

I could hear Thunderfoot chuckling behind me, but I kept my cool and walked back ten yards to the ball and lined it up again. I aimed, swung, and up the ball went, up and up, and "whop" hit the same tree in almost exactly the same spot, then bounced back about ten yards over my head and behind me.

"Mfffff, mffff," came the muffled chuckles from behind me.

I looked at the ball, looked at the club and looked to the right of the fairway at the cornfield that bordered the golf course. I wound up and threw the club as hard as I could into the cornfield.

"Mffff, mfff..."

"Bring the rest of the clubs when you get done, I'll see you at the car," I said and walked calmly off the course.

A while later, Thunderfoot came walking up to the car carrying the golf clubs and my nine iron.

"I went out in the corn and found your club," he said, not looking at me.

"Oh yippy. How nice," I said.

He turned away, and I could see him shaking from laughter. When I began to see how foolish I looked, I said, "Go ahead and laugh, I'm not mad at you."

He cracked up and laughed till tears came out of his eyes. "I don't think I've ever seen you so mad," he said. "There was smoke coming out of your ears almost."

We loaded up and drove home. When we got to his house, I pulled in to let him off. "Just take those clubs home with you."

"What? You want me to take them?"

"Yup, take them and play with them or take them and throw them in the river. I don't care. Just never let me see them again."

He looked pretty pleased but stopped just short of the house. "I hope you're not mad at me," he said.

"Nope, I'm not mad at you, but from now on, we'll stick to something that I'm good at, like fishing."

He opened his mouth and started to say something about him being a better fisherman, too, but thought better of it and went into the house. Some days it's better to just shut up and let well enough alone.

Thanks, Thunderfoot.

The Big One Didn't Get Away

The official end of summer was upon us, and Thunderfoot and I decided that we should go fishing for northerns one last time. It was Labor Day weekend, and it was blistering hot, threatening to storm, just the way we liked it for fishing for big, toothy northern pike. For some reason, northerns always were hungry or maybe angry, on those hot humid days, so we thought it was a good idea to take advantage of the weather and spend the day fishing before hunting season started and our minds strayed to other endeavors.

"This is way better than going to some softball tournament and wasting the whole day doing nothing," Thunderfoot said as we slid the canoe into the lake.

Normally, we used the little flat bottom johnboat, but this lake didn't have a good place to put a boat in. It was a long carry through the woods to get to the water, so we had decided to use the canoe that we used for duck hunting. The johnboat was too heavy for such a long carry but was more comfortable to fish from. The other thing was that the johnboat was longer and roomier and much more stable when fishing, but we really wanted to fish this particular lake, so the canoe had to suffice.

"Get up in the front," I said, "and I'll push off."

Thunderfoot stepped lightly to the front of the canoe and sat down, and I pushed it off the bank and climbed into the back seat. We wobbled and tilted like crazy until we got our "sea legs" and began paddling toward the first weed bed that looked like it might have a few northerns hiding in it. Thunderfoot laid his paddle down and began getting his rod ready before we were near the weeds, and as soon as we were in range, he rifled his bait across the lake and into the weed cover. He had hardly begun to retrieve his lure when the water exploded and a nice northern grabbed his bait and headed back into the deep weeds.

"Yahoo! First fish of the day," he yelled.

He fought the fish and I moved the canoe into the weeds to help him get closer to it, and he finally brought a nice northern to the surface along with about ten pounds of weeds. He reached over the side and lifted the fish out of the water, removed his lure, and turned to see that I was appropriately impressed, then released the fish back into the lake.

"The old Pike Killer does it again," he said, admiring his lure. "Oh, that's the Pike Killer this week," I said.

"Yup, this one's been my favorite for quite a while."

We moved back out of the weeds and began working through the rest of the weed bed, and soon I was fighting a bass and Thunderfoot caught another northern.

This particular lake was about a mile long and only about a hundred yards wide, so we usually worked our way to the end of the lake on one side and then planned on working back on the other side.

The sun was becoming almost unbearable, so we tried to stay in the shade of some of the tall trees on shore. A short time later, Thunderfoot got his Pike Killer in a tree as he cast, and the lure was hanging down in the water with the line up over the branch, about six feet off the water.

"I'm gonna just reel it up as close as I can, and then just flip it over the branch," he said.

He began reeling up the slack line and the lure was dipping back and forth on top of the water, when a nice bass came up and inhaled it.

"Whoa, holy cow! I got a fish on!" he shouted.

He was fighting the fish back and forth under the branch that his line was dangling from. Finally he pulled the fish from the water and lifted it up in the air.

"Paddle over there so I can get that fish off," he said, grinning.

I paddled over to the fish and he reeled up his line as we went to keep the fish in the air. When we got there, he reached out and took hold of the fish and unhooked it and let it go back into the lake. Then he reeled his lure up to the branch and flipped it over and into the boat.

"The master at work," he said, grinning from ear to ear. "Paddle me back to a respectable casting distance, would you?"

"Why, yes, of course, Bwana."

Big grin.

We got to the end of the lake and paddled across to the other side to begin our trip back. There was a good-looking spot back under some overhanging branches coming up just ahead.

"Watch me side arm one into that hot spot," he said, swinging his rod to the side, so his lure would go under the branches.

Just as he swung, I bent over to pick up my tackle box, and as he swung the rod forward to cast, his Pike Killer hit me in the top of the head and imbedded itself there. Smack!

"Yeeeeouch, don't pull, don't pull!" I screamed.

He was sitting with a stupid look on his face, trying to figure out where his lure had gone. He turned toward me and his mouth dropped open.

"Goooh, yikes, I think you got your head in my way."

He began to reel up the tangled line, and the lure began to pull and twist in my scalp.

"Stop, stop, don't pull! It's in there tight," I said.

He quit immediately and laid the rod in the bottom of the boat carefully.

"Let me come back there and see how bad it is," he said and began crawling back toward me.

"Take it easy, don't tip this thing over. I don't want to be on the bottom of the lake with a rod and reel attached to my head," I said.

He got back to me and I tipped my head forward, so he could see the lure.

"Oooh, uh, I think it's pretty far in," he said.

"Oh, great. Well, let's paddle over to the bank and see if we can get it out," I said, thinking that it would be better on dry land than in the unstable canoe.

We paddled over to the bank, and Thunderfoot got out to guide the canoe alongside the bank so he could take a clipper and cut the line, freeing me from the rod and reel. I climbed out and sat in the grass. Immediately, the air was full of mosquitoes. They came up out of the grass in clouds, and soon we were covered with the blood thirsty little monsters, adding to my misery considerably.

"See if you can pull it out with the pliers," I said.

"Are you sure? You really want me to pull on it?" he said, brushing mosquitoes away.

"Well, try it, and we'll see if I'm brave enough."

He took out his needle nose pliers and parted the hair so he could see the hooks.

"One isn't in very far, but the other one, oh man, it's in a long way."

"How far, past the barb?"

"Yup."

Oh, great, that wasn't the news I wanted to hear. "Well, see what you can do."

He took a deep breath, and I could feel him gripping the hook and then he pulled quickly and let out a sigh.

"One is out."

"Try the other one," I said.

I could feel him gripping the other hook, and it hurt like the devil. I held my breath, and he took a deep breath and suddenly, he plopped down in the grass, his face deathly white and with a confused look on it.

"Are you OK?"

"Whew, I got kind of woozy, I guess," he said.

"Try it again."

He gripped the hook again and the same thing happened. He sat down and got real pale and pasty looking.

"I don't think I can do it. It's in a long way and when I grab it with the pliers, the skin kind of puckers up and wow, it's really gross."

Well, now what to do. I knew I couldn't get the hook out by myself, and we were almost a mile from the truck on a Monday of a holiday weekend.

"Let's paddle back and see if we can go and get some help," I said. We climbed back into the canoe and paddled back to the end of the lake where the truck was waiting. We carried the canoe and gear up to the truck and drove back to town. By now, the top of my head was kind of numb feeling, so I was doing OK. Poor Thunderfoot didn't dare look at my head, or he began to feel faint.

I didn't know of anything else to do, so I drove to the hospital and went to the emergency room.

As we walked in, an older lady came to the reception desk. "How may we help you?" she said.

"I need to get a fish hook taken out," I replied.

"OK, we'll need you to fill out these forms," she said. "Where is the hook?"

I bent my head down so she could see.

"Oh, my God, forget the forms, come this way right away," she said.

That made me feel real confident.

I went down the hall to the examining room and sat on a bed until the doctor came in.

"So, a little fishing accident," he said, surveying my head. "Nice job," he said, looking toward Thunderfoot, who looked down but had to grin.

He cleaned off the area with something that stung like crazy and then said the dreaded "this might pinch a little" as he stuck a needle into the top of my head. Pinch, my butt; it hurt like heck.

Thunderfoot couldn't keep a straight face as I grimaced in pain. The doctor waited a few minutes and visited with us about how our day had been prior to the hook being imbedded in my skull. Then he took a pliers and I could feel him doing something up on top of my head. Thunderfoot looked away. In a couple of seconds, the Pike Killer was back in its owner's hands.

Thunderfoot took the lure and looked pretty upset when he saw the doctor had cut the barb off the hook that had been in my head.

"Jeez, you ruined the hook," he said. "Oh, sorry, that's OK," he said, smiling.

The doctor bandaged up the top of my head and we went out to the desk, completed the forms and I paid the lady for the services.

"Well," I said. "That was an expensive fishing day."

"I suppose you know I'm sorry," he said.

"Well, I didn't think you did it on purpose."

He patted me on the back. "Of course, my Pike Killer is ruined."

"I'll give you a new hook, and it'll be as good as new."

"Cool, you know, we still have half of the lake to fish, and it won't be dark for quite a while," he said.

"OK, let's go, but I want to stop home first and get my old football helmet and safety glasses."

"Oh, real funny."

I wasn't trying to be funny.

Thanks, Thunderfoot.

Surely There Will Be Better Days

The ducks had abandoned us for the past two weeks at our regular hunting place. We had our blind and all our gear on our favorite pond in the marsh, but for some reason, the ducks had stopped coming there.

"I think we scared them all, and they're too smart to come back near us," Thunderfoot said.

I wasn't so sure and didn't know what the reason was, but I did know that we weren't getting any action, so we needed to try a new plan.

"There have been a lot of ducks flying into the Goose Pond," he suggested.

"Yeah, so what? How do you suppose we're going to get to the Goose Pond?"

"We'll wade and push a canoe over there, and hunt from the canoe," he said, like it was as obvious as the nose on my face.

Now the Goose Pond was about a half mile from our duck pond, and the only way to get to it was across the swamp. It was smack dab in the middle of the marsh and was surrounded by water, tall grass and floating bogs. Of course, that was why the ducks had decided to make it their home.

"Oh, I don't know about that. It's got to be half a mile, and there isn't much dry ground between here and there. That would be an awful lot of work."

Just then we saw a nice flock of mallards flying along the river and watched them turn and circle the Goose Pond once and then set in.

Thunderfoot looked at me and nodded his head. "See, what did I tell you? We'll get lots of action there. Are you ready to go?"

I wasn't ready, but I knew that every time a duck even flew close to the pond, I'd get an earful of "I told you so," so I gave in. We tossed a couple of decoys into the canoe and the water jug, and told Katy to get in, then paddled the canoe to the end of our pond. When we got to dry ground at the end of the pond, we began carrying the canoe across it until we got back to mud and muck. Then we slid the canoe through the grass and pushed and pulled it toward Goose Pond. Katy walked along for part of the way, but then the muck got too deep, so she had to ride in the canoe, making it even harder to push.

When we had gone about a third of the way, I called for a rest break. I was sweating like a camel driver in the Sahara and puffing and gasping for breath, waiting for the "Big One" to take me from this incredible situation that I had agreed to. Thunderfoot, of course, was barely breathing hard and chomping at the bit to get going.

"If we take breaks all day, we won't get there before dark." "If I drop dead, you'll have to push the canoe by yourself."

We began again and pushed for another hundred yards or so before I had to stop again. This went on for almost an hour, and finally we made it to the pond.

Goose Pond was only about twenty yards across and almost a perfect circle. It was surrounded by tall cattails and in the center of the pond was a huge beaver lodge. Of course, all of the ducks that had been on the pond were now gone, scared away by the noise of a canoe being pushed through the marsh and an old man gasping and wheezing, trying not to drop dead.

The pond was deep, so we had to get into the canoe. We paddled to the center and put out the decoys, and then we slid back into the cattails and maneuvered the canoe sideways, so we could both shoot without shooting over each other's head.

I was drenched in sweat and began to get cold as I sat there.

Thunderfoot and Katy were both real comfortable, since they hadn't worked up a sweat between them.

We had been sitting there for about fifteen minutes when we spotted a pair of ducks coming our way.

"Here comes a pair," I whispered, and Thunderfoot nodded.

I turned toward my right a bit, so I could get a better shooting angle, and just as I did, the front of my right thigh clamped tight with a huge cramp. I gasped a quiet "Arrrrgh" and tried to straighten my leg out when suddenly the left one cramped up in the same place.

I let out a bellow, tried to get my legs straightened out, and began thrashing around in agony.

Thunderfoot looked back over his shoulder with panic on his face. He was gripping the sides of the canoe, which was swaying side to side, as I fought the cramps and tried to get into some position that would allow me to work them out of my legs.

"Jeez, be careful, you'll tip us over," he shouted.

Just then my left calf cramped, and I let out another agonized bellow. Now I had three cramps at once, and I was rolling around in the bottom of the canoe like one of those big Nile crocodiles that you see that crazy guy from Australia trying to slip a noose around his snout. Once the noose is on, the croc goes into a series of "death spins" and writhes around thrashing and wrecking everything in sight, which is just what I was doing now. Katy moved to the front of the canoe, where Thunderfoot was hanging on for dear life, when my right calf cramped.

"AAAAArrrrrrgh!" I screamed.

Now Thunderfoot was becoming alarmed. "Are you fooling with me? Hey, what's wrong? Are you dying?"

"Cramps," I managed to say through clenched teeth.

I was doing my best to get my legs straightened out, but it wasn't working very well. Finally my right front thigh loosened up and then I got my right calf to stop cramping. I was able to lay on my side and eventually got both of the other cramps to stop.

When the cramps finally quit, I was panting like a dog and pretty well spent.

"Are you OK?" Thunderfoot asked, genuinely concerned.

"Well, so far. If I can sit back up without cramping again, I'll be alright," I said.

Cautiously, I slid back toward my seat and carefully lifted myself up onto it. Very carefully, I slid my legs back under me, expecting at any moment for them to seize up again. No cramps.

"Wow, I hope that's the end of that," I said.

"Me, too. You almost tipped us over," Thunderfoot said. "Thanks for your concern for my welfare," I said sarcastically.

"I was concerned, but what could I do? Shhhh, here comes some ducks."

We crouched down and the ducks came sailing into the pond.

Thunderfoot shot and missed. I didn't shoot because it would have required me to twist too far to the left, and I didn't want to take a chance on another cramp from that position.

We did some shooting and got a couple of ducks as the day wore on, but soon we began to notice that there were many ducks landing in the woods about fifty yards from where we were sitting.

"Is there a pond back in there?" Thunderfoot asked.

"Must be. Those ducks wouldn't go in there if there wasn't water." "Let's sneak over there and see," he said, shaking his head yes.

I was pretty well rested now and had dried off, so what the heck, I might as well get all sweated up again, so I agreed.

We backed the canoe out of the reeds and paddled as close to the woods as we could get before we had to abandon the canoe and go on foot. Fortunately, we found a good trail that the beaver who lived in the Goose Pond had made, dragging brush and small trees to and from the pond, so it was pretty easy walking.

I had Katy with me and told her to heel, and Thunderfoot was behind us. As we got close to the pond, Katy began to get excited and got ahead of us.

"Kate, heel." She stopped and waited for us.

Off we went another ten feet, and she snuck ahead again. "Kate, heel."

She waited and in another ten feet she was sneaking ahead again. I grabbed her tail and took off my cap and popped her on the butt with it.

"Heel!"

She looked up at me and sat down on the trail.

"Come on, Kate. Let's go," I said and started down the trail. Katy stayed sitting. Thunderfoot passed her and she still sat there, looking peeved at me.

"Katy, come."

She laid down.

I looked at Thunderfoot, and he was doing his best not to laugh. "I think she's mad at you for hitting her with your hat," he said. "Let's go on to the pond. When she hears us shoot, she'll come running."

We snuck up to the pond. Thunderfoot went to the right and I went to the left. & we cleared the cattails, about twenty-five ducks took to the air. I lost my balance trying to turn to shoot and before I could get my feet out of the sticky muck, I tipped over and fell down. Thunderfoot began shooting and managed to bring down one duck.

"Nice shooting," he said, laughing as I got up covered with sticky black swamp mud.

"Kate, come here!" I shouted. No Katy.

"She's still sitting there," Thunderfoot said.

The duck wasn't far from me, so I decided I could get it myself. I took a couple of steps and soon realized that the pond was deeper than my hip boots. Now I was at the very top of the boots so I stood on tiptoes and as I tried to turn around, I sunk in just enough that both boots filled with water.

"Now you might as well go get it," Thunderfoot said, snickering like a fool.

He was right, so I waded in up to my belly and got his duck. When I got back to dry ground, Katy got up and started down the path toward the canoe.

"Best we don't hit her with a cap again," Thunderfoot said. "No kidding."

We hiked back to the canoe and then decided it was time to start back to our regular hunting pond. It didn't take quite as long going back because we had made a pretty good trail through the swamp on our way over. We finally got back and put the canoe away in its little hiding place and started back up the trail to the truck.

Thunderfoot was hiking merrily along with his duck, and I was plodding along looking pretty sad. I was limping on both legs, cut and bleeding from hundreds of grass cuts from the saw grass I had sloughed through, wet from the top of my head to the middle of my body, and from there down, covered with mud. My boots were making a slurping sound as I walked with them still full of water.

Thunderfoot got ahead of me and then stopped to wait where the bank rose up to the truck.

"Didn't have a real good day, did you?"

"Not the best," I said. "At least I came out alive. I thought I was going to have a heart attack when I got the cramps."

Thunderfoot began to snicker. "I'm sorry. It was pretty funny with you wallowing around in the canoe like a head shot cow."

I had to grin a bit, too.

"Just think how mad the rescue squad guys would have been if you had died out there. They would have had a heck of a time dragging your body out," he said.

That was a cheery thought.

We got to the truck and I went to the driver's side door to get my gun case.

"Uh, maybe you better ride in the back and let me drive home.

With all that mud on you, you'll stink up the truck real bad."

The perfect end to a perfect day. A ride home in the back of your own truck with a wet dog as a companion.

Thanks, Thunderfoot.

We've Had Better Ideas

After the debacle of pushing the canoe across the marsh the previous weekend, I was not exactly looking forward to any more expeditions to the duck swamp the following Saturday morning. Thunderfoot was heading across the backyard with his camouflage duck hunting clothes on, and I knew he would be pestering me to go duck hunting. The problem was that the duck population was almost non-existent at this particular time.

We had had a dry fall, and many of the good potholes in the marsh were dried up, or what little water there was was just a puddle in the middle of what used to be a nice sized lake. There were a few that were tended by beaver that had remained pretty full, but most of those were almost inaccessible. I was still sore from the previous weekend and wanted nothing to do with any more long hauls across the marsh.

"So, what ya doin' today?" Thunderfoot said, as he opened the refrigerator and began rummaging.

"Not pushing the canoe across any swamp."

"Oh, come on, don't be such a baby. That wasn't so bad."

"My legs are still sore from all the cramps, and my arms are just healing up from all the cuts from the saw grass. No more of that for me."

"I've got a better idea," he said, grinning and shaking his head up and down like one of those little plastic baseball player souvenirs you buy at the ballpark.

"Oh Lord, what now?"

"Let's take the canoe and go out by the bridge by the old Lockhard farm and put it in and cruise down the creek to Blue River. It's only about two or three miles, and we can take turns sitting in the front. We should be able to jump-shoot some ducks that are sitting in the creek. I figure that since the marsh is so low, a lot of the ducks will be using the creeks." His head was really going up and down now.

"How are we going to get back?" I asked.

"My mom will come and pick us up a couple of hours after we go, and she can take us back to the truck and then we can go back and get the canoe."

Well, it didn't sound like too bad of an idea at that. An hour or two paddling the canoe downstream on the creek wouldn't be so bad. He probably was right; there would be ducks sitting on it because of the low water conditions in the river bottoms.

"OK, that sounds pretty good. Let's try it."

He let out a whoop and grabbed the phone to call his mom.

"What time should I tell her to come and get us?"

"Well, let's see. It's almost ten now. An hour to get everything loaded and ten minutes to drive to the bridge, and what, two hours to paddle three miles? Tell her to pick us up at around 2:30. That will give us some extra time so we don't have to hurry."

He thought that was fine and called his mom and asked her if that would be OK with her. She agreed to meet us at the highway bridge just outside of Blue River, a small town just west of us, at 2:30 that afternoon.

We loaded the canoe and a couple of seat cushions, two paddles, our guns and a couple of boxes of shells. We debated whether or not to wear our hip boots. Since we would have the canoe to pick up any ducks we might get, we might not need them. After thinking about it, we decided that we might need to get out of the canoe to stretch and to switch places from front to back when it was time for one or the other to assume the gunning duties. So we decided to wear our hip boots after all.

It was a beautiful fall morning, so I decided just to wear a short sleeve shirt and a vest to hold my shells instead of my heavy canvas hunting jacket. Thunderfoot already had his heavy coat on, so he decided to use it rather than run home for his vest.

We had a hard time convincing Katy that she couldn't go. The creek was pretty deep in some places and was the lower end of a trout stream, which had very cold water. I didn't want a dog getting excited and tipping us over into that cold water. Besides, we would be able to pick up any ducks ourselves, so she had to stay home and rest for the day.

It only took a few minutes to drive to the creek and park by the bridge. The creek was about 12 to 15 feet wide with high muddy banks and it wound through some woods along a hillside for a couple of miles. Then it took a turn to the north and went under the highway bridge where we would be picked up, and from there it emptied into the river. The water was pretty fast and real cold, and we wobbled a little as we took off from the bank. After a few hundred feet, we got our "sea legs" and the canoe settled down. We began to paddle leisurely along a pasture where a dozen cows stared at us, probably wondering what kind of strange critter we were. Thunderfoot was in the front of the canoe with his gun loaded, and it was propped up in the bow of the boat between his feet. My gun was uncased and unloaded and laying in the bottom of the canoe.

The idea was that we would paddle silently, with the back person doing most of the paddling and steering, while the front person would be ready to shoot at any ducks we might surprise. If we got a duck or two, we'd pull up someplace and switch places, letting the back person move to the gunning position. That way we wouldn't be shooting over each other's heads. I felt much better doing it this way, because as much as I trusted my little buddy, I didn't like the idea of him following a flying duck through the air and forgetting my head was just a few feet below the muzzle of his gun.

We had paddled about three hundred yards when the stream turned and headed into the woods. About fifty yards into the woods, the stream turned sharply to the right and on the corner was a big logjam.

"Whoa, we can't go over that," Thunderfoot said.

I back paddled the canoe so we wouldn't get swept into the jam.

"We'll have to pull out and carry it around."

I maneuvered us to the bank, and Thunderfoot stepped out onto a log and held the canoe steady while I stood up. I stepped out onto the mud and sank up to the middle of my thigh. Now I had one foot buried deep in the mud and the other up in the canoe.

"Hold this canoe steady. I'm stuck." I struggled to get my dry foot out of the canoe and tried to get it to solid ground but only managed to get it a bit higher than my stuck one. Now I had both legs mired in the sticky goo.

Thunderfoot was snickering as I pulled first one then the other leg up and slopped my way up to dry ground. The bank was real steep, so I had to hang onto a small tree to keep myself from flopping back into the stream.

"Can you lift your end up?" Thunderfoot asked.

"Yeah, I think so." I lifted the end of the canoe up onto the bank and as soon as I let go of the tree, I slid into the mud again. Thunderfoot walked the log over to the bank and put his end of the canoe up on the bank.

Meanwhile I was pulling myself out of the mud again and as soon as I was out, I climbed up onto the bank.

We picked up the canoe and carried it around the logjam and down a less steep bank and put it back into the stream.

Thunderfoot climbed in and then I got in. We began our journey again. We went about fifty yards, and the stream turned again and there was another logjam.

We paddled into the bank again, but this time it wasn't so steep, and we managed to get the canoe out, up over the bank and back in without me getting any muddier. We continued down the stream and this time we went almost a hundred yards before we found a big tree that had tipped over in a storm and fallen across the stream.

"Should we try to go under it?" Thunderfoot asked.

"No way. We'll get part way under and get stuck and then we'll really be in a mess. Let's portage again," I said.

We slid the canoe in next to the tree, and Thunderfoot stepped out onto the trunk while I waited for him to slide us closer to the bank. Then I carefully stepped up onto the trunk and we tight roped the canoe across the tree trunk to the bank. We carried it to the other side and set it down in the grass.

"Before we put this back in, I want to walk ahead a little way and see if there are more obstructions," I said.

I walked down to the next corner and it was free of any brush, but there were six wood ducks sitting in the corner who flew away as I walked up.

"Oh, that was good. Why don't you just go ahead and chase all the ducks away and then I won't have to shoot," Thunderfoot said.

We got back into the canoe and paddled for about six or seven minutes until we got to the next brush pile. This time it was really steep so I maneuvered the front of the canoe to the bank and Thunderfoot stepped up onto the bank from the seat of the canoe. Then I tried to walk to the front of the canoe while he held onto the bow while laying on the bank. I got almost to the front before I tipped and had to step out into the water. It was about six inches deeper than the top of my hip boot, and cold, real cold. Now I was standing in the water with my right leg hanging over the side of the canoe. Of course my left foot was stuck in the bottom, so the only solution was to step into the water with my right boot, which instantly filled with the ice water, too.

I pulled and tugged and made my way up onto the mud and then crawled up over the bank to dry ground. Thunderfoot pulled the canoe up and over the bank while I laid on my back and held my legs up in the air, so the water could run out of my boots. At least, the water cleaned the gooey mud off the outside of the boots.

I could hear Thunderfoot snickering as he dragged the canoe around the brush and slid it back into the stream.

I sat there, feeling kind of sorry that I had ever started this journey and glanced at my watch.

"Jeez, it's almost 1:30 already," I said.

"Holy cow, you can still see the bridge where we put the canoe into the creek," he said, looking back toward the hill.

I looked, and we had probably only come a couple of hundred yards as the crow flies but had probably gone a mile by creek.

"If the rest of the stream is like this, we'll never make it by 2:30," I said.

"Best we get going."

We paddled another seventy-five yards and turned the corner to our next obstruction. By now, it was no surprise. We got out and slid the canoe up the bank and then climbed up ourselves. There was a lot of brush along this stretch of stream, and as we began carrying the canoe through it, we realized it was prickly ash. Thunderfoot, of course, had on a canvas coat, and I was bare armed. We had to carry the canoe through the torturous stuff for about twenty yards before we could get back into the stream, and by the time we got back into the canoe, I was bleeding profusely from about fifty gouges in my arms and face.

We had just gotten into the canoe and began downstream when a small flock of mallards rose up out of the tall grass ahead of us, and, of course, Thunderfoot was paddling instead of shooting, so they flew off without even a shot being fired.

The next three hours were a nightmare of mud, logs, nettles, prickly ash, sweat, and an occasional duck that went on its way unbothered. I lost count of how many times we dragged the canoe up and down the bank, but it was beginning to get dusk when we saw something moving through the brush along the creek ahead of us. Soon we saw that it was Thunderfoot's mother walking along the creek looking for us.

"I thought you two goofs had drowned yourselves," she said. "We couldn't be so lucky," I said.

"Well, it's about a half mile to the car," she said.

"Hey mom, how many brush piles between here and the car?" Thunderfoot asked.

"None that I saw. Why, are there some upstream?"

He looked over his shoulder at me and we both began laughing like fools. His mom shook her head and began walking back toward the car. I was as tired as I had ever been, covered with mud and sweat and dried blood and hadn't fired a shot all day. Thunderfoot was still dry but pretty pooped, too, and he still had all of his shells.

"Well, this was a good idea, huh?" he said over his shoulder. He turned and gave me a big grin.

"It won't rank as one of our best, but who knows, we'll probably come up with something just as stupid one of these days."

He got a silly look on his face and said, "Let's race home." "Take Your Mark, Get Set, Go!" We began paddling like we were in the Olympics and quickly passed his mom, throwing a big wake up along the creek bank and laughing like a couple of maniacs.

I bet she wondered about us sometimes.

Thanks, Thunderfoot.

A Friend In Need

Thunderfoot and I were really glad to see deer hunting season arrive. We had been on some pretty fruitless duck hunting excursions during the past fall. Hopefully the deer season would provide us with a little more hunting action, instead of all the hunting we had done previously without much luck.

We had scouted the farm where we would be hunting and had chosen our stands the previous Saturday. I would be sitting at the corner of the fence where two neighboring lands joined our hunting farm and watching a huge field. Below me, there was a logging road that wound up the hill, and I could watch the ridge above the road and the top of the field, which was wide open but would require a long shot.

Thunderfoot was below me, where a patch of woods extended up into the field. He would be sitting right on the corner of the patch of woods where many deer trails came together. When deer came into the field, most of them went toward the patch of woods so they could get back into cover faster rather than cross the open field. That was where I wanted Thunderfoot to sit, so he could have a good chance at a deer and wouldn't have to make such a long shot. It also gave me a good view of him, so I could keep an eye on him.

The night before season, he came over and stayed in the spare bedroom where he slept before most major hunting or fishing trips. We had supper and then tried to watch a movie but kept losing interest and began telling deer stories. He was talking about the huge deer that he had seen the previous season that had "been behind some does" so as not to afford him a good shot. I kept accusing him of having "buck fever," and we were arguing about that for most of the evening. Finally, I thought I was sufficiently tired to go to sleep, so we went to bed.

It seemed like just minutes had passed when the alarm went off, and I looked at the clock, which read, 4:30 a.m. I laid there a minute and then sat up on the side of the bed. As I sat there, I imagined that I could smell toast and bacon, and suddenly realized that I actually could smell toast and bacon. I got up and went to the kitchen, and there was Thunderfoot making breakfast.

"I was awake, so I thought I'd get us a good breakfast," he said, as he broke eggs into the frying pan.

"Who are you?" I said. "What did you do to the grumpy kid that usually sleeps here?"

"Oh, ha, very funny," he said. "I'm always ready to go when it comes to hunting or fishing."

I sat down and he put a plate of bacon and eggs in front of me and we had our breakfast. Afterward, we cleaned up the kitchen quickly and loaded our lunch into our backpacks. We had made the lunch the previous evening, and it was an integral part of any outdoor trip that we took.

I always felt that a backpack full of lunch was essential to keep the hunter content and made it easier to sit longer. This was especially important during deer season. If you sat still longer, the odds were that a deer would walk by you eventually. Those that could sit would see deer. Those who lost patience and began to walk around would spook the deer. Of course, we needed some of those less patient hunters in the area to make the deer come past us, too.

We each had a backpack and each had a thermos of hot chocolate.

Thunderfoot had packed four sandwiches for himself and made three for me. Plus, we each had a sack full of chocolate chip cookies, a bag of salted in the shell peanuts, and the most important item of all, some Kit Kat candy bars. The first year I ever shot a deer, I was eating a Kit Kat as the deer came to me, so I decided that Kit Kat was my lucky charm and always made sure I had some with me on every deer hunt. Of course, my lucky hat may have had something to do with it, too, so I made sure both were packed and ready to go. I had bought a new hat that same year and, like many hunters, felt I would be jinxed if I didn't have my lucky hat along, so I was still wearing the old dilapidated thing, despite all the nasty names Thunderfoot had called my precious headwear.

We loaded up the gear and drove through the darkness to the farm.

We parked at the old buildings and gathered up our gear and began hiking up the hill. Of course, Thunderfoot was going like it was a cross-country race, and soon I began to huff and puff, trying to keep up with him.

"Hold it," I gasped. "I've got to slow down or you'll be dragging me back to the truck like a dead deer."

He turned around and I could see the grin on his face in the low light from the stars. "Sorry, I was in a hurry to get to my stand," he said. "I guess we've got time. It's over an hour till we can shoot."

I removed my outer jacket to keep from getting all sweaty, and we began hiking again and made several more stops on our way to the top. When we got to the top of the road, we stopped and looked out over the field.

"Well," I said, "I'll talk to you later. Good luck."

He punched me in the arm, "You too," he said and walked along the top of the woods to his stand. I walked up the hill farther to my corner and sat down. We each had a folding chair with us, so with our comfortable chair, lunch, hand and foot warmers, and lucky candy bars, we were ready for a day in the outdoors.

I arranged my food and gear and loaded my gun and stood it against the fence. It was about twenty degrees out, so my breath was scope. He followed them and must have been imagining he was goose hunting. I noticed movement out of the corner of my eye, and coming across the field, directly above Thunderfoot, were three deer. One was a buck and the other two were does. They were walking along, going straight at him. By now, the geese were right overhead, and one of the does actually looked up at them. Thunderfoot was still watching the geese through his scope, and the deer were walking closer and closer to him.

I couldn't do anything but watch. It wouldn't do any good for me to shoot at them and I didn't want to anyway, since they were going to him. So I just lowered my gun and watched the fun.

The deer were about thirty yards from Thunderfoot when he lowered the gun and laid it in his lap. He stretched his neck from side to side and looked up the hill. You could see him stiffen up as he saw the deer standing there looking at him. The deer, of course, saw him move, too, and were alert and ready to bolt back up the hill. Both hunter and hunted faced each other for several seconds, and then Thunderfoot tried to slowly raise his gun. That movement was all it took for the deer to decide the game was over, and they turned and bounded up over the top of the hill as Thunderfoot struggled to get them in his sights.

As he lowered his gun, I could see him shaking his head. Then, he stopped and looked slowly my way. I was sitting there laughing, and you could see the look on his face. He shook his head from side to side, as if to say, "I'll never hear the end of this." Score two for the deer.

He looked at his watch and then stood up and began hiking up the hill to me. 1 couldn't suppress the grin on my face as he got to my stand.

"I can't believe you let those deer walk up to me while I was watching those geese," he said.

"What? How does this suddenly become my fault?" I said, laughing.

"Why didn't you get my attention and warn me?" "What was 1 supposed to do? Fire a warning shot?"

"I just can't believe it," he said. Then he sat down on the ground and began rummaging through my lunch sack.

"What are you looking for?"

"Something to eat. Mine is all gone."

"Maybe if you did something besides eating and bird watching, you might actually get a deer."

Killer look.

We sat there a while and he tried to make me promise that I'd never tell anybody about the incident, and finally he went back to his stand. My lunch was now all gone anyway, so there wasn't any reason for him to stay.

We sat there until the last hour of the day and never saw another deer. I whistled to him as the time ran out, and we both folded up our stools and leaned them against a tree. We would leave them there because we would be back tomorrow, and there wasn't any reason to carry them back and forth up and down the hill.

We began walking down the hill, talking in hushed tones, and as we got to the bottom, I laid my gun and backpack on the ground by the gate and began to climb over. I put my left foot on the second wire up from the bottom and swung my right leg over the top wire. I put my right foot on the third wire up and as I put my weight on it, the wire came loose from the post and I fell over the fence with my left leg still on the other side. A barb from the top wire had dug into my crotch and ripped into my pants and leg and firmly impaled me on the top wire.

Instantly, I was hanging upside down from the top wire, with a sharp spike of metal imbedded in my leg.

"Yeeeeow!" I screamed. "Help me, I'm hooked."

I was looking upside down at Thunderfoot who was laughing so hard he could hardly stand up. He was trying to help me upright from the wrong side of the fence.

"Climb over and help me," I said.

He went to the other end, hopped over the fence like a gazelle and came over to where I was hanging. By now, I had managed to get hold of the fence post and had partly righted myself.

"We gotta get you off that top wire," he said.

He examined my leg where the barb was imbedded. "Oh, yuck, it's stuck right into your leg."

"Can you get it out?"

"It's right next to your, uh, you know, not a place I want to be messing with."

Now was not the time to be worrying about anything like that.

"Forget that. I don't care where it is. Get me off it and hurry up; the blood is rushing to my head."

Perhaps his fear of my wrath was greater than his fear of getting too close to another guy's crotch area, because he grabbed hold of my leg and lifted as much as he could and then took his other hand and manipulated the barb out of my leg and torn pants. When he got me loose, I flopped to the ground like a darted elephant.

"Holy cow, that is a nasty hole in your, well, you know."

"What do you mean?" I asked, not knowing exactly where the hole was but knowing it made my whole crotch hurt.

"Well, it's kind of in that little area that is kind of right below everything. Actually you're pretty lucky it wasn't a little farther in front. You would have had to wait for the EMTs to help you if it was there," he said, grinning.

I got up and had to walk like a bowlegged cowboy. Thunderfoot gathered up all the gear and loaded it up. I let him drive home because it hurt like heck to move my legs, so I just sat quietly in the passenger side.

When we got home, I took my clothes off and tried to examine the damage with a mirror. I couldn't get a good look at the puncture but washed the area as best I could.

"I need you to help me," I said from the bathroom. No answer.

"Hey, come here."

He came to the door, but didn't open it. "What?"

"Come in here and put some iodine on this for me. I can't see it and it needs some kind of disinfectant so I won't get an infection."

"Put iodine on where?" "On the cut, where else?"

"No way, I got as close to that as I ever want to get, back at the farm." "Well, then I guess we'll have to forget hunting tomorrow so I can make a doctor's appointment to get it done."

The door opened. "Give me the iodine."

I was watching him in the mirror as he tried to dab the iodine on without looking.

"You're gonna have to watch where you are putting it," I said.

"Come on, it's just a butt. Don't be such a sissy."

"Yeah, but you're not looking at it from the angle I'm looking at it." Finally he got some iodine on the wound, and I got dressed and we sat down to have something to eat.

We were eating quietly when he began laughing. "That was a real smooth move on that fence."

I moved a little on my chair and my crotch gave me a little stab of pain. "I'm glad you liked it," I said. "Tomorrow I'm going to open the gate and go through."

He laughed again and we ate in silence for a while.

"Sorry about the crotch thing. It's a guy thing, you know."

"Yeah, I understand. But thanks for helping me," I said.

"No problem."

"You know," I said, "I'd do the same for you anytime." He turned pale. "Jeez, I hope you never have to."

Thanks, Thunderfoot.

Over the River and Through the Woods

We were experiencing one of the snowiest winters we had seen for many years. Thunderfoot and I had just finished clearing out my driveway and had come into the house for something to eat.

"Jeez, snow shoveling makes me hungry," he said, opening the refrigerator and snooping around inside.

I moved him out of the way and began getting the ingredients out for a couple of omelets while he went into the living room and turned on the TV I whipped up a couple of ham and cheese omelets and a pile of toast and called him to eat. I didn't have to call twice, as he came on the run.

"Boy, that smells good," he said, smearing jam onto a piece of toast and plowing into his eggs. "Hey, I was watching a show about fishing crappies at night through the ice."

"Oh, yeah," I said, "I've done that, up to the park. They have a lot of crappies, and a guy I used to work with had a shanty up there. We used to go up after work and fish them. It was fun, and we did pretty well."

"How about Gutwielers?" he asked. "What about it?"

"It's full of crappies, and I bet we could go down there tonight and set up the tent and catch some."

"I've never seen anybody fish at night on any of these lakes."

"That doesn't mean it can't be done. Come on, let's have a little adventure," he said, grinning and nodding yes.

We decided to give it a try, so we went to the hardware store and got some mantles for the lantern and filled it and the heater with fuel. Then we got some minnows and, of course, prepared a snack to take along. Thunderfoot never went anywhere without a snack.

We waited for the afternoon to pass, and I took a nap while Thunderfoot watched fishing shows and ate me out of house and home.

We loaded up the ice shanty and the rest of the gear and started for the river bottoms just as the sun was going down. By the time we got everything loaded onto the shanty, it was dark, and we began pulling it down the path to the lake. The path was made by people walking in the snow. We were pulling a shanty that was four feet wide and six feet long, and it was piled with about a hundred pounds of gear. There hadn't been many people on the lake that day, and with the snow from the previous night, it was tough going.

I was in front pulling and Thunderfoot was in back pushing. "Are you pushing or just hanging on?" I panted.

"I'm pushing. Try pulling a bit more and talking a bit less," he retorted.

The snow was almost up to my waist in places and it was like pulling a refrigerator that was tipped over on its side. I was struggling and sweating, and we were only a few feet from the bank.

"There's no way we're going to get this thing out to the lake," I said as I stopped to catch my breath.

"Oh, come on. We're almost there."

"We aren't even half way."

"Let's take the gear off and just pull the shanty, and then come back and get the gear."

I knew that he was determined to get to the lake and do some fishing, so I agreed, and we pulled the empty shanty off into the darkness. As we got to the lake, we tried to get our bearings so we could set the tent up in the right area, where we hoped the crappies would be.

We finally decided on the spot and popped the tent up, and then waded back through the snow to the rest of the gear. By the time we got back, I was sweating up a storm and just about done in.

First we had to shovel off a space on the ice for the shanty to sit, and then we drilled four holes in a line that would accommodate the cutout section of the floor of the shanty, and slid it over the holes. Thunderfoot kicked snow up against the outside edge of the shanty to make a seal and we crawled inside. I carried my bucket in first and positioned it on the far side, and then Thunderfoot came in and sat on the other side by the door. He brought the lantern in, and I was trying to get situated when he struck a match to light it.

"Be sure you have it pumped up and the little pumper-thing locked," I said.

"Yeah, yeah, I know how to do this. Do you think this is my first time?"

I could hear him pumping and things clanking as he struck a match and held it up to the lantern. As the flame entered the little hole in the bottom of the chamber where the mantles were, there came a huge "Whoooof" sound, and the lantern exploded into a huge ball of flame.

Thunderfoot dropped it on the bottom of the shanty floor and dove out through the door. I was on the wrong side of the shanty and the blazing lantern was between me and the door, really shooting flames up into the air. I managed to get my heavy mittens out of my bucket and grabbed the thing with mittens on my hands and tossed it out through the open door into the snow.

There was a "Shhhhhhhhhh" sound as the lantern sunk into the snow and went out.

"Jeez, what are you trying to do, cremate me?" I shouted.

I could hear him at the door. "Maybe you better light that lantern after all. I think there's something wrong with it." I could see his grin in the starlight.

"No kidding. I think I'll light it outside this time," I said.

I picked up the lantern and found that he had forgotten to turn the little valve that lets air into the mixture and that was what caused the flare-up. I lit the lantern and got it adjusted so it was working perfectly and then took it into the shanty and sat down.

"Whew, that was pretty exciting," he said, grinning.

"Yeah, real exciting, especially from the inside of the shanty.

Thanks for your concern for my well-being. I see you abandoned me like a rat leaving a sinking ship."

He looked at me and shrugged.

We got our fishing gear out and cleaned the ice chips out of the holes, baited up and lowered a baited hook into each of our four holes. Thunderfoot's bobber had hardly hit the water when it went down and he grabbed the pole and lifted a nice crappie out of the cold water.

"See, I told you it would work. Look at this beauty."

Things were looking up. I watched my bobbers expectantly for a bite, and he re-baited his and put it back into the ice hole. We picked each pole up and jigged it every so often to entice a fish into biting, but got no more bites.

A half hour passed and not another bite. Then an hour had passed.

"That was kind of a short feeding period," I said.

"Either that or a small school of crappies," he said, laughing.

I sat there and shook my head. "I have to admit, I thought we'd get some fish, but one is just an insult."

We ate our snacks and decided to call it a night. Thunderfoot had put his crappie in the minnow bucket so it was full of life, and he put it back down the hole. "Go tell all your buddies how well you were treated," he said to the fish as it swam down the hole.

By now the moon had come up and it was pretty well lit outside, so we could turn out the lantern and work by moonlight. We decided it wasn't worth the effort to try to take everything in one trip, so we carried the gear back first, and then came back for the shanty. I got rid of my heavy coat on the first trip, so it was a little easier the second time back to the truck.

We pulled the shanty up over the high bank and to the truck and slid it inside the box. I was puffing a little, and we just stood there catching our breath when a coyote howled a few hundred yards away in the river bottoms.

"Wow, that was cool," Thunderfoot said quietly. "Yeah, it was."

"You know, I saw a show on TV the other day about calling in coyotes at night," he said.

"Well, that sounds like fun. I'll lend you my coyote calls, and you can try it and tell me about it afterward."

"Oh,funny."

Thanks, Thunderfoot.

Say Meow

Thunderfoot had a couple of days off from school because of teacher conferences, so he was at the shop with me, helping me get the spring turkey hunting merchandise out and priced. I was working on the clothing and he was arranging the calls and accessories when the delivery man came in with a package for me.

We chatted a bit and he fed the dogs a cookie each, and then he told me of a strange encounter he had just that morning.

"I was coming down the road out by Castle Rock when I saw something walking up out of the ditch on the right. I slowed down, thinking it was probably a deer or dog, and as I got right up to it, it stepped into the road. It was a cougar," he said.

When Thunderfoot heard that, he dropped what he was doing and came over by us. "A cougar?"

"Yup, a full grown cougar."

"You're sure it wasn't just a big cat? You know, there are some big barn cats around." I said.

"This wasn't a barn cat. It was probably four to five feet from nose to butt and then had a three foot tail behind that," he said. "It was a cougar, no doubt."

Thunderfoot was dumbfounded. "There aren't cougars in Wisconsin."

"Well, then this critter was doing a good cougar impression," the delivery man said.

"You know," I said, "I heard of a county cop who has seen a cougar on his property, and I think he lives right in that area."

"You guys are foolin' with me," Thunderfoot said.

"No fooling, I saw it," the driver said as he started for the door. Thunderfoot was shaken.

"So what?" I said. "If there's a cougar, it's not going to hurt us any."

"Yeah, but they're like lions. They could eat people."

"I'm sure we're not in any danger from a cougar, if it exists."

We went back to our work and nothing more was said about the incident. About two weeks later, a man came in to look at pistols, I showed him what I had in stock and he decided on one that he wanted to buy.

"I have my service revolver, but I want to have a back up gun, and this will do fine," he said.

"You're a cop?"

"Yes, I'm on the county sheriff's department," he said, and laid down his driver's license for identification for the paperwork for the pistol. "Are you the deputy that I heard about that has seen a cougar on his farm?" I asked as I saw the name on the license.

"Yeah, that's me. I've seen him three times."

"So it is real," I said.

"Oh, yeah. I was in the barn about three weeks ago, and he walked right through the barnyard not fifteen feet from me. He's real alright."

I told him about the delivery man, and he told me that the place he had described when he saw the cat was just over the ridge from his farm.

"It's wild country up in there," he said. "There are some big rocky areas that are real steep and deep valleys that are almost inaccessible, so there are lots of places for him to hide. Plus, lots of deer, rabbits, squirrels and raccoon probably make it pretty easy for him to eat, so he's probably pretty content."

I was impressed with this new account of the cat. Now I really began to believe in it and couldn't wait to tell Thunderfoot about my new information.

That day after school, he came into the store to see what was going on, and I told him about my visit from the county cop.

"Oh sure, you're just trying to spook me," he said.

"No fooling. He's coming back on Saturday to pick up the gun, after the waiting period. You can ask him yourself."

Saturday came and Thunderfoot was there, waiting for the man to come in and get the gun. When he arrived, I asked him to tell Thunderfoot what he had told me. By the time he was done with the story, Thunderfoot was standing, listening with his mouth hanging open like a simpleton.

"See, I told you," I said.

He seemed to be more upset about the cat than necessary, so I asked him what was wrong.

"Have you ever looked at a map of that area? If you go across the hills instead of by road, that place is probably only a half mile from where we turkey hunt," he said, grabbing a county map and opening it. "See here, there is where we hunt, and here is the road where the guy saw the cougar. Notice how short the distance is from here to here?"

"So what? That cougar isn't going to bother us."

"Oh, that's easy for a big guy like you to say, but I'm just the right size for a good snack."

I began laughing, thinking he was making a joke, but he was dead serious. I had never seen him get so shook up over something like this, so I dropped the subject.

A couple of weeks went by, and our turkey season was on us. We were hunting in the same place we had hunted for years, and we knew the terrain and where the turkeys lived, so our scouting was minimal. We made our plans for where we would hunt opening morning and left that morning in the darkness for the turkey woods.

It took us about twenty minutes to get up into the woods and to get situated by two large oak trees. It was still dark, and the turkeys hadn't gobbled yet, so we sat in the dark about ten feet away from each other and waited for dawn to come. I was getting pretty drowsy and my eyes were getting heavy when I heard a sound behind me like something had fallen from a tree or someone had taken a step and stepped on a twig. I came fully awake now and listened carefully. The sound came again. It sounded like a real soft step on leaves and grass.

I looked over at Thunderfoot but couldn't see him. He was sitting on the backside of a big oak tree, and I could just make out his fanny pack sticking out alongside the tree.

There was another step, this time much closer. I tried to think what could be making such a noise. There were no cattle in the woods. Squirrels were still in bed. Turkeys were still sitting on their roosts. Raccoons made a shuffling sound as they worked their way through the woods, and this was a stealthy step, and then another, not raccoon-like at all.

I leaned my head back and tried to ignore the sound and suddenly it came again. This time it sounded like it was just few feet behind the tree. Then I could hear a quiet breathing sound, too. My heart was beginning to hammer, and I was listening so hard that my ears began to hurt. Then I heard a sound like a low hum. Like a cat purring!

I sat perfectly still, and my mind began to play tricks on me. I was sure that there was no danger from anything that lived in the woods, except maybe poison ivy or a very seldom seen rattlesnake, but I was sure that if I turned my head and looked over my shoulder, I would be staring face to face with a cougar. The sound came again, and this time it was right behind my tree.

I began to breathe in little gasps, and my heart was racing. I looked over at Thunderfoot's tree and he hadn't moved. His fanny pack was still laying where it had been. He was probably asleep. The thought went through my mind that it was good that he wouldn't see his hunting buddy torn limb from limb if he was sleeping.

I decided that I had to turn and look. I moved my head to the right and leaned out to see around the tree. As, I cleared the tree, there came a scream, "Yeeeeeeooooow!" and Thunderfoot pounced on me! I tipped over and almost had a heart attack. He was laying on top of me, laughing like a maniac.

"You little fool, are you trying scare me to death?" I whispered.

"You, ha, you, oooh, almost, ha ha!" He was having some kind of fit. Finally he calmed down and sat up. "I thought you said that a cougar wouldn't come near us. You sure were scared of something."

"You maniac, what did you think I would do? You're lucky I didn't take my gun off safety and blow your fool head off."

He lapsed into fits of laughter again.

"How did you get back there in the first place? I didn't see you walk past me," I said.

"Of course, you didn't see me. You were sleeping like a hibernating bear, only you sounded like a fog horn. I just got up and walked right past you, oh mighty hunter."

Hmm, maybe that drowsy spell I had was more than I thought.

"Well, now that you've had your laugh for the day, would you mind sitting yourself down and shutting up, so we might have a chance at a turkey?" I said.

"Yes, Bwana," he said, and he got to his feet and walked back to his tree. As, he went past me, I gave him a punch in the leg.

"Snot!"

He sat down, got situated and things quieted down. I settled down and began to doze off again, when I heard the purring sound. I opened my eyes instantly and looked over at him. He was sitting there, shaking with laughter.

"Here kitty, kitty," he whispered. Sometimes he could be such a wise guy.

Thanks, Thunderfoot.

Never a Borrower Nor a Lender Be

I'm one of those people who take good care of their stuff. I have a place for everything in my home and keep my things in their proper places. I take good care of my guns, cleaning them after each use, and storing them in a gun cabinet to keep them safe, free of dust and dirt. Most of all, I take especially good care of my fishing equipment. Rods and reels are cleaned and greased as needed. New line is almost a religious experience. I check my line after every fishing trip and any that is frayed or looks bad is replaced. My thinking has always been that no matter how much money you spend on tackle, the line that attaches you to the fish is the most important part of the whole system.

Thunderfoot, on the other hand, is about the most careless person I know when it comes to taking care of his equipment. You can always pick out his rods and reels. They are the ones with a dehydrated gob of night crawlers still on the hook from the last trip. Most of his walleye jigs have a desiccated minnow still hanging grotesquely on the hook. His rods are missing guides. He has one that has about four inches broken off the tip, but he still uses it, and uses the first guide as a tip. His reels are full of sand and most of them will only cast a short way because they have such little line left on them. He never replaces his line and after a time, he doesn't have enough to make a decent cast. Usually I can't stand it any longer and I fill his reels with new line.

Tackle boxes are a whole story by themselves. My lures are cleaned, dried, and sorted into their assigned little cubicles after each fishing trip. Hooks are sharpened, line is snipped from the eye of the lure, and bent or damaged hooks are replaced. There is no reason for Thunderfoot to own a tackle box. Tackle boxes have little compartments for lures; he stores everything in the bottom of the box in a big gob. His lures are all tangled together in a big cluster. Most of the hooks and baits have pieces of line hanging from them, and every hook he has still has dried worms or dehydrated minnows still hanging on them, looking like a little collection of miniature mummies. Lures, twister tails, and bobbers all are thrown together in a large tangled mess. For him to get something out of his tackle box, everything comes out at once. And, the bottom of the box has things in it that I wouldn't even touch without rubber gloves. All in all, it's a disaster area.

He calls me a "neat freak," and I may be, but there is order in my fishing, and I want to keep it that way.

Hunting isn't quite as bad. He does wipe down his guns with an oily rag after most trips, but full cleaning isn't such an important issue with him. "They'll only get dirty again when I shoot next time" is his philosophy. Of course, his boots and other gear are normally just strewn around until we get ready to go hunting, and then he has to tear the house apart to find the things he's looking for.

Once, a few years ago, he came over and asked me if I could take a look at his shotgun, which had a crack in the stock. I said sure, bring it over. He walked in with his gun in a cloth gun case, which looked like it contained a hockey stick. When he took the gun out, the stock was bent off to the side at about a thirty-degree angle from the centerline of the gun.

"What in the world did you do to this?" I asked.

"Well, I went up to my grandpa's farm, and we were hunting, and I got back to the truck first, so I just laid my gun in the grass. You know it's against the law to lay it against the truck. So, then I took a little nap, and when grandpa came to the truck, he got in and we left. When we got back to his house, I remembered my gun, and when we went back to get it, we found it. But it looks like he ran over it when we left."

I took the butt plate off the gun and got a wrench on the screw that held the stock on. It was a struggle to get it off, and when I did, we found it was bent beyond fixing. The stock was broken too badly to repair, and the forearm was crushed. I looked in some gun books and found a replacement stock and forearm and ordered them for him. Then we had to call an 800 number to order another bolt for the stock. A week later, we had all the parts and he had a new gun.

So, to say he was careless about equipment wouldn't be an overstatement.

I was thinking about all of the wrecked gear he owned as we fished for walleyes along the rocky rip rap that ran along the railroad tracks on the Mississippi River. In late summer, the rocks were walleye magnets. There were many aquatic insects among the rocks, and they drew in the small fish and minnows that feed on insects. Of course, small fish and minnows attract predator fish, such as walleyes and bass, and the rocks were the best place at that time of year for us to spend a day fishing.

We would go to the upper end of a long stretch of riprap and then position the boat about ten yards from the shore and cast crank baits toward the shore. You had to almost get the bait on dry ground, as the fish were right up in the shallow water waiting for some minnows or crawdads to feed on.

I was using a level wind bait casting rod and reel. The advantage of this type of reel over a spinning reel is that I could put my thumb on the spool and stop my bait just where I wanted it. With a spinning reel, you often cast too far, and your lure ended up on the bank in the brush. That was the problem Thunderfoot was having, and he had just lost his last crawfish colored lure.

"OK, that's it. I need to borrow a lure from you, and unless you want me to lose all your lures, you better lend me a bait caster, too," he said, matter-of-factly.

"If you'd take care of your stuff, you'd have a bait caster of your own. What happened to the one I gave you last year for your birthday?"

"You know exactly what happened. It fell overboard when that monster fish grabbed my lure last spring."

"And why weren't you holding on to it?"

He looked at me with a peeved look. "I forgot to reel it up all the way, and it fell in. Are you happy now?"

"So, now you want to use one of mine?"

"Wow, Sherlock, you figured that out really fast," he said, grinning. I wasn't sure I wanted him to use one of my good rods and reels, but it was that or give him an endless supply of crank baits that he would throw up into the brush, so I relented and gave him one.

He grinned from ear to ear as he tied on one of my baits and began casting toward the rocks. He was good at it, especially with a rod that had all the guides and a reel that was full of good line.

"Hey, this works better than the one I had," he said.

"That's what happens when you take care of your gear," I said. "Mine just gets worn out faster because I catch a lot more fish than you do," he said. "I'm just ... whoa," he said, as he set the hook into a fish that grabbed his lure. "Holy cow, this is a good one," he said.

I watched him fight the fish for a minute or so and then moved to the back of the boat with the landing net. The water boiled next to the boat as the fish was almost at the surface. Thunderfoot raised the rod again and up came a really nice walleye. "Get him, get him!" he shouted.

I slid the net under the fish and hauled it into the boat. It was a dandy, probably about seven or eight pounds.

"Let's get a picture of him," I said, laying the net and fish in the bottom of the boat. I went forward and grabbed my camera. Meanwhile, Thunderfoot was getting the fish and lure untangled from the net.

"Leave the lure in its mouth and hold it up," I said as I knelt in the bottom of the boat. Thunderfoot stuck his first three fingers under the gill flap of the fish and held it in front of him.

"Say cheese," I said as I snapped the picture.

"Cheeee." Just as I snapped the shutter, the fish took a violent shake, and Thunderfoot lost his grip. His hand came out of the gill flap, the lure swung around and one of the treble hooks sunk into his thumb. The fish fell to the floor of the boat with Thunderfoot attached to the back treble hook.

"Yeeeeeoooowww, the hook's in my thumb! Help! Help!" he yelled. The fish was thrashing around in the bottom of the boat, and Thunderfoot was trying to subdue it and keep it from jerking on the hook that was imbedded in his thumb.

I grabbed the fish and tried to quiet it. "Get the fish off the bait," he said, through clenched teeth.

The other hook was still deeply into the fish's jaw, so I had to lay it down to go get my needle nose pliers. The fish started thrashing again, and Thunderfoot went to his knees on the bottom of the boat.

"Hurry up, hurry up."

I found the pliers and grabbed the fish and removed the hook.

Then I lifted the fish and slid it back into the water.

Thunderfoot looked at me in disbelief. "You let my fish go."

"We aren't going to kill that big fish. We'll keep some small ones to eat, you know that."

"Well, you could have asked me first."

"Let me see that hook," I said.

One of the hooks from the treble was sunk into the meaty part of Thunderfoot's thumb, next to where it was attached to his hand. The barb was not visible.

"Ooo, it's past the barb," I said.

"Oh, great. What are we gonna do now?"

"Well, I can try to get it out, or we can quit for the day and go find a doctor."

"Get it out. It's too early to quit."

He turned his head to the side, and I pushed on the hook to see how much it would move. As I pushed, he grimaced and gritted his teeth but didn't say anything.

The hook was just past the barb, so I pushed down as hard as I dared on the shank and then pushed backwards. It moved out past the barb and then popped out of his thumb.

"There, that wasn't so bad," I said.

Thunderfoot was sweating and as pale as a ghost. "Oh, no that was just a lot of fun. I don't suppose it was too bad from your point of view."

"Jeez, I didn't do it to you, you did it yourself. Don't blame me," I said, kind of hurt after my lifesaving surgery.

"Sorry," he said, wiping his forehead and giving me a grin.

I moved back to the front of the boat and positioned it so we could begin fishing again.

I cast to the shore and was retrieving my bait when I heard his reel go "whirrrr" and then there was a "sploosh" sound.

"What was that?" I said, turning my head to look back.

Thunderfoot was standing there with his mouth hanging open, with his hands out in front of him.

"What was that sound? What fell in?" I repeated.

He looked at me and then at the water. Then I noticed that my rod and reel weren't in the boat.

"My hand is kinda numb, and well, it kinda slipped when I cast and fell in," he said.

I took a deep breath. When I finished my retrieve, I cast again and retrieved the bait again.

Yelling wouldn't bring the rod and reel back; it could be replaced. Thunderfoot felt bad already and it wouldn't serve any purpose to make him feel worse. "Grab another one out of the rod box and try again."

He stood there a minute and then came forward and got himself another rod. He tied a lure on and then punched me in the shoulder as he went back to the back of the boat.

I turned and grinned at him and he said, "Next big one, you hold it. I'll take the picture."

Gladly.

Thanks, Thunderfoot.

Heave Ho

Thunderfoot picked up the phone on the first ring. "Yo."

"Geez, that's a nice way to answer the phone. Did you ever hear of saying hello?"

"I knew it would be you," he said. "Just how did you know that?"

"Because it's Thursday, and we always plan what we're gonna do on the weekend on Thursday night."

He knew me pretty well. "OK, smart guy, what do you think I've got planned?"

"I hope it's going to Lake Michigan and catching some salmon," he said expectantly.

I had been cooking up a trip to the big lake with a friend of mine who had a brother-in-law who lived on the lake and had a big boat for salmon fishing. Thunderfoot knew that we had a chance to go and was waiting for the call.

"We leave at 3 a.m. Saturday morning."

"Three! That's the middle of the night. Will there be any place open that early for breakfast?"

"We'll take some donuts and then stop later so you won't starve." That seemed OK to him, and he said he'd be over in a minute to get things planned. Since we didn't need to take anything with us except a lunch for on the boat, it didn't take long to get ready.

Friday afternoon, he came to my house right after school and we made sandwiches and packed cookies and chips and fruit for the next day's fishing. That evening he stayed over and we both went to bed early. My alarm woke us at 2:30; it took a little coaxing to get Thunderfoot out of his warm bed.

"You know, these salmon will average over ten pounds," I finally said after having little luck getting him motivated.

"Average? You mean there might be bigger ones than ten pounds?" he said, sitting up in his bed.

"Some over twenty, but if you don't get your lazy butt up, we'll miss the boat and have to fish from shore and catch perch."

He was out of bed like a shot and after a trip to the bathroom to get "civilized" he was ready to leave. We stopped at my friend's house and picked him and his son, Travis, up and off we went toward the big lake.

The two boys were in the back seat and soon we could hear paper rattling as they dove into the sack of donuts. They each ate three or four donuts, leaving us with one each, and guzzled in a couple of quarts of milk. Then it got quiet and they both were slouched down in the seat sleeping.

"It never fails," I said, "ten miles into the trip, nap time."

We drove for another three hours and pulled into a truck stop for breakfast. The two sleeping beauties took a little rousing to get awake, but as soon as the smell of food from the exhaust fan in the restaurant got to them, they were up and ready for some breakfast.

"I need a lot of vittles to give me strength for hauling in those big old salmons," Thunderfoot said as he perused the menu. "I believe I'll have a large stack of pancakes with bacon and a large milk." He looked up at the waitress and gave her one of his famous smiles. She took our orders and in a short time we were all digging into huge plates of food. We finished breakfast and went looking for our host, whose boat was tied up at a slip down by the lake. It was just getting light as we pulled in and met our captain, and it only took a few minutes to load our lunches and get the boat untied and off into the mist that hung over the water.

We motored slowly down the river that led to the big lake. As we did, Thunderfoot was asking the captain lots of questions about all the fish we were hoping to catch. The captain explained that we would be about three miles from shore in two hundred feet of water. Thunderfoot's mouth dropped open at that comment. "How we gonna pull them up from so deep water?" he said.

The captain explained that our baits would be up higher and that the fish would be suspended above the bottom, so it wouldn't be that deep where we were actually fishing. Once we got to the open lake, the captain opened up the throttle and we took off out into the huge expanse of water. Thunderfoot was watching the depth finder, and it kept dropping and dropping and soon it read two hundred feet.

He looked at me with a kind of worried look on his face. "It's mega deep here."

We slowed the boat and the captain asked my friend to take the wheel and keep the boat going in a straight line, and then showed the rest of us how to rig the lines and let the baits back to the correct depth. We began setting the baits and rods in their trolling positions. Each bait was let back a certain distance and then the line was hooked into the clip of a downrigger and lowered to a measured depth. It was all quite impressive.

"Pretty scientifical," Thunderfoot quipped.

Once we had the four lines out, the captain took the wheel and we began trolling.

"We should decide who takes the first fish," I said.

It was decided to draw straws, so we cut four toothpicks into four different lengths and took turns picking them for the order in which we would take turns fishing. Longest went first, and then on down the line.

Thunderfoot drew the longest toothpick. "All right, let me at them."

About ten minutes later, one of the lines popped out of the downrigger and the pole began bucking. "Fish on!" yelled the captain.

"Take him," I said to Thunderfoot, but he just looked at the bucking rod and shook his head no. "You take the first one."

There wasn't time to argue, so I grabbed the rod and began playing the fish, which was about three hundred feet behind the boat. The rod doubled over and the fish fought like a whale. In its first run, I thought it would pull the rod out of my hands or me overboard, but I managed to gain line slowly but surely and in five or six minutes we could see the fish shining like a silver-blue streak in the water behind the boat. My friend grabbed the long handled net and when I brought the fish to the surface, he skillfully slid the net under it and lifted it into the boat.

"Whew, that's a beauty," Thunderfoot said, admiring the nice salmon.

"It should be yours," I said. "Why didn't you take the rod?"

"I guess I was just kind of wanting to see how it was done first. You know, these things are pretty big and I thought they might pull me overboard, and the water's too deep for me."

"They're strong, but not that strong. You take the next one. You'll be fine."

It didn't take long for the next fish to hit, and this time Thunderfoot grabbed the rod and began fighting the fish as soon as "Fish on!" was yelled. He did a good job and after a good fight, he raised the fish to the net and it was in the boat.

"Whoa, that's the biggest fish I've ever caught," he said, admiring the salmon that would weigh close to twenty pounds. I grabbed the camera and took his picture with the fish; then we heard another "Fish on!" It was Travis' turn.

The next three hours were almost non-stop action. We would barely have one fish landed and another would be on. At one time, we had two fish hooked at once but, with all the confusion, lost both of them.

The boys were having a great time and were consuming the entire lunch, bit-by-bit, between their turns on the rods. As the sun got higher, the wind began to pick up, and by the time we were getting close to our limit, it was getting pretty hard to stand in the boat without holding onto something.

The lake was getting rough, so our captain suggested that we begin to work our way back to the harbor. We made a wide turn and began trolling back into the big rolling waves. Up we went, down we went, up we went, down we went.

Thunderfoot and Travis were sitting on the bench at the side of the boat and had suddenly become quiet. They were both holding onto the railing and had a definite pale look to their faces.

"Are you guys sick?" I asked.

"No, we're fine," Thunderfoot said. "I think we ate too much lunch, and maybe we've got a little upset stomach."

As he said that, Travis bolted to his feet and hung his head over the side and "prayed to the lake god." When Thunderfoot saw his pal hanging over the side, he suddenly turned green and joined him. I walked over and held onto both of the boys' belts to keep them from taking a swim. After a short while, they both stood up, shakily.

"You didn't bring a gun along, did you?" Thunderfoot asked.

"No, why?"

"I thought if you did, you could just shoot me and put me out of this misery," he said, as he leaned over the railing and said another prayer to the lake god. Travis followed him.

The boys "prayed" a couple of more times each, and then were done for. They both went down into the cabin and sprawled out on the bunk. The rest of us, who hadn't consumed enough food to feed a gang of lumberjacks, were feeling fine.

We worked our way back to the harbor and then to the slip. When we got there, we loaded the fish into our coolers and got the boys from their deathbeds. We all thanked the captain for a great fishing trip, and took off for home.

The boys were still kind of groggy, but as they got their land legs again, they began to come around.

"Holy cow, that was fun. Well, all except the sick part," Thunderfoot said.

"It's a lot different than what we usually fish for, isn't it?" I said. "No kidding, and the lakes we fish don't get so bumpy either. By the way, when are we gonna stop for something to eat?"

"As sick as you two were, I didn't think you'd want to eat anything."

"Obviously you didn't notice that our donuts, breakfast and lunch are floating in the lake. We're faminished."

Of course, how silly of me.

Thanks, Thunderfoot.

Just Like a Cannon Ball

"Go and look in the hunting closet," I said to Thunderfoot. He was in need of some old shoes to use for helping me with some roof repair. His feet were as big as mine, so I thought he should use some old castoffs instead of getting tar all over his good shoes.

"Jeez, there's a lot of junk in here," he said. "I thought we cleaned this out a while ago."

"About three years ago," I replied.

"Whoa, what's this? You got a bowling ball? I didn't know you could bowl."

"I can't; that's why it's in the closet," I said.

He came into the living room carrying my bowling bag and sat down and opened it and took the ball and shoes out. "Hey, this is cool. Why don't you bowl anymore?"

"Remember golf?" I said. "I was the same with bowling. At first I wasn't any good at it, then I got fair and then got pretty good. Then, I couldn't get any better than I was and started getting worse again. Rather than take all that frustration, I quit bowling. I should have thrown that ball in the river and forgot about it."

"No way, this is cool, and I like these white shoes, too. Quite snappy," he said, grinning from ear to ear. "Let's go try it out."

"No way, you remember me throwing a golf club into a corn field? I don't think I want to take the chance of throwing that bowling ball through the wall of the bowling alley when I do poorly."

"Oh, come on, let's go tonight. We can take Scott along; he's a real bad bowler so you won't be worst," he said, speaking of his buddy Scott who often went along with us.

"Oh, so Scott is worst, and does that mean that you're a good bowler?"

"Well, of course, I hate to brag, but I have been known to throw a few strikes," he said as he puffed up his chest and rolled an imaginary ball through the living room.

"OK, smart guy, we'll see. Call Scott and tell him we'll pick him up at seven."

He was grinning like Sylvester the cat after he had popped Tweety into his mouth as he called Scott.

We got the roof tarred and had some lunch and then I took a little nap so I'd be ready to show these two kids how to bowl. We picked up Scott and drove to the bowling alley, and the boys rented shoes. But I, the old pro, had my own. We went down to the alley and changed shoes and then the boys picked out a house ball while I got out my ball and polished it up. I felt pretty smug with a couple of rookies like these two, and didn't think I would have any trouble beating them.

"Can we take a practice roll first?" Scott asked.

"Sure, go ahead," I said.

Scott stepped up, put his toe on a dot on the floor, raised his ball to eye level, concentrated for a second, took five practiced steps and rolled the ball down the lane, right into the pocket and smashed the pins. "Strike!" he shouted.

He turned around and walked back and sat down. "Go ahead," he said to Thunderfoot.

Thunderfoot stepped up, put his toe on the next dot over, raised the ball, took his five steps, and rolled another perfect strike, the twin to Scott's. "Steeeeerike," he said, grinning like mad.

"Your turn," he said to me as he walked by.

Suddenly, my haughty air was gone. I was pretty stunned by the form and ability of these two kids. "Where did you learn that?"

"Learn what?"

"How to bowl like that."

"Physical Ed class, they teach us the way to do it and we just do it," Thunderfoot said matter-of-factly.

Oh, boy, I was in trouble. I picked up my ball and put my toe on my spot and sized up the pins. Being left handed, I had a natural curve, so I had to throw the ball real close to the left gutter to keep it from going too far to the right and missing the pocket. I took a deep breath and started my steps.

One, two, three, four, and Bang. My right foot slid out from under me at the foul line just as I let the ball go. I landed on the floor on my butt, with my legs sticking over the line, and the ball bounced down the gutter and into the back of the lane. BZZZZZZZZZZZZ went the foul buzzer.

I got to my feet as quickly as I could so the whole bowling alley wouldn't see me laying on my back and turned to go back to the seats. Thunderfoot and Scott were doubled over with laughter, tears running down their cheeks. As I approached the seats, they both got up and scurried out of the way.

"Maybe, you better, he he he, check your shoes, he he, they seem to be a bit slick," Thunderfoot managed to say. Scott was speechless, laughing too hard to talk.

My butt hurt but my pride was much more highly damaged, but I tried to put on a good game face. "Well, at least I got that over with so now we can bowl," I said.

"Don't you want another practice?" Thunderfoot asked before falling over with laughter again.

"Just bowl!"

Well, after the first disastrous throw, I did quite a bit better. I threw a couple strikes and picked up a few spares. The boys were a little cooler, too, both bowling pretty well but not running away from me. By the time we got to the eighth frame, Thunderfoot was leading Scott by eleven pins and me by eighteen. He threw a strike in the eighth and so did Scott, so I had the pressure on me. I took extra long to get ready and as I was thinking about my shot, I could hear Thunderfoot whispering in the background. "Don't choke."

I took my steps and threw a perfect ball and got a strike. As I turned around, I gave him a "did you see that" look. He was impressed by the look on his face.

In the ninth frame, Thunderfoot had a bad ball and left himself with a spare. He took careful aim and picked it up. Then Scott threw a split and missed picking it up, so I had a chance to catch up a bit. I got as serious as I had ever been about a non-fishing event and threw another strike. As I got back to the boys, sitting on the bench, I raised my hand for a high five, but they weren't in the mood apparently.

Frame ten, Thunderfoot stepped up and threw a bullet that turned into a smashing strike. His second ball picked up only eight pins, and then he picked up the other two. Scott split again and was done. If I struck out, I could win, but I had to strike out. The first ball went into the pocket like it had radar and made a perfect strike. Thunderfoot was noticeably shaken. "Don't choke," he whispered. I ignored him.

My second ball was a twin to the first, and all the pins flew like leaves in a fall windstorm, except for the ten pin which stood there and teetered back and forth. "Fall down," I shouted, and the pin tipped over.

Now Thunderfoot was really worried. His lead had vanished, and if this ball struck, I would beat him. In fact, I only needed eight to tie and nine to win.

"You better check your shoes again," he said. "I'd hate to see you fall on such a crucial shot."

I ignored him. I got ready for my shot and took a deep breath.

"The shoes are fine," I thought to myself "Don't worry about the shoes."

I started my steps, and as my fifth step came in contact with the lane, my shoe slipped out from under me. My ball went down the alley much too far to the right and as my butt hit the alley, the ball hit the ten pin.

BZZZZZZZZZZZ went the foul buzzer.

I had done the splits when I threw the ball and as I got up, I could feel a draft and reached around to feel the seam in my pants. It was split from the belt loop to the bottom of the zipper. My plaid boxers were now in view of everyone in the alley.

I would have done anything rather than turn around and see the whole place snickering and laughing, but there was no place to go but back toward Thunderfoot and Scott, who by now were both laying on the floor clutching their stomachs.

I sat down to cover up my exposed backside and began to take off my shoes.

"What, don't you want to play another game?" Thunderfoot cackled.

"This is quite enough for one night," I said, as I packed my shoes and ball into the bag. "If you guys are riding with me, you better get your shoes changed. I have a stop to make on the way home, and I want to get there quickly."

They changed their shoes and we got into the truck and headed out.

As we got close to home, we started across the bridge that crosses the Wisconsin River on the way into town. I stopped the truck in the middle of the bridge, put on the flashers, and got out, taking my bowling bag with me. I walked up to the railing of the bridge and zipped open the bag, took the ball out, extended my arm out over the river and dropped it. Kersploosh!

Then I picked up the shoes and bag and dropped them over the rail, too. I got back into the truck. The boys were dumbstruck.

They sat there looking at me like I was insane. "Go ahead, say it, and no, I'm not crazy. I just don't want to bowl ever again, and without that miserable ball and shoes, I won't be tempted to do it again."

They never said a word. We finished driving home and dropped Scott off at his house. He thanked me for a nice time and walked slowly to the house, probably thinking that I had finally lost my mind.

When we got to my house, Thunderfoot got out and stopped.

"Are you mad at me."

"No, not a bit."

"Well, I don't want us not to be pals," he said.

I put my arm around his shoulder and gave him a hug. "That's not gonna happen over some silly game. Don't worry about it. It's water under the bridge, so to speak."

He grinned at that. "More like bowling ball under the bridge." At least it wasn't cluttering up the closet anymore.

Thanks, Thunderfoot.

Close Quarters Camping

The summer was almost over, and Thunderfoot and I had decided to go on a camping and fishing trip over the Labor Day weekend. I called ahead to a campground and made a reservation for a campsite and we were in the backyard, getting things ready.

"First, we've got to dean up the pickup," I said.

Thunderfoot was busy unrolling the hose, and I went to the house for a bucket of soapy water so we could wash all the dust and dirt from the box of the pickup. I had an old topper shell, and we were going to put it on the pickup box and use it for a place to sleep. A double mattress fit just perfect in the box, and this would eliminate the need for a tent and all the extra work that was involved in setting it up and then having to sleep on the ground.

"This will work great and give us more time to fish instead of working at setting up a camp," I said.

Thunderfoot dove right in and soon we had the truck sparkling clean. We waited for it to dry out and then put the topper shell on and damped it down. We took the mattress off the bed from Thunderfoot's room, which used to be my spare bedroom and outfitted it with some sheets and blankets and pillows.

"Wow, that's cool," Thunderfoot said as we finished up the bedroom in the back of the truck.

We packed a cooler with some food and pop and loaded up a few pots and pans for cooking, some lawn chairs for lounging at the campsite and the dogs' dishes and some dog food. We had decided to take Katy and Kirby along, and they were frantic when they saw their dishes going into the back of the truck, knowing that they were going along. We finished loading and backed the pickup up to the boat and hooked it on, and we were ready to leave.

About an hour later, we pulled into the campground and I went to the office to find out where our campsite was. Thunderfoot hooked the dogs up to a couple leashes as required by the campground and took them for a short walk while he waited.

When I got back, we drove down the crooked road that roamed through the park to our site and looked it over. There was a picnic table and a fire pit and not much else at the site. We had everything else that we needed, so we just set our cooler and box of groceries on the table and went down to the boat landing to unload the boat. After I unhooked the straps from the boat and backed it down the ramp, Thunderfoot jumped in and started the motor and drove it off the trailer. I went back to the campsite and unhooked the trailer and left it parked there, while the dogs and I waited for Thunderfoot to pick us up. Our campsite was right on the water's edge, and in a couple minutes, he pulled up along the shore and I carried each dog through the shallow water and put them into the boat. Then I climbed in and we took off for an afternoon of fishing.

It was a glorious fall day and we had great luck fishing, catching many walleyes and some northerns and bass. The dogs lounged in the boat and barked at the other dogs in passing boats who had the nerve to be on 'their' lake, and all in all it was a great day. By late afternoon, Thunderfoot was getting "faminished" so we went in for something to eat. We pulled the boat up and tied it up to a tree, unloaded the dogs and started a fire in our fire pit. We had a little grate to put over the fire and soon our potatoes were sizzling and the beans were boiling. Thunderfoot was grilling two hot dogs on his weenie stick that he had cut from a nearby tree.

The dogs were waiting for their share, and we cooked and ate for quite a while to get everyone filled up.

"Give the dogs their dog food, too," I said, "and I'll make sure the boat is secure for the night."

When I got back, the pans and plates were all taken care of, and the two dogs were snoozing by the fire. It was getting dark by now, so we sat in our lawn chairs and talked and visited with some people who passed by.

About an hour later, Thunderfoot was rummaging around in the back of the truck. "What are you looking for?" I asked.

"My Jiffy Pop. There's nothing like fresh popcorn around a campfire," he said, emerging from the truck with two Jiffy Pops in his hand and a grin across his face.

He took the paper off the first one and held it in the fire. It didn't take long until the pan began sizzling, but he kept pulling it out of the fire because the wire handle was getting too hot to handle. "Jeez, this thing gets hot all the way up," he complained. Then he got an enlightened look on his face and took off his shoes and socks. He put a sock on each hand and used them as potholders. He turned to me and grinned at his own brilliance.

"You better hold that thing back a little, you'll burn it."

"I've done these a hundred times. The secret is to get them hot and then they pop better."

OK, who was I to argue. In a little while, the popcorn began popping and soon smoke began to billow out of the growing aluminum balloon on top. Thunderfoot pulled the popper out of the fire and shook it, trying to keep the corn from burning, but by the time things cooled down, most of the popcorn in the pan was a tan color and smelled pretty smoky.

"Ooch, this one got a bit hot," he said, handing it to me. "Here, this one is yours."

He ripped the paper cover off the second one and held it back away from the fire farther, and soon it began to pop and of course, it turned out beautifully.

He opened it and began eating the corn as I picked through the burnt hulls in mine.

"Sorry, I got yours a bit hot. Too bad I didn't bring another one along."

I tossed my cremated corn into the fire and took a handful of his. He started to protest but thought better of it.

We sat for a while and then decided it was time to go to bed.

I let the tailgate down and we lifted the dogs up into the back of the truck. Then we climbed up in and raised the tailgate. Then I lowered the door of the topper and there we were, a truck full of dogs and people. Thunderfoot and I were trying to get out of some of our clothes and to get under the blankets, and the dogs were trying to find a good place to curl up. We finally got everyone situated. Thunderfoot was on the right side of the bed, I was on the left, Katy was between him and me, and Kirby was curled up by our feet. It was a tight fit.

"This is a pretty cool camper," Thunderfoot said. "What do you think, Kate?" he said as he patted Katy on the back. Katy grunted her approval. "Well good night all," he said.

The campground was settling down for the night and most of the noise was dying down. I was almost asleep when I smelled the most awful smell. I raised my head just as Thunderfoot sat up in bed. "Holy cow, you stink."

"That wasn't me. Don't try to blame me for your smell," I said. "Whew, I can't breathe," he said, turning the crank on the louvered window on his side of the topper. "Open your window." I opened mine, too, and soon the breeze carried the malodorous smells out into the night.

Just as I was drifting off again, there came another blast of the same smell. "Come on, quit that," I said.

"Me? Me? Don't blame me. I didn't do that," he protested.

Just then Katy groaned in her sleep and let one go. "Oh, no, it's Katy," I said.

Another blast of dog essence filled the camper. "Holy cow, why is she doing that?" I said.

"Umm, maybe it's the beans," Thunderfoot answered.

"Beans, what beans?"

"Well, after supper, I gave the dogs the leftover beans. They liked them."

"Oh, great, pretty soon Kirby will start, too. We'll be gassed before the morning gets here."

Just then Kirby let one go.

Thunderfoot started cackling with laughter and soon I joined in.

The dogs looked at us like we had gone insane.

We settled down again and began to drift off to sleep but left the windows open, just in case.

About midnight, I woke up and had to go to the bathroom. I tried to go back to sleep, but there just wasn't any way I was going to be able to hold it until morning, so I decided to get up. Of course, I was pinned down by Katy on one side of me and Kirby on the other, laying on top of my blanket. I managed to move them, amid much protesting and yawning, and made my way to the back of the truck.

The latch on the tailgate had been broken earlier in the summer when Thunderfoot dropped an anchor on the metal handle, so it wasn't easy to open it, especially from the inside. I raised the topper door and decided to crawl over the tailgate. I straddled the tailgate and swung one leg over. Just as it got on the other side of the gate, the back of my thigh muscle cramped up.

"Ooohf," I said, trying to get my leg straightened out, and in doing so, my other leg cramped up, too. "Arrrrgh, oh, uh, ahhhh!"

Here I was, one leg on each side of the truck tailgate, and each had a cramp in the back of the thigh. I wallowed around like one of those big sea lions crawling up onto a rock and managed to fallout of the truck onto my back. The grass was all wet with dew, and I stretched my legs as best I could and finally got the cramps to loosen up. I was panting like I had just run a marathon and all wet from rolling around in the grass when I heard a chuckle.

I looked up and there was Thunderfoot resting his chin on the tailgate with Katy on his right and Kirby on his left. All three were watching me like I was some circus act.

"Uh, what exactly are you doing out there at this time of night?" he said, grinning from ear to ear.

"I had to go to the bathroom and got a cramp," I answered.

"I thought we were having an earthquake," he said. "Do you need some help?"

"No thanks, I'm all right now. Go back to bed."

I walked over to the toilets and got my business done and then returned to the truck. I carefully climbed back in and worked my way through the dogs who had taken over my bed while I was absent. I got snuggled down again when I heard a distinct noise coming from Thunderfoot's side of the camper.

"I heard that. Whew, now I smell that. You're rotten," I said.

I could feel the truck shaking from his laughter. "Katy, shame!" he chuckled.

Katy, indeed.

Thanks, Thunderfoot.

No Fool Like an Old Fool

Thunderfoot was trotting across the backyard as I put my .22 rifle in the back of the truck. We had made plans to do a little squirrel hunting that afternoon, and he had just called to see if I was ready. To be honest, I was sitting in my recliner having a nap when he called, but it didn't take me long to get my gear out and get ready, and I was waiting as he put his gun into the back of the truck.

"Let's be off then," he said, grinning at me. "OK, boss, where do you want to go?"

He thought a while and then suggested a farm that we hadn't hunted yet this season, so off we went. When we got to the farm, I drove past the house to an old logging road that was about a half mile farther down the way. Thunderfoot got out and took his gun from the back of the pickup.

"What are you doing with that shotgun? I thought we were after squirrels," I asked.

"Just in case I see a grouse, I want to be ready. Besides, I'm such a good shot, I can put nary a BB in anything but the squirrel's head." I didn't want to argue, so I told him I'd go back and park at the farm, then take the trail down the valley and meet him up on the ridge somewhere. That was fine with him and as I pulled out, he was sauntering down the logging road towards the woods.

I watched him go and had to remember back to our first squirrel hunting trip, many seasons earlier when he managed to step on every stick, rock and leaf on the road, earning him his nickname of Thunderfoot. Now, he walked along confidently, silently watching ahead and looking for movement that would give away the position of some unsuspecting squirrel. He had come a long way since that first trip.

I drove back up to the farm, crossed the fence and followed a well worn deer trail down into the valley. At the bottom, there was a nice open woods where several wild apple trees stood, and often you could find a free snack of an apple or two that the deer weren't able to reach. This time the majority of the apples had already been harvested by the deer. Tracks and deer pellets were everywhere.

I continued on down the valley, and the path crossed a dry creek bed. I carefully worked my way down the steep side of the ditch and stopped in the bottom to look at the smooth washed stones that littered it. I wondered how often water actually ran down that ditch. As I was standing there thinking about it, I looked up to see a ten point buck walking down the trail from the other side of the ditch, right at me. He had his head down and was sniffing the ground as he got to the edge of the ditch. He looked up and there I was, standing less than six feet away. I was looking up at him, my head being about level with his knees.

He stopped and stared at me, not knowing what this thing was that was standing in his path. My heart was beating so fast I was sure he could hear it, and I was holding my breath, so as not to let him see me move. It seemed like an eternity as he stood there, watching me for movement. Then, he raised his right foot about a foot up in the air and stamped it hard on the ground. I kept completely still. He raised his foot and stamped again. Nothing. He looked at me for another minute and then turned his head to the left and took a step that way. Just as soon as his left foot touched the ground, he turned real quickly to look back at me. I stood stone still. Then he took another couple steps and turned again, trying to catch me moving, but I was onto his game and kept still as a statue. Finally, he gave up the game and walked off through the woods.

I let out a breath and found that my knees were shaking like I had just run a marathon. That was the closest I had ever been to a live buck, and it was a pretty awesome experience. I continued on down the path and worked my way up on the hillside where I found a nice place to sit, and sat down for a rest and to watch for squirrels.

Now, if the truth be known, I really hoped I wouldn't see any squirrels. Not that I had anything against hunting them, I just liked it better when Thunderfoot did the shooting. After all, I fed the little critters at home in my bird feeders, so I wasn't too excited about finding any.

As I sat there, I could hear a squirrel barking up on the hill above me.

He barked almost constantly, and I listened for quite a while before I decided to try to sneak up on him. I wasn't sure if I would shoot him or not, but it was good practice to see if I could get close enough, without being seen or heard.

I worked my way slowly up the hill and toward the barking squirrel.

He was having a good time, making lots of noise, so it was easy to tune in to the area where he was. As I got closer, I expected to see his tail jumping up and down as it usually does when a squirrel barks. The barking not only gives their position away, but the tail action usually pinpoints them.

The barking was plenty loud and seemed to be just ahead, but I couldn't see the squirrel. I figured he must be on the other side of the tree, so I snuck up close and began to look real hard. I leaned back against a big oak tree and looked up into the trees around me, looking for the now silent squirrel when suddenly there was an explosion in the tree above my head! Leaves, branches and bark, came raining down on me. Startled, I jumped away from the tree and stepped backward, and fell over a pile of brush onto my butt. I was laying there looking up into the tree, trying to figure out what had happened when I heard the snickering and sobbing coming from my left.

I couldn't see him, but Thunderfoot was over there someplace, and I could hear him laughing and choking.

"He he, uuu, he he, cuu, mmmfff, he he."

"You little snot, where are you?" I said, as I got to my feet. "Ohohohoh, he he, jeez, whoooo, he he."

I walked over and there he laid on his back in the leaves, tears running down his face, laughing his fool head off. He couldn't talk but held up a little wood tube with a rubber bulb on the end. A squirrel call!

"Oh, you little devil. You almost gave me a heart attack," I said, now grinning at my own foolishness.

"Oh, man, that was so funny, he he he, you were looking up at the trees and almost walked right up to me." More fits of laughter.

He had let me get right next to him and then shot his shotgun into the tree above my head. I was completely fooled by his squirrel call and walked in like a rat to a cheese baited trap.

We sat there a while and he finally calmed down enough to show me the call. It sounded pretty good, and after I inspected it, I put it in my pocket.

"Hey, give that back."

"I will, when we get home," I said. "I just got stared in the face by a huge buck and almost scared to death by a little brat, and I don't think my old heart will stand any more pranks. So I'll keep it until we're safely out of the woods."

"OK, my stomach hurts too bad from laughing to do any more stuff to you anyway."

Good, I had enough fun for one day already.

Thanks, Thunderfoot.

Not the Way to Start the Day

When we built our first duck blind several years ago, it was standing in the cattails at the edge of the pond. We had been able to walk right up to it and climb a little set of steps and we were ready to hunt.

Over the years, the beaver who shared the pond with us had built a dam at the lower end. The pond had grown by almost a third. Now, our duck blind was about twenty-five feet from the hard ground and we had to wade through mud and water to get to it.

"You know what we should do," said Thunderfoot, "is build a bridge to the blind, so we don't have to get wet when we go out."

It sounded like a good idea so we began to scrounge around for some material to build the bridge that wouldn't cost us, or rather me, a lot of money. We happened to be driving past the hardware store, when Thunderfoot yelled for me to stop. "Look there, those pallets. Do you suppose they'd give us some of them?" he said, pointing to a huge stack of used pallets that the store had out back.

"Let's go see," I said, and we went inside to ask. The storeowner was happy to let us have all we wanted, so we loaded up the pickup with as many as we needed and went home to do some preliminary work on the bridge project.

We got the chainsaw out and cut each of the pallets in half, making them just about two feet wide and about four feet long. Then we removed some boards from one end of each pallet, so the one before it would slide inside the end of the second one, and the two could be nailed together, one after another after another. We then got some wooden posts and a few two by fours to make the base. Our bridge was ready to install.

"Cool, we got most of the work done already," Thunderfoot said as we drove though the woods to the river bottoms. We parked the truck in our parking spot on the high bank.

"Now, if we only had all of this material out there in the marsh, we'd be in good shape," I said, looking at the hundred yards or so that we had to haul all the material.

"Oh, it won't take long," said Thunderfoot, as he hoisted a bridge section out of the truck and took off for the swamp. I followed with another and we made about six more trips each before we had all the lumber at the edge of the pond.

"Whew, that's it for me," I said, panting. "We'll come back tomorrow and do the building. I'm pooped."

Thunderfoot didn't argue, as he too was tired out from all the work. The next morning he was waiting for me in the kitchen when I got up. "Thought we should get an early start, right after some eggs and bacon?" he said, nodding his head up and down.

"Don't you have eggs and bacon and a frying pan at home?"

"Yeah, but you make them so much better than I do."

Big grin.

I made us some breakfast and then off we went to the swamp. We carried a saw and a bag of nails and a couple of hammers with us and began constructing the bridge. Actually it went together much faster than I had anticipated, and in a couple hours, we were done.

Our bridge snaked its way through the cattails from dry ground right up to the blind. We had attached a full sized pallet to the side of the blind by the door, for a kind of porch, and from that we could just walk on a dry bridge back to the hard ground. It was really nice and would make it easy to get into and out of the blind without getting wet and muddy. Plus, we could sneak into the blind quietly and not disturb any ducks that might be on the pond when we got there.

"A masterpiece of engineering," Thunderfoot exclaimed proudly as he looked over our creation. I had to agree and couldn't wait to try it out the following weekend.

The weather turned decidedly colder that week and on Saturday morning, there was a good coating of frost on the windshield as we started up the truck for the trip to the marsh. Thunderfoot scraped the windshield and as soon as we could see through it, we left for our blind with Katy, my golden retriever, sitting between us on the seat. We gathered up our gear and walked out across the marsh to the pond.

As we got to the bridge, I stepped up on it and it was covered with frost. My foot slid off into the water. "Wow, this thing is slippery, be careful," I said, as I stepped back on and slid my way out toward the blind. Thunderfoot came along behind me, walking carefully and Katy followed him.

We slipped and slid our way to the blind and when we got to the little porch, I unhooked the door to the blind and stepped to the side to let him and Katy into the blind first. He preferred the right side of the blind, so it was easier if he got in before me. As I took the step to the side, my foot slid off the edge of the porch, and in trying to recover my balance, lover did it and lost my footing on the other foot and in an instant, I was going over the side, into the water, head first!

I hit the ice-cold water and went straight down, about to my waist. My feet were up in the air and tangled in some button ball brush that grew next to the blind. I began to thrash around like a wildebeest caught in the jaws of one of those huge Nile crocodiles. I was running out of air and was trying to get my head above water. Finally I got my feet loose and flopped over on my back into the ice cold water. I tried to get up and out of the water as fast as I could, so I wouldn't soak through, but I'm just not the most graceful person and by the time I was able to climb back up onto the bridge, I was wet from head to toe.

I knelt there gasping for breath and dripping like a drowned rat for a while and then stood up. Thunderfoot looked dumbstruck. He stood there with his mouth hanging open with the most stupid look on his face. "I'll put out the decoys," he said as he climbed down the ladder into the canoe, which was parked in a little blind of its own. I nodded OK and climbed up onto the porch and stumbled into the blind and sat down.

My gun had gone into the water with me, so I opened the chamber and looked down the barrel to see if it was full of mud or grass. It was OK, so I loaded it and stood it against the front railing of the blind. Then I took off my hat and wrung the water out of it and turned down my hip boots and emptied them out. I took off my jacket and wrung as much water out of it as I could, just as Thunderfoot came back from putting the decoys out on the water.

He climbed back into the blind and edged past me to his side and sat down. He looked out over the pond and to the sky and didn't look my way at all.

There was complete silence, not a bird, not a duck, not a sound.

I began to shiver, and the blind began to shake. Thunderfoot was still looking toward the end of the pond, away from me.

I stared at him; he didn't look my way. Katy was sitting looking out the little dog hole in the front of the blind, and she didn't look at me either.

"Go ahead," I said.

"What?" he said, still looking away.

"Go ahead and laugh. I know it's killing you."

He turned and the tears were running down his face, and he began to laugh and laugh and laugh. "Holy cow, that was the funniest thing I've ever seen you do. Jeez, your feet were flying around, it looked like somebody had killed a moose or something." Tears were running down his face, and he was having a wonderful time telling me how stupid I looked upside down in the water. "I thought you were gonna knock the whole bridge down."

I let him have his fun for a few minutes and actually joined in.

I could just about imagine how it must have looked with me standing upside down in the mud.

"I'm sorry, did you get hurt any?" he finally said, wiping the tears from his face.

I showed him my right hand, where I had torn the skin off the palm when I made an attempt to grab the blind. "Just tore the bark off my hand. I think I'll live."

We sat there for a while and I began to shiver. The cold was beginning to go deep into my body.

"You're froze, aren't you?"

"Yeah, I'm getting pretty cold."

"Let's go home, and get you dry."

I didn't argue, and stiffly got to my feet and shuffled off the bridge while he picked up the decoys and closed up the blind.

We walked back to the truck and by the time I got there, I was feeling a little better, being warmed up by the walk.

As I got to the side of the truck, I could see my reflection in the window. My face was almost black with mud, and my hair was standing up straight on top and out on the sides, stiff with dried mud. "Jeez, I look like the Creature from the Black Lagoon," I said.

Thunderfoot cracked up again.

"You know, it might be better if you rode in the back of the truck and let me drive. You'll have mud allover the truck," he said, trying to suppress a grin.

I agreed that he was right and climbed into the box of the pickup for an undignified ride home.

"And, you know what? When we get home, I think we should get some more boards and put a handrail on that bridge."

I could hear him chuckling as we drove off.

Thanks, Thunderfoot.

Patience, My Boy, Patience

Thunderfoot and I had been scouting for our deer stands the previous weekend and had decided to hunt the woods on the high bank above our duck hunting marsh. Nearly every time we drove down the dirt road to the marsh, we had seen deer in one of the two fields that bordered the road, so we felt pretty confident that we would see some during deer season. At least, I felt confident. Thunderfoot wasn't convinced that we would see anything, but we enjoyed hunting in the area so he went along with the idea.

The woods that we were hunting were an impenetrable jungle of berry briars, prickly ash and scrub oak. It was a great place for deer to hide, and a terrible place for a hunter to walk. That's why I chose to sit in the edge of the fields that bordered the woods. We found two deer trails the came from the woods into the field on the west side of the lane and placed Thunderfoot's stand in between them, right at the fence. I went on the other side of the lane and decided on a stand under a huge pine tree in the corner of the field. It afforded a good view of the land, and was only about a hundred yards from where I would park the pickup, which was an added bonus.

"If you sit and stay put, I guarantee you'll see a deer," I told Thunderfoot.

"Yeah, but will it be during this season, or do I have to wait many years?"

My young friend wasn't the patient type. "Just be patient, you'll see," I said. "Years ago, I decided to sit in the same spot until I got a deer, and I did it. It took six days, but he came along finally. Then, after that, for the next ten years, I got a buck in the same spot every year. It's just a matter of waiting. One will come along, if you wait long enough."

I could tell he wasn't convinced, but he agreed to give it a try. On Friday before the season opened, I got all our gear out and ready. When he came over after school he couldn't believe his eyes. "What's all this stuff? We going to the moon?"

"This is all essential stuff. If you're comfortable, you'll sit longer," I said. He began sorting through the two piles of gear. I had a folding lawn chair for each of us, and a duffel bag full of food and other essential things. He began unloading the duffel bag. "The food I can understand," he said, "but what's all this other stuff?"

"The hand warmers, for your hands, foot warmers, same but for your feet, rope, obvious, knife, same, shells, obvious, paperback book, something to pass the time, and toilet paper, again, obvious. Plus the salted in the shell peanuts, to pass time."

"Pass time?"

"Yeah, they give you something to do to keep you alert."

He just shook his head. "Do we really need all this stuff?"

"Leave it if you don't want it. You only have to walk a couple hundred yards across a flat field, and it'll make you more comfortable."

That night, Thunderfoot spent the night and we made sandwiches for the next day and then turned in. The alarm went off at 5 a.m., and we soon were driving down the road to the woods. It was still dark as midnight, but I wanted us to be on our stands and ready when it got light, so we walked down the lane until we came to the spot where we went different directions and as we parted to go to our stands, I whispered, "Good luck."

"You, too."

I crawled under my big pine tree and set up my chair and put my gear in strategic places on the ground around me. That way I was ready for the day and wouldn't have to do a lot of moving around for whatever I might need. As the daylight increased, I could just begin to make out Thunderfoot's orange jacket over on the other side of the field across the lane. He was right where he was supposed to be.

Dawn turned to day and morning turned to midday. We heard some shots in the area, but not a deer showed itself in either of our fields. I settled back and "rested my eyes" for a couple minutes and when I opened them, I just got a glimpse of a deer between two trees on the other side of the field I was watching. That was it, the only deer action we had for the day.

At closing time, Thunderfoot came walking across his field toward the truck. "Boy, this is a good spot. I saw lots of squirrels, but, oh, that's right we're DEER hunting."

"I never said we'd see one the first day," I said. "There's always tomorrow."

He just rolled his eyes and crawled into the truck.

The next morning we got up and began getting ready to leave.

"We're gonna do the same thing again?" he asked.

"Be patient, you'll see a deer." I could tell his patience was getting pretty thin.

We deployed as we did the previous day and the morning dawned and the sun rose and warmed things up and it was a gorgeous day. At about eleven o'clock, the clouds began to roll in and I saw Thunderfoot moving around and gathering up his gear and soon he was at my stand. He unfolded his chair and sat down next to me. "Did you miss me?" I said.

"No, you said if it started raining, I should come over here and we'd go home."

"Is it raining?" I asked.

"Yeah, it is out there," he said, pointing to the field, "but not under this big tree." I hadn't noticed the rain because of the big pine tree I was sitting under.

"Fine, you watch, I'll read for a while," I said, and opened my book. "Don't you think we'd see more deer if we took a little walk through the woods?"

"Nope, you remember what this woods is like? Prickly ash and berry briars are not my idea of a stroll through the woods."

"Do you think there's a deer within two miles of us right now?"

"Yup."

"Do you think there's a deer within a mile?"

"Yup."

"A half mile?"

"Why don't you shut up and let me read. Be patient, there could be a deer laying right over there in that little patch of brush right now. Just watch and suddenly there'll be a deer, I guarantee it."

"Yeah, but when? Today, next year?"

"If we sit here long enough, there'll be one."

"But ..."

"Shut up, and watch."

I began reading and looked up every couple of minutes to see if anything was happening. Thunderfoot had slid back in his chair, watching, but with little enthusiasm.

I had just turned the page when I heard him say, "Holy cow, there's some deer!"

I looked up and there, about twenty yards from us, was a doe, followed by a nice buck, trotting right toward us. "Shoot him!" I whispered. Thunderfoot raised his gun and aimed. "Shoot him!" I dropped my book and reached for my gun. When I did that, the deer saw me move and began trotting across the corner of the field, away from us.

"Shoot him!" I said, getting my gun up and aiming at the deer.

Thunderfoot was still aiming, so I took a quick aim and shot. The deer began running then, and Thunderfoot ran out into the field after him. "Get back! Get out of the way!" I yelled, as Thunderfoot ran between me and the deer. "Shoot him!"

Finally, he shot, and the deer fell down. "You got him!" I shouted, but the deer got up and ran off into the brush between the fields. Soon he appeared in the field that Thunderfoot had been watching and ran across the end of it and disappeared into the woods on the deer trail that Thunderfoot would have been sitting by, had he been patient and stayed on his stand.

"Oh, no, he got away!" he said.

"Let's see if we can find blood. I think you hit him."

We walked to the field and searched and searched but found no blood. The field was full of mole burrows, and the best that we could figure was that the deer must have tripped in one of them and had just fallen down. We found where he had crossed the lane and found no blood, nor did we find any along the deer trail that he had escaped on.

"Well, he got away clean, at least," I said. "I'd have hated to wound him and let him get away."

Thunderfoot was still dumbstruck, not saying two words since the deer had run in front of us.

"You OK?" I asked.

"Jeez, they just popped up like ghosts. I can't believe it."

"I told you that's what would happen, didn't I?"

He nodded his head. He hated being wrong.

"What took you so long to shoot?"

"I was aiming and he kept moving and I don't know what I did. I guess I got too nervous."

"Why didn't you shoot again, when you were out in the field?"

"I forgot to eject my empty," he said, sheepishly.

I began to laugh. "Well, we really did a good job of that. One reading a book, with no gun in his hands, the other with buck fever. Any deer that crosses in front of us is pretty safe."

"Yeah, you and your book."

I looked at him, and he grinned. "Of course, you may remember that I wanted you to sit right over there, about twenty feet from where the deer went into the woods. Had you been patient, he would have run right up to you."

He just shook his head and sat down. "I'm gonna hold my gun in my lap from now on. Do you think they might come back by again?"

"I doubt it, but there could be another any minute."

"Yeah, yeah, I know, be patient, be patient."

He was learning.

Thanks, Thunderfoot.

Here Yogi

"You know, this is the last year that you can just go buy a bear hunting license. Next year you have to start applying for them with a lottery type drawing, so it might take a long time to get one," Thunderfoot said, as we drove down the road toward the river. "1 read about it in the paper the other day."

"So, why do I care? We're not bear hunters," I said.

"We could be," he said. "My uncle has a cabin up in the north and he has bears there all the time, and he said we could go up there and use his cabin if we wanted to, so it won't cost any money for a place to stay and we can hunt right from the cabin and don't even have to drive some place to hunt, and it's a real cool place."

"You've been rehearsing that little speech for a while haven't you?" I said.

"Well," he grinned, "yeah, but it's still a good idea, huh?"

"Bear hunting? You've seen bears, right, those big black things with lots of teeth? They're not like ducks and squirrels. They bite back."

"Yeah, but think how exciting it would be to get one. We could bring it back and drive around town and let everyone see it. Way cool," he said nodding his head up and down.

"I'm not sure I want to shoot a bear; they never did anything to me," I said.

"Yeah, but this will probably be our only chance to ever go, and you wouldn't want me not to ever experience the glory of an autumn day in the north woods, hunting for bear."

He was sitting there with a miserable look on his face.

I just shook my head. "You poor, pitiful little thing."

He grinned; he knew he had me.

"When does the season open?" I asked.

"Next weekend, and I called Uncle Jim and nobody's gonna use the cabin and we can have it; in fact, I've already got the key," he said, digging in the pocket of his jeans and producing a key to the cabin.

"You were pretty sure I'd go," I said.

He just grinned; he knew I was easy.

The rest of the week we read up on bear hunting, watched some videos that we rented about bear hunting, and by Friday noon, we were loaded and on our way north. It was about a five-hour drive to the cabin, so we would probably get there after dark and not be able to scout, but we figured we could worry about that when we got there. On the way, we stopped at several sport shops to buy a bear license but were always told we had to get farther north because they didn't sell them. Finally we got to a shop that had the licenses and we both got one.

The terrain changed from steep hills and deep valleys to flat, low rising swells in the landscape. The north had been flattened by the last glacier and all of the hills had been ground down to little low rises that undulated along like the swells on a lake.

The last time we had come this way, we had seen a large bear lying alongside the road that had been hit by a car. As we drove past the place, Thunderfoot kept a sharp watch out just in case another one was in the area. "Could be a crossing," he said.

We got to the little town near the cabin and turned off on a county road that ran north toward our destination. The county road turned to a town road that was just gravel and not too wide, and then we came to the end of the dirt lane that ran to the cabin. "Just turn in here and we follow it for a while till we get to the cabin," Thunderfoot said, reading the directions on the slip of paper he was holding.

I turned down the dirt road and we drove for almost a mile and came to a fork in the road. "Which way?"

"Hmmm, the paper doesn't say anything about a place like this," he said.

We looked at the roads and they both looked about the same, so we flipped a coin and took the one to the right. Of course, it went about a quarter mile and ended at a cabin that looked as if it hadn't been occupied for many years. "Well, now we know which road to take," Thunderfoot said merrily.

We got turned around and backtracked to the fork. We took the left fork and went another mile or so and there was the cabin. It sat in the middle of a large clearing in the woods, was built of logs and was quite a nice place. It had a well cared for lawn and there was a shed next to it that housed a gas generator and a water pump and stored firewood for the huge stone fireplace. "Wow, your uncle has a nice place here," I said.

"Yeah, he has a guy who lives up here take care of it, so when he comes up he doesn't have to work all the while he's here."

We unloaded the truck and went into the shed to start the generator and soon had the cabin unlocked and the lights on and a fire going in the fireplace. It was furnished like most cabins, with a couple of couches that opened into beds, a kitchen table that served as a dining table and a place to play poker on a cool fall evening. There were two bedrooms, and each had a set of bunk beds in it, so with the couches opened, eight people could sleep comfortably there. We put our stuff in one of the bedrooms, unloaded our food into the refrigerator, and then sat in a couple of big comfortable chairs by the fireplace. I slid off my shoes and was toasting the bottom of my feet when Thunderfoot went over by the big picture window that looked out over the lawn and stopped by a light switch.

"Watch this," he said. "Uncle Jim said to turn this on after it gets dark, and we'll see some cool stuff"

He flipped the switch and a spotlight burst to life that was aimed at a shallow hole in the ground about a hundred feet from the cabin. Mineral salt had been dumped into it for years, and there were nine deer at the salt lick, digging and pawing and not paying any attention to the light. "They're used to it," Thunderfoot said, as we watched the deer. Most were does but there was one huge buck and a couple smaller ones. All seemed to be taking turns enjoying the salt and were oblivious of us watching them.

"We better get some supper and then get to bed if we're going to hunt in the morning," I said, and we began fixing some food. We hadn't planned anything fancy, and I opened a can of stew and put it in a pan to heat. We got out some bread and butter to go with it and soon we both were full and ready for bed.

Dawn was about six the next morning, so I set the alarm for five to give us time to get a little breakfast before we left. We got up, ate some eggs and toast and soon were walking across the lawn toward the woods. The wind had come up during the night and there was a distinct nip in the air. We followed a fire lane for a while and soon it intersected another.

"Why don't one of us stay on this lane and the other go down that one?" I said, not having the faintest idea of how to go about hunting bears in the north woods. "If you can find a good looking spot, sit for a while and I'll do the same. If you find any sign, like bear poop, that's probably a good thing."

"Do they always poop in the same place?" Thunderfoot asked, grinning.

"No, dummy, but it means there was one there and he might still be around. How do I know, you're the expert here."

We separated and walked off, each down our own fire lane and soon I was all alone in a forest that probably ran for a hundred miles in any direction, in a gale force wind, without the faintest idea of what I was doing, looking for a bear. What was I thinking?

A short way down the fire lane, I ran across a deer path that crossed the lane. I was looking at the tracks in it when I realized that I was looking at a bear track in the middle of it. There was another and another, and they were following the deer trail into the woods to my right. Hmm, maybe this wasn't going to be so hard after all. I followed the trail into the woods and I had only gone ten feet when I began to feel closed in. There was no open area to see what was ahead or to the side of you. The trees and brush were so dense that you could only see a foot or so in any direction around you. These woods weren't like the ones I was used to at home. There we had big trees and some underbrush, but the woods were open, so you could see for a long way. Here the trees were all medium size and real close together, and so dense that you could only see a few feet ahead of you. I followed the trail for what seemed like a long way, and suddenly came to an area that was fairly open, compared to the rest of the woods. Here I could see, maybe, twenty feet around me. The trail went on into the thick stuff again, so I decided that this was where I was going to make my stand. I moved off the trail and found a stump to sit on and sat down. If the bear was planning on going past on the deer trail today, I'd be waiting for him.

I sat there trying to hear any movement, but it was almost impossible because of the wind. The trees swayed and danced and leaves flew like yellow snowflakes. Many of the trees were aspens and birch, and their leaves were flying through the air like a yellow and brown snowstorm. If a bear came by, he was going to be right next to me before I had any indication that he was coming. I was not very comfortable with my situation, and was thinking of getting the heck out of there, when I heard a noise right behind me that sounded like a large animal crashing through the brush. The hair on the back of my neck stood straight up and I whirled around to meet the charge. All I could see were the trees and bushes swaying in the wind. No more sounds came but, suddenly, there was a crackling and breaking of brush from the other side of the clearing. "Oh, my God," I thought. "He's charging from the other side."

I spun around to meet the charge and, again, no more sounds came from that direction. "I must be losing my mind," I thought.

By now I was thoroughly spooked and decided that this was insane.

I really didn't want to shoot a bear anyway and wasn't going to sit here any longer and end up being a meal for an angry bear, so I crossed the clearing and followed the deer trail back to the fire lane. When I got to the open lane, I felt much safer and stopped to catch my breath. I looked down and saw a familiar foot print in the soft sand next to mine where I had been following the bear print. It was Thunderfoot's boot track, and it was following mine into the woods. The little fool had followed me into the woods and was sneaking around pretending to be a bear!

I was about to yell at him when I had a better idea. I took off running down the fire lane back towards the cabin. I ran into the cabin, picked up the duffle bags, still empty, and ran from the cabin and threw them into the back of the truck. Then I jumped in the truck and flew out of the driveway and down the lane spinning gravel and making a huge cloud of dust.

I drove till I was out of sight and then parked the truck and snuck back up the road toward the cabin. As I got near, I could see Thunderfoot pacing back and forth in the front yard, obviously thinking I had been so scared that I had left him behind. I snuck around the shed and got as close as I dared and then let out a loud ROAR!!!! He almost jumped out of his boots and spun around in mid air, with his gun pointed at me.

"Whoa, whoa, I surrender," I said, raising my hands above my head. He dropped the gun immediately and stared at me. "You, uuu, you, I thought you dirty bugger. I don't believe you did that."

I was laughing myself silly by now. "What, can't take your own medicine? I knew that was you in the woods. You sneaky little snot."

He began to grin. "Yeah, you knew, my foot. You were ready to pee yourself. You were jumping around like a scared chicken. How did you know it was me?"

"Your foot prints on the deer trail. Do you think I'm blind?" "Darn, never thought of that. What do you think of this bear hunting? Man, I got into those woods and couldn't see anything, so I came looking for you. Want to keep at it?"

I turned my thumb down.

"Me, too. You know, that stream over there is full of trout and I saw a monopoly game in the cabin."

"Good idea," I said. "Tell you what, you hike down the road and bring back the truck and I'll make us some lunch and then we'll just take the rest of the weekend and relax and let the bears alone."

"Sounds cool to me," he said and began walking toward the truck.

"Hey Yogi, hey Booboo, don't worry, you're safe," he yelled.

Thanks, Thunderfoot.

Yo Quero Taco Bell

Thunderfoot and I had been planning this trip for many weeks. We were in Escanaba, Michigan, on Little Bay de Noc, which was a part of the upper end of Lake Michigan. Several weeks earlier, we had watched a TV show that showed the host catching walleye after walleye on the bay, and we had decided it was worth the six-hour drive to give it a try.

We arrived on Friday afternoon, checked into our motel, and then went down to the waterfront to look over the lake.

"Wow, that's big," Thunderfoot said. "A little bigger than what we're used to fishing."

"No kidding," I said. "You can barely see the other side. You think we can find walleyes in all that water?"

He looked apprehensively at me, but grinned. "Why not? If those TV dudes can, why can't a couple of experts like us do it, too?"

I hoped he was right. We went back to town and decided to stop for something to eat before we headed back to our motel.

"Let's stop at the Taco Bell," he said, pointing to the restaurant on the left."

"No way. Tacos will keep me up all night. I want something that's not so spicy."

He grumbled and griped a while, but we settled on a mom and pop cafe. We had a good supper and then went back to the motel for a good night's sleep.

Next morning, we stopped at a bait shop and got a map of the bay and some advice, and soon we were motoring across the big water. Thunderfoot looked a bit uneasy as we got farther and farther from shore.

"Boy, I hope we don't get lost out here," he shouted over the noise of the motor.

"Don't worry," 1 said. "I set the boat landing as a way point on my GPS.

We just have to tell it to take us to number one and it will point the way, just like a video game."

He perked up at that bit of information. "No kiddin', it can do that?"

"Yup, you just push this button, and it remembers the latitude and longitude of the spot and stores it for you. Then when you want to go back there, it shows you the pathway from where you are, to the spot. We can lock in spots that we find fish, too. It's a cool gizmo."

Thunderfoot was fascinated and seemed to feel a little less apprehensive about being on such big water.

We checked out some reefs and sandbars on the map and soon found one that was full of walleyes. It didn't take long for us to catch several nice ones. "Let's lock this in on the GPS and go look for some other places," I said. "I hate to catch too many and have to quit so early."

Thunderfoot agreed and we took off down the lake for another spot on the map and some more walleyes. We kept it up all day and soon had about four really good spots locked into the machine.

"So, tomorrow we can just push number three and come back here?" he asked.

"Yup, tomorrow I'll show you how it works," I said.

We went in and cleaned our fish and went back to the motel and put them in the freezer, and then cleaned up for a trip to town and some supper.

"Hola, senor. Tengas un Taco?" he said as we approached Taco Bell.

"Excuse me?"

"I'm taking Spanish at school, you know. I asked you if you had a taco." He grinned.

"You're gonna pester me till I stop at Taco Bell, aren't you?"

"Si, senor," he said, grinning.

We turned into the Bell and went inside. As I looked over the menu, Thunderfoot got into line and began ordering in Spanish. "Want me to order for you, too?" he asked. "Yeah, go ahead. But don't get me anything too spicy." What a bad mistake that was.

He picked up the tray and I paid, as usual, and we went to a table and began to eat. The food was good, but way too spicy for an old guy. But I was too hungry to be sensible, and I ate my share of the tacos, refried beans and whatever else he had ordered. We hadn't even left the restaurant and I was already feeling the aftermath of the food.

"Oh, I'm gonna regret this," I said, finishing off my last taco.

We went back to the motel and watched TV for a while and then went to bed. I had hardly laid my head down when I felt the first wave of heartburn and had to get up for some Turns. That went on all night, up and down for Tums and Alka Seltzer. By morning, I was more tired than I had been the evening before and worn out from all my traveling between the bathroom and my bed.

Thunderfoot was smiling and real chipper, ready for a big greasy breakfast as I staggered from our room to the truck.

"Boy, you look like crap," he said cheerily.

"Thanks, and thanks for talking me into those tacos. They almost killed me during the night."

"What a weakling."

We had breakfast and took off for the water. We motored up the lake and stopped at our first waypoint and found our reef real easily. We began to catch fish right away.

"Wow, that thing works pretty darn good," Thunderfoot said as he reeled in a nice walleye.

We fished at the first place for a while and then continued along our path of waypoints and caught fish at each of them. As the day wore on, I could tell that I was going to have to pull into shore someplace for a bathroom break before long. The tacos had worked their way down to the lower part of my system and were going to be parting company with me soon.

"We're gonna have to go in pretty soon; I'm gonna have to visit the latrine," I said.

"What? You're surely kidding. Do you know how far that is?

We'll waste a whole hour going all the way in."

"Well, I'm gonna have to go and pretty soon, so get ready," I said. "What you gotta do? Can't you just do it over the side?"

"It's not that. I've got to sit to do this."

"Oh, no! Why didn't you do it before we left?"

"I did, and I did it all night, thanks to you and your tacos, but I have to go again and pretty darn soon, so you better reel up," I said, feeling a particularly bad cramp coming on.

"Oh, man, what a baby. Sit on the back of the boat and let her rip," he said.

Suddenly I had another cramp, and I knew he was going to get his wish. There was no way I was going to make it all the way to the shore.

"OK, you win. Get in the front and keep me pointed away from the other fishermen," I said. I squatted down and lowered my pants and carefully sat on the back edge of the boat, next to the motor.

Thunderfoot was sitting on the front seat, running the foot control electric motor and began turning the boat so the back end was facing toward a bunch of boats off on the other side of the submerged reef.

"Hey, quit that! Turn us back the other way," I said.

He began laughing and kept turning us so my bare backside was going to be shining in the direction of the other boats. "Hey, you little snot, turn us back the other way," I said, as I tried to pull my jacket down to cover my obvious asset, and in doing so, lost my grip on the motor. In less than a second, I went over backward into the lake. Now, it was bad enough to fall into Lake Michigan, into water that was about fifty-five degrees, but it was even worse with my pants around my ankles.

I did a somersault as I hit the water, and when I came to the surface, I grabbed the back edge of the boat. I couldn't see Thunderfoot sitting on the front seat, but could hear him laughing from the bottom of the boat. He was laying in the bottom, clutching his stomach and laughing crazily.

"I'm gonna drown you, I said."

"Oh, ho, ho, not if you can't get in the boat, you're not," he laughed.

"Come here and help me in."

"No way."

"Come on, this water is cold as heck. I won't do anything to you. Promise."

He came back and grabbed the back of my shirt and pulled as I gripped the motor and lifted myself up. As I cleared the water, he began howling again as my bare butt came up into view.

"If the other boats didn't see your butt when you fell in, they sure do now," he said, laughing and crying.

Right then I didn't care; I wanted to get out of that cold water and back into the boat. I finally made it in and flopped on the floor of the boat like a harpooned walrus. Thunderfoot scampered past me to the front seat and began to fish, like nothing had happened.

I crouched in the bottom of the boat and got my pants up and everything situated and then stood up. The people in the other boats all began applauding.

I felt pretty foolish, but what the heck. I took a graceful bow.

The sun was out and it didn't take me long to dry out, so we fished for several more hours before we loaded up for the trip home. As we were driving through town, we were coming up to the Taco Bell, which was just on the right ahead of us.

"Ahhh, senor " he began.

"What's the Spanish word for 'no way'?"

"Hmmm, we haven't learned that one yet."

"Well, I'll use English then... no way. Que Pasa?"

"Si, senor."

Gracias, Thunderfoot.

In the Heat of the Night

The thermometer outside read 96 degrees, and it was only ten 0' clock in the morning. We had been having a hot spell that was about five days old, and I was planning on taking it easy for the day and sitting in the air conditioning with a good book when the phone rang.

"Whatcha up to?" It was Thunderfoot.

"Staying cool. Have you been outside yet?"

"No kiddin', it's like the desert out there. Say, you wouldn't want to give me a ride to the appliance store later, would you?"

"What are you buying?"

"Well, Mom ordered a new air conditioner and they called and said it's in, but she's gone for the day, and I want to get it and cool off the house and surprise her when she gets home."

That sounded like a noble idea, so I got some shoes on and went out to the van to go pick him up. It was like a sauna in the van, but it cooled off fast as soon as I turned on the AC. The pickup didn't have air, so the van was much nicer to drive in the summertime. Thunderfoot was waiting and sprinted out to the van as I pulled up. "Whew, it's nice in here," he said.

We drove to the appliance store, which was just down the road in the next town. As we drove along, we passed a roadside fruit stand and there was a big pile of watermelons on a cart in front of it. "Yum, those look good," Thunderfoot said.

I had to admit that a nice slice of cold melon would be nice, so we made a U turn and went back to get one. Thunderfoot thumped and shook about a dozen melons and pronounced one "perfect" and picked it out of the pile. He was standing with it balanced on one hand on his shoulder while I paid for it. "Be careful with that thing," I said. "If you drop it and bust it, you bought it."

He looked at me with a mock worried look, and started back to the van. I talked with the melon salesman about the weather for a bit and then went back to get into the cool van, which was idling so the AC would keep it cooled off. Thunderfoot was sitting in the back seat. I opened the door, and there, sitting on the front seat, was the watermelon, strapped in with the seatbelt!

"Is that safe enough for you?" he said, chuckling from the back seat. "Oh, real funny," I said. "Put this back there and come up here."

I had to laugh even though he was being a smart butt.

We got back on the highway and soon were at the appliance store.

His mom had paid for the air conditioner so all we had to do was pick it up. I backed up to the delivery door, Thunderfoot put it in the back of the van and we turned around and headed for home.

When we got to his house, I asked him if he needed help unloading the AC and installing it. "Nope, I can do it just fine. You go put the melon in the fridge and I'll come over and sample some of it when I get done here."

That was OK with me, and I drove home, put the melon away and settled down for a nap in my recliner. A couple of hours later, I was awakened by the noise of the refrigerator door being shut. I looked into the kitchen and there was Thunderfoot with a huge knife, carving at the watermelon.

"Man, you were snoring up a storm," he said.

"Have some melon," I said.

Big grin. "Thanks, I think I will. Can I cut some for you?"

He cut me a slice, and we sat at the table and enjoyed the cold melon. His hair was all wet and his clothes looked damp, too. "Did you just shower or are you still sweating?"

"I'm sweating. It's still really hot in the house; the new air conditioner doesn't seem to work very well."

"Really? It sure looks big enough. Are you sure you installed it right?"

"What's to install? You plug it in and it's installed."

"Yeah, but did you seal it up real well around the window?"

A stupid look came across his face. "Window? What do you mean?" "You have to put it in the window and then seal up the space around it so hot air doesn't come back in."

He chomped down his melon and headed for the door. "I'll be back later."

I was curious about what made him leave so fast, so I put away the melon and dishes and walked over to his house. As I walked up to the door, I could see Thunderfoot measuring the window in the living room, and the air conditioner, sitting on a small table, in the middle of the room, running.

He looked up and saw me staring at the AC and shook his head.

He knew he was in for it.

"Uh, I know what to do. You go chill the melon," I snickered. "I'm so smart, you don't have to tell me anything."

"Oh, man, you can be so sarcastic sometimes," he said.

The house was as hot as an oven, so we unplugged the air conditioner and opened a window. Then we put the unit in the window opening and slid the little accordion-like things on the top and bottom out to fill the open space. We plugged it in and soon nice cool air was filling the room.

"Hmm, it seems to work pretty well now," I said.

He just looked at me. "OK, for once you're right, but once in a while you're bound to be right. It's just the law of averages."

Sure, sure, but it was sure nice for a change.

Thanks, Thunderfoot.

You Should Model For Calvin

"Let me use it. Please, please, please," Thunderfoot pleaded.

"It's the last one left, and I paid for them, so ..." I said.

"Oh, come on, that's my favorite bait in the whole world. I'll be careful with it, I promise. You can use it after I catch a couple on it, honest."

We were arguing about our last Mississippi Swamper. It was new bait that we had found earlier that summer that we had been having fantastic luck with. It was a soft, plastic bait that had a great wobbling action as it came through the water, and drove northerns and bass wild. I had bought a half dozen of them and this was the last one. The only problem with them was that since they were made of soft plastic, the teeth of a northern ripped them up and after a while, they fell apart. Also, we lost them more than regular baits, because we didn't use a steel leader with them. The action wasn't as good with a leader, and the teeth of a northern often cut our lines, so the life expectancy of a Swamper was kind of short.

I knew Thunderfoot would bug me all day if I didn't give him the bait, so I tossed it to him in the front of the boat. "Now be careful with it."

He was all grins as he tied it on and cast to an opening in the weeds. He had hardly taken two turns on his reel when a fish hit and took off toward the weeds. He set the hook and the line went limp. The northern had cut his line. "Oh, no, the Swam- per!"

Our last Swamper was gone. Thunderfoot was looking pretty dejected. "We might as well go home," he said.

"Oh, come on, don't be such a baby. We've got other things that'll catch a fish."

He tied another bait on but his heart just wasn't in it. The Swampers were his favorite, and others just didn't give him any confidence. We fished another couple of hours and only caught two small fish. "See, we need some Swampers," he said.

We pulled the boat out of the lake and went back to town to look for Swampers. There were none to be found, so we went home for the day. The next day I was driving through another town a few miles away and happened by a sport shop, so I stopped in to see if they had any Swampers. Much to my surprise and delight, they had two left, so I bought them both.

When I got home, I went to the boat shed and tied one on Thunderfoot's rod, which he had left in the boat. I tied the other on my rod. Then I went into the house and called him. "Hey, it's a nice day. Let's go down and see if any northerns are hungry."

"Yeah, I suppose. I'll be over in a minute," he said. He didn't sound too enthusiastic.

We put the boat in the back of the pickup and drove down to our favorite slough and carried it down over the bank. When he went to get in the boat, he saw the Swamper on his pole. "Holy cow, you got some! Oh man, let's get on the water." He was in a much better mood now.

We pulled out onto the lake and began casting. On his second cast, Thunderfoot put his Swamper right in the top of a tree that hung out over the water. "Oh no!" He jerked and twitched and did everything he could to free the bait but it was wrapped around a limb and was a goner.

"You might as well kiss that one goodbye," I said.

He shut his eyes and wrapped his line around his sweatshirt sleeve and began to pull. Suddenly with a crack, his line broke and fluttered down into the water. His Swamper was hanging in the tree, probably forever.

"Oh, that's it. Take me home," he said.

"No way. We're gonna fish for a while now that we're here," I said. We fished toward the middle of the lake and I swung my rod back for a long cast. As I threw it forward, I got a backlash and my Swamper flew about forty yards, hit the end of the line, snapped off and landed in the water, not attached to my pole anymore.

"Holy cow, you lost yours, too," Thunderfoot said, kind of happily.

"I watched right where it landed," I said. "Let's see if we can get it."

We paddled the boat over to the spot and suddenly I could see the Swamper laying on a clump of weeds under the water.

"There, I see it," I said, pointing down into the water.

"Oh, yeah. I can reach it, I think," Thunderfoot said.

He pushed up the sleeve on his sweatshirt, laid over the side of the boat, and reached down. Soon he came up and pushed his sleeve up as far as it would go. Then he laid down and reached and reached, and went in too far and got his sleeve all wet. "I'm so close," he said. This time, he hung over the side and put his head and shoulder into the water. He almost tipped the boat over trying to get back up. No lure.

"I can see it down there; I'm just a little short of getting it."

"Well, let it go then," I said.

"No way," he said. He was wearing bibbed camouflage overalls; he stood up and took them off. "What in the world are you doing now?" I said.

"Maybe I can get it with my toes. My legs are longer than my arms, and my pants are already wet."

He sat up on the side of the boat and put his feet into the water and fished around, trying to get the lure. "Darn, can't grab it," he said, sliding back into the boat.

"Let it go," I said.

"No way. I'm all wet now, I might as well go in after it." And, with saying that, he took off his sweatshirt and jumped over the side.

The water was about mid-chest deep, and he stood there on the bottom for a few seconds to let the mud and debris clear so he could see the bait, and then went under water. A half a minute later he came up, with a huge grin on his face, and then held up the Swamper. "See, I told you I'd be able to get it."

He put the lure in the boat and I sat on the opposite side to balance the boat while he climbed back in. Thankfully, it was a nice warm sunny day, because he had gotten every stitch of clothes he had with him soaked in the process of retrieving the lure. There he sat on the front seat, grinning from ear to ear in his underwear, holding his prize Swamper.

"Well, I have to give you an A for effort. You're persistent," I said. He grinned and began tying the Swamper onto his line. "Hey, what are you doing? That's my Swamper," I said.

"Oh, really? Apparently, you don't know about the maritime salvage laws, do you? It would appear that I have salvaged this bait from the deep, and it is now my property."

"Oh, really?"

"Yeah, really," he said, defiantly.

"Well, if you want to be that way, fine with me," I said.

"Thank you very much. Now will you row me over there? I think there's a hungry northern laying there with my name on it." Huge grin.

Oh well, what the heck, I guess he did deserve it. There wasn't a northern in the whole lake that would make me get into that cold water.

Thanks, Thunderfoot.

A Typical Day in the Marsh

The early duck season was in full swing, and Thunderfoot and I were in our blind, planning on hunting all day long. We had grassed our main blind, carried the canoe and the decoys out the previous week, and had just settled down for the day's hunt. We had the decoys out, and Katy was sitting by the little dog door in the front of the blind, waiting for us to shoot a duck so she could do her job. I had made a sack full of sandwiches and had packed cookies and some chips to keep Thunderfoot happy. The early flight of ducks was just starting, and we were ready.

"There's some, over by the woods, and some more. Cool, here comes a couple from the lake," Thunderfoot said as he watched the skyline, looking for birds that might be interested in our decoys.

A minute later, a pair of ducks came by and we stood and shot at them, missing both cleanly. "Well, that's the way to start," I said, laughing. "We educated that pair, so we won't have to worry about them coming back here for a while." Less than a minute later, a small flock of mallards looked at the decoys but weren't convinced, and decided to go on down the marsh.

There were small flocks of ducks everywhere and it was hard to keep track of them. Suddenly, a flock of about twenty teal came right in, low over the grass and were setting their wings into the decoys before we even saw them.

"Holy cow, look," Thunderfoot said as he stood up to shoot. The teal saw him instantly and began to rise up instead of dropping onto the water, and the flock quickly turned into a whirlwind of darting and wheeling birds, making for a getaway. Meanwhile we each tried to pick one duck from the mass and shoot at it. We both shot all three of our shells, and one duck fell from the flock over at the right end of the pond. Katy had been watching the fracas and jumped out of the blind and went back toward the dry land behind us.

"Kate, no, go fetch," I said as I pointed to the end of the pond.

She stopped and stood a minute and then went to where I was pointing, sniffed out the duck and brought it in. Then she took off for the back of the blind again. "Kate, no, come here." She stopped and stood for another minute and then obeyed me and came back to the blind. "Good girl," I said, patting her on the head. She grumbled a bit and then lay down.

"That was some good shooting," Thunderfoot grinned. "At this rate we'll need about twelve boxes of shells each for a limit of ducks." Oh, well, so what; shooting was the fun part anyway.

The next hour or so was pretty busy, and we shot at a couple dozen more ducks without taking so much as a feather from any of them. Things started to slow down as it got mid-morning, and soon I needed to make a trip back to the bushes to say hi to Mother Nature.

"Go way back," Thunderfoot said as I climbed out of the blind.

I was back about a hundred feet from the blind when I noticed a hawk, hovering over the right end of the pond. As I watched it, I began to believe that it was a peregrine falcon because of its size and shape. I had only seen them on TV; but a friend of mine was a birdwatcher and he had recently told me that he had seen one in this general vicinity a few weeks earlier. As I finished my business, I began walking back through the willows and tall grass and as I got near the pond, I saw a lone blue wing teal coming from the left. It was just skimming the tops of the grass and came across the end of the pond going about sixty miles per hour. Thunderfoot saw it just as it got even with the blind and jumped up to shoot, but by the time he got his gun to his shoulder the teal was at the other end of the pond. It started to rise up to clear the grass, and the falcon moved to its right, so quickly that I wasn't sure if I had even seen it make the move, and caught the teal in mid air! There was a puff of feathers, the teal's head flopped over and the falcon carried it off down the marsh.

I got in the blind and Thunderfoot was still sitting there with his mouth hanging open. "Did you see that duck run into that hawk? It got killed and the hawk carried it away."

"That was a peregrine falcon, and we just saw something that probably very few people in the whole world have ever seen."

"How do you know it's a falcon?"

"They're the only hawk-like bird in our area that can catch a duck in mid-flight. And, it's the right size and shape, and I heard there was one around here, so I'm pretty sure."

"Wow, cool. He sure was quick, a lot quicker than me. I didn't even get my gun off safe," he grinned.

Well, that had been an interesting event, so we sat and chatted about it for a while, and Katy began whining to get out of the blind. "Maybe she needs to go potty," Thunderfoot said.

"Yeah, she hasn't been out, since we haven't shot any ducks.

Come on, Katy, go potty," I said, opening the door.

Instead of going potty, Kate took off for the brush behind the blind. "Kate, where are you going?"

"Sometimes, I think she's not so smart," Thunderfoot said, shaking his head.

"No fooling. Come on, Kate, get in here." I couldn't see her but the weeds and grass were moving where she was fooling around.

"Kate, get back over here!" I yelled, getting impatient.

Soon we could see the grass moving as Katy came back toward the blind, and when she got to the edge of the pond, we could see she was carrying a dead teal in her mouth. "Holy cow, she's got a duck," Thunderfoot said.

Katy brought the duck into the blind and laid it down next to the one we had shot from the flock of twenty that had come by a couple of hours ago. She looked up at us, gave us a grunt and then lay down to watch out of her door.

Thunderfoot looked at me. "You suppose one of us got that bird and didn't see it fall?"

"Probably, and Kate saw it and didn't forget. Hmm, makes me feel a little stupid for yelling at her." I gave Kate a pat on the head and she grunted back at me.

Mid-day was pretty slow for duck action so we just sat in the sun and enjoyed the beauty of the marsh. A couple of ducks had landed in the pond just west of us and Thunderfoot was bound and determined to go over there and see if he could get them. "Leave them. It's too soupy over there; you'll just get stuck and all full of mud," I said.

A while later, a small flock of mallards landed in the same pond, so now there was no stopping him. He took Katy with him and began sneaking up to the pond. I could tell he was having a tough time going, because I could see his head and hat above the grass and it wasn't moving very fast. He made slow progress toward the pond, and all of a sudden, I could see him standing on top of the tall grass. When he stood up straight, the ducks flushed and he shot a drake mallard as it cleared the marsh grass. I could hear Katy sloshing through the water and heard Thunderfoot say "good girl" as she brought him the duck. He turned to me and waved. I still couldn't figure out how he got up high enough that I could see him. The grass was at least five feet tall and with his feet in the mud, he wasn't much taller than five feet himself Suddenly he disappeared and then I could see his hat coming my way just above the grass again.

When he got to the blind, he proudly held up his mallard. "A beauty, huh?"

I congratulated him on a nice duck and then said, "How did you get so tall over there?"

"There's an old hay rake sitting there in the mud. I climbed up on the seat and I could see everything in the marsh."

"A hay rake? I heard there was one out here somewhere, but never have seen it. So that's where it is."

"Yup, sitting there like somebody is gonna make hay tomorrow, but they'll have to put inner tubes on the tires, because there's water all around it. How did it get way out here?" he asked.

"In the old days, before the beaver got so thick in these river bottoms, this was all dry ground around these ponds and they used to make marsh hay to use for bedding for the cattle. I suppose it got left one year and never got back to high ground."

"A 'one of these days' things that never happens?" he grinned.

"Probably."

We sat for the rest of the day and didn't fire another shot. All the ducks were flying too far away for good shooting, and they didn't seem interested in our little spread of decoys.

"Well, I guess I'll go out and pick up the decoys," I said, and I got up and stepped into the canoe.

"I'll get the rest of the stuff ready," Thunderfoot said.

By the time I had the decoys in the canoe, he had walked back to dry ground with Katy and was waiting for me. The sun had just about set and the western sky was turning a beautiful red. We stood there for about ten more minutes and watched the red fade and night begin to fall on the marsh. Soon the evening star, actually Venus, began to shine low in the ever-darkening sky.

"Well, we didn't get many ducks, but it was a pretty interesting day," Thunderfoot said.

"Yeah, no kidding. Better than chasing around after girls, right?"

"Ummm, I'm gonna have to think about that for a while," he said with a big grin.

The boy was growing up.

Thanks, Thunderfoot.

Where the Wild Goose Goes

It was getting close to the end of the goose season, and Thunderfoot and I had decided to make a trip to the Horicon Marsh for some late goose hunting. We had been to the marsh many times before, during other years, and always much earlier in the season. This was the first time for us this year, and we had waited until nearly the end of the season. We called our farmer friend with the goose blinds, and he told us we were lucky because he had just had a cancellation and we could have the number one blind.

In the part of the Horicon Marsh designated as the Intensive Zone, hunters must hunt from a blind. This rule is in effect to help the farmers who surround the marsh to recoup some of the money they lose to the hundreds of thousands of geese that feed from their cornfields during the fall. Each farmer is allotted a certain number of blinds according to the acreage he has, and hunters must rent these blinds to be able to hunt. Some farms have elaborate blinds, but most have a plywood structure that is four feet by eight feet and four feet high. There is a little wooden bench and that's about it. Some make their blinds out of bales of straw or hay, but basically they are just a place to sit and hide while waiting for geese to fly in or out of the marsh.

We were pretty excited because the number one blind is the prime blind on the farm where we hunt. It is about one hundred feet from the boundary fence of the marsh, where no one is allowed unless he has geese for parents. The blind is on a knoll overlooking the marsh and is nothing more than a hole dug in the top of the knoll, with a wooden bench in the bottom of it. Actually it looks like a foxhole from WWII. But, what it lacks in accommodations, it makes up for in being in the prime spot on the farm.

Normally, we get one of the blinds that is in the fourth or fifth tier of blinds and have to work our way up, as other hunters fill their limits, until we get to the front of the pack and get some good shooting. We had never gotten the best blind, so we were really excited about having it for the day's hunting.

It was still dark, and the wind was whistling out of the north across a frozen landscape. We didn't have much snow yet, but what little there was lay in little drifts behind clumps of corn stubble and clods of frozen dirt in the fields surrounding the blinds. We stopped and talked to our farmer friend and paid for the blind use, and he told us to drive out through the pasture and park by the cornfield so we wouldn't have such a long walk to our blind.

I drove through the darkened barnyard and down a lane past some cattle to the iron gate at the pasture fence. Thunderfoot hopped out of the truck and went up to the gate and took the chain off from around the fence post and swung it open. I drove through the gate and stopped to wait for him to close it and get back in the truck.

He was pretty groggy yet from the long nighttime drive, and as I watched him, he trudged over and took hold of the gate and swung it back to the closed position, took the chain and wrapped it around the post and clipped it shut, and then looked up with a look of confusion on his face. He was on the wrong side of the gate! He had closed it and stayed on the other side. I was laughing, watching him in the rear view mirror. He stood there a second and then realized what he had done, and then looked up at the truck to see if I had seen him.

He shook his head as he saw me laughing. He was caught doing something that I would surely never let him forget. He climbed over the gate and came to the truck. "I don't want to hear about it. Kindly drive us to the cornfield and shut up," he said. I could see him grinning, even though he wanted to try to keep a straight face.

I never said a word. We drove to the cornfield, parked, got our guns and gear from the back of the truck and started out across the picked corn stubble to the blind. The north wind bit into our faces and stung our ears as we crunched across the frozen snow and corn stubble. We finally got to the edge of the knoll and found the blind. "Wow, this is cool, like in the movies, a foxhole," he said, surveying our little hiding place. He raised his gun and began softly going "tchu, tchu, tchu" like someone firing a machine gun at the enemy. "Take it easy, John Wayne, you'll scare all the geese. They're just down there on the other side of the fence," I said.

He grinned and sat down on the bench, loaded his gun, and then stood it against the front of the embankment. "Ready and able, sir," he reported. I shook my head; he'd been watching too many war movies.

The wind continued to sting our faces and redden our cheeks, and soon the darkness began to fade into grayness as dawn crept over the marsh. In a few minutes we could hear an occasional honk of a goose or a "whaaa, whaaa, whaaa" of a hen mallard. The silence of the night began to give way to many bird calls, and the sounds soon rose in intensity to a quite loud noise. "Wow, they're making a lot of noise. Sounds like there's still a lot of them in there," Thunderfoot said.

Pretty soon a small flock of geese rose from the marsh like a puff of gray smoke drifting up from a campfire, slowly formed a loose V shape and began moving north toward a far off cornfield that was to be their breakfast. They were going to be too far out for us to shoot at, but soon more began rising up and flocks began forming all over the marsh. Soon one of these flocks was headed our way. "Get ready, and don't forget to lead them," I said. Thunderfoot nodded.

The geese crossed the boundary fence and continued on in front of us. "Take them!" I whispered, and we both stood up and picked out a goose and shot. I aimed at the lead goose and hit the second one back. Thunderfoot shot at, well, I'm not sure what he shot at, but nothing happened. We both were using our single shot ten-gauge shotguns, so one shot was all we had. Actually, that was good because a box of shells lasted a lot longer when you used them one at a time.

"Wow, you got one," Thunderfoot said, as he jumped to his feet to run out and gather up the downed goose. He raced to the pasture and brought my goose in for me. I put a sticky tag around its neck and laid it in the bottom of the blind. "That was almost too easy," I said. "My aim was a little off, though. To be honest, I was aiming at the lead goose and got the second one."

Thunderfoot looked at me. "How far are you aiming ahead?"

"Oh, I don't know, maybe fifteen or twenty feet."

"Oh, come on, twenty feet? You gotta be kidding me."

"No, I'm not. Those are big birds and they look like they're going slow, but they're not. You have to shoot a long way ahead of them."

I knew he wasn't convinced so I didn't push the issue. In a short time, another flock came in range and we both shot again, and this time I got the lead goose. Thunderfoot, again, missed. He ran out and picked up my goose and brought it back. I tagged it and I was done for the day. I had my limit.

"Well, I guess I'll put my gun away and watch you," I said. "That's what you get for being such a smart pants. Now you have to just watch," he said.

The next flock started our way, and I said to Thunderfoot, "Now, be sure to just pick one bird. Don't flock shoot and then lead him."

He nodded and aimed his gun. He was leading the first bird in the flock, and I watched from behind him as he led the bird and then shot. The fifth goose back, ducked his head back as the shot buzzed past his nose.

"You were way too short on your lead. Did you see that other goose duck his head?"

"Jeez, I can't believe I was that short. Are you sure that was me that made him duck?"

"Pretty sure. You see that log laying on the ground over there?" I said, pointing to an old fence post. "That is about seven or eight feet long. Shoot about three logs in front of the first goose."

He shook his head but agreed to try it. The next flock started drifting our way and he got ready. "Now remember, three logs," I said.

I squatted behind him and watched as he got a lead on the lead goose and then swung the gun ahead and pulled the trigger. The second goose back from the lead dropped from the flock and crashed onto the frozen pasture. "Holy cow, will you look at that?" he said, as he climbed over the edge of our foxhole and ran out to pick up his goose. He held it up proudly and then came back and tagged it and laid it in the bottom of the blind with the others.

"As much as I hate to admit it, you were right," he said, grinning.

"As usual," I said.

"Don't wrench your arm patting yourself on the back."

We let a few questionable flocks go by and soon another lowing bunch was coming right toward us. "Well, here comes the last shot of the season," he said. "I calculate them at about 3.25 logs." He took aim, swung ahead and dropped the lead goose.

He turned to me with a huge grin on his face. "Old dead eye strikes again."

Then he jumped over the side of the blind and ran out to get his goose.

I would have liked to stay and sit and watch the geese fly for a while, but there were other hunters in the back blinds who were waiting for their turn in the front blind. "Man, this is a good place to hunt," Thunderfoot said. "Now I see why people try to get it all the time."

"Yeah, it's almost too good," I said. "We got done pretty fast."

"Well," he said, "the way that wind is freezing my ears, I'm kinda glad, and besides, my belly is calling for some pancakes, and sausage, and maybe a couple of eggs for a kicker."

As usual he was faminished.

"Well, let's go then," I said, and we carried our gear back to the truck. The group in the blind behind us waved as they moved up, and the group behind them moved up to their blind, to wait for them to finish.

When we got to the gate, I stopped and Thunderfoot sat in the truck instead of getting out to open it. "What are you waiting for?" I said.

"Aren't you gonna make some smart remark about being on the right side when I close it?"

"Who, me?"

Thanks, Thunderfoot.

Black powder hunting had been gaining in popularity for the past few years, and Thunderfoot had been pestering me to get a black powder gun so we could hunt the extended deer season with our muzzleloaders. I finally broke down and bought one, and he had conned his grandpa out of one, so we now had an extra week to hunt.

I bought my gun a few weeks earlier and had been going to the range to learn how to load it and figure out which type of bullet and how much powder made the best shooting load. Thunderfoot already had that worked out for him by his grandpa, so he came along to shoot and to practice with his gun, too. These modern guns were pretty accurate, and with the invention of the new powders and bullets, were safe and effective for killing a whitetail deer, moose, elk, or even a bear. The only drawback was that you had only one shot, so you wanted to make that one shot count.

Boom! "Whooie, that was a good one," Thunderfoot said, as he fanned the huge cloud of smoke away from his shot. We looked through binoculars and saw that he had hit almost dead center in the bull's-eye that we had painted on the side of a cardboard box that was sitting about fifty yards away. "Give yours a try and see if you can do that."

I aimed, touched off the ignition cap, and half a second later there was a boom, and the gun recoiled and smoke bellowed out of the barrel. After the smoke cleared, we looked down range and saw my bullet had hit within an inch of Thunder foot's. "Not bad for a rookie," he said, grinning.

"Well, I've put about a hundred practice shots through my gun now, so I feel pretty confident that I can hit a deer with it," I said.

"I know I can," he said, matter-of-factly.

We went home and cleaned the guns and made them ready for the next day, which was opening day for the muzzle loading hunt. His grandpa had invited us to his farm, and Thunderfoot was going to stay the night at my house so we could get an early start in the morning. We made our mandatory lunch and packed it before we went to bed, and what seemed like a very short time later, my alarm was beeping. I went to the spare bedroom and woke Thunderfoot, who grumbled about being awakened until it dawned on him that he was going hunting and not to school. We had a quick breakfast and headed out for grandpa's farm.

I had been at the farm before, so I knew the lay of the land. I was going to go up to the left side of the valley and sit until a couple hours after dawn. Thunderfoot was going up the right side to a stand that his grandpa used for the regular deer season. It was a really luxury stand. It was built about ten feet up in the lower limbs of a huge dead oak tree and was like a little house with a window cut into each side. The windows were just window holes, with no glass, so the hunter could shoot right through them. It had a corrugated tin roof and a couple of chairs inside for the hunter or hunters to sit in while they watched the end of the valley. There was a nice ladder permanently attached to it so even an old, not so agile guy like me could get up with ease.

Thunderfoot was going to sit in the little house and after I got cold, I was supposed to work my way up the left side of the valley and then walk slowly toward him, possibly chasing a deer or two toward the house.

We parked in the farmyard and crossed the gate behind the barn. The valley was about a mile long and pretty narrow. There had been a cornfield in the bottom of it all summer, but that was now picked and grandpa had about fifty head of beef cattle in the valley to clean up the missed corn and use the pasture on the sides of the hills.

"Good luck," I whispered as we parted and each went up one side of the valley. "You, too," he said.

It was a cloudy night, so there was no moon or starlight, and it was as dark as it could possibly be. I could just make out the forms of the lighter colored cattle moving ahead of me and almost bumped right into a big black one. She mooed at me and I said, "so boss" quietly, so as not to alarm her. I crossed the valley floor and started up the side of the pasture on the hillside. It was pretty steep, but I was going across pasture so it was easy walking.

Suddenly, in less time than it takes to tell, both of my feet were in a fresh puddle of pasture pudding, which was as slick as a puddle of fresh oil but smelled a little more fragrant. Both feet went out from under me so fast that I didn't even have time to put my hand down to stop my fall. I was carrying my gun in the crook of my left arm and when I hit the ground, my arm came up and my forehead crashed down on the gun with a crack. I don't know if the crack was audible or just inside my head, but it was real loud and I hit my head real hard on the gunstock.

The next few minutes were kind of fuzzy. I don't know exactly how long I laid there, but the next thing I knew, I could hear a soft, "mooooo." I raised my head a bit and stared right into the wet nose of one of the black cows. She was standing over me, probably trying to figure out if I was alive or dead. It was somewhat light now, so I figured I must have laid there for a while.

My head hurt like crazy and I tried to get up, only to have my feet slide again in the same pie I had slipped in in the first place. Well, actually it wasn't a pie anymore; I was wearing most of it on the front of my pants and coat.

My guardian cow moved back when I began to move and I finally staggered to my feet. Now I could see much better and could see what had happened. The pasture was like a minefield with meadow muffins everywhere. It was a wonder that I had made it as far as I did without stepping in one and sliding on my face.

I continued up to the edge of the woods and sat on a stump for a while to watch for a deer. After a while I began to get cold, so I thought I'd take my little trek up the hill and around the end of the valley to where Thunderfoot was sitting in his nice little house.

It took me about an hour to make the hill trip and soon I could see Thunderfoot sitting, looking out the window of the house on the tree. He waved, held up a sandwich for me to see and motioned for me to come up and join him.

I walked across the end of the valley and climbed up the ladder into the house. "Holy cow, what happened to your head?" he said.

"I fell down in some cow poop," I said.

"Whew, I guess you did, you're wearing most of it. Did you know you've got blood allover the side of your head?"

"No, is it still bleeding?"

"Nope, it's all dried. You look like heck."

"Thanks."

"Want a sandwich?" he said, offering me the last sandwich.

"What, you're not hungry? What happened to the other five of them?"

He just grinned and patted his belly.

I opened a can of pop and took the sandwich, and we both sat down in the chairs. I was telling him about my adventure in the pasture when suddenly he began looking really hard at the hillside across the valley. "There's a deer coming down the hill," he whispered.

I looked and, sure enough, a nice buck was working his way down a trail on the side of the hill. "Don't move, or he'll see you," I said.

Thunderfoot nodded, and raised his gun slowly. I was just about to say, "Don't shoot it inside the house, stick it out the window," when he touched it off. Now, to say it was loud is the understatement of the year. Imagine setting off a huge firecracker in your bathroom and that might be close. The muzzle blast displaced a huge amount of air and made the leaves and debris on the floor fly around the house like a hurricane had hit. Then the smoke from the gun filled the little house, and I couldn't even see Thunderfoot three feet away from me. "Holy cow, my ears are deaf!" he said.

My ears were ringing like mad, and I could barely hear what he had said. I waved the smoke away with my hat and soon the wind cleared it enough so we could see each other.

"I was going to tell you not to shoot inside the house," I said, shaking my head.

"Good idea," he said, nodding his head. "I wish you would have said it sooner, so I wouldn't be totally deaf now."

Despite our hurt ears, we both began to laugh. "Whew, that was loud," he said.

"Hey, did you get the deer?" I asked.

We both looked out the window and, sure enough, there laid the deer.

"Cool, what a marksman I am," he said.

"Well, you better go field dress him and we'll get him tagged," I said.

"Eh? Can't hear you."

"I said ... " Then I saw him grinning and handing me his knife.

"Could you, just this one more time?"

Oh well, at least I wouldn't be able to hear him pestering me for the next couple days to do some other fool thing.

Thanks, Thunderfoot.

Wisdom From Thunderfoot

When Dan nicknamed me Thunderfoot many years ago, I never dreamed that we would become such good friends and have so much fun together. I think maybe I was lucky to have a friend like him, but he always says it's him who was lucky to find a hunting and fishing buddy like me. Who knows, maybe we were meant to meet and have all these great times together so we could share them with you.

I've been places, seen things I never thought I'd ever see.

And I've done things, wow, so many things, that I never ever dreamed I'd do. Sometimes I almost wish I hadn't done some of them, because at the time, they weren't too much fun, but after we got dry or washed the mud off of us, we thought they were pretty funny.

We've had lots of fun and done some pretty crazy things, but most of the time we just ~ere doing something that many people do, enjoying the outdoors. No matter how normal your plans are for a day, there are lots of things that can happen to make a little fishing trip or hunting trip into a day you'll never forget. Especially when you hunt and fish with someone who never forgets a thing, like Dan. He seems to be able to remember every time I made a mistake or had a little accident. And, of course, I think he makes it look like most of the things that went wrong are my fault. Of course, I'm totally innocent of all such charges.

And I've learned so much. I've not only learned to catch a fish or shoot a duck, I've learned about life and, of course, death, and friendship. I wish I could count the times we just watched a deer or duck or squirrel and never even shot at it and still had the fun of being there. Or, the hundreds of fish that we caught and then put back, to fight again. And, the sadness of Lucy leaving us, and the funny feeling in my stomach when I've shot a nice deer or duck. It's a feeling that I am happy that I got the game I was after, but also the feeling of sadness that I took the life of such a beautiful thing. Of course, death is part of life, and also part of hunting.

And the friendship. I don't know how many people have a friendship with another person like we have. I can't imagine how many hours we've been together in a cold duck blind or an ice shanty. Or the hours we sat under the hot sun in the boat. The hundreds of sandwiches and cookies we shared; the hours just sitting quietly watching for game to come to us; enjoying every minute of it. We have a bond that has lasted many years and hopefully will last for many more.

No matter how cold or hot or bored you get, being with your best friend makes it enjoyable. And, we've sure enjoyed a lot of those special times.

Dan keeps complaining that he's getting too old for some of these little adventures we go on. I keep telling him that as long as he is still upright and breathing, I expect him to keep going with me, and he said he thought maybe he could. So, we're looking forward to lots more fun in the outdoors.

I thank you for reading this book and hope you had a laugh or maybe a tear. If you enjoyed reading about us, just think how much fun it was to be there. So many memories, and hopefully so many more coming in the future.

We'll see you on the water or in the woods, and as always, I'll be the one with the grin on my face.

Your Buddy, Thunderfoot

Thanks
Thunderfoot

Here We Go Again

The setting sun was a shimmering orange globe that was just about to sink into the silvery water on the western horizon. I was standing in the middle of the river, casting a small surface bait to an old bridge piling where I hoped to get a small mouth bass to strike. It was the middle of the summer and the water was bathtub warm, so I was barefoot and clad in some old cut offs and a tee shirt. I was carrying my rod and reel, and without getting them stuck in the fabric, an extra lure and a couple of jigs hung from the top of my shirt pocket. That allowed me to fish without having lots of stuff to carry. I could wade and cast to the rock piles, remnants of old bridge piers from long ago, lined up across the river just above the new bridge. I cast my little imitation crippled minnow just past the rocks and pilings and gave it a twitch. I let it rest a couple of seconds and then twitched it again. The water exploded before the rings from the motion of the second twitch had even begun to radiate across the water, and a nice small mouth bass jumped halfway out of the water as it engulfed my bait. I snapped the rod up and set the hook. The bass took off like a rocket for the deeper water. I held steady pressure on my rod, and suddenly the bass jumped out of the water, shaking its head, trying to throw the lure free. A hundred drops of water flashed against the red-orange sky and looked like little sapphires as they fell back into the river. I kept working the fish and it jumped a half-dozen more times, but finally gave up as it tired from exertion. The water came just to the bottom of my cut off shorts, so I led the fish close and carefully grabbed it by the lip and lifted it from the water. It was a typical river smallmouth; bronze sided with dark bars running from top to bottom. I took the hook from the fish's lip and bent over to hold it in the water – to let the current flow through its gills so it revived before I released it. After a short time in the current, the fish began to swim. I let go and watched it lazily sink away, back to the rock pile to fight another day.

I started to stand up straight, but I heard a ripping sound. I looked down to find that the extra lure I had hanging from my shirt pocket had caught on the bottom hem of my shorts, and I was hung up, bent over in the middle of the river. I tried to get the hook from the denim, but it was past the barb, and the more I struggled with it, the deeper it became imbedded. I tried to free the other end of the lure from my pocket, but that hook too, was past the barb. I needed two hands to get out of this mess, but there was no place to set my rod and reel down without dropping them into the river. I was trying to figure out how to get loose from the lure when I heard Thunderfoot snickering a few yards away. He was standing in the river just above the next piling.

"Got a little problem there, old fella?" he snickered.

"That's *Mr.* Old Fella to you!" I said.

He laughed and started wading toward me. "Jeez, this is just like taking someone from "The Home" out fishing. I should get college credit for my work with you."

I looked over at him from my upside down vantage point and I could see his grin and the sparkle in his eyes. He loved seeing me in unflattering situations; he was really enjoying this. When he got next to me, I handed him my rod and reel and began working the hook out of my shirt pocket – ripping a hole in the pocket, but at least I was finally able to stand up straight. Then I worked on the other hook in my shorts, and soon I was free of the lure.

"That was a real good idea to hook that extra bait on your shirt," Thunderfoot said.

"Yeah, I thought so, too," I said. "Why don't you go back over to your rock pile and fish and quit making wise-crack comments."

He looked distressed. "Ouch! Touchy! Here I came all the way over to rescue you... and that's the thanks I get?"

"Yup. That's it. Take it or leave it."

He grinned, punched me in the arm and began wading back to his rock pile. I watched him going slowly through the current and thought back to when I had met him over four years earlier. I owned a sporting goods store, and one day this new kid came through the front door with a younger kid tagging along. He introduced himself and his younger brother, and told me that his mom and dad had split up, and that they had just moved to town. He was hoping to find some new fishing spots, and he said that he had just passed Hunter Safety and was planning on going hunting the next season for the first time. About a week later, we took a day off and went squirrel hunting. He was just 13, tall and pretty skinny. I had lots of old hunting gear that I had outgrown over the years, and being one of those people who never throw anything away, I was able to outfit him with some hand-me-downs that worked quite well. His feet were as big as mine, so I lent him an extra pair of my hunting boots. As we walked along a ridge road up the first hill, he managed to step on every stick that was lying in the road. If he wasn't stepping on sticks, he was dislodging rocks that rattled down the hill, causing lots of noise and probably scaring away every living critter for a mile around. I slowed my pace and watched him from behind. He was walking bent at the waist, like he was sneaking up on someone, but never looked down to see where his feet were going.

"Hey, Thunderfoot! Why don't you look where you're putting your feet so you don't scare every squirrel away in three counties?"

"Thunderfoot?"

"Yeah. Your big feet make as much noise as thunder. Try sneaking a little."

Well, the nickname stuck, and we became best friends. Over the next weeks, he came around often, and before long he was helping me around the shop and watching things when I needed to run errands or take a little time off. Now, four years later, here we were, still enjoying the great outdoors together.

Although his real name was James – or Jamie, as his family called him – he was "Thunderfoot" to me. During the past four years, he had grown and matured to a fine young man. He wasn't much taller than when I first met him but he had filled out and had passed that gangly stage, and was now a handsome kid. He had a perpetual smile on his face and the brightest blue eyes I had ever seen. He loved the outdoors, and no matter how successful we were with our fishing or hunting – whether we caught a lot of fish or no fish, or got a lot of game or none at all – he always enjoyed himself. We just liked being there, and being together made it even more fun. Of course he was always ready to pull a fast one on me, and we enjoyed a lot of laughs from our pranks on each other.

He cast a small spinner to the rock pile he was fishing and after about three turns of the reel his rod bucked and the line took off for the current. "Whooie!" he beamed, as a nice smallie jumped and then made another hard run. He played the fish for a while, and then released it. He looked over at me and gave me one of his famous grins. "The Bass Master strikes again."

We fished for another fifteen minutes. The sun was almost gone when he suddenly yelled, "Holy cow, did you see that tail come up by the rocks?"

"What tail?"

"A fish tail. It was a foot across!"

"A foot across? Oh, come on. Are you sure the sun wasn't in your eyes and you just saw a ripple?"

"Ripple my eye! It was a fish tail and it came up out of the water and it... there, there, see?" he said, pointing to the rocks. There it was: a fish tail that was easily eleven or twelve inches across came up out of the water and then disappeared again.

"Wow! You weren't exaggerating," I said.

"What do you suppose it was?"

"Probably a shark," I said.

He just gave me a glare. "No. Really. What's in this river that's that big?"

"I don't know – maybe a big sturgeon or one of those paddle fish. It's a big one, that's for sure."

By now the sun had disappeared and twilight was settling in. I thought about a fish that was big enough to have a foot-wide tail, and it suddenly gave me a spooky feeling to be standing in the same water, only a few yards away from that monster. Thunderfoot must have gotten the same thought, because he began wading toward me as fast as he could go. "I don't know about you, but I'd feel safer on the bank," he said. I reeled up and we both headed for the sandbar a few yards from us. The closer we got to the sand, the faster we waded, until we were almost running through the water.

Once we were safely on the sand, I began to feel pretty foolish about getting spooked by a fish. "You know neither a sturgeon nor a paddle fish would hurt you. Neither one has any teeth. The sturgeon is a bottom feeder and the paddle fish is a filter feeder, so I don't think we were in any danger."

"I know. But it was just scary thinking of that big thing in there with us," he laughed.

Just then the tail appeared at just about the same spot where Thunderfoot had been, and it slapped the water like a cannon shot as it dove down. "Well, what do you think?" I asked. "Want to go back for some night fishing?"

"I believe I'll pass, thank you," he said. "But go right ahead if you want to. I'll just sit here on the sand and watch."

I decided that I wasn't that brave either.

We walked back to the pickup and drove back to town, stopped at the gas station for an ice cream and a pop, and then headed home to put our gear away. It was just another typical evening and another little adventure in the outdoors that can change a regular day into something special, where you just never know what will happen next. Of course, that's what makes each day in the outdoors fun. And boy, we sure have our share of that.

Thanks, Thunderfoot.

The Carperee

I peered out the window that overlooked the back yard. Thunderfoot was on his way over to my house with the local newspaper clutched in his hand. He was walking as fast as he could go without running, so I knew he was on a mission.

"Did you see this ad about the Carperee?" he said as he walked in the front door and handed me the paper. He had opened and folded it to the ad. I took the paper and began reading.

"Carperee," the headline said. "A fishing tournament for everyone. Two person teams will fish for rough fish only. No game fish allowed. Winning teams will split all of the entry money."

"Now there's something we can do good at," he said. "We always catch a lot of junk fish when we fish the river."

We looked the ad over some more. The contest was scheduled for the Saturday after next. We didn't have anything planned for that day, so we decided to enter and see if we could win some money. The entry fee was $25 per team, and the top three teams with highest weights of rough fish would split the pot: 60% to the first place team, 25% to second place, and 15% to the third place team. "If there are a lot of teams," Thunderfoot said, "we could win hundreds of dollars."

"Don't be counting the winnings just yet," I said. "We still have to catch some fish to win."

"Yeah, yeah, I know," he said. "But two experts like us should have no trouble winning a carp contest."

I wished that I was as sure as he was about it, but I thought it would be fun anyway, whether we won or not, so I wrote a check for the entry while Thunderfoot cut the entry form from the paper. We put the check in an envelope with the entry form and mailed it to the local fishing club that was sponsoring the event.

"We've got a lot of time to practice, so maybe we should put the boat in the river and go find some hotspots," Thunderfoot suggested.

"Practice? You think we need to practice fishing?"

"Yeah, sure. We need to find some places where there are lots of carp and stuff."

Well, I knew I wasn't going to talk him out of that idea, and it was a nice day to spend fishing, so we packed a lunch, picked up some night crawlers and headed to the river. We motored downstream to a likely looking spot. We set out the rear anchor and then tied the front end of the boat to a small tree that was hanging out over the riverbank. Then we let out some more anchor rope so the boat turned sideways, giving us each unobstructed fishing. We rigged our rods and reels with heavy sinkers and plain hooks, baited them with night crawlers, and tossed them out into the current. It didn't take long before Thunderfoot had a bite. He cautiously picked up his rod and concentrated on the tip, watching for the telltale sign of the fish eating the night crawler. The rod tip bumped again and he reared back to set the hook. "Got him! Hey ya!" he shouted as his rod doubled over and he began playing the fish. I grabbed the landing net and waited for him to bring it alongside the boat. Soon a good-sized carp was thrashing in the water below me. I scooped it up into the net.

"What do you think? About 4 pounds?" he said.

"Yeah, probably. Maybe a little more. That would be a good one to catch in the Carperee," I said.

He would have given himself a pat on the back if he could have reached it. We removed the hook from the fish and put it back into the river. Just as I laid the net down in the boat, one of my rods began bucking like mad and I grabbed it and set the hook into the fish. I fought a good-sized fish for several minutes and then led a sheepshead into the net. "Those count too," Thunderfoot said. "Any rough fish – carp, sheepshead, blue buffalo, suckers, gar – anything that isn't a game fish. Oh boy, oh boy! This is a good spot. We're gonna do good here."

We decided that we should move from the spot so we didn't "sore mouth" all of the fish in the area, and so none of our competitors would see us there and steal our spot. We pulled up the anchor and untied the front of the boat and motored down the river for a while, looking for more similar spots.

"That looks like a good drop off over there," Thunderfoot said, pointing to a sandbar just ahead. There was about a foot of water running over the sandbar and at the lower end you could see that there was a deep pool. We slowed down and I maneuvered the boat below the shallow bar. We anchored cross current again at the top of the drop off.

"This looks good. Deep water and good current," I observed.

We each baited up and cast out our lines. It didn't take very long for Thunderfoot to catch a big white sucker, and then I caught another just like it. "Both about two pounds – not huge but not bad either," he said. We both re-baited our hooks and cast out again.

It was a gorgeous morning. There were a few big cotton candy clouds scattered here and there across the sky, and the temperature was just about perfect mid-70s. There was a gentle breeze blowing across the water that was just enough to keep the bugs off us without bothering our fishing. We each had two rods and reels propped against the side of the boat, and after a while without a bite, I picked up a boat cushion and laid it against the up-river side of the boat. I slipped my shoes off and put my feet up on the other side and laid back to rest in the sunshine.

"You better not go to sleep," Thunderfoot said.

"Don't worry. I'm alert and ready for a bite." My eyes were getting kind of heavy when Thunderfoot whispered, "Your right pole." I looked. The tip of the right rod bounced once. I watched it for a few seconds and it bounced again. I took my feet down from the rail of the boat and began to sit up and slowly put my hand down to pick up the rod. Just when I was about 6 inches from it, the rod bounced three times really hard and shot out over the side of the boat like a javelin hurled by an Olympic champion. It all happened so fast that I didn't have time to think. The rod hit the water about five feet from the boat, and I hit the water right behind it. As I dove toward the bottom of the river, I opened my eyes and the first thing I saw was my sunglasses falling toward the bottom. I hadn't thought of taking them off when I dove into the water. I reached down to grab them and when I did, I also grabbed the line from my rod, completely by accident. A second later the rod came sliding up into my hand.

Now that I had my rod, I swam for the surface and came up about twenty feet downriver from the boat. I put the sunglasses into my mouth and began swimming on my side toward a sandbar downstream, holding my rod in my other hand. I looked back at the boat. Thunderfoot sat there with his mouth hanging open. "I'll swim over to that sandbar and walk back up," I shouted. He just sat there, his mouth agape, amazed.

I swam to the sandbar and waded onto the sand. The fish that had pulled my rod overboard was still hooked on, so I reeled and played him until I drug him up on the sand. "About a 10 pound carp," I shouted to Thunderfoot. He *still* was just sitting there looking stupidly at me.

I released the carp, walked back up on the sand bar and then across the shallow water. I stepped into the boat from the upper side. "Jeez. You could give a guy a little warning if you plan to go over the side," Thunderfoot said. "I thought you had a heart attack and died or something."

"I didn't have time to say anything," I told him. "If I had taken time to inform you of my plans, my rod would have been downriver and I'd have never caught it."

He just shook his head. "Well, it was a nice carp at least."

We spent the rest of the day fishing and found some pretty good places where we caught quite a few rough fish. That following week we went out two more times "practicing." Friday evening we got our gear ready and made lunch for the Carperee the next day.

We arrived at the village park where the contest was to be held and got in line with lots of other teams to get our boat number and an official weigh-in bag. In about half an hour all the teams were ready and we got the rules and regulations and all took off for the river. There were boats going every which way and soon we were at our first hot spot. We tied up with the boat across current so we could cover the maximum amount of water and not be in each other's way. We laid the landing net on the seat between us so it would be ready when we needed it.

Thunderfoot got a bite in just a short while. He picked up his rod and waited for the fish to bite again. When it did he set the hook and fought it up to the boat.

"Oh nuts. It's a walleye," I said as it came to the surface.

"We don't want any walleyes today," Thunderfoot said, and took the fish off the hook and slipped it back into the river. I got the next bite and caught a real nice smallmouth bass.

Then Thunderfoot finally caught a catfish. "What happened to our carp spot?" he said.

"I don't know. But it's full of *good fish* now."

We fished for another hour and caught one sheepshead, three more walleyes and two bass.

"We'd better try another spot."

We went to the sandbar drop off where my rod had been pulled in and caught one small carp right away. Then walleyes, catfish, and bluegills plagued us. "I'm not believing this!" Thunderfoot said. We tried another spot, and another with the same luck, and then we tried one final spot and before we knew it the time was getting close for us to be back at the riverside park for the weigh-in. "Let's just go home," Thunderfoot said, "we don't have enough to even go back for the weigh-in."

"You never know. Maybe everyone had the same luck as we did." That brightened his spirits. We pulled the anchors and motored back to the park.

The fishing club had a dump truck backed up to the weigh-in station and had made arrangements with some farmer to spread the fish on one of his fields for fertilizer. There were many teams bringing their strings of junk fish to the scales. We had managed to catch three small carp, one fair buffalo, one gar and two sheepsheads. Our total weight was 16 and a half pounds. "That puts us in third place," Thunderfoot said. Our hopes were pretty high until we saw my next-door neighbor and his wife pull up in their boat.

"What do you think of this one?" his wife said as she held up a sheepshead that looked to weigh about 25 pounds.

"Jeez. They got one fish that's bigger than all of ours put together," Thunderfoot groaned.

When all was said and done, we ended up in 8th place. As teams kept coming in our weight got lower and lower on the chart. "Oh well," I said. "We had fun, anyway."

"Yeah, I guess so," Thunderfoot said. "I think we ought to enter some walleye or bass tournaments. We seem to catch more of them than anything."

"Yeah, but you know what would happen then," I said.

"Of course. We'd catch carps and suckers," he said grinning.

Well, anyway you look at it, catching any fish is fun, as long as they pull and give you a fight. And spending a day on the river fishing is way better than working.

Thanks, Thunderfoot.

Bank Poling

I was reading the morning paper when Thunderfoot came in through the front door. He was instantly mobbed by Katy and Kirby and spent a couple of minutes wrestling with them until they were properly assured that he had noticed them. He came into the kitchen, retrieved the cereal and a medium-size mixing bowl from the cupboard and sat down at the table to have his breakfast.

"Are you out of cereal at your house?" I asked.

"Nope. I just like yours better," he grinned. "What do you know about bank poling?"

"What do you mean? How to do it, or what it is?"

"Both. I heard some guys talking about it and I wondered if it was something we should be doing," he said.

"Well, it's not rocket science," I said. "You cut down some small trees, strip the branches off them, find a likely looking spot and shove them into the riverbank. Then you tie some 200# braided nylon line on each one with a big heavy sinker and about a 10/0 hook, and bait them with a bullhead. Each fisherman can have five poles, but he has to buy a license that gives him five metal tags to tie onto each pole. You set them in the evening, and then check them for fish in the morning."

Thunderfoot was sitting there poking cereal into his face and nodding his head up and down as I talked. When he'd finished the first bowl, he poured another.

"Why can't you bait them in the morning when you check them for fish?" he asked. "That would seem to be a lot less work."

"If you bait them in the morning, turtles and gar will eat your bait. They don't feed during the night. But that's when the big catfish are active, and they have a better chance of getting your bait then."

He nodded some more, thinking over all the information. "So, have you ever done it?"

"No, but I went with a friend a few times when he baited and raised his lines. It was fun, but I guess I just never got the bug to do it myself. When I was a kid, my dad's friend caught a catfish that was almost 5 feet long. It weighed over 60 pounds."

"Sixty pounds!" Thunderfoot's eyes were as big as his cereal bowl. "Holy cow! That's a big one! Why don't we try it?"

"Sixty pound fish are pretty rare. I haven't heard of one that big for years," I said. And there's a lot of work in this. You have to catch a lot of bullheads, and cut all the poles, and find spots to set them and then go to the river twice a day."

"Oh boy, that sounds like work," he replied with a little sarcasm thrown in. "Let's see... use a hatchet to chop some poles, fool around on the riverbank, catch bullheads, and then go out on the river two times a day? What a terrible thing to have to do."

"Ok, smart guy. I guess it's not so terrible. You want to try it?"

"I'm almost finished with my breakfast. Lets get started," he said, pouring his third bowl of cereal. I picked up the box and there was about a tablespoon of cereal left in the bottom. I poured it into his bowl and threw the box away.

"You better get more cereal. You're out," he said grinning.

Regular license stations didn't have Bank Pole licenses, so our first mission was to drive forty miles to the County Clerk's office for the license and tags.   Then we took the ax and hatchet, drove down to the river bottoms and found some appropriately sized small willow trees that would make good poles. They were about 12 feet tall and about as big around as a baseball bat, and being willows, they were really tough and springy. Thunderfoot attacked the trees, cutting them off at the bottom. I trimmed all the branches off with a small hatchet, and cut them all off at about ten feet long. By the time we had ten of them, we were pretty tired out and went home for some lunch and a rest.

My eyes had gotten heavy right after lunch and I was snoring in my recliner when Thunderfoot shook me awake. "We've got no time for a nap now. We have to get the rest of the stuff and get our poles out."

"Jeez. Don't be in such a hurry. We have to catch bait yet. We won't have time to get them out today, so just be patient." Thunderfoot was not the patient type.

We tied braided twine on all the poles and rigged them with big, heavy sinkers and huge hooks. Then we wrapped the lines around the poles and stuck the hooks in the butt end. Our poles were ready. Now for the bait.

"A friend of mine has a pond on his farm that's full of nice sized bullheads," I said. "I'll call him and see if it's ok for us to catch some." I went in the house and placed the call. My friend told me to take all we wanted, so Thunderfoot and I grabbed a couple of rods and reels and some plastic buckets for the bullheads. Off we went to the bullhead pond. We arrived at the farm and drove through the pasture to the pond. It was about an acre of water and was a great place to fish because the cattle had kept the weeds and grass chewed down. It was almost like a little park. Besides the cows, there were several ducks and geese, and one huge tom turkey waddling around.

"Holy cow! Look at that big turkey," Thunderfoot said.

"That's a tame bird," I said. "He's way too big to be wild. He'd be quite a trophy if he was a wild one."

We baited our hooks and began fishing. In no time at all we began catching bullheads, and as we caught them, we put them in the pails. We had about ten bullheads in one pail, so Thunderfoot volunteered to haul it back to the truck. He carried the pail across the pasture and as he got near the turkey, he began talking to it and tried to reach out to pet it. Wanting no part of such activity, the turkey quickly ran away. Thunderfoot put the bucket in the truck and started back to the pond. As he got near the turkey again, he said something to it, and it puffed all up and began strutting. "Hey look," Thunderfoot said. "He thinks I'm a girl turkey and he's trying to impress me."

Thunderfoot sat down in the grass by the pond again and resumed fishing. Soon the turkey came waddling up to the pond and began strutting and drumming next to his new best friend. It would run at him all puffed up, and then spin around and make a spitting and drumming sound. "Pfffft, boooom!"

"You'd better watch out," I said to the boy. "He'll be trying to mate with you if you're not careful." I had no more than said that when the turkey rushed forward and jumped up on Thunderfoot's back. Thunderfoot jumped to his feet and almost fell into the pond.

"Hey, you big bugger. Get away from me!"

I was laughing my head off as Thunderfoot backed away from the bird and it kept coming at him, spitting and drumming and making itself look as big and beautiful as it could. "You're his choice of a mate," I said. "He thinks you're looking pretty foxy."

"Oh, ha ha. You're really funny," Thunderfoot said. The turkey chased him around the pond for a half-hour. When the bird finally got tired of his advances being ignored, he wandered off to pester the geese that were lying in the sun, enjoying the day.

"I wish you'd quit fooling around and help me catch these bullheads," I said. He just glared at me and baited his hook and cast out. He kept looking over his shoulder every few minutes to make sure his suitor wasn't coming back. In about another half-hour, we had enough bullheads for the time being. We loaded our poles and the fish into the back of the truck and drove home. It was too late in the day to try to set the poles, so we decided to set them out in the morning, and bait them the next evening.

The next morning we motored slowly up the river just after breakfast, looking for deep water along the bank – areas that looked like a place where a big catfish would live. We found a good-looking spot and tied the boat to a tree, and began trying to shove one of our poles into the bank. It wasn't an easy task. When we tried to stick the pole into the ground, the boat slid away from the bank and we didn't make any progress. "One of us has to get out and work on the river bank," I said.

"I'll go," Thunderfoot said. "There might be a snake out there and I wouldn't want you to have a hissy fit."

I didn't argue with him.

We finally got the first pole into the bank, found the water depth, tied the line at the correct length, and then wrapped it up on the pole. "There, one down," I said. "Only nine more to go." It was a good thing we started early because it took us all day to get the poles all set. We worked straight through without lunch, and Thunderfoot was so weak from hunger that I had to get out on the bank, despite the threat of vipers, and shove the last three poles into the dirt.

"I'm feeling faint from lack of food," he said as he lay limply in the bottom of the boat.

"You poor baby. I feel so bad for you."

"If I loose consciousness, shove a hamburger or something in my mouth and move my jaw, and maybe I'll come back to life," he said as he tried to raise his head.

We loaded the boat and went home for some food. Thunderfoot fired up the grill and soon had a dozen hot dogs cremated. He stuffed them into his face as fast as he could lay them in a bun and squirt ketchup on them. "I think I may survive after all," he said as the 7th hot dog disappeared.

"I was worried about you for a while," I said, "but I knew how tough you are, so I knew you'd pull through." Big grin as hot dog number 8 began to disappear.

After we finished eating, Thunderfoot said, "Do you think we have time to bait the hooks yet?"

"It's getting pretty late. I don't know."

"Let's try. Otherwise we'll have to wait a whole day more."

Making sure there were ten bullheads in the pail, we took off for the river again. One by one, we baited the poles with a bullhead on each line. It was nearly dark when we got back to the boat landing and loaded up. It had been a long day.

The next morning I could hear cupboard doors slamming and the refrigerator open and close so I knew Thunderfoot was having his breakfast, and doing it as noisily as possible so I'd get up. "Can I pour you some cereal?" he said cheerily as I walked into the kitchen.

"Have the dogs been out yet?"

"Yup. I took them out half an hour ago."

"Again, I must ask: are you out of cereal at your house?"

"Of course not. I just enjoy your sunny smile every morning, so I come over here for breakfast," he said, with a grin from ear to ear.

I couldn't help myself from smiling, and cuffed him on the side of the head. "Pour me some cereal and give me the newspaper."

After we ate, we hopped into the truck and headed for the river. The boat was still hooked on the back of the truck from the evening before. We launched the boat and began motoring upriver to the first pole. As we got alongside the pole, Thunderfoot reached out and took hold of the line, lifting it carefully. The bullhead was gone. "Wow. We got robbed on this one."

"Hook it up on the pole and we'll check the next one."

The next two poles had live bullheads on them so we just left them in the water. As we approached the fourth pole Thunderfoot took the line and began lifting it up. He had raised it about a foot when his hand was jerked down into the water. "Holy cow! There's a fish on here!" he shouted.

"Pull him up!" I said.

He pulled and the line jerked down, and then he gained a little on it only to have it pulled back down again. "It's a big one," he said. Finally he began to gain on the fish as the water boiled beneath the line. I got the net out and prepared to net the fish. Suddenly a catfish that weighed about ten pounds came to the surface and I slid the net under it. "Whooie," Thunderfoot said. "Our first bank pole fish."

"Not bad."

"Jeez. If that one pulled that hard, how would you ever get a fifty pound one up?"

"Very carefully," I said.

The next two poles were minus their bullheads, and the next one was snagged up on some roots or something next to the bottom. We pulled and pulled and finally had to cut the line. We decided to move the pole to a new spot. Pole number eight was just ahead, and as we came near, the pole began bucking like a bronco. There was a fish on it, and it had to be a big one – it was pulling the pole right down into the water. "Holy cow," Thunderfoot said. "I'm scared to grab it."

"Just go slow and steady," I said as I held onto an overhanging branch to steady the boat. He took hold of the line and began cautiously lifting it. It came up easily. He looked at me. "Maybe it got off."

"Doesn't look like there's anything on it now," I said. He shrugged and began hauling the line up hand over hand. Suddenly the sinkers appeared and then the head of a huge catfish appeared on the surface of the water.

"Holy smokes!" The fish's head was about a foot across with a mouth big enough to swallow your arm, clear up to the shoulder. The catfish dove for the bottom, ripping the line through Thunderfoot's fingers. He tried to stop it and almost got pulled over the side. "Come here and help me," he yelled. "It's gonna pull me in!"

I raced to the front of the boat and grabbed the line and together we fought the fish. It was a grand battle. We would gain a few feet of line and then the fish would drag it back through our hands and we'd have to work to get it all back. This went on for a long time, before the fish began to make shorter and shorter runs to the bottom.

"He's tiring out," I said.

"So am I," Thunderfoot panted.

Finally, the fish came to the top and lay on its side. There was no way it would fit into our net. "How we gonna get it in the boat?" Thunderfoot asked.

"Just a minute. Hold it." I stepped to the back of the boat and put on a pair of gloves I kept ub vgnbvcncnder the seat. Then I went back to the front and reached over the side, grabbed the fish by its lower jaw, lifted and drug and finally slid the monster into the boat.

We both fell back onto the floor of the boat panting. "Jeez!" Thunderfoot said. "That's the biggest catfish I've ever seen."

"It's a big one, for sure. The biggest I've ever caught."

The huge catfish was over three feet long and must have weighed 30 or 40 pounds. It lay there breathing air through its gills, wiggling from side to side every so often. We watched it for a couple of minutes and I think we both had the same idea at once. Thunderfoot looked at me. "Are you thinking what I'm thinking?"

"Let it go?"

"We think alike," he grinned. "A fish that's been in the river for as long as that one has deserves to go back and live for a while longer."

"Get the pliers and let's get the hook out and turn her loose," I said. We removed the hook and I took the fish's lower jaw and Thunderfoot lifted its tail, and we put it over the side. We held it in the current for about a minute, and then it began to struggle to be free. We let go and watched it swim into the depths of the river.

Thunderfoot slapped me on the back. "We did good."

"Yeah, we did," I said. We both were exhausted and sat down in the boat to rest. I was sitting there just catching my breath and began to notice that Thunderfoot had red welts on his arms and legs. "You look like you got into some poison ivy or something."

He looked at his arms and legs. "Wow! You're right, and you've got it too." I looked and sure enough, I had little red welts on my arms and legs, too.

"We probably got into it when we were jamming those poles into the bank yesterday," I said.

"Whatya think of this bank poling?" Thunderfoot asked.

"I think catching the bait was the best part, except for releasing that big fish."

"Me too. Let's pull up the poles and go back to regular fishing. This was fun, but I don't think I want to do it every day."

I didn't argue. We pulled up all the other poles on the way back to the landing, turned the rest of our bullheads loose and stacked the poles in back of the garden. "They'll be good for building duck blinds this fall," Thunderfoot said.

We cleaned the ten-pound fish and chunked it up so we could deep-fry it later that evening for supper. Then we went to the pharmacy and got a couple of bottles of Calamine lotion.

We probably looked a little funny as we sat on the patio with the deep fryer. We'd fry a batch of battered catfish chunks, then a batch of French fries, and then a batch of onion rings. We ate as we fried, and we kept it up until we were both stuffed.

We both were covered with pink spots where we had dabbed the Calamine to take the itch out of the poison ivy. "Well, that was quite an adventure," Thunderfoot said as he chewed on a piece of catfish. "We got to be lumber jacks; I got attacked by a lovesick turkey; and we caught Jaws. And now, here we sit looking like a couple of clowns with pink spots all over us."

I glanced over at him and smiled. "So, why is this much different from most of our adventures.?"

"I guess you're right," he laughed. "Nobody can say we aren't willing to try something new."

So true, so true.

Thanks, Thunderfoot.

You Should Be On TV

Thunderfoot and Katie were playing ball with an old half-flat soccer ball and Kirby was lying in the sun snoozing. I was puttering around in the greenhouse when the phone rang. I ran for the house to answer it, and as I went through the front door I noticed the peeling paint on the trim that had been in need of a coat of paint for a quite a while. But I had kept talking myself out of getting the painting job done for quite a while, too. As I hung up the phone I decided to go to my workshop, get the paint scraper, and begin the dreaded task. Finally, the trim would be repainted.

Well, the scraper made short work of the chipped trim, but then I noticed that the edge of the roof overhang was looking a little shabby, so I started scraping that, too. When that was done I saw a couple of places on the siding that needed a little touch-up, and soon I had a pretty large area all scraped and ready for painting.

Meanwhile, Thunderfoot had made it a point to ignore me. "You wanna help me paint this?" I asked.

"I knew you were making work for me when I saw you starting that," he said.

"Oh, come on. It won't kill you to paint a little."

He grudgingly sauntered to the porch. "Where's the paint?"

"I have some in the closet from a couple of years ago. I'll get it," I said. Well, of course, the paint in the can was as hard as a stone, so we hopped in the truck and went to the hardware store for some new paint.

"Might as well get a gallon, so we have enough," I said.

Thunderfoot gave me an apprehensive stare. "We're just gonna paint the door frame and stuff, right?"

"Of course."

We bought a handful of disposable foam paintbrushes and a piece of plastic sheeting to catch the drips, too, and soon we were back at the house painting the door frame, the fascia board, and the rest of the trim. "That looks good," I said. "But now the siding looks shabby. While we're at it, let's paint just this area by the door."

Thunderfoot shook his head – like he knew what was coming – and kept on painting.

As the siding on the wall we were painting was almost finished, I decided to move to the adjoining wall and spruce it up, too. While we worked, we heard the honking of a flock of geese. We both stopped and looked up. A flock of about thirty geese flew overhead. "There they are," Thunderfoot said, pointing up to the northwest. "Have you ever noticed that when geese fly in a V, one side of the V is longer than the other?" he asked.

"Well, yeah, I guess you're right. I never really thought about that before."

"You know why one side is longer?" he asked.

"Nope. Why?"

"Because there are more geese on that side!"

I just looked at him, trying to figure out if he was being smart, or if he was serious. Suddenly he burst out laughing. "Jeez. What a fish. You fell for that hook, line, and sinker."

I had to laugh, too. He got me on that one.

We continued painting, and Thunderfoot said, "Do you think one of those big military helicopters with a propeller on each end could lift your house?"

I stared at him. Another joke? "What?"

"Do you think one of those big helicopters could lift your house?"

"Are you serious?"

"Yeah. Of course."

"What is going on in your head? Where did you get that idea?"

"I don't know. It just came to me," he said grinning. "Do you think they could lift it?"

"I have no idea. And just for the record, you scare me," I said.

"How many people do you think are dead in the cemetery?"

I stopped painting again. "How many people are dead in the cemetery? Did you have a sharp blow to the brain recently?" I asked.

Thunderfoot looked at me as seriously as possible. "How many people are dead in the cemetery?"

"I don't know."

"All of them!" He doubled over with laughter. Score two for Thunderfoot.

We finished the adjoining wall, and then I was looking at the trim above the front window. Thunderfoot moaned. "I knew it. I just knew it. We're gonna end up painting the whole house before we're done."

"Oh, quit griping and paint."

"Know what the white part of bird poop is?" he asked.

"Are you trying to drive me crazy?" I said. "Because if you are, you're doing a good job of it."

"You majored in biology in college. I'm just thirsting for knowledge."

"Sorry," I said. "I thought you were being smart again."

Thunderfoot just shook his head.

"I'm not sure. I guess we never studied bird poop," I said.

"Well, I just happen to know what the white part of bird poop is," he said. "It's bird poop, too!" Again, he burst out laughing and slapped his knee. "Jeez, you're so easy."

A little while later he said, "Knock, knock."

"Ok. You win. Let's quit," I said. I began putting the lid on the paint can and gathering up the plastic tarp. Thunderfoot just stood there watching.

"You don't have to be mad. I was just trying to make a little joke."

"I'm not mad. We already painted three times as much as I planned, and I don't like painting any more than you do. So let's quit."

We threw the disposable brushes away, woke up the dogs, and started into the house. I stopped by the front and looked at our paint job. "It looks a lot better, but you know, it really could use a second coat."

"Let's have some lunch, and then we'll do it," Thunderfoot said. "I've got lots more material to try on you."

Well, at least his jokes were better than his singing.

Thanks, Thunderfoot.

Just Call Me Oliver Twist

During the summer, my Sport Shop had an added sideline business. I had ten canoes and rented them to people to canoe the Wisconsin River. Part of the rental business included a shuttle service. I had an old van and a canoe trailer to haul the intrepid paddlers upriver to a drop-off point so they could start their journey, and then I picked them up at the time and place they wanted to leave the river.

Now that Thunderfoot was old enough to drive, he was my canoe hauler for the summer, which was just fine with him. I charged the renters for the service and gave Thunderfoot two-thirds of the charge for his time, and kept one-third for gas. It worked out to some real good money for him on some weekends, for not too much work, and he occasionally got a tip for his help unloading canoes and giving advice to the tourists on how to read the river and to be safe.

Usually, most of the canoe business was on the weekends, but occasionally some people would show up during the week wanting to take a canoe trip. It worked out really well for me to have Thunderfoot living so close, and he was usually home. And if he wasn't home, he was usually at my house, anyway.

Such was the occasion when a couple showed up one Wednesday and wanted to spend the day on the river. I called Thunderfoot's house and his mom answered. She told me that he was outside painting the picnic table and she'd send him right over. I took care of the rental forms and in a couple of minutes, Thunderfoot came trotting across the back yard, wearing an old pair of cut off jeans and a tee shirt that was torn and covered with dark red paint. "Jeez! Don't bother dressing up just for work," I said jokingly.

"I thought you wanted me right away. I didn't take time to clean up."

"Well, take these folks up to the Lone Rock landing, and then work out a time to pick them up," I instructed.

"Okie dokie," he said, and went out to load up the voyagers.

After about an hour he came back and parked the van. "I'll be back to go get them at about five," he said. "Oh, hey. By the way... I keep all tips that I get, don't I? Or do I have to share them with you?"

"Tips? Nope. You get all tips. Why? Did they give you a tip?"

"Yup," he said, pulling three dollars from his pocket and grinning like a cat with canary breath.

"They were probably entranced by your lovely wardrobe and quick wit," I said.

"Actually, I think it was because I looked like a pauper, and they felt sorry for me."

I didn't think much more about it, and later that day he picked up the people and put the canoe and other gear away. A couple of days later, two couples came to the store and wanted a couple of canoes, so I called Thunderfoot. He came right over and hauled them to the river. I noticed he was wearing the same old cut off jeans and another equally tattered tee shirt, but thought he was probably painting or working for his mom, and I didn't give it much attention.

That day, when he returned from picking up the tourists, he was strutting like a peacock as he came into the shop. "I did good again," he said, pulling five dollars from his pocket.

"Another tip?"

"Yup. This is getting to be a good racket. I think these people think I'm real poor and feel sorry for me." I just shook my head. What a con man.

The weekend came and we had three groups of canoe renters coming on Saturday morning, so I told Thunderfoot I'd call him when some of them arrived at the shop.

When the first group showed up, I called, and told him to get three canoes ready with paddles and life jackets. He was out back loading the gear when I took the people out to meet him. I couldn't believe my eyes. He was wearing some old dress pants that looked like the legs had been cut off with a chain saw, about 6 inches different in length, and had strings and pieces of cloth hanging from them. One sleeve was torn from his tee shirt, and the pocket was partly ripped off and hanging down. But the clincher was his feet—one tennis shoe and one beat up, old, brown dress shoe.

"I... uh... this is Thunderfoot. He'll take you up river," I said to the people.

They looked at him and I could see the pity in their eyes.

"Hello," Thunderfoot said, giving the tourists his most wonderful smile. He glanced and winked at me as he turned toward the van. I just wished the people a good trip and went back to the shop.

A while later, the second group came, and just as soon as Thunderfoot came back from dropping off the first group, he loaded up the next bunch and took them up river. The final group arrived, and again he took off for the river with them. It was nearly noon when he returned, and he came in to the shop for some lunch.

"Please sir. May I have some porridge?" he mugged.

"Jeez. You're unbelievable. What is that get-up you're wearing? Is it Halloween?"

He grinned from ear to ear. "I figured if they thought I was real poor, I might get some bigger tips."

Late in the afternoon, when the canoe renters began arriving at the boat landing, Thunderfoot picked them up and returned them to their cars. He was in the back putting the paddles away and hanging up the life jackets to dry when I walked out. "Everyone back safe and sound?"

"Yup. All accounted for," he said.

"And how did poor Oliver Twist make out?"

His grin was as wide as the river. "Well, the first group gave me five dollars, that group of three couples gave me a ten, and the last ones – with the lady who looked at me so sad? Well, they gave me ten dollars too." He reached in his pocket and pulled out two wadded up tens and a five. His share of the charges for the shuttle amounted to 46 dollars, so he had a pretty good day.

I handed him his share of the money and he sorted and turned all the bills facing the same way. "Hmm. Not bad," he said. "Seventy one dollars for about five hours' work."

"But don't you feel bad about making those people think you're so poor?" I asked.

"Oh, yea. I feel real bad... Not."

I had to laugh at him as he grinned like the little miser he was.

"You know," he said in a pondering sort of way. "I wonder if I could get a cast on my hand or one of my feet? That would work pretty good, too, huh?"

I just walked away shaking my head. Next he'd be trying to sell someone a building site in the river bottoms.

Thanks, Thunderfoot.

Houseboating

I had been talking with my friend Lumpy about another trip to Canada, and we had looked into some new ideas for our annual upcoming vacation. The fly-in trip had been lots of fun and we caught plenty of fish, but we wanted to try something else this summer. We checked into renting a houseboat on Lake of the Woods. We thought it would make a great summer trip, so we booked it, and now we were going to tell the boys. Lumpy's son, Chris, had been with us the year before, and he and Thunderfoot got along well. Both were died-in-the-wool fishermen, so we got together on a Sunday afternoon to break the good news to them.

We were sitting in the back yard, grilling hamburgers and relaxing while the boys played with the dogs. "Hey, you guys. Come here," I called to them. "We're kicking around an idea, and we want to see what you think of it."

They came running and plopped down in lawn chairs, panting after the roughhousing with the dogs. "What's up?"

"Well, we've been thinking of a fishing trip this summer, and wanted to see if you guys thought it would be okay."

"Trip? What trip?"

"Well, we thought since last year we did a fly-in, we'd take a houseboat trip on Lake of the Woods this year."

Their mouths dropped open. They both looked as though they had been struck in the head by a blunt object. "Lake of the Woods! That's huge. It's like an ocean. A houseboat? Holy cow!"

They were both just about ready to bust.

"Here's how it will work," I said. "We drive up to the houseboat place, and we take our own boats along. We can piggyback them on one trailer since Lumpy's boat is a little smaller than mine. Then, when we get there, we tie our boats behind and tow them with the houseboat out on the lake. The houseboat has a kitchen, shower, toilet, and bunks, and we just live on it, like in a cabin for the week. When we fish, we take our boats out and then come back to where we've tied up the houseboat – on an island or beach. And we can always move the houseboat closer if we find some good fishing spots. What do you think?"

Both of the boys were ready to jump up and leave for the north instantly. "Ohmygosh," Thunderfoot said, jumping to his feet. "I gotta get my stuff ready. When are we leaving?"

"Relax. We're not going for two weeks. I don't think you have to pack just yet," I said, laughing. We spent the rest of the evening talking about what to bring and made our grocery list, and after a while, we had our plans pretty well figured out.

We began checking our tackle and rods and reels, and readied the boat and trailer for the trip. The time passed quickly, and all of a sudden, there were only a couple of days left before we were going to leave.

Thunderfoot and I were in charge of grocery shopping. We went to the grocery store to get the things we needed for a week on the big lake. Having had the experience of getting pretty tired of fish on the last trip, we were taking enough meat and food for breakfast, and one other meal a day. We planned on eating a shore lunch each day, so we needed food for the other meals. Not that there's anything wrong with fresh fish, but after half a dozen meals of it in a row, we wanted something a little different.

We also had a list for snacks. On that list were chips, cheese, crackers and SITSPN. "What's SITSPN?" I asked.

"Hmm. Let's see," Thunderfoot said.

"You wrote the list, and you don't know what you wrote down?"

"I can't remember what that was suppose to mean."

"Well, let's keep shopping. Maybe it'll come to you," I said.

When we had about everything on the list gathered up, Thunderfoot still couldn't remember what SITSPN was supposed to represent. "Well, we'll have to just forget it if we can't remember what it is," I said.

"I hope it's not something important."

We took the groceries home and packed all the dry stuff in a box, and put the meat and everything that had to be kept cool in the refrigerator. We called it a day. Thunderfoot went home, still trying to remember what it was that we hadn't gotten. I watched TV a little while, and then went to bed. I was sleeping soundly when I could hear a bell sounding, and I tried to ignore it. It kept ringing and ringing, and suddenly I realized that it was the phone. I jumped up and looked at the clock. It was just after one o'clock in the morning. I raced for the phone, fearing the worst. After all, who calls at one in the morning if it's not bad news? "Hello?" I said, as I picked up the phone.

"Good. You're up."

"Of course I'm up. I had to answer the phone!"

It was Thunderfoot. "I know what SITSPN is!"

"What? You called me in the middle of the night to tell me that?"

"Uh... well... yeah, I guess it is a little late. But I remembered what it is."

I sat down in my recliner, my heart racing from the mad dash to the phone, with the expectation that I was going to hear someone had been in a car wreck... or worse. "Well, you have my attention now. What the heck is SITSPN?"

"It's Salted In The Shell Pea Nuts," he said calmly. "Boy, it's a good thing I remembered that. I'd hate to go on a trip like this without them."

"Well, now I can sleep soundly, knowing that we didn't forget our peanuts," I replied.

"Jeez... you don't have to be such a grouch," he said, sounding a little hurt.

"Sorry. I'm like that when I get woke up from a deep sleep to be told such earth shattering news."

"Well fine. Next time I'll just not call you."

I had to laugh a bit, and said, "Oh, never mind. I'm glad we figured it out. I'll talk to you tomorrow. And if you think of anything else we missed, just write it down and tell me in the morning. Okay?"

"Okie dokie. Nighty night," he said.

The big departure day finally arrived. We loaded up all of our gear in the boat and in the back of the van, and met Lumpy and Chris. We finished loading all of their stuff, and then we strapped down Lumpy's boat upside down on top of mine. It was quite a sight to see how much gear four people needed for a fishing trip. But soon we were off toward the great north woods.

The drive would take about eleven hours, so to avoid getting too tired, Lumpy and I took turns driving. Of course, the boys kept volunteering to drive, but neither Lumpy nor I were too keen on riding with someone their age and with their limited driving experience. We stopped for a late supper. After we finished and were walking back to the van, Thunderfoot said, "Why don't you let me drive for a while? You guys are tired, and I'm a perfectly good driver."

"Oh, that's okay. I'm not too tired," I said.

"You could barely keep your eyes open when we were eating," he said. "I drive the canoe trailer all the time and it's no different than the boat trailer."

Well, he did have a point. "Okay. You can drive and we'll take a little rest. But be careful."

Thunderfoot and Chris sat in the front seat and Lumpy and I crawled in the back. Off we went, again, into the darkness.

"You'd better get some gas pretty soon," I said. "The towns are a long way apart up here, and we don't want to run out."

"Okay. As soon as we come to a gas station, I'll stop," Thunderfoot said.

I was dozing a bit when I felt the van make a turn and saw that we were pulling into a gas station. We slowed down by the pumps and then sped up again and back out onto the highway. "What are you doing? Why didn't you stop for gas?"

"It was too expensive. It was about five cents a gallon higher priced than the gas at home," Thunderfoot said.

"Well, don't go too much farther, or we'll run out."

My eyes were heavy again, and soon I was asleep. The next thing I knew, I could feel us pulling off the road and stopping. I opened my eyes and there was no gas station; there was no town; there were no lights; there was nothing but darkness. "What's wrong?" I asked.

Thunderfoot and Chris were huddling in the front seat, looking at the map.

"What's going on?"

"Well," Thunderfoot said, "We're about half way between that town with the expensive gas and this town here," he said pointing to the map.

"But we don't have enough gas to get to that town, so I think we gotta go back to the last town."

"What? Are you serious? How far have we gone past that town?"

"About fifty miles," he said so softly that I could barely hear him.

"Fifty miles! And how far to the next town?"

"Maybe seventy, give or take a few miles, and we're below an eighth of a tank, so we can't make it that far."

I was about to blow my top when I realized that Thunderfoot had just made a mistake, and it wasn't worth making a big fuss over. "Okay. Well, turn around and we'll go back."

Thunderfoot shot Chris a quick glance, and they put the map away. He turned our rig around and started back to the expensive gas station. I looked at Lumpy and he just grinned and shrugged his shoulders. "Oh well, what the heck?"

After another short nap, we were slowing down again. I sat up in the seat. We were at the expensive gas station, but it was closed. Of course. It was two o'clock in the morning, so that was no surprise.

"Uh oh. It's closed," Thunderfoot said.

"No foolin, Sherlock. What was your first clue?" We all got out of the van and were standing there trying to figure out what to do next, when a police car pulled into the station.

"You fellas got some trouble?"

"We're just about out of gas, and I don't think we can make it to the next town," I said.

"You should have filled up earlier in the evening," the policeman said.

"Yeah. No kidding," I said as I shot a scowl at Thunderfoot.

He shrugged his shoulders. "I was just trying to save you some money."

"Well, there's an all night station about twelve miles east of here. Can you make it that far?" the policeman asked.

"Well, I think so," I said. "If not, one of these young lads will be glad to jog down the road with a can to get enough gas to get us to the station." I looked right at Thunderfoot who nodded his head like an obedient puppy.

"Well, good luck then," the policeman said and drove off.

"Well, let's go and find this station," I said. We all got back into the van. I drove this time, and we must have been running on fumes as we finally saw the lights of the gas station up ahead.

"We made it!" Thunderfoot said from the back seat.

"Yeah. How nice. We only wasted two hours and sixty miles of driving the wrong way. And hey, look! It's three cents cheaper than the last place," I said.

"Jeez... you don't have to be so sarcastic," Thunderfoot whined.

We gassed up, got some pop and snacks and then headed back into the darkness. This time we were going north again, which was a big improvement.

We reached International Falls at about eight in the morning and decided to stop before we crossed the border. At a neat little trading post type Tourist Stop, we had our money changed to Canadian currency. The place displayed lots of souvenirs and funny tee shirts. Thunderfoot and Chris each bought a shirt that had a picture of a walleye on the front and said "Walleyes, eh?" Thunderfoot snuck around and bought something else that he wouldn't show us.

"What are you buying?" I asked.

"Just a little souvenir for mom," he replied.

With our new Canadian money, we headed for the border and then on up into the country toward Lake of the Woods.

We crossed the border with little trouble. The border guard looked under the boat on top of the trailer as best he could, and then waved us through. He probably thought we looked too bedraggled to be smugglers.

We pulled into the houseboat rental place at about eleven that morning. We were a pretty motley looking group, having driven all night. But we were all full of enthusiasm, ready to get our boats in the water and our gear on the houseboat. The man who rented the boats helped us stow our gear and food on the boat, and then took us out in the lake for a lesson on how to drive the houseboat. He showed us some good places on the map to tie up at night for a camp. We took him back to shore and he wished us a good trip. Then, off we went for our first day on the lake.

"Can I drive?" Thunderfoot asked as we pulled away from the dock. I glanced Lumpy's way. He shrugged his shoulders.

"I guess so, but keep it slow for a while till you get a feel for it. We'll put all the gear away and tidy things up. And remember – this doesn't have brakes like a car, so if you think you have to stop, start doing it ahead of time."

"Aye aye, captain." Thunderfoot grinned from ear to ear as he sat on the stool behind the steering wheel inside the cabin. We started out across the bay, and Lumpy and I studied the map to decide on a place to park the boat for the first day. The outfitter had marked several locations on the map with a little red x – good places to tie up. He had also given us some pointers about good places to try the fishing. We decided on a spot and showed it to Thunderfoot.

"Can you follow this map to that spot?"

He peered at the map a few seconds and said, "I guess so. It can't be that hard."

The rest of us got busy and put the food into the refrigerator and stored our clothes and other gear in the little bedroom at the back of the boat. Our two boats were trailing along in the wake of the houseboat, and seemed to be riding just fine, but we checked the knots holding them, anyway, just to make sure we wouldn't lose one on the way. It had taken about an hour to get everything ship-shape, and when I went back to the main cabin to check on Thunderfoot, I noticed he was reading the map upside down. "What are you doing? That map is upside down."

"Yeah, I know. I like it that way," he said.

"Why are you doing that?"

"What's the difference? Don't worry. I know right where I am."

By then we had gone past several islands and I had no idea where we were, so I had to rely on him being right. "You know, there's 14,000 islands in this lake. Don't get us lost."

He gave me one of those looks, and then a while later he said, "Right around that island should be where we want to go. That's Rabbit Island." Well, sure enough, just as we got to the other side of the island, there was a nice sandy beach that was shown on the map as a good place to tie up. Thunderfoot just gave me one of his famous *"see, I told you so"* looks. We pulled up on the sand beach and the boys hopped out. They tied the boat to two trees by long ropes that were attached to the back of the houseboat.

"Let's go fishing," Thunderfoot and Chris said.

"That's what we came for," I said, and I began putting gear and our poles into the boats. Soon we were off, and we decided to all go to the same place to fish, since the day was almost shot and not a lot of time left to explore. We found a little bay that had a small stream running into it from one end, and we started casting walleye jigs up into the moving water. In no time at all we had enough fish for supper. We decided to call it a day.

The houseboat was just like a large motor home, but with pontoons instead of wheels. The kitchen was small, but it had everything we needed. There was a stove, oven, small refrigerator, and an eating area that could be converted into a bed. There was another sitting area that could be folded down to form another bed, if needed. The bathroom was just a little larger than a phone booth with a small sink, toilet and shower, all of which were supplied with water that was pumped from the lake, and heated by a small, concealed water heater. Wastewater was collected in a tank under the boat and would be pumped out when we returned.

The bedroom was in the back of the boat, and it wasn't what you'd call roomy. There was a set of bunk beds on each side of the room, with a narrow walkway between them. Against the back wall was a closet for storing clothes and gear. Outside the bedroom was a small deck with a rail around it to keep any sleepwalker from taking a drink, and a ladder that led to the roof, where one could soak up the sun. And there was a gas grill bolted to the floor on the roomy front deck. So, overall, it was a pretty nice little self-contained home on the water.

The boys cleaned the fish while Lumpy and I peeled some potatoes and opened a couple of cans of beans. Soon the smell of frying fish and potatoes filled the kitchen.

While the food was cooking, I decided that I'd try the shower. I found a towel, clean clothes, and my bathroom kit in the bedroom, and squeezed into the phone booth bathroom. After I shaved, I decided to see how the shower worked. I turned the water on, adjusted it to just the right temperature, and then squeezed in. It was a tight fit. I managed to wash my hair, and as I began to soap up my body, of course I dropped the bar of soap trying to reach my back. I tried to bend over to pick it up, but there wasn't room in the shower to bend, at least not for me. I had to open the curtain and step out into the bathroom to be able to bend far enough to pick up the soap, and then hit my butt on the sink while doing it. This was definitely not the bathroom for a full sized guy like me. I finally managed to get clean and rinsed off, and by the time I was dry and dressed, the supper was ready.

"How'd the shower work?" Thunderfoot asked.

"Not bad. The water was nice and hot, and it came out pretty good, but it's a little cramped for me."

"Maybe you could just rub soap on the walls and then spin around," he said, laughing.

That didn't sound like a bad idea.

It didn't take long for us all to start yawning and stretching after supper, and as soon as we had the kitchen cleaned up we all began preparing for bed. The bedroom wasn't big enough for four people to get undressed at once, so we took turns until we all were in bed. I was the last in line, and I turned out the light.

"G'night Lumpy."

"G'night Thunderfoot."

"G'night Chris."

"G'night Dan."

The quiet settled in.

Then Thunderfoot said, "G'night Mary Ellen. G'night John Boy." The whole boat was shaking from our laughter. Then it was quiet again and I began to dose off. Then someone farted. We were all laughing again like we were on drugs or drunk. Then it was quiet for a while.

"G'night Grandpa."

"G'night Mary Ellen." We all laughed again. Quiet again.

"Burrrrrrp!" Raucous laughter filled the bedroom again. This went on for the next several minutes until exhaustion finally took us all off to dreamland.

Sunlight poured into the bedroom through the glass door, rousing our sleepy bunch the next morning that came much too quickly. It wasn't long until we all began yawning and scratching. Thunderfoot was the first out of bed and heading for the bathroom. "I'm gonna get in there before it gets all fouled up," he said. The rest of us arose and dressed, and soon Lumpy and I were busy in the kitchen making breakfast. In about an hour, all of us had gotten our bathroom duties out of the way, filled our bellies with hash browns, bacon, and eggs, and were ready for a day of fishing.

Off we went again, in both our boats, in search of the elusive walleye and northern pike. It was a grand day with little wind, and we found a spot about four miles from the houseboat that was just full of fish. "I'll go back and move the houseboat to that bay over there," Lumpy announced. He and Chris left to bring our house closer to the good fishing while Thunderfoot and I stayed and fished. That evening we had fresh walleyes with fried potatoes and beans on the side. We ate until we all just about exploded. Then we played a few games of cards, and at bedtime, the same old routine was replayed as we all "G'nighted." until we were nearly sick with laughter.

I was sleeping soundly when I thought I felt the boat moving a little, but it didn't wake up enough to cause me to worry about it. I was just dozing off again when I heard a loud bang outside the back door of the bedroom. That woke me up completely, so I sat up and swung my legs over the side of the bed. Lumpy and Chris seemed to still be asleep on the two bunks across from me, so I stood up to see if Thunderfoot was still in his bunk above me, but his bed was empty. I walked to the front of the boat and checked the bathroom to see if he was there, but he was nowhere to be found. Then I remembered the bang I had heard at the back of the boat. I walked back to the bedroom and out onto the deck. There was Thunderfoot, sitting on the deck in his underwear.

"What are you doing out here?" I asked.

He stared up at me with a dumbfounded look on his face.

"What are you doing?" I asked again.

"I... uh... I came out here to pee, but somehow I ended up on my back on the deck," he said. There was enough moonlight to see his footprints on the dew-covered deck, and the skid marks where his feet slid out from under him.

"You must have slipped on the wet deck," I said.

"Jeez... it's a good thing I didn't fall in the water," he said.

"It's a good thing your head is so hard, or you might have hurt yourself."

"Oh, funny," he said. I gave him my hand and helped him up. He was all wet on his backside, but he seemed okay otherwise.

"Why didn't you go in the bathroom?" I asked.

"I didn't want to wake you guys up."

"Well, you succeeded partly on that. Lumpy and Chris are still asleep," I said.

"No we're not," Lumpy called out from the bedroom. "Mr. Graceful woke us up, too, when he banged his head against the deck."

"Well, I had good intentions," Thunderfoot whined.

He dried off his back and changed into some dry underwear. He climbed back into his bunk and we all settled down for the rest of the night.

The next two days were spent fishing, eating and just having a grand time. The weather was perfect, the fishing was great, and the companionship was the best. On the morning of the fourth day, we decided to split up and explore more of the lake. So Lumpy and Chris headed north, and Thunderfoot and I headed west. We had our map and were looking for a river that ran into a huge bay a few miles west of our camp. We had been having some good luck fishing near creeks, so it seemed that a river must be even better.

At about mid-day we found the river and began fishing, catching some really nice northern pike. But then, the wind began to pick up. The surrounding timber sheltered the bay, so it wasn't too windy to fish, but I kept looking out past the point, and the big lake was getting pretty rough. "I think we'd better get back a little closer to home," I said.

Thunderfoot looked out toward the lake. "I think you're right. Those waves are getting pretty big."

We reeled up, put everything away, and decided it would be a good idea to put on our rain gear before we tackled the big waves coming at us across the lake. When we came out from the sheltered cove, we realized that the waves were much larger than we had thought. Many of them were three or four feet tall, and it was a long way across the lake. "Oh boy. Hang on!" I told Thunderfoot.

We started out slowly – going to fast just meant smashing the boat into the bone jarring waves. As it was, the cold water driven by the wind came splashing over the sides of the boat, and we were soon soaked even though we wore rain gear. And worse yet, it was impossible to see the other side of the lake, so we weren't sure where we were going.

"Once we get to the other side, we'll have to find our way between the islands to our houseboat," I yelled to Thunderfoot. He nodded in agreement. On we went... slowly.

After a few minutes, Thunderfoot turned quickly toward me and pointed to another boat, splashing and cutting through the waves, and coming in our direction. I steered toward the boat that carried just a lone person. As we neared, I recognized the old Indian guide who we had met back at the houseboat rental place. He looked to be about 70 years old and was barely over five feet tall. His face was brown and weathered, and now, in this weather, it looked like a wet catcher's mitt. He slowed down his boat and we pulled along side. "Yutta Hey! A bit bumpy out here, eh?" he said as he grinned at us with his three teeth that he had left, and the water dripping from his chin.

"Yeah, just a bit," I said. "Do you know which way it is to Deer Island?"

"Sure," he beamed. "Straight that way – two, maybe three miles." He pointed in the direction he had come from.

"Okay. Thanks," I said.

"Have fun, boys!" he said. He revved up his motor and headed out across the lake, seeming not to have a care in the world.

"Jeez... he's brave being out here all by himself," Thunderfoot said.

"He's probably been doing this his whole life," I replied.

"Well, two maybe three miles and we're home," Thunderfoot said just as a big wave slammed into the boat.

We pounded on ahead, and after about a half hour of being tossed among the surf and drenched with wind-driven spray, we reached the sheltered shoreline of the lake. We followed a cut between two islands, and eventually arrived at the houseboat. Glad to see that Lumpy and Chris were already home safe and sound, we noticed that the gas grill was sending out clouds of the most delicious smelling smoke. "Yutta hey!" Thunderfoot yelled as we drew near.

"Where you guys been?" Lumpy asked.

"Yutta hey. Two, maybe three miles yonder," Thunderfoot said, mocking the old Indian guide.

I knew we wouldn't hear the last of that for a while.

We tied up our boat, stowed away our gear, and changed into dry clothes. Lumpy had fired up the grill a few hours earlier, and as we walked to the front deck of the houseboat, he opened the grill lid, revealing the most beautiful golden brown turkey that I had ever seen.

"Holy cow! That's beautiful, Lump," Thunderfoot exclaimed.

"I think it's ready," Lumpy said. "And the rest of the meal is ready in the galley, so let's eat!" We sat down and ate like famished pagans, and in a half-hour or so, all that remained of the turkey was a skeleton, and

Thunderfoot was gnawing on that like a hyena.

"That was the best turkey I've ever had," he said, wiping the grease from his chin. "Burrrrrp."

I don't know if it was the sleep inducing affect that turkey has on people, or just the wind and waves, but in a short while after the meal we were all rather tired. One by one we drifted off to the bedroom, and soon we were all fast asleep.

The map that had been left with the houseboat had markings on it from other groups of fishermen who had found good angling spots. "Look here. There's a place where they marked a crappie spot. I didn't know there were crappies in Canada."

I studied the map. "That's quite a ways from here. Do you think it's worth the boat ride?"

"It says fourteen-inch crappies. I think that would be a lot of fun," Thunderfoot said. "But if you guys don't want to go, Chris and I can go and check it out."

I wasn't absolutely sure that I trusted Thunderfoot and Chris on the lake by themselves, but Lumpy thought it would be okay, so I gave my approval, too. The two boys jumped in Lumpy's boat and took off out across the lake. Lumpy and I went searching for a bay that had the promise of holding some toothy northern pike.

We found the bay, and after a few hours we had caught a lot of pike. About mid-afternoon, we decided to go back to the houseboat for some lunch. As we came around the island to the bay where the houseboat should have been parked, we both were quite shocked to see that it wasn't there. "What the heck?"

"This is the right bay, isn't it?" I asked.

"I'm sure it is," Lumpy groaned. "Go closer and we can see if there are tracks in the sand."

I drove up closer to the beach, and sure enough, there was a groove in the sand where the houseboat had been beached, and footprints in the sand where we had walked to tie it up.

"Where do you suppose the boat is," I asked.

Lumpy just shook his head.

We sat there trying to figure out what to do next when I noticed a piece of paper pinned to a tree branch with a clothespin. "Look, there's a note," I said, pointing to the tree. I moved the boat close to the beach. Lumpy jumped out, retrieved the note and read: "Moved the house to the crappie hole. They're huge and millions of them."

"The boys moved the boat," Lumpy said. He jumped aboard and handed me the note.

"Did you happen to look at the map to see where that crappie hole is?" I asked.

He shook his head.

"Oh, that's nice," I said. "They moved and we don't know where they moved it to."

Here we were on Lake of the Woods, with over 65,000 miles of shoreline and 14,000 islands, and our house had moved without us. "Well, I know that they took off to the north," I said. "I guess we'd better get to looking for them before it gets dark."

We fired up the motor and started up the lake toward where we had last seen the boys. It was like looking for a needle in a haystack. We drove for about two miles and then started looking around each island that we came to. If the boys had parked the boat on the backside of an island, we could easily miss seeing it. We looked at dozens of islands, and finally we came around the bend of one, and there was the houseboat pulled up on a beach. Thunderfoot and Chris were out on the deck with the fish cleaning board on a table, cleaning crappies. They waved enthusiastically at us as we drove up.

"Hey, look at these huge slab crappies." Thunderfoot held up a couple of them, grinning like madman.

"Those are real nice," I said calmly.

"Well, don't go overboard to compliment us," he said, his ego obviously bruised.

"Do you know where Lumpy and I have been for the last three hours?"

Thunderfoot glanced at Chris. "Fishing, I suppose. What else would you be doing?"

"We were searching for you two," I said. "Trying to find the houseboat."

"But we've been here for a long time, and we thought you knew where we were going."

"How would we know that?" I asked.

"Well, because we told you we were going to the crappie hole."

"Yeah, but we didn't know where that was."

It was then that he and Chris instantly realized that we had had no idea where they were going. A grin came to Thunderfoot's face. "Oops. We didn't think of that. We thought we were doing good to move the houseboat close to the crappies."

Lumpy and I just shook our heads. "Well, we're here now, so let's see those crappies."

We tied up our boat and inspected the huge crappies the boys were cleaning. "They'll be pretty tasty tonight for supper," Thunderfoot said rubbing his stomach.

"We'll get some potatoes ready. You guys finish cleaning the fish."

That evening, the boys told us about the bay just around the corner where they had caught all the crappies, and we declared the next day would be a crappie-fishing day. The next morning, Thunderfoot and Chris thought they would go in the same boat again, and they were off before we had even untied my boat from its mooring. We followed them to the crappie bay, where we set the boats to drift, trailing a bobber with two crappie jigs suspended underneath. It didn't take long until we began catching huge crappies, one after another. We would drift across the bay and then fire up the motor and go back to the other side and drift again.

Thunderfoot and Chris had just completed their drift and were motoring past us. As they went by, Thunderfoot, in the front of the boat, stuck his feet up on the side of the boat and yelled, "Yutta hey! Two, maybe three miles." On his feet were two big, brown, pillow-like slippers that looked like bear feet, with little beige claws and spots like the pads on a bear's foot. He was grinning like a madman. "Yutta hey!" Now we knew what he had bought in the gift shop at the border. Lumpy and I laughed until our stomachs ached.

The next day Thunderfoot was with me again, and we were a few miles from the houseboat, fishing for walleyes. The sky darkened and the wind came up.

"Looks like a storm coming," I said.

"Did you see that trappers cabin back there?" Thunderfoot said. "Let's see if we can go in it until the storm is over."

We motored back down the lake and beached the boat on an island where there was an old cabin. The door was unlocked.

"I don't think they ever lock these, so people who need shelter can use them," I said.

"Well, we need shelter, 'cause here comes the rain."

We watched the storm rage from inside the cabin. The wind riled up the lake into huge whitecaps, and the rain pounded on the tin roof of the cabin that had a few leaks, but nothing too serious. In the corner was a pile of dry firewood, so Thunderfoot decided to make a fire in the potbelly stove. In just a short while, a fire crackled and the cabin was getting nice and cozy.

"Now if we only had some food, we'd be in good shape," Thunderfoot suggested.

"I planned on going back to the houseboat for lunch, so I didn't bring anything to eat," I said.

"Well, I'm getting faminished," he said rubbing his belly.

There was a little lull in the storm, and suddenly Thunderfoot bolted out the front door. "Be right back." He ran down to the lake and grabbed the stringer with three walleyes that was tied to the oarlock. He came running back to the cabin. "We can have fish for lunch," he said as he bounded through the door.

"How are we going to cook them," I asked.

"Just you wait and learn," he said. He picked up an old weathered board that had once been driftwood and placed it on the table. Then he got out his knife and filleted the walleyes. He ran down to the lake again with the fillets and rinsed them off. When he returned to the cabin, he put the fillets on the table, ran out to a bush near the cabin and cut a couple of branches. Then he came back in and whittled the branches so they each had a fork on the end. Next, he cut a piece of fillet and skewered it onto the fork of one stick, opened the potbelly stove door and held the fillet over the coals. He turned to me, grinning. "Fish on a stick."

I watched as he carefully cooked the fish, and then slid if off onto the bare table. He picked it up and took a careful bite. "Mmm, not bad. Could use a little salt and pepper, but not bad."

I just shook my head. He never ceased to amaze me.

We ate all the fillets, and by the time we were done, the storm had passed, so we went back out on the lake and fished the rest of the day.

We had to return the houseboat back to the dock by eleven o'clock the next morning, so we started packing that night. Next morning we made a good breakfast before we started down the lake. Thunderfoot insisted on driving, and as surprised as I might be, he managed to find his way right back to the dock.

We loaded up the boats and gear, and much too soon we were heading south, toward home. The trip was uneventful, and many hours later we pulled up to Lumpy's house and unloaded his stuff. We bid Lumpy and Chris farewell and drove the last few miles home. As we pulled into town, Thunderfoot said, "Looks the same as when we left."

"Yeah. What did you expect to change?"

"Oh, I guess nothing," he said. "It seems funny that when you're on such an adventure, that the rest of the world just goes on the same."

We pulled into my driveway and the dogs came running out slobbering and jumping all over us. My dog sitter had done a good job of taking care of them, but they were glad to see their Dad and Thunderfoot. "Let's just leave the stuff and put it all away tomorrow," I said.

"Yeah. Good idea. I think I'd better go home and let mom know I'm still alive." Thunderfoot put his arms around my shoulders and gave me a bear hug. "Thanks for taking me."

"You're welcome," I said. That was all we needed to say about the subject, and he went walking across the lawn toward home.

Part way across, he stopped and put his hand up over his forehead, like he was looking for something. "Yutta hey! Three, maybe four miles," he said.

Yutta hey, Thunderfoot.

Do It Yourself

Shortly after we returned from our Canada excursion, a friend of mine offered me a roll of heavy-duty cyclone fencing. It had been a dog kennel, but his old dog had died and he wouldn't need it anymore. Of course, I couldn't turn down such a good offer, so I drove over to his house and picked it up. When I came home, I called Thunderfoot to tell him that I had a project for him.

"What ya gonna do?" he asked as he trotted into the back yard.

"I got this fencing for free, and I thought we could make a kennel for Katy and Kirby. Then, if we go someplace that they can't go along, they can lounge in the nice weather instead of being cooped up in the house."

"Cool. What you got in mind?" Thunderfoot asked.

"Well, I thought we'd mark out a rectangle here next to the garden shed and have someone come and pour a cement pad. Then we'll build a frame and put the wire on it, and if we cut a hole in the side of the shed, the dogs could go inside if it rained, or if they just wanted a nap."

"Why hire somebody to make the cement pad? *We* can do it. My grandpa has a cement mixer, and we can just frame it up and mix our own cement."

"Oh, I don't know," I said. "That sounds like more than we're capable of doing."

"What do you mean? You take sand and cement and water and roll it around in the mixer and it becomes concrete. How hard is that? Besides, just think of the money you'll save if we do it ourselves."

Well, I agreed to think about it. While I was pondering the idea, we rolled out the wire and measured it, to determine the size of the kennel. There was 28 feet of wire. We allowed space for a gate, and then measured out the size of the cement pad.

"That doesn't look so bad," Thunderfoot said. The area didn't seem that big, and after all – how hard could it be to mix cement? I agreed to give it a try.

The next day, Thunderfoot's grandpa drove into the driveway with a cement mixer in the back of his pickup truck. Thunderfoot and I drug the thing to the back yard, and then we went to the lumberyard for some two-by-fours for the form, and some sand and bags of concrete mix. The guy at the lumberyard helped us figure out how much of each ingredient we needed. We loaded it all in the pickup and headed for home.

The ground was kind of uneven where we wanted to build the kennel, so we had to shovel some of the dirt out to get it level.

"Where are we gonna put this extra dirt?" Thunderfoot asked.

I was standing there thinking about where to dispose of the dirt when he suddenly appeared quite enlightened. "Hey! Let's put it over there in the back of the yard and make a little hill, so the water can run down like a little waterfall into the pond."

"What pond?" I asked. (He had been pestering me for years to dig a pond in the back yard so we could put some bluegills in it during the summer.)

"Lake Thunderfoot," he said with a big, foolish grin.

"Oh, I don't know. This is gonna become a bigger job than we want – real fast."

"Oh, come on. It'll be fun." I knew he'd never let up, so I agreed.

We dug down so the kennel would be level, and dumped the extra dirt in a pile in the corner of the yard with a wheelbarrow. Then we built the form for the concrete pad. By the time all of this was done, it was time for lunch, and a nap for me, I hoped. Thunderfoot would not hear of it though, and kept hounding me until I agreed to pour the cement right away. "The sooner we get the kennel done, the sooner we can put in the pond."

We moved the mixer next to the form, began shoveling sand and concrete mix into the agitator and then added water until it became a soupy concoction that looked like cement. Once it was all mixed, we dumped it into the form.

"Holy cow! It's gonna take a lot of batches to fill this," Thunderfoot groaned as we surveyed the little puddle of cement. I just shook my head. I knew this was going to be one of those jobs that *seemed* easy at first, and then turned into a nightmare.

About fifteen batches of cement later, we finally had the form filled. We leveled it off with a two-by-four, and did our best to smooth it out with trowels when it started to harden. It wasn't exactly professional, but it did turn out pretty good.

"Well, are you ready to admit you were wrong?" Thunderfoot asked.

"We're not done yet. Let's wait until this is all finished, and then maybe I'll consider it."

We left the job for the day, while the cement dried, and the next morning, Thunderfoot was here bright and early for breakfast. When we removed the forms, the cement pad looked pretty darn good.

"Not bad for a couple of rookies," Thunderfoot said as we admired our handiwork.

We got out the saw, hammers and nails, and built the frame for the kennel, and fastened the wire to the frame. It fit like a glove. Then, with an old wire panel that I had saved for some reason, we built a frame and made a very nice gate for the kennel.

Thunderfoot stepped back and admired our work. "Very nice. All it needs now is a swimming pool, and the dogs will have their own spa."

I had to agree, but I wasn't too sure about the swimming pool.

"Well... let's go get the liner for the pond, and finish that up, too," he added.

"You still insist that we make a pond?"

"What? Did you think I'd forget?"

We went to the hardware store and looked over the choices for pond liners. Of course, Thunderfoot wanted to get one that was twenty feet by thirty feet – so we could have a *for real* pond. I was looking more at the little pre-formed ones that held a couple hundred gallons of water.

"Oh come on," he prodded me. "That thing is just a puny little puddle. We need a *real* pond."

"Well, I'm *not* going to turn the entire back yard into a lake," I advised. So we finally agreed on a compromise, and I bought it, along with a filter, hose and pump to keep the water circulating. We took it home and set it on the ground where we decided it would look best. We drew an outline in the dirt around it, and started digging. The dirt went up onto the ever-growing pile that we had started the day before. When the pond finally fit the hole and was level, I informed Thunderfoot that I had had enough for one day. "I'm pooped."

"Okay," he agreed. "But let's start early tomorrow so we can get the pond finished... and get some bluegills in it."

The next morning Thunderfoot was in the back yard bright and early backfilling around the pond and smoothing out the little hill we had created with all the extra dirt.

"You know," he said, "we should get some rocks and cover the dirt with them, and then maybe put in some plants and stuff so it looks nicer."

That sounded like a good idea, so I called a friend who had a quarry on his land and asked if we could get some rocks from him. He told me to take all we needed. In fact, he told me that he had an old trailer built from a pickup box hooked on the back of his truck, and that I should just use that to haul the rocks, so my pickup wouldn't get all scratched up. This was looking better all the time.

Thunderfoot and I drove out into the country to my friend's farm, got his pickup and trailer, and backed into the quarry. The stones were flat and of many different sizes – just what we wanted. The trailer was looking pretty squat after we had loaded up a lot of stones, so we decided to take what we had to the house and see if they would do the job. Thunderfoot drove my pickup back to town in case we needed it for another errand.

After we had backed the trailer into the yard and were ready to start unloading, we decided it would be a good idea to cover the dirt pile first with some of that porous cloth for gardening, so the weeds wouldn't grow up through the rocks. We got it all covered and began piling the rocks on the little hill and around the pond, to hide the liner.

"Wow!" Thunderfoot said. "We're gonna need a lot more rocks."

"No kidding. This isn't going to make a drop in the bucket. Aren't you glad we made the little hill so large now?"

"Oh, gripe, gripe, gripe," Thunderfoot said, grinning.

It took two more trips with the trailer to get enough rocks to cover the hill. While we were unloading the last load, my friend and his wife pulled into the driveway, and said that he needed his pickup, and that I should just pull the trailer back to the farm with mine. I thanked him for everything. We unhooked the trailer and he left.

When the last rocks were unloaded, we stepped back to admire our work. "Boy, that does look good," I said.

"Umm, see? What did I tell you? Now in the evening, you can come out here with a book and a beverage and sit and listen to the water cascade down the rocks and splash into the pond."

"And swat mosquitoes until I'm exhausted."

His face brightened. "Maybe we should build a little screened in house out here."

"I think we've done all the building we're going to do for a long while."

I had lifted enough rocks to last a lifetime. My back was sore, my hands were bruised and scraped, and my old body needed a shower and a rest. I insisted that we quit for the day.

The next morning, I heard water running and I went out to the garden to see Thunderfoot with the hose, filling the pond.

"We'll get it full, and then see how the pump works," he said with one of his big grins. We had hidden a length of hose under the rocks from the submerged pump to the top of our little hill, and placed three large, flat rocks as steps for the water from the pump to flow over, back into the pond, like a little waterfall.

Soon Thunderfoot was pestering me back inside the house to come and look. He had the pond filled and the pump turned on, and it was working like a charm.

"Not bad if I say so myself," he said proudly.

I had to admit – it was nice. We buried the electrical wire from the house to the pump and tidied up the rest of the area.

"Well, let's take the trailer and the cement mixer back and then get some bluegills for the pond," Thunderfoot said. "I'll drive the truck around and hook up."

A few minutes later he was honking the horn and I went around back to help him take the trailer back to my friend's farm. I decided to drive, since I wasn't real comfortable with him pulling the trailer. We had only gone two blocks, when we came to an intersection with a little dip in it. As we went through the dip, I suddenly heard a horrible screeching sound. I slammed on the brakes and looked in the side mirror. The trailer had come off the ball hitch and was passing us on the left side, streaking down the street all by itself. The tongue had dropped to the road and was making the screeching noise as it slid along. It passed us, then veered off to the left, plowed a furrow into my neighbor's yard, continued across the yard, and slammed into the side of his garage.

"Holy smokes!" Thunderfoot yelled. "It came off!"

By then I had the truck stopped and was surveying the mess we had made in the neighbor's yard.

"Didn't you hook it down?" I asked.

"Yeah. I had it real tight."

My neighbor had come out of his house and was walking toward the trailer. "It's a good thing my garage was here, or you might have lost your trailer," he said.

"Jeez, I'm so sorry. I thought it was fastened down," I said.

"Don't worry about it," he said. "Nothing that a little paint and a couple of pieces of siding won't fix."

Well, at least he wasn't nasty about it. We pushed the trailer back to the road and set the hitch on the ball of the truck. Then I realized what the problem was: my truck had a one and seven-eighths inch ball, and the trailer had a two-inch coupler. "Didn't you see that this was the wrong size?"

"I didn't think an eighth of an inch would matter."

We rigged the hitch with a chain wrapped around the whole thing to keep it from popping off again, and then continued on to the farm... very slowly. We dropped off the trailer and thanked my friend for it and the rocks, and then drove back home.

I backed up my truck to the cement mixer. We put down the tailgate, laid some planks on it, and then slid the mixer up into the box of the truck.

"I think we should lay it down on its side," I said. "Your grandpa brought it here laying down."

"It's real sturdy," Thunderfoot assured. "I don't think it'll tip. Grandpa is just an old, cautious guy."

I was too tired to argue, so we slid it up to the front and started off to Grandpa's.

I drove slowly across the grass. At the edge of the driveway there was a little bump where my yard and the pavement met. As I drove onto the pavement, I looked in the rear view mirror to see how the cement mixer was riding, and just at that very moment, it tipped over and came crashing through the back window of the truck. In one second – BANG! – the rear window turned from one clear pane of glass to about ten thousand little chunks.

"Holy cow!" Thunderfoot cried as he put his hands over his head and ducked. The inside of the cab was covered with bits of glass that looked like thousands of ice chips.

I stopped and stared at my astonished passenger. "Grandpa's just a cautious old guy."

"He is!"

"Do you suppose he was cautious because he thought it might tip over?"

"Well, possibly."

I shook my head.

He picked up a handful of glass chips and let them trickle from his hand. "Well, you know, you've been talking about getting one those sliding glass windows for a long time. I guess now is the time."

We both started to chuckle.

"I knew we made it through this project too easy," I said.

"Yeah," he said laughing. "*Something* had to happen."

We brushed the glass off the seat onto the floor and took off down the street. "By the time I buy paint, siding for the neighbor's garage, and a new window, I think we could have hired somebody to do this and had a lot of money left over."

He nodded. "You're probably right, but just think of the bonding we've done with this. And besides, that cool breeze feels pretty nice coming through the hole in the back of the truck. Someday we'll think back and laugh about this." I glanced over at him and we both cracked up laughing. No time like the present.

Thanks, Thunderfoot.

Little Shop of Horrors

During the summer, the river became low enough that taking a boat and motor on it for fishing was more trouble than it was worth. The Wisconsin has dozens of hydroelectric dams along its length and they all hold back water to generate power. The last dam is many miles above our town, so in the summer when thousands of air conditioners are running, there isn't much water being allowed to flow down to the lower parts of the river. Consequently, sandbars begin to show and soon there is as much surface area that is sand as there is water surface. No matter how small your boat, you spend as much time pushing it across sandbars and shallow water as you do actually driving it or fishing from it.

So when the river gets low, the fishing gets more difficult because it's so hard to get to the good places to fish, but while it's hard to get around, the shallow water concentrates the fish, so when you find a fish, he usually has many friends with him.

These were the conditions that we faced as Thunderfoot and I set out with one of the canoes to spend a day fishing for small mouth bass. The canoe would still float over pretty shallow water, and was much easier to push if we did come to some places that were too shallow to paddle. The only problem with a canoe was the size of the thing. We usually took enough tackle and poles to outfit a small hardware store, but we had to scale back our selection because there just wasn't enough room to put a lot of gear. And, of course, a canoe is a tippy craft, and we had, a time or two, dumped the whole thing over into the river, and we didn't want hundreds of dollars worth of tackle to end up on the bottom.

When the water was warm, as it was at this time of year, the bass would congregate along steep banks with trees hanging over the water, and where there were brush piles and log jams. We often found bass and walleyes congregated below sandbars, feeding on minnows in the deeper water.

In the summer, Thunderfoot and I always looked forward to a day of canoeing and fishing for bass with fly rods, and today was the day. We left Thunderfoot's mom's car at the boat landing at home, and then hauled the canoe, two fly rods, and a couple dozen poppers and streamers upriver about fifteen miles. Of course, we had lunch, pop and cold water along so we could spend the whole day on the river.

"Look down there. See that island?" Thunderfoot said, pointing at an island a short ways ahead. "Lots of trees hanging over... should be a bass paradise."

We paddled toward the island and positioned the canoe just out far enough that an easy cast with our fly rods would place our poppers right next to the trees. My popper had hardly gotten wet when the water exploded and a nice small mouth engulfed it and bulldogged toward the treetops. "Whoa! Come back here!" I yelled. Just then Thunderfoot had a smashing hit on his popper, and he was fighting the twin of my fish.

"Jeez, I wonder what the poor people are doing today?" he said as he turned and grinned at me while stripping in his line. His fish jumped and threw the hook. "Dang. Got away." He made a false cast and then settled his popper back amongst the treetops. He had another fish on the hook before I had gotten mine to the boat.

"This is the day," I said.

"No kidding. Three casts, three fish on," he said with a huge grin.

It surely was the day. We fished our way down the river and caught bass after bass. We stopped at a few good sandbars and caught more bass and some real nice walleyes, too, using streamers that looked like minnows. "This is the way fishing is suppose to be," Thunderfoot beamed.

It was truly a great day of fishing, but costly. When you're drifting with the current, you have little time to cast, so your cast must be perfect. If you're off just a little, you usually don't have time to get your popper back from the treetops before the canoe has gone past and your popper is a goner. The current is swift, so paddling back upriver to retrieve the popper is almost impossible. The consequences are that you go through a lot of poppers in one day.

We had lost a couple dozen of them and were down to the last few as we brought the canoe in at the boat landing. "Whew. I thought we were gonna be out of baits before we got home," Thunderfoot said.

"It was close," I replied.

We took his mom's car back upriver, retrieved the truck, came back to the landing, loaded up the canoe and went home.

"You know, I think I could make some poppers for us to use," he said.

"They're not that expensive," I reminded him.

"Yeah, I know. But it'd be fun to make something that we could catch fish on." Well, that did sound okay. But I didn't think he'd pursue it, so I just forgot about it.

The next day, Thunderfoot came over to the shop and asked if he could take a box of hooks home and try making some poppers with them. "I have a fly tying kit that I got for my birthday a few years ago, and I think I can make us some good poppers."

"Go ahead. Take what you need," I told him.

The subject didn't come up for a while, and about a week later he called me. "Hey, come over and see what I've got ready for the bass." I walked over to his house and his mom said he was in the basement. "Go on down," she said. "He's in the closet."

"The closet?"

She just shook her head.

I went down the stairs and walked across the basement to the door of a little closet that was against the back wall, next to the laundry room. The door was closed, so I tapped on it.

The door opened and there sat Thunderfoot on a little stool. It looked like the workroom of a voodoo witch doctor. Squirrel tails, chicken skins, pheasant tails, rabbit fur, and the skins and feathers of other critters that I didn't want to know about were tacked to the back of the door and the walls. Thunderfoot sat at a little workbench that he had built against the wall, with a fly tying vise mounted on it and a bare light bulb suspended above the work area. He was tying a popper. "Hey, come on in," he said cheerfully.

"Come in? Where would I come in? There's no room in there."

"Oh, yea. Well, what do you think of my little fly making shop?"

"Where did you get all these dead animals?"

"Oh, around. I just keep an eye out for stuff that looks like it would make a good popper. I found this pheasant run over out near the bridge, and this was off a chicken that my grandpa butchered. This is a squirrel tail that I found on the street – he must have been out practicing dodging cars and didn't dodge when he should have. And this..."

"Never mind. I get the picture," I said. "Why are you sitting in this closet?"

"Mom is acting like a girl about all this stuff, so I had to put it in here where she couldn't see it."

I could understand that.

He showed me the poppers that he had made, and some of them were pretty impressive. "Boy, this one looks great," I said, peering at one that was a good imitation of a small frog.

"That's my favorite," he said. "I'm trying to find something to make an imitation of those silver minnows in the river. I'd like to make one that looks like it's crippled and flipping around on the top of the water, but I haven't found the right stuff yet."

"That would be a good bait. There's lots of them on the river, and the bass love 'em."

I scanned over his creations a while longer, and then left him to his little room and went home. The next day, I had to meet the guy who prepared my taxes, so I called Thunderfoot and had him watch the shop for a while. When I returned, he was in a big hurry to get back to his popper business, and took off for home. That evening, I was getting the dog's supper ready when I noticed that the long silver hairs on Kirby's tail looked different. His tail usually had long, whitish hairs mixed with the blonde of his golden retriever hair, but most of the white hairs were gone. "Kirby, are you shedding already?" I asked. Kirby looked at me, without a clue as to what I was saying, but he wagged his less hairy tail enthusiastically anyway.

"I got enough poppers for another fishing trip," Thunderfoot said as he walked through the door later that evening.

"How about tomorrow," I said. It didn't take much coaxing to get me on the river when the fish were biting.

The next day we went through the same procedure with his mom's car, and soon we were coming up along the first island where we were going to fish. "Flip your line up here," he said from the front of the canoe, "and I'll tie on a popper for you." I did, and he tied on a popper just as we came up to the island. I didn't even look at the bait, but as he dropped it over the side of the canoe, I took up the slack, flipped it back and forth a couple of times, and then dropped it between two trees next to the island. Just like it was planned, a small mouth bass slammed the popper and the fight was on.

"Hey! That popper works great," I said. Thunderfoot just beamed. He cast his popper and soon we were both battling fish. I worked my fish in next to the canoe and lipped it. I took the hook out and slid the fish back into the water. Then I took a good look at the popper. It was a pretty nice bait. He had carved a piece of cork to make the dished face of the popper and then fit it on the long shank of the hook. Then he had tied some short white feathers – probably from grandpa's chicken – and then some long white hairs behind the feathers made it look like a small minnow. The head was painted white with big red eyes. "Looks like a professional job," I said.

He was proud as could be. "See? You made fun of my fly shop, but I did pretty good, huh?"

"Yeah, you did," I said.

We began fishing again, and then something occurred to me. I reeled in my popper and studied it some more. "Where did you get this long white hair?"

He glanced over his shoulder and grinned. "Recognize it?"

"Kirby?"

He grinned again. "Yup, and do you know what I named this popper?"

"What?"

"The Kirbinator."

Thanks, Thunderfoot.

The Things We'll Do for a Duck

The days were growing shorter and cooler – the early duck season was only a couple of weeks away.

"You know, we'd better get working on the duck blinds," Thunderfoot suggested.

"Yeah, I guess so. It'll be Duck Eve sooner than we think," I said. Duck Eve was a big day for us. The season opened at noon, and it was our tradition to go the day before to set up camp on the high bank above the duck marsh, and then spend the evening camping while we waited for the opening hour. It was great fun for us, and for Katy, my golden retriever.

We had two blinds built on the marsh. Each year we went to the river bottoms and cut saw grass, wove it into mats, and then fastened them to the chicken wire around the outside of the blinds. The blinds made us invisible to the ducks – or, at least close enough for them to be lured to our decoys so we could shoot at them.

We usually spent one evening cutting a pickup load of grass, and then another two or three evenings weaving it into three mats – one for each blind, and one for the boat house that hid the canoe in the tall grass below the big blind. It was a lot of work, but when we were finished, we had some dandy blinds that would last all season.

"Well, let's go cut grass this evening and then we can work on the mats as we have time," I said.

Thunderfoot agreed, and late that afternoon we drove down to the river bottoms, and wearing our hip boots, we cut bundles of tall grass with big pruning shears, stacking them in the back of the truck. One of us would gather up a big double handful of grass, and the other would cut it off just above the waterline. When we had a good pile made, the holder would pick it all up and carry it to the truck. We'd take turns cutting and bundling. That gave one of us a little rest between trips to the truck.

"This is some good grass," Thunderfoot said.

"Yeah, it's nice and thick this year... and tall. This'll make a good blind," I replied.

Just then Thunderfoot gazed over my shoulder toward the pond. "Look, a loner! Two of them!"

I turned to see two wood ducks as they glided down and lit on the water. I bent over to cut the grass Thunderfoot was holding, and then the thought hit me, and I laughed. "Two loners?"

Thunderfoot started laughing, too. "Two loners. Yeah. That's sort of like a pair, I guess." We cackled about that for a while.

When the sun had set, we decided that we had enough grass, so we packed up and headed for home.

We parked the pickup in the back yard and left it for the night. During the next three days, we wove three large mats, and rolled them up so they looked like big green corn shocks.

"We can haul them down tomorrow evening, do a little repair and get at least one blind finished," I said, "and then do the other one the next night."

"Sounds good to me."

The next evening we loaded a couple of hammers, a saw, a few pieces of scrap lumber, and the grass mats into the pickup and drove down to the marsh. While we were getting ready, Katy, my golden retriever, was galloping around, begging to go along.

"Kate wants to go. Can we take her?" Thunderfoot asked.

"I guess so," I said. "She knows it's getting close to duck season and she probably thinks we're gonna hunt. She loves exploring the marsh, so load her up."

"How about Kirby?"

"Well, the part of him that's golden retriever isn't much into hunting," I said. "And I think the collie part of him likes napping better than hunting." I called to the dog, "Kirby! D'ya wanna go?" Kirby just looked up from his shady spot, rolled over and closed his eyes.

"I think he'd rather nap," Thunderfoot said.

So, off we went to the marsh, with Katy sitting in the front seat between us, panting and slobbering like a fountain. When I had parked by the marsh, we decided to take the tools, lumber and one roll of grass out to the blind. We could come back for the others.

I hefted the roll up onto my shoulder, and Thunderfoot hauled the rest of the stuff through the marsh to the blind. The first trips out each year were hard going. The grass was almost head high, and there weren't any paths to follow, so the lead person had to forge a new trail. I was, of course, that lead person. By the time we had gone the hundred yards from the high bank to the blind, I was pooped.

"Holy cow. I think I'm gonna have the big one," I panted. Thunderfoot was huffing and puffing, too, and we both stood there a few minutes to catch our breath. "Let's see how many repairs we have to make before we haul all the grass out," I said.

With the lumber and tools we walked out onto the narrow bridge we had built from the hard ground to the blind. We stopped to nail down a few loose boards, and proceeded the rest of the way.

The blind was merely an open box on posts, with the plywood floor about a foot higher than the water. The sides were just chicken wire stretched over a frame. There was a small hole for Katy in front so she could see the pond, and where the ducks fell when we shot them. We had built a little ramp for her to get out of the blind and into the pond.

On the bridge side of the blind, a little landing was just above our boat hide. We had driven three posts into the marsh about four feet apart in a straight line, and attached a three-foot by twelve-foot cattle panel to the tops of the posts. The result was a hinged trap door covered with wire. We could pull the canoe right up to the landing on the blind, climb out onto the landing, and then lay down the trap door covered with one of the grass mats to camouflage the canoe. It was a slick set up.

I had run across an old bus seat at a garage sale several years earlier. It was just the right height and quite comfortable to sit on while waiting for ducks. So when we built the blind, we included the bus seat.

"I'm gonna rest for a minute," I said. I opened the door of the blind and sat down on the bus seat. Thunderfoot was busy driving nails into loose boards, and Katy was exploring the marsh. It felt good to sit for a few minutes. The duck blind was one of my favorite places in the whole world. I had probably sat there for hundreds of hours, and enjoyed every minute of it, whether it had been during the hot, early season when we took off our boots and sat barefoot and in tee shirts, or during the late season when we wore so many clothes we could hardly move. It was just a special place for me.

I was sitting there enjoying myself when I heard a far off hum. I listened for a few moments and was trying to determine what was making the noise. It sounded like a far away chain saw, or it was possibly one of those three-wheeled trail bikes. "What's that noise?" I said to Thunderfoot.

Thunderfoot stopped his hammering and listened. "I don't know for sure... it sounds like it's getting louder... Holy Cow! It's bees!"

Just when he said that, I saw the first bee land on my arm. Then there was another, and then about ten more, and suddenly the air was full of bees. I jumped up and ran for the door. Thunderfoot cleared the end of the bridge and disappeared into the tall grass just as I started across the bridge. I was heading for the hard ground, but the bees caught up to me – hundreds of them, swarming around me and landing on me and stinging me. I tried to swat them away as I ran down the narrow bridge, but I had only gone a few feet when I accidentally stepped off the edge and fell into the marsh. It didn't take long for the bees to find me again, as I went slogging through the mud and water as fast as I could go, heading for the tall grass.

I made it onto the hard ground and ran as fast as I could for the high bank. The bees followed me for a ways, and then left and went back to their nest, which was most likely under the bus seat in the blind. Finally, I could stop, and I nearly collapsed from exhaustion.

"Are they gone?"

I looked around for Thunderfoot, but I couldn't see him. "Where are you?"

"Down here."

I saw his hand come up from the grass a few feet away. "Yeah, they're gone. You can come out now," I said.

He slowly rose up from the grass and looked out over the marsh. "Jeez! That was a lot of angry bees. Did you get stung?"

"Yeah, I got stung," I growled. "What did you think they'd do? Just escort me to land?"

He started to laugh. "I'm sorry. It was pretty funny though. Wow! You've got a bunch of red welts on your face and arms."

"Yeah, I was lucky," I said. "I fell in the water. That probably saved me from a lot more stings."

He laughed again. "For once, being clumsy paid off." We both had a good laugh over that.

"Well, we're gonna leave this blind until it cools off... so those bees are a little slower."

"Yeah," Thunderfoot said, "and we can spray them, but I think I'll do the spraying. I can run just a little faster than you can."

I certainly wasn't going to argue with that.

"Hey, where's Kate?" he asked.

"Katy?"

"Katy?" She didn't seem to be anywhere around.

"Let's go back to the truck and blow the horn. She'll hear that and come," I said. I figured she was exploring the marsh and had just wandered off. We walked our new path back to the truck and there was Katy, sitting in the seat. She had apparently decided to make a hasty retreat when the bees came after me, and must have jumped in through the open window.

"And who says a dog is a dumb animal," Thunderfoot remarked. Then he turned to me and said, "Well, you better sit in the back of the truck. You're all covered with mud." That was nothing new to me. I'd ridden home in the back many times. In fact, I was getting pretty used to it.

When we got home, Thunderfoot took delight in making a careful count of all seventeen bee stings, and then helped me put some ointment on the stings that was supposed to make them feel better. "Well, that was fun," I said.

"Yeah," he laughed. "Oh, by the way... when we go to the other blind tomorrow, I'll go first."

"I was just about to suggest the exact same thing." I said.

Thanks, Thunderfoot.

You Gotta Be Nuts

"Chello!" Thunderfoot said as he answered the phone on the first ring.

"Sometime you're gonna do that when somebody other than me calls and you'll look kinda stupid." I said.

"Oh, I can tell when it's you. I've got ESP," he said.

"Oh? Well what did I call about if you're so perceptive?"

"Hmm. Well, I'd say it was about duck hunting... probably on the Mississippi river because the diving ducks are there and we should go over to Gus' cabin and try to shoot some of them."

I stood there with the phone in my hand and my mouth gaping. "Jeez. That's just what I *was* calling about. How did you guess that?"

He laughed. "I saw Gus at the gas station after school, and he told me he had already talked to you. Sheesh, you're easy."

I should have known. "Well, we'll leave right after supper, so get your stuff ready... and don't forget your chest waders," I said.

"My stuff is on the porch already. And by the way... what's for supper?"

"Why? Is your refrigerator empty?"

"Always."

"Well, then come on over. We'll find something to fill you up." I put a couple of frozen pizzas in the oven, and after we ate, we gathered up my stuff.

We met Gus at his house and off we went into the night over the hills to the Mississippi. His cottage was right on the river just above Lynxville. The river is about three miles wide there, and a huge stump field for the first two miles of it on the Wisconsin side. The stumps were usually just under the water, which was only about three feet deep in normal river stages. Before the Corps of Engineers built the dams on the river, the area had been a forest that extended across the bottoms all the way to the river channel along the Iowa border. Much of this forest was logged before the valley was flooded by the dams, leaving hundreds of stumps, some as big as the top of a car, just under the water's surface. It made for some tense boating, especially in the dark. In cold weather, like it was now, the water was only about 45 degrees – way too cold for a dip if you managed to upset your boat by running up onto a stump.

"We'll take the boat up the shore a ways," Gus explained. "There are two willow blinds built in the bay up there. I'll let you two off in the blinds, and then go sit in the boat in the willows by the lower side of the bay. These are bluebills and ringbills... they're not real smart, and they come to decoys real easy. You guys shoot them when they come in, and I'll pick them up with the boat."

Well... that sounded like a good plan.

The next morning we loaded up our gear and took a short boat ride up along the shoreline to the bay where some willows stuck up out of the water about a hundred feet from the shore. Gus pulled up by one of the stands of willows and told Thunderfoot to get out. "It's only about waist deep," he said, "and there's a wooden pallet anchored to the bottom of the river so you have something solid to stand on. When the ducks come by, just stand still, and when they're close enough, let 'em have it."

Thunderfoot gave us a big grin and slid over the side of the boat. He reached back in for his gun and a box of shells, which he slid down into the pouch in the front of his chest waders. "Okie dokie," he said. "See ya later."

Gus took me to the next blind up the bay a short ways. I got out of the boat and waded to the blind. The pallet made it much nicer to stand than it would have been, had I stood in the mud, but it was still a bit awkward trying to hold my gun up so it didn't dip into the water. And it didn't take long for the cold water to chill my feet and legs.

Gus dropped off a half dozen decoys between Thunderfoot and me, and then parked the boat in some thick willows with the back pointed out into the river. He sat down in the bottom of the boat. We were ready.

In only about ten minutes we saw ducks winging down the river. They were bluebills, as we call them, because of the bluish color of their beaks. Actually, they were Greater Scaup, only distinguished from Lesser Scaup by their size. They are diving ducks, meaning that they live on bigger water and dive for their food, rather than living in small ponds and tipping for their food like Mallards and Wood Ducks. We hardly ever saw a bluebill on our ponds, so this was going to be a treat for us. The diving ducks seemed to be less wary than puddle ducks, probably because they saw less of humans in their usual habitat on big water. Anyway, they were fun to shoot at, and easy to decoy.

About twenty-five ducks made up this flock, and as soon as they spotted our decoys, they veered right toward us from Thunderfoot's side of the bay, passing in front of him first. He let go with his three shots and one duck dropped to the water. They flew on toward me, and I missed with all three shots.

Gus pulled the starter cord on the motor, backed out of the willows and went after the duck on the water, which was now floating downriver on the current. He had just picked it up and returned to the willows when a low-flying flock of ring necked ducks, which we call ringbills, came buzzing by. I managed to drop one, and Thunderfoot hit two. Gus fired up the motor again and retrieved them.

This went on for the next couple of hours, and by then we had a pretty good bunch of ducks. But my feet and legs were getting so cold I could hardly stand it. My feet ached, and when I tried to move around to get some blood circulating into them, I nearly fell down from the stiffness in my knees.

A lone bluebill came past and Thunderfoot took a shot at it. The duck continued on toward the middle of the river and looked as if it were joining its friends somewhere out there, when suddenly its wings folded up and it crashed to the water. It was a long way out in the river, and I wasn't sure if Gus had seen it fall.

"Hey Gus. Did you see that one?" I yelled to our retriever.

"He missed, didn't he?"

"No. It fell way out there." Thunderfoot said.

"I didn't see it. I'll come and pick you up, and you can guide me to it," he yelled back to Thunderfoot.

Gus backed the boat out of the willows and drove to Thunderfoot's blind. Thunderfoot waded to the side of the boat and pulled himself up into it. "We'll be back in a bit," he said, and they took off for the middle of the river.

I was about to yell to them to pick me up, too, so I could get out of the cold water, but the motor roared to life and it was too noisy.   I just watched as they drove away. Thunderfoot was standing in the bow of the boat as they slowly went back and forth, looking for one lone duck floating on the dark water. They kept getting farther and farther away down river. It seemed like hours passed, and they were still getting farther away, and I was getting colder.

"Well, this sure is fun," I thought to myself, standing there in the middle of the Mississippi River like an idiot, freezing to death.

By now, I was so stiff I could hardly shuffle my feet, and I was so cold that shivering was beyond my control. Finally, I saw Thunderfoot and Gus heading back. They pulled into the bay and Thunderfoot held up the duck. "Great! Hey, let's take a break and thaw out," I yelled to them. "I'm about frozen to death."

"Ok. We'll come and get you."

I turned and stepped off the pallet onto the muddy river bottom. My legs were so stiff and my feet so cold that I could hardly get them to go one in front of the other. I took about two steps toward the boat when my feet snagged on some underwater root or sunken log. I was tipping forward – and I was going down! I hit the water face first and went all the way to the bottom. The cold was like getting slapped with one of those tasers used to subdue criminals. My whole body shook as I scrambled to my knees and then to my feet.

Thunderfoot and Gus looked pretty worried as I came to the surface like a breeching whale. Gus pulled the boat along side me and I tried to climb in. My waders, now, were not only holding me, but about twenty gallons of water, too, and there was no way I could get over the side of the boat. Gus and Thunderfoot each took an arm, grunted and pulled, but they couldn't haul me aboard. "Hang onto him," Gus said. "I'll drive us over to shallower water so we can get him in." He started the motor.

I must have looked like one of those big elephant seals as they drug me through the water toward shore. When the water was shallow enough for me to touch bottom, I sprang up and flopped into the boat. I lay in the bottom of the boat, shivering and shaking, and we headed off to the cabin.

At the cabin, I managed to crawl to my feet and out of the boat. I unhooked the straps and pulled down my waders, letting the extra water run out onto the ground. "Sit in that lawn chair," Thunderfoot said. "I'll pull your boots off."

I waddled over to the lawn chair and collapsed into it. Thunderfoot took hold of the boot part of the waders and pulled them off, taking my socks with them. My feet were red as beets and all shriveled. Then I slowly walked, stiff legged because my knees wouldn't bend, yet, to the cabin deck. I stripped off my outer clothes and left them in a wet pile on the deck, and stiffly went into the cabin. Gus had run ahead of us and had a fire going in the fireplace. "Go in and take a warm shower," he said. I'll get some hot soup cooking."

I just nodded.

I took a nice, hot shower and toweled off. I looked like a lobster – bright red from head to toe. I put on the warmest clothes I could find in the bedroom, and then settled in a chair about three feet from the roaring fireplace. After a couple of bowls of hot bean soup, I thought I might just live to hunt another day.

"Jeez! You sure disappeared fast," Thunderfoot said, laughing. "All I could see was the tip of your gun barrel sticking up out of the water."

"Oh! My gun!"

"Don't worry," Gus said. "I took it apart, dried it off and oiled it."

"And I've got your clothes hanging on the clothesline out back," Thunderfoot said, "and your boots are turned inside out and are drying on the deck."

"Thanks guys," I said. "Sorry for being such a party pooper."

"Don't worry about it. The extra work was worth seeing you come up out of the water. You looked like Moby Dick," Thunderfoot laughed.

I finally began to feel my toes again, and after some lunch we dressed the ducks and put them in the freezer. Then we settled in for a few games of three-handed cribbage. Soon after, we all had a nap.

"What have you got in mind for tomorrow?" I asked Gus.

"What?" Don't you like the willow blinds?" he asked.

"Well, if that's what you want to do, I'll be the dog," I said.

Gus laughed. "No, I thought tomorrow we'd go out by the channel and do some stump hunting. The main rafts of ducks are way out, and usually fly up and down the channel. So what we'll do is find a couple of nice high stumps – ones that are up out of the water – I'll let you guys out on them, and then we'll do the same as today, except we won't use decoys. We'll just take passing shots at ducks that are flying by."

"We won't have to stand in the water?" Thunderfoot asked.

"Nope. You just sit on a stump, nice and dry." Gus said.

Well, that sounded like a much better idea to me.

The next morning we got up early, ate breakfast and then headed out across the river to the channel on the other side. Thunderfoot and I had taken this route to the other side a few years earlier, ran up onto a stump and almost sank the boat, so both he and I were a little nervous. Gus seemed to know his way quite well, and except for a slight glancing blow off one stump, we managed to get to the channel intact.

We cruised up river a little ways and saw some stumps that were up out of the water, high enough that the hunter would not be wet. Gus pulled up to one of them. Thunderfoot stepped out onto the stump and sat down with his feet resting on the roots that were just at water level. "Piece of cake." he said, grinning.

About fifty feet away, I stepped out onto the next stump. Then Gus parked the boat against a little willow island a couple of hundred feet downriver.

In just a little while, ducks began flying by us quite regularly. Almost all were bluebills and ringbills, but we saw some buffleheads and golden eyes, too. Both were ducks that we rarely saw on our marsh at home. We had some great shooting, and we managed to get a few ducks.

As the morning went on, the wind switched from the west to the north. The temperature dropped, and nasty looking clouds began to build up in the northwest. Soon the wind was making some pretty significant waves that slapped at my stump, splashing on my gear and me. Just minutes later, a few flakes of snow drifted by.

I looked over at Thunderfoot. He was all hunched down inside his waders and his down jacket like a turtle. I could see his grin as he shrugged his shoulders.

Just then I heard a boat and I thought, "Good, here comes Gus."

But as I turned to look, I saw three late season walleye fishermen in a boat going up the channel. They waved at us as they went by, and we waved back.

When they were just past us, the one in the front leaned back toward his buddies and said, "Look at those idiots sitting there on those stumps. They must be nuts." Of course, he didn't realize that in talking loud enough to be heard by his friends, his voice carried across the water to us, too.

His buddies yucked and laughed as they motored away.

"Maybe I should fire a volley across their bow," Thunderfoot yelled to me.

"Why across it? Just shoot a hole in their boat," I yelled back.

We had a good laugh at that, and then I heard another boat. It was Gus. Thank God!

"I think it's gonna get pretty cold out here pretty soon," Gus said. "You guys had enough?"

"Plenty," I replied.

By the time I had stepped into the boat, Thunderfoot was on his feet and more than ready to be picked up.

"That was fun, but I think it's time to put away the shotguns and get out the ice fishing gear," he said.

We motored back to the cabin, dressed the ducks, cleaned up ourselves and went to town for dinner. When we arrived back at the cabin it was just about dark. Gus and I went inside, but Thunderfoot walked down to the riverbank.

I saw him down by the water, so I slipped my coat on and ventured down to the edge of the river in the cold evening air. As the light in the sky faded, one late flock of ducks was just landing out near the channel.

"Well," he said, "we got our money's worth out of this duck season."

"Yeah, no kidding. I don't think I've ever hunted so late in the season. This was kind of fun, but I still like our duck blind and our decoys and our mallards and wood ducks."

"Yeah, me too," Thunderfoot said. "The early season is more fun... and the water's not so cold, and our duck blind is lots more comfortable."

He sure had that right. "Up for a little cribbage?" I put my arm around his shoulder and we walked back to the cabin.

Thanks, Thunderfoot.

Northern Adventure

We were enjoying the beautiful late October weather. Although there had been a few cold days, the fall had been unseasonably warm, and the forecast for the following weekend was a beauty. I happened to run into a friend at the hardware store one day, and he started telling me about how amazing the small mouth bass fishing was at this time of year near the cottage he owned in the Drummond area. Good friend that he was, he offered me the use of his cabin for the weekend.

I called Thunderfoot and told him I was planning a little trip, and to come over if he was interested. As I hung up the phone I looked out the window. Thunderfoot was already on a dead run across the back lawn. He burst through the front door a few seconds later. "So, where is this trip?"

"Jeez. That didn't take you long," I said.

"I'm a speedy guy when it comes to hunting or fishing. Which one are we doing on this trip?"

"Well, I think a little of both," I said. "You know Jim, don't you? He's got a cabin up near Drummond, and I was thinking of going up there this weekend. We can hunt ducks during the morning, then fish for small mouth during the day, and then hunt ducks again in the evening. That is, if you're interested."

"When are we leaving?" he said.

"Oh, so you approve? I was thinking Friday after school. We'll get up there pretty late, so maybe we won't get an early start Saturday morning. But we'll still hunt and fish Saturday, and part of Sunday, and then we'll come home. Not a big trip, but I think it would be fun."

"Let's make a grocery list," Thunderfoot said, "and I'll get my stuff over here later. Then all we gotta do is jump in the van on Friday, and off we go." It seemed that groceries were always his first concern when we were packing.

Thunderfoot raced home from school on Friday afternoon, changed into his traveling clothes, and was at my house a few minutes later. Everything was ready and loaded in the van. We had decided to take the van because it got much better gas mileage, and with the back seats removed, we could take a nap if we got too tired to keep driving the entire six hours to the cabin.

We loaded up Katy and Kirby, and off we went. Katy came along so she could retrieve our ducks – if we got any – and Kirby came along for the ride. He had some Golden Retriever in him, but one of his parents was probably a Collie, and he didn't like swimming in the cold water, and he didn't have a clue about finding a dead duck. But he liked to ride, and he would have been horrified to be left behind.

Dusk came pretty early at that time of year, and by then we were getting into the "northy" woods. At home, our hills were full of oak, hickory, maple, and pine trees. But this far north, there was only flat ground, pines and poplars. The biggest hills were just slightly rolling high places, left over when the glaciers had passed and scraped the land down to the remaining sandy soil.

We stopped at a hamburger joint and ordered from the drive through window. The dogs were barking with excitement, and the kid at the other end of the speaker had a little difficulty hearing our order. When we drove up to the window, he was rubbing his ears. "Jeez. Your dogs about made me deaf," he said, good-naturedly.

He handed me the bag of goodies and our drinks, and then he smiled politely as I handed him the dog's dish for some water. "I can't fill that. My boss would have my head," he said. "But I *can* give you a large cup of water."

"Boss must not be a dog guy," Thunderfoot said, shoving a handful of French Fries into his mouth.

We pulled into the parking lot and ate, sharing our meal with the dogs. I had ordered a hamburger for each of them – Kirby's with no pickles – and an extra order of fries that they shared. They loved trips like this.

Then off we went, once again, into the darkness.

Thunderfoot and the dogs were sleeping, and I was getting a little drowsy, too. I closed my eyes for just a second, and abruptly found myself on the shoulder of the road. I jerked the steering wheel back to the left.

Thunderfoot sat up. "Did you fall asleep?" he asked.

"Yeah. I'm getting real tired. You wanna drive?"

"Not really. There's lots of deer up here, and I'm afraid I'll crash and then you'd never let me hear the end of it."

"Well, then we'll have to pull over and sleep a while," I said.

We were just outside of a little town that was built right on the shore of a small lake. A sign pointed the way to the town park, so I turned. Just down the street we found a nice little park with picnic tables, a beach, a toilet and changing house. "Let's just crawl in the back and take a nap," I said.

"Sounds good to me," Thunderfoot said, yawning. "I'll take the dogs out for a potty while you get out the pillows and blankets."

A makeshift bed in the back of the van was ready when the three of them returned. Everyone was ready for a nap. We all climbed in, and I pushed down the buttons on the doors, to make us snug and safe. The dogs snuggled down between us, and soon we were all sleeping.

I awoke a couple of hours later to the overhead light in the van coming on, and then off again. I sat up and saw Thunderfoot in just his under shorts and barefoot tiptoeing across the cold grass to the toilet. I lay down again and started to drift off, when a devilish idea just popped into my head. I sat up again, and snapped down the lock on the door. Then I watched as he tiptoed back to the van. I lay down and pretended to be asleep. My eyes were open just enough to see what he would do. He grabbed the door handle and pulled. Nothing happened. He pulled again, and then he realized it was locked. He stood there for a bit, and gave it one more unsuccessful try. Then he tiptoed around to the other side and pulled on that door handle. Locked!

By now he had his arms wrapped around his chest, trying to ward off the cold night air. He went to the sliding side door of the van – it was locked, too. I could tell he was getting worried. He cupped his hands around his face and pressed it up to the window, trying to see inside. I heard him talking to the dogs: "Kate. Come pull this thing up," he said, pointing to the door lock button. Kate just yawned and laid her head back down. Thunderfoot was jumping up and down, shivering as he pulled on the door handle again.

By then I was laughing so hard, the entire van must have been shaking. I tried to pretend I was still sleeping, but he could see my sides heaving with laughter.

"Oh, you're real funny," he whined.

I tried to lie still, but Kirby got up, went to the window and looked out at Thunderfoot. "Hey, Kirby, buddy! Pull this thing up, will you?" Thunderfoot said, once again pointing to the door tab. Kirby just stood there, and then he licked the window.

Thunderfoot rapped on the window. "Come on, I know you're awake. I'm freezing out here."

Finally, I felt sorry for him and I acted as if I just had awakened. I sat up and looked around. "What are you doing out there?" I said, trying to sound surprised.

"If you don't let me in," he said, "I'm gonna strangle you in your sleep next time I get a chance."

"Well, get in. I'm not stopping you."

"The door's locked... as if you didn't know."

"Oh, maybe Kirby did it. He must have been worried about where you went."

"Kirby, my butt. Now let me in. I'm freezing!"

I reached over and lifted the lock tab. Thunderfoot climbed into the van and quickly slid under the blankets. He pulled Katy and Kirby down to snuggle on both sides of him. "Jeez! I almost froze to death out there."

"Well, I didn't tell you to go running around in the night almost naked," I said.

"Oh, you're a barrel of laughs," he said. "Why don't you go back to sleep and shut up?"

"Ooo. Touchy," I teased.

"Just wait," he said. I heard him mumble something about shaving off one of my eyebrows as he snuggled under his blanket. I was probably in for some retaliation, but oh, it was worth it.

I just about jumped through the window A few minutes later when he put his ice cold feet on my back. "There! See how cold the grass is?" he said.

I guess I deserved that.

We woke up early, but we got to my friend's cabin just a little too late for the early duck hunt. "Well, let's have a good breakfast," I said. "Then we'll go down to the river and see if the smallies are hungry."

We made a huge breakfast of bacon, eggs, pancakes, and toast – enough for the dogs to each have a big plateful, too. After the kitchen was cleaned up, Thunderfoot took the dogs for a walk, so they would be ready for a nap while we went fishing. I didn't want to take them to the river for two reasons: Katy would be in the water all the time, scaring the fish; and there were a lot of bears around – I didn't want the dogs to get them riled.

I made a fire in the fireplace while they were gone, and when they returned, both dogs picked a spot in front of the warm fire. They were sound asleep before we walked out the front door.

"Jim told me the river is about three quarters of a mile north," I said. "It's like a big trout stream, but instead of trout, it has smallies and northerns. He said spinners and small crank baits are all we need."

Thunderfoot went to the driver's side of the van. "I'll drive while you pick out a few lures. How about putting them into one of those little plastic boxes, so we don't have to be lugging a tackle box along."

That sounded like a good idea. I sat on the floor in the back of the van and sorted out a few lures. We hadn't driven very far when Thunderfoot turned right onto a narrow road.

"Is this three quarters of a mile?" I asked.

"Pretty close. It's the only road I've seen on the right."

I went back to the sorting, and then I heard a lot of leaves scraping and brushing on the sides of the van. "Pretty narrow, isn't it?"

"Yeah, it is. But most of these roads into lakes are like this," the driver said.

The brushing and scraping got to be real noisy. "Are you sure this is the road? It seems like it's getting pretty narrow."

"Well, it is narrow. But I think it's right," Thunderfoot replied.

When I finally I had the small pocket tackle boxes ready, I climbed up between the seats and sat down on the passenger side. There was a trail ahead of us, but it was just barely wider than the van. It looked like it hadn't been traveled in years.

"Whoa. Wait a minute. This isn't a road."

"Well, it was a lot wider back farther, but it's gotten pretty narrow, now."

"Stop. Let's walk ahead and see. I don't want to find out that it just ends, and then have to back all the way out," I said.

He stopped and turned off the engine. I tried to open my door, but it would only open about four inches before it hit a tree. It was the same on Thunderfoot's side. "We can't open the doors," he said. "How're we gonna get out and look ahead?"

"Pop the tail gate door," I said. He pushed the button and the tailgate snapped. We crawled through the back of the van, and pushed it opened. "Whew, at least we can get out of here."

We made our way through the trees and brush to the front of the van, and then followed the "road" about twenty feet where it stopped dead against a big spruce tree.

"Well, there's the end of our road," I said.

"Who would make a road like this?" Thunderfoot said. "Just go in half a mile or so and stop."

"What do you mean? Half a mile? Are we that far in?"

"Yeah, I think so... maybe a little more."

"Oh, boy. We're gonna have to back the whole way out."

"I guess so. There's no place to turn around," he said. "You drive."

Oh thanks! That's just what I wanted to hear. We got back in through the tailgate and Thunderfoot pulled it shut. I got in the driver's seat and he knelt in the back and tried to guide me as I backed through the trees and brush.

It was slow going. Many times I had to stop and pull forward because I had gotten off track, and one of the mirrors was against a tree, or the rear bumper had smacked into a tree that was quite close to the trail.

The *Mother of all Cricks* lodged in my neck by the time we finally reached a place wide enough to turn around. Thunderfoot climbed back up to the front. "Whew, that was pretty tight," he said.

"No kidding. It's a good thing I'm not fussy about my van, or I'd be going nuts about what's left of the paint job."

"Oh, that'll buff right out," Thunderfoot said.

We pulled out onto the road again, and about fifty feet farther, there was a gravel road to the right – *and a sign* that said "To the River."

"That other one must be that road less traveled... that Robert Frost was talking about," Thunderfoot laughed.

A ways down the road we came to a beautiful little stream. The road continued on over a bridge, but we could see no reason for going any farther. We pulled over and parked, took off our shoes, put on our hip boots and gathered up our fishing rods and little plastic tackle boxes of lures.

"I think I'll cross the bridge and fish that side," Thunderfoot said.

"That's a good idea. I'll fish this side," I said.

The river was like something from a movie, about ten yards wide with crystal clear rapids tumbling over boulders. Parts of it were bordered with trees right down to the water's edge, and gravel bars out in the middle. Other places were more open with grass and brush along its banks, and shallow enough that if you couldn't make your way along the banks because of brush, you could just wade along the edge of the water. It meandered back and forth for as far as I could see.

Thunderfoot emerged from the brush on the other side. "This is just about perfect," he called out. "What do you want to do? Go upstream or down?"

"Let's go upstream, today," I said. "Maybe tomorrow we can try downstream."

He signaled an okay, and we started working our way up the river, casting to pockets behind boulders – likely looking eddies where a smallie might be – and casting to the bottom of riffles where the water dumped into a small pool. It didn't take long until Thunderfoot let out a whoop, and a nice small mouth bass made its first jump, and then took a screaming run downriver with his spinner. The fish jumped another half-dozen times during the fight, and finally Thunderfoot brought it up to his feet, reached down and lipped it. "Look at this beauty," he beamed, holding up the little bronze torpedo.

I was just about to compliment him on his fish when one hit my spinner and almost took the rod out of my hands. It made a jet-like run upstream and jumped three times in about three seconds before it made a run back toward me. I reeled as fast as I could, caught up to the fish and turned it. It jumped again, fighting, but I soon had it lying on its side next to my feet. It was a twin to Thunderfoot's fish. I took the hook out and slid it back into the water.

By then, Thunderfoot was upstream from me, wading along the shoreline toward a bend in the river. There was a deep-looking cut along the bank on my side, so I stepped out of the water and worked my way past it so Thunderfoot could cast to it. I emerged from the brush about ten yards beyond and stepped into the river again, casting up toward some boulders. Thunderfoot, meanwhile, was standing on the point at the bend, casting toward the opposite bank. He quickly had a strike and began playing a nice fish. I had a strike just then, too. My fish jumped and put up a good fight until I finally got it close enough to pull it out of the water. I released the fish and waded upriver to cast again. I turned to see if Thunderfoot was still fishing the point.

Sure enough, he was in knee-deep water at the point, fighting another fish. I was just going to start upstream again when I saw something black moving through the brush near the point. I stopped and looked more carefully, and then I realized that a pretty large black bear was tramping through the willows right toward Thunderfoot. I wasn't exactly sure what I should do. I was afraid that if I yelled, it might startle the bear into running Thunderfoot over. So I just stood there, waving, trying to get Thunderfoot's attention.

He was intent on his fishing, but after a few long, nervous moments, he looked my way and saw me waving. He raised his hand, returning the wave. I pointed behind him. He looked confused and shrugged his shoulders. I pointed again, and made a gesture with my arms, trying to convey the idea that something big was there. He turned slowly toward the bank, and just as he did, the bear stood on its hind legs, looking through the willows right at him, from about ten feet away.

Thunderfoot froze. The bear dropped back down on all fours and took a couple of steps forward. Thunderfoot began backing away. The bear heard him splashing in the water and stood up again to see *what* he was. That did it. When the bear stood up the second time, Thunderfoot waded backwards as fast as he could go, right into the deep hole on my side of the stream. The water was about mid-chest depth, but that didn't stop him. He kept wading and sloshing backwards until he was up against the bank. When he felt the bank against his back, he threw his fishing pole up into the weeds, climbed up out of the river, and took off running through the tall grass for the van.

The bear watched him go, calmly walked down to the river, got a drink, and then ambled off into the woods. I just stood there quietly enjoying the entire performance.

I fished a while longer, and then I decided to see if Thunderfoot had stopped at the van, or if he had kept running all the way back to the cabin. I picked up his rod and reel and strolled back downriver to the parked van. Thunderfoot was sitting on the floor with all the windows rolled up and the doors locked, peeking out the rear window.

He reached to unlock the door and whispered, "Get in... and lock that door behind you!"

"What? Are you afraid that the bear knows how to open car doors?" I laughed.

"I'm not taking any chances. Did you see that thing? Jeez! I'm lucky I'm not bear supper right now! Did you see him stand up and charge?"

"See him charge?" I was laughing so hard I could barely get my breath. "He wasn't interested in your scrawny body. All he wanted was a drink of water."

"Yeah, right! He looked pretty hungry to me. Besides... what do you know? You were a long ways from him. I was right there, looking him right in his evil eye."

"If he'd taken a bite of you, he would've spit it right out," I laughed.

"Oh, real funny," Thunderfoot pouted.

"I really don't think he intended to bother you. He was just out for a drink of water, and you just happened to be where he was going," I said.

"Well, let's go back to the cabin. I need some dry clothes," he growled.

"You probably need some fresh underwear, too."

"Oh, ha, ha!"

We drove back to the cabin. Thunderfoot changed into dry clothes and hung his wet ones on a clothesline strung between two pine trees. We had some lunch, fed the dogs, and settled down for a little nap before the evening flight of ducks.

The little duck boat tipped up against the backside of the cabin was longer than the inside of the van, so we had to leave the tailgate up, but didn't have far to go and we'd drive slow. When the boat was loaded, we changed into camouflage clothes, grabbed our hip boots, shotguns, and shells, put the dogs in the back with the duck boat, and headed out for the evening hunt.

Katy and Kirby were all excited about going someplace, even if they didn't know for sure where. We drove down a little country road to a small lake. The dogs jumped out and immediately ran around exploring. We unloaded the boat and the rest of the gear, called the dogs, and pushed off for the cattails on the opposite shore of the lake.

We hid among the cattails, and pulled some of them across the open boat to camouflage it better. Then we just settled back to wait for some evening ducks. Katy watched the sky for her first duck. Kirby curled up in a ball and took a nap.

It didn't take long for a small flock of Wood Ducks to slip over the tops of the trees and circle the lake. "There, to the right," Thunderfoot whispered.

I nodded. The ducks circled again, right over us. We both rose up and shot. The ducks went from four little steady targets to a swarm, flying every which way as they scrambled for altitude. I missed with my first shot, but one fell with my second. Thunderfoot missed both the first and second, but got one with his third shot. "Kate, go fetch," I said.

Katy jumped into the water and swam out toward the first duck. She picked it up and swam back, got her front paws up on the side of the boat, dropped the duck in, turned and went after the second duck. Now Kirby was awake. He sniffed the duck, sneezed, and curled up again for another nap. Apparently, he wasn't interested in getting wet. Kate came back with the second duck and we helped her back into the boat. Of course, she brought a lot of water in with her, so now there was a puddle in the bottom of the boat. Kirby got up and moved closer to Thunderfoot where it was still dry. "Kirby's not real excited about hunting, is he?" Thunderfoot said.

"Nope," I laughed. "His hunting is mostly for a place to sleep."

After a couple more flocks had flown past, it was time to call it quits. I rowed across the lake and let the dogs out of the boat, drug it onto the shore, tipped it and drained the water out. We loaded up and headed back to the cabin.

I made supper – steaks and raw fried potatoes – while Thunderfoot cleaned the ducks and fed the dogs. It had been a long day for us, and after we ate, we were feeling pretty tired. "I think it's time for bed," Thunderfoot said.

"No argument from me."

We let the dogs out for a potty break, and then the four of us settled down for the night, Thunderfoot and I in the bunk beds, and Katy and Kirby sprawled out in front of the fireplace.

It was still dark when my alarm went off. Katy was hogging my bed – stretched out taking her half out of the middle, leaving me on a little sliver. "Kate, move over!" I said. She grumbled and groaned but moved a bit so I could straighten out my legs. "Hey, wake up, there's daylight in the swamp."

No answer. I pushed on the mattress above my head. "Wake up, lazy. Time to go hunting."

"You know, you can sure be irritating so early in the morning. How can anyone wake up and be so cheerful?"

"I'm going hunting, and if you want to go along, you'd better get up, or I'll go without you."

"Well, if you put it that way... okay, let's go," Thunderfoot said. He hopped down from the top bunk.

We washed up and went to the van. We'd hunt for an hour or so, while the morning flight was on, and then come back for some breakfast.

We went back to the same lake and got in some pretty good shooting, collecting two more ducks for our bag. Then we went back, cleaned the birds, and had a big breakfast.

Thunderfoot kept the dogs entertained while I was washed the dishes. "Well, what do you think?" I asked. "A couple hours of fishing before we head for home?"

"Fishing? Where?" he said.

"The stream we fished yesterday."

"Are you insane? There are hungry bears out there. I'm not going near that place again."

"Oh, don't be such a baby. Those bears won't hurt you."

"Easy for you to talk. You're almost the size of a bear. I'm just a snack size."

I laughed, and then I decided it was fine with me if we prepared for the trip home. It was a long drive; we could take our time to enjoy scenery that we had missed on the way up during the night.

"And besides... I need to do some homework before school tomorrow," Thunderfoot said.

"Oh, you just remembered that, did you?"

"Yes, I did. And you know I'm a very conscientious student. I want to get good grades to make my mom happy."

I just shook my head. Now I had heard it all.

Thanks, Thunderfoot.

Covered Coveralls

Thunderfoot and I were getting our deer hunting gear laid out for opening day. As usual, before a big hunt, he stayed overnight at my house in the spare bedroom that he had claimed as *his room.* He kept several changes of clothes and had a lot of his junk stored there, so, for all intents and purposes, it *was* his room.

He was making sandwiches and bagging up cookies as I laid out my clothes and boots. All of his outer clothes, his gun, shells, and other gear were all piled up and ready to go.

"You'd better go and roll up some TP," he suggested.

"Oh, yeah! I can't go without that," I said. I went into the bathroom and unrolled a long strip of toilet paper, rolled it up into a small roll, and stuck it into the pocket of my jacket.

"You got enough? You know how you always have to go when you get to the woods," he said.

"I think so. There's always leaves in an emergency."

"Oh, yuck," he groaned.

I turned on the radio to hear the weather report. The weather lady was talking about possible rain, and temperatures in the upper 60s, possibly low 70s.

"Holy smokes. It's gonna be warm tomorrow," Thunderfoot said.

"Yeah. I don't think I want to wear my insulated pants and coat. I'll cook in them."

"I've got that thin jacket I can wear over anything, so I'm in good shape," Thunderfoot said. He packed the sandwiches into a couple of duffle bags.

"You know, I've got those old red coveralls. Maybe I can just wear them... so I won't be so hot."

"You can't wear red. That's illegal."

"Yeah, but if I wear a blaze orange vest over them, I'm okay. One half of the top of me in blaze orange is all that's required."

"Yeah, that might be a good idea. After we meet Jerry and Scott at noon, and make some drives, you'll be cooked in those heavy clothes."

I found my old red coveralls and an orange vest, and transferred the stuff from the pockets of my heavy jacket and pants. Now at least I wouldn't get overheated.

It was still quite dark outside when the alarm went off. Thunderfoot and I ate a quick breakfast, and then off we went to the woods. We were hunting on the high bank near the area where we usually hunted ducks. There were two nice alfalfa fields for us to watch, and even better for me, it was only a short walk, on flat ground to my stand. I was getting to like flat land hunting more, rather than climbing the hills that seemed to be getting steeper every year.

I carried a lawn chair to my stand under a huge white pine, cleared off the branches in a five-foot area and settled down. The blanket of needles under my feet felt like a carpet. It was still dark and the wind was blowing just a bit, making mournful sounds through the pine branches, but it was a real cozy spot. I slid down and leaned back in my chair, and closed my eyes just for a second.

Quite surprised to see that it was fully daylight, I opened my eyes again when I heard a thudding noise. I looked out into the alfalfa field; two big does and a really nice buck had made the noise that awakened me. They stood about forty yards away. My heart beat a little faster, and then I realized that my gun was laying on the blanket of pine needles on the ground. Slowly, I moved my right arm off the chair rest and toward the gun. The deer watched as my hand got closer, and just as I reached it, their tails went up and they bounded off into the edge of the woods.

I didn't bother to jump up and make chase. They were headed right toward Thunderfoot, across the lane and at the other end of the woods, watching another alfalfa field. I waited and listened, but there was no sound of gunfire. I grinned to myself, thinking that Thunderfoot was probably asleep, too, and the deer had probably tiptoed right past him without waking him.

Oh well. No hurry. It was opening morning. Lots of time left.

I did pick up my gun and lay it across my lap. I was just finishing a sandwich and a cookie when a coyote trotted across the field, and a few minutes later, six turkeys ambled out of the woods, picking their way across the alfalfa, having their breakfast. A couple of hours later, two does snuck across the other end of the field, but no more bucks showed themselves.

I was enjoying the morning when I heard leaves crunching and saw Thunderfoot coming through the brush toward me.

"Seen any?"

"Yeah," I said. "Real early, but I was dozing. They came your way... did you see them?"

He shook his head. "Yeah, but not till they were almost in the woods. I was resting my eyes, too. I heard them and woke up, but it was too late. My gun was laying on the ground, anyway."

I laughed. "We seem to hunt alike."

"Well, it's almost noon," Thunderfoot said. "Let's go back to my house. Mom said she'd make lunch for us. Jerry and Scott will meet us there. We'll hunt some more this afternoon."

"Sounds good to me.

I picked up my gear and my chair, and we walked down the lane to the truck. When we got to Thunderfoot's house, Jerry's old beater of a pickup was already there. He and Scott had been on stands all morning without any shooting, either.

"You guys see any?" Jerry asked.

"Yeah, but we were both snoozing, and neither of us shot," Thunderfoot said.

Scott and Jerry laughed, and couldn't resist giving us a lot of static about being such poor hunters.

"Just wait till this afternoon," Thunderfoot said.

Thunderfoot's mom had a huge pot of chili on the stove, and a big plate of ham and cheese and a couple of loaves of bread on the table. "Sit down and make some sandwiches," she told us. "I'll dish up the chili."

She sat the bowls of scalding chili in front of us and we all dug in. The chili was hot in both ways – scalding hot off the stove, and spicy hot, too. But it was delicious after a morning of fresh air. I had two bowls, and with a little coaxing, I was talked into a third.

"Boy! That is the best chili I've had in ages," I said.

"You'd better watch out with that stuff," Thunderfoot warned. "You know how those kidney beans react with you."

"Just be sure to stay upwind of me," I said.

"No doubt about that!" he said, laughing.

After we ate, we made our plans for the afternoon. A patch of big pine trees on the edge of town usually had a few deer in it. With only four of us, we'd be better off sticking to a smaller woodlot to make a drive. We decided that Jerry and Scott would go to the east end of the pines and find a couple of places to sit. Thunderfoot and I would go to the west end and do the same. Then, at 3:30, Thunderfoot and I would walk slowly through the pines, hoping to scare out any deer toward Jerry and Scott.

"You guys watch for us at about 4 o'clock," I said.

"Okay. We'll be ready," Jerry replied.

Off we went in the two pickups. Thunderfoot and I parked along the highway and walked along the fence at the end of the pine plantation. Thunderfoot stopped about a third of the way in and looked at his watch.

"I've got 1:44," he said.

"Okay. I'll set mine for that, too. We'll start walking at 3:30 sharp. But take it easy, and don't rush," I told him.

He nodded an okay. I walked on for a while, found a nice spot, and sat down.

Of course, with a full belly and a nice sunny afternoon, my eyes soon began to get heavy. I was at a nice big tree with a cushiony bed of needles on the ground, and I couldn't resist the temptation of a little nap. I was dreaming about deer and ducks, and then all at once I felt like I was having a heart attack. I woke up, sweating, and realized that my heart attack was really heartburn from the chili.

My stomach was churning and I thought I was going to blow up. Oh, boy! I had an upset stomach. I would have given anything for a *Tums*. I looked at my watch. It was nearly 3:30 already, so I stood up and carefully tried to let a little gas slip out, just to take off the pressure. I felt a little better.

It was time to start the drive toward Scott and Jerry. I walked slowly, working my way to the east. As I walked, I must have stirred up the chili again, because I soon had some terrible gas pains again. I stopped, concentrated, carefully vented and moved on.

Now I was half way through the woods, and suddenly I had a pain like what I imagined it would be like to give birth. I doubled over in pain and tried to bleed off a little more gas. But I knew that the previews were over.

The big show was inevitable, and it was not far off.

I looked around for a log to sit across, but found nothing. The danger of an unwanted discharge was getting closer with every step, so I decided that the moment had come to release the beast, and by that time, it was almost too late. I laid down my gun and unzipped the front of my coveralls. Underneath was just a tee shirt and a pair of jeans, so I hurried the coveralls off my shoulders, dropped my jeans and let fly.

Because of the tremendous backpressure, it didn't take long for the job to be done. I reached in my vest pocket for my roll of TP and took care of things. When I bent over to pull up my pants, I saw what had happened. In my haste, I hadn't thought about the coveralls lying on the ground behind me. The backpressure had been great, but not great enough to take the main event past them.

"Oh, no," I groaned.

Well, there was nothing to do now but to get them off. I removed my boots and carefully slid my feet out of the legs of the coveralls. I used a stick to roll them up into a ball, and tied my deer dragging rope around them. I picked up my gun and started off through the woods again, dragging my coveralls behind me.

When I reached the other end of the woods, I heard voices.

"Maybe we should look for him… maybe he had a heart attack or something." It sounded like Jerry talking.

"He's probably in there someplace… sleeping," I heard Thunderfoot say.

"I'm not sleeping," I announced as I emerged from the woods.

"Jeez! You took long enough. What you been doing?"

"I just took my time," I said.

I had left the coveralls at the edge of the woods, planning to return later to get them… to save myself a little ridicule.

"Well, okay. Let's go," Scott said.

We started walking toward Jerry's truck when Thunderfoot stopped abruptly. "Hey, where's your coveralls?"

The other two stopped and looked me up and down, too. "Yeah. You were wearing coveralls when you went in there."

My brain was working overtime trying to think of a plausible explanation for why I was without my outer clothes.

The others just stood there waiting for an explanation.

"Well, I had a little accident with them, so I left them behind," I said.

"What did you do? Rip them?" Scott asked.

Thunderfoot began laughing like a fool, staggering around and clutching his belly.

"He pooped them. I'll bet you a dollar he pooped them."

The other two began laughing, too, so I hiked back a few yards, picked up the rope and pulled my bundle toward the truck. They all howled like mad when they saw me dragging the coveralls out of the woods.

"Ho, ho! Is that a buck or a doe?" Thunderfoot gasped between laughs.

"Need some help taking that to the locker?" Jerry said.

I just ignored their sophomoric behavior, walked to the truck and got in the passenger seat. Jerry was going to take me to my truck, and then I'd come back to pick up Thunderfoot.

When I drove my truck back, Thunderfoot and Scott had hoisted my bundled coveralls over a branch of a tree with the rope, and tied a deer carcass tag on the zipper.

"Come over here and stand by your trophy," Thunderfoot said. "I'll get the camera and take your picture."

Sometimes, he could be such a wise guy.

Thanks, Thunderfoot.

Lutefisk

Winter was just around the corner, and Thunderfoot had agreed to help me with my winterizing chores. There were still a few leaves to finish raking, some pots to move to the greenhouse, and most important of all, we had to winterize the pond in the back yard.

Pond might be a bit of a misnomer. Earlier in the summer, he and I had built *Lake* Thunderfoot, with some potted water lilies in the water, some arrow root plants, and, of course, some bluegills. The instructions that had come with the pond liner said to remove about half of the water and the pump, and leave it that way for the winter. So, that was our main chore for the day.

I saw Thunderfoot coming across the back yard. "Hey. You ever ate lutefisk?" he asked as he came through the front door.

"Nope. Why?"

"My grandpa gave me two tickets to a lutefisk dinner tonight. I thought you and I might go to it."

"Why isn't grandpa going?"

"He has to go to some meeting, but he already bought the tickets, and he doesn't want them to go to waste."

"What about your mom?"

"She said she doesn't like it."

I had never tried lutefisk, but I'd heard from some of my friends that it was great, and from others that it was awful. "Do you know what it is?" I asked.

"It's fish, isn't it?"

"Yeah. It's dried cod that's been soaked in lye," I said.

"Lye? Don't you make soap with that?"

"I guess they used to. I've heard it's good, and I've heard it's nasty. I really don't know, for sure, what it's like."

"Well, let's try it," Thunderfoot said. "We got free tickets."

Well, how bad could it be? I agreed that I'd go with him to the supper.

We started our chores for the day out in the yard. By a little after noon, we had finished and I offered to make lunch, but Thunderfoot just wanted a snack, to save room for the lutefisk.

"I love fish," he said, nodding his head. "I don't want to miss out, so I'm gonna go *real* hungry."

We goofed around cleaning the boat and straightening up the garage for the rest of the day until it was time to go to the lutefisk supper.

The supper was at the Five Points Lutheran Church – a country church way out in the middle of nowhere. We knew *about* where it was, and when we came closer to the area, we saw signs pointing the way to the lutefisk supper.

"Wow! This must be a big deal," Thunderfoot said. "They've got signs all over the place."

When we topped the next hill, there was the church, sitting next to a small cemetery, and a parking lot with about a hundred cars in it.

"Holy smokes. Look at all the cars," Thunderfoot gasped.

"No foolin'. People must come from all over the place for this stuff. Maybe it's better than I've heard about," I said.

Kids with flashlights were directing cars to parking spots. People were going to and coming from the church it in steady streams. We parked and walked toward the church. As we got closer, we both began sniffing the air.

"Whew. What's that?" Thunderfoot said.

"It smells like a dead carp on a sandbar," I said.

"I hope that's not what were eating," he whispered.

"Me too."

We went in the door of the church and the aroma was even stronger. I looked at Thunderfoot and he just shrugged his shoulders. A man inside the church directed us to the pews in the main part of the church. "The next seating will be in about twenty minutes," he said.

"Seating?" I asked.

"Yes, we can seat about forty people at a time. You can wait in the church, and when the last group is finished, you can go down to the basement to eat. This will be our twentieth seating today."

"Twentieth? You mean there have been eight hundred people here to eat?" Thunderfoot asked.

"Oh, yes. We started at eleven o'clock this morning. By the time we're finished, we usually will have served about a thousand people."

We were both kind of amazed at those statements. We walked into the church, found a pew and sat down. Soon we were chatting with some people in the next row.

"So, this is your first time eating lutefisk?" the man asked.

"Yeah, my grandpa usually comes, but he couldn't make it, so we're using his tickets," Thunderfoot said. "Where are you folks from?"

"We're from Janesville," the man answered.

"Janesville! That's a hundred miles from here. Are you just visiting the area?" I asked.

"No, we drove up here just for the lutefisk," the man replied.

An older couple was sitting behind us, and the man smiled and said, "My wife and I are from Green Bay. We drove down here just for this, too."

Thunderfoot looked at me. "Maybe we've been missing out on something really good all this time."

I was beginning to think that he was right.

A few minutes later, the man from the front door stepped in front of the pews and told us that we could go to the basement and be seated. We got up with all the rest of the people and walked down the stairs to a big room that had long tables set up with plates and silverware and everything we would need for our lutefisk supper.

We sat at the table with the folks from Janesville and Green Bay, and within just a little while, the ladies of the parish started bringing bowls and platters of food to each table. First came a big bowl of mashed potatoes, and one of meatballs. Then came some green beans and one of corn. Then a girl brought out a plate of sweets and another brought bread and rolls. Finally, like a king entering his court, a lady brought out a big bowl of lutefisk and handed it to Thunderfoot. "Here, young man. You can start the main course."

The lutefisk *looked* kind of like fish, but it had a jellylike wiggle to it as Thunderfoot took hold of the bowl and spooned a medium sized chunk onto his plate. He had a worried look on his face as he passed the bowl to me. "Here. Have some lutefisk."

I was careful to take a piece that was not too big. I slid some of the wiggly stuff onto the plate and quickly passed it to our Green Bay friend. He shoveled about four big pieces of the stuff onto his plate and passed it on. The rest of our tablemates did the same.

The rest of the food was passed around and when we all had some of everything, we began eating. I cut off a small piece of fish and put it in my mouth, just as Thunderfoot did the same.

As soon as I bit down on the lutefisk, I knew why it wiggled so much. It was like tough jelly – like fish-flavored rubber bands. My throat constricted as my stomach tried to keep my mouth from sending the strange stuff down to it. I chewed and chewed and did my best to try to swallow it. I looked at Thunderfoot and he was doing the same, chewing like he had a hand grenade in his mouth. He looked at me with horror in his eyes. Both of us chewed for a long time, and we finally managed to swallow the lutefisk.

"How do you boys like the lutefisk?" Mr. Green Bay asked.

"I think somebody should be put in jail for doing that to perfectly good fish," Thunderfoot said.

Green Bay burst out laughing, and soon the whole table was in stitches over Thunderfoot's remark.

"It's an acquired taste," Green Bay said.

"How long have you been eating it?" I asked.

"Oh, for about thirty years," Green Bay said.

"You must be a glutton for punishment," Thunderfoot said.

Again the whole table had a good laugh.

I ate some of the meatballs and potatoes and gravy just to get the taste of the fish out of my mouth. The rest of the food was great, and both Thunderfoot and I ate several helpings of the other stuff, but we politely passed on extra helpings of lutefisk.

I hated to leave the fish on my plate, so I kind of hid it under some beans and potatoes. I could see Thunderfoot was doing the same thing. But our friends at the table ate lutefisk until I thought they would all blow up and make a terrible mess. Finally, we all were full.

"Well, what do you guys think? Will you be back again for lutefisk?" Green Bay asked.

Thunderfoot glanced my way. "I don't know about Dan, but I believe this will be my first and last time for it."

"I sure don't want to hurt anybody's feelings," I said, "but it would take a bunch of big, mean guys to ever make me come to another lutefisk supper."

"Big guys with big guns," Thunderfoot added.

Well, at least we gave it a try.

Thanks, Thunderfoot.

Wheels

I was just about to drift off into an afternoon nap when I heard the loud vroooom, vroooom of a car in the driveway. I knew who it was. He had been waiting quite a while for this big day. There sat Thunderfoot in his new car. He waved for me to come out and have a look.

"Come and see my new wheels," he said as I stepped out onto the porch.

"Jeez! It looks like a racecar."

"You bet! And it runs like a racecar too."

He had been saving his money for the last two years for a car, and he had finally found the one he wanted, and the one that he could afford to buy. I kept trying to steer him toward something small with a tiny engine, that wouldn't go past about 50 miles per hour. Of course, he wanted just the opposite.

The car was a Dodge Charger, and it looked like something that should have been on a racetrack instead of in my driveway. It was gold, with stripes down the side, and it even had a couple of stripes from the windshield to the front of the grill. It sounded like a racecar, too, as Thunderfoot kept gunning the engine and making it roar.

"Turn that thing off. You're making me deaf," I said.

He grinned, shut off the engine, and stepped out of the car. "Well what do you think of her?"

I looked it over, and while I checked out the upholstery, he popped the hood. "Look at this engine," he said.

I tried to act impressed as I stared into the engine compartment. The extent of my knowledge about cars and how they ran was confined to the fact that gas went into the hole in the back, and the key started it. If it didn't start, I called someone to fix it. "Yeah, that's a big one," I said.

"It's got some real kick to it."

"Yeah, well you'd better be careful with it... at least until you get used to driving it. It's supposed to snow tonight, so take it easy."

"Yes, Mom."

He was grinning as he dropped the hood. "I'll be careful. You know I didn't save for two years just to wreck it the first day."

"Yeah, I know. I just worry that you'll get hurt," I said.

"Don't worry. Jerry and Scott and I are going to take her for a spin tonight, and we'll be careful. I promise."

I went back into the house, and he went to show off his car to anybody else that would look at it.

It started to snow later that afternoon and it kept on snowing all evening. I spent a quiet evening with a book and the dogs, and after I had taken them out for their last potty session, I went to bed. As usual, about two thirty I had to get up to use the bathroom – one of the joys of getting older.

When I was finished in the bathroom, I turned off the light, opened the door, and ran right into a man standing in the hallway. I jumped back and shouted something incoherent at him, and began to look for something with which to defend myself. My shouting woke up the dogs and they came barking and growling from my bedroom, and the dark, quiet house quickly evolved into bedlam. I tried to grab the intruder in the dark, and then he started yelling at me. "Wait, wait, it's me!" Thunderfoot yelled.

I stopped short and turned on the light. "Holy Criminey! What the heck are you doing here? You almost gave me a heart attack," I said.

"You! Jeez! I about pooped when you came out of there and attacked me."

"What are you doing here at two thirty in the morning?" I asked again.

"I had a little problem with the car, and I came here to see if you can help."

Then I noticed that he was dripping wet and shivering. "What happened? Why are you all wet?"

"Well, Jerry and Scott and I were out driving around and we came to this place in the road where you had to turn right or left. But it was real slick, and we went straight. We went through a fence and out into a field."

"Good God! Are you okay?"

"Yeah. But the car is stuck in the field."

"Where are Jerry and Scott?"

"They're out on your front porch."

"Go and bring them inside before they freeze to death," I said.

He went to the living room and called to his pals to come in. They both looked like drowned rats, too, wet from head to toe.

"You guys get those wet clothes off, and I'll get you something dry to put on," I said. I went to the bedroom that Thunderfoot used when he stayed over and found some of his tee shirts and jeans. Jerry and Thunderfoot were about the same size, but Scott was a little huskier, so I found a pair of sweat pants for him. I got out some towels and took them to the boys. The three of them were standing in their underwear, shivering like crazy. "You guys jump in the shower for a few minutes and warm up, and then put on these dry clothes," I said.

They all trooped off to the bathroom, and while they were taking turns in the shower, I gathered up all the wet clothes and tossed them in the dryer. Then I put a big pan of water on the stove to make some hot chocolate. By the time the water was hot, they all were wearing dry clothes and had warmed up a bit. The hot chocolate finished the job.

They were sitting side by side on the couch, and I was sitting across from them in my recliner. "Well, you guys have been busy tonight. Where did you wreck?"

"Out by Sand Branch creek," Scott said.

"You walked all the way from there?"

"We didn't have much choice," Jerry said. "It was that or sit there in the middle of the field for the night, after Mario Andretti, here, drove us through the fence."

"Well, we'd better call your folks and let them know where you are, so they don't worry," I said. I stood up to get the phone.

"Uhhh, we can't do that," Thunderfoot said.

"Why?"

"Well, I'm supposed to be staying over at Jerry's, and he's supposed to be staying over at Scott's, and Scott is supposed to be staying over at my house."

"So you little connivers fixed it so you could stay out all night and not get caught?"

"Yeah, and it would have worked, too... if we hadn't crashed."

"Well, I'll help you get the car out of the field, but not until morning. You guys can sleep here, and we'll see what we can do then, okay?"

They all agreed. Thunderfoot went to his room, and I found some pillows and blankets for Jerry and Scott to sleep on the sofa that opened to a bed. I went back to bed, and the house was dark and quiet once again.

The next morning I fried a pound of bacon, scrambled a dozen eggs, and toasted a loaf of bread. My young midnight hikers polished it all off in just a few minutes. Their own clothes were dry by then, so they got dressed. I put on some boots and found extra ones for them, and off we went to rescue Mario's racecar.

The snow had stopped falling, but the roads were still covered. In a short time we got to the scene of the wreck. "How fast were you going?" I asked as I peered at the car sitting in the middle of the field, about fifty yards from the highway.

"A little too fast, I guess," Thunderfoot said, grinning.

"Will it run and drive?" I asked.

"Yeah. It's not hurt... just some scratches on the hood where we went through the fence."

I contemplated the situation and decided it would be easier to get the car out from another road on the back side of the field. The car was closer to it than it was to the road we were on. "I'm going down to the house and tell them what's going on," I said, "and meanwhile, a couple of you go out there and hook this chain under the car someplace on the frame. One of you can come with me to open that gate on the ridge road."

Jerry went with me, and I drove down to the farmer's house and explained what we were doing. The farmer said that if I couldn't get them out, to come back and he'd come out with his tractor. Jerry told him that they would be back and help repair the fence. The farmer was real nice about it. "That would be just fine," he told Jerry.

I drove back past the field and stopped at the ridge road. Jerry opened the gate and I drove through, gunning it a little because it was kind of steep. I stopped about half way up the slope and waited for Jerry to get back into the pickup. Then I gave it some gas and began to climb up the steep road. I got almost to the top and the tires began spinning. "Uh, oh," I said. I gave it a little more gas, but that only caused the truck to slide sideways, over the side of the hill. I braked and we stopped.

"We've got problems," I said.

Jerry nodded. "See if you can go backward," he whispered, as if talking out loud would cause us to slide down the hill.

I put the truck in reverse and gave it a little gas. We started to slide again, and now we were even closer to the edge of the bank.

"That's not going to work," I said.

We sat there, afraid to move, trying to think of a way out of our predicament. "I'm afraid we'll slide over the edge if I try to go any farther."

Jerry nodded, his face nearly as white as the snow.

"But we gotta do something," I said.

I put the truck in Low and gave it a little gas. We moved uphill about a foot and then the truck started sliding over the edge. It only took a couple of seconds for us to slide down the hill sideways, but it seemed like hours. Jerry and I were both screaming like thirteen-year-old girls at a horror movie. When we reached the bottom, the truck tipped up on its side, hovered there a few seconds, and then fell back onto its wheels. Jerry was almost sitting in my lap by then, and when we stopped, he let out a breath like he had been holding it for hours.

"Holy smokes! I don't believe we did that," he said.

I could barely speak, let alone release the steering wheel. "W... w... we almost tipped this thing over," I managed to say.

We sat there a few moments, recovering from our trance-like stupor, when Thunderfoot started blowing the horn on the racecar. Jerry gave me a big grin. He slid over to the other side of the seat. "I think we'll go out through the hole in the fence," he said. I nodded and grinned, too.

We drove along side the hill to the pasture where Thunderfoot and Scott were waiting. "Jeez! What took you so long?"

"We had a little adventure trying to get to that ridge road," Jerry said.

"Yeah... just a tiny flaw in our plans." Jerry and I laughed, but Scott and Thunderfoot, though, failed to see the humor in the joke.

We hooked up the chain to my trailer hitch, and although it took some time and effort, I managed to tow the racecar back toward the hole in the fence, and we finally got it back on the road. Thunderfoot started it up and vroomed the engine. It seemed to be okay to drive.

"Okay," I said. "You guys go down to the house and see when he wants you to come and help him fix the fence. I'm going home."

The boys all thanked me and I drove away. I was still shaking from the ride over the side of the hill.

About mid-afternoon, the phone rang. It was Thunderfoot. "We got the fence fixed and the car is okay... except for two big scratches on the hood where the barbed wire scraped it."

"Well, that's good. And it's even better that you guys didn't get hurt."

"Yeah. That was pretty stupid, to take the car out on a snowy night. Maybe I learned a lesson... you think?"

I grinned. "Maybe. At least, I hope so," I said.

"You going anyplace tonight?"

"Nope. Why?"

"The guys and I are coming over. Don't make any supper. We're buying."

"Ok. See you then."

A couple of hours later, the three of them got out of the car in my driveway. Jerry and Scott were each carrying a huge pizza box, and Thunderfoot had a case of sodas. They came in, took off their shoes and coats, and we all sat around the kitchen table, laughing and talking and eating pizza.

"That was pretty cool of you not to nark on us last night," Jerry said.

"Yeah. Thanks for that, and for a hot shower, dry clothes and a warm bed," Scott added.

Thunderfoot just punched me in the arm. "These guys don't know you like I do," he said. "That's why I hang around with you. You're a pretty okay guy."

I grinned at him. "And the best fisherman in town, too."

He grinned. "Second best."

Thanks, Thunderfoot.

Runaway Ship

When it came to fishing, Thunderfoot and I really didn't care what we caught. We enjoyed fishing for anything that swam in the area lakes and rivers. No matter if we were fishing small mouth bass or carp, as long as they pulled on our line, we liked it. If we had to choose a favorite, though, it probably would have been the spring walleye.

There is nothing like sliding the boat across an icy landing and into water that has chunks of ice floating in it, and then feeling the faint tick of a walleye inhaling your jig, especially after a long winter of fishing through a hole in the ice. Walleye fishing was our first chance to get out and fish on *soft* water again.

The first places to fish each year are below the dams on the Mississippi and Wisconsin rivers. Due to the fast moving water, the ice melts sooner below the dams, and they're the first places to see boats each spring. I had received a call from a friend who lived near Genoa. He told me that the dam was open and the boat landings were free of ice. So, Thunderfoot and I were heading for the big river at first light for our first day of open water fishing. Riding between us, with his head tipped back, his mouth open, snoring loudly, was Thunderfoot's buddy, Scott, who often went with us on our adventures.

We arrived at the river and prepared the boat for it's first launch of the year. Someone had scattered pea gravel and salt on the landing ramp, so it was quite safe backing up to the edge of the water, where we slid the boat off the trailer and into the river. I jumped in the boat while Thunderfoot parked the truck, and Scott held onto the bow rope. I wanted to be sure the motor would start before we got away from the landing. It started right away, and it was nicely warmed up by the time Thunderfoot sprinted back from the parking lot. "Cast off, mate!" he said to Scott as he climbed into the boat.

We idled away from the landing out into the current, and then motored upriver to the dam. We weren't alone, as there were already twenty or more boats already there. When we got up into the pack of boats, I stopped the motor. Thunderfoot jumped up onto the front seat and lowered the bow mount trolling motor and worked us downriver through the maze of other boats. I didn't have my line in the water very long when I felt that slight tap on my jig. I set the hook into a walleye of respectable size.

"Ah! Boy that felt good," I said as I lifted the first fish of the season into the boat.

Just as I said that, Scott set his hook into another fish, and just a second later Thunderfoot did, too. They glanced at each other with that competitive look in their eyes, and both began reeling as fast as they could, eager to be the first with his fish in the boat. Thunderfoot's fish was rather small. It came up fast, and he won the challenge. "Okie, dokie, Scotto," he said with a huge grin. "You buy the ice cream!"

"That's okay," Scott replied with a smile. "It's worth a couple of ice creams just to be here on a beautiful day like this." He enjoyed the fishing too much to let a little thing like buying ice cream bother him.

It was, indeed, a beautiful day. The sun was up over the hills, now, and the air was warming into the 50s – just about perfect for a day of spring walleye fishing.

We drifted slowly downriver until we were no longer getting bites. I started the big motor again, and we went back to the dam and started another drift. It didn't seem like much time had passed when Thunderfoot announced that he was faminished. I checked my watch – it was already past noon. We pulled over to the shore, drug the boat up on the sandbar, stretched our legs and ate some sandwiches.

While we were eating, Thunderfoot took notice of the western sky and said, "Boy, those clouds over there look like they're gonna rain or snow on us."

Sure enough. A bank of really dark clouds was rolling in, and they looked wet. "Well, we've got plenty of fish right now, but I'd like to fish a while longer," I said. "We'll keep an eye on the clouds, and if they look like they're gonna rain on us, we'll get out of here."

I took over the trolling motor and Thunderfoot ran the gas motor when we went back on the river. I was on my pedestal seat fishing, running the trolling motor, and minding my own business when I heard Thunderfoot say to Scott, "Crack kills."

They both laughed.

Then Scott said, "Say no to crack."

Another big laugh.

I turned around. "What are you guys talking about?"

They were snickering and Thunderfoot pointed to my lower back. "Every time you lean over, don't you feel a draft?"

I reached behind me and then I understood. My jeans had slid down a little, and my butt crack was showing, and they were making fun of me. "Quit picking on my butt crack. My jeans just don't stay up very good... I'm all belly and no butt."

"Well, from where we're sitting, there's enough of your butt showing that it makes us just about lose our sandwiches," Thunderfoot teased.

I laid down my pole, stood, and hiked up my pants. "There. Now you ladies won't have anything to whine about."

"Thanks. You're so kind."

I have had a problem with my pants sliding down for most of my adult life. I'm kind of built wrong for good pants position. I'm top heavy, with a much smaller behind than I have belly, and there's just no way to keep my pants from sliding once in a while. I'm not to that stage, yet, when I want to wear them up under my armpits, so I just have to put up with a little slippage now and then.

We fished for about another hour, and then the wind picked up, swirling around a few snowflakes. "Let's reel up and get out of here," I said. "If it starts snowing heavy like it does sometimes in the spring, I'd rather be on the other side of the big hills between here and home before the roads get slick."

The boys agreed. We reeled in our lines and headed back to the landing. By the time the boat was on the trailer, heavy snow was coming down. Luckily, enough salt on the landing kept it from getting slick, so we made it up from the water and onto the highway with no problems.

We had planned to drive downriver to Lynxville, then up the Lynxville hill, and on home. But by the time we got there, the snow was piling up on the road. "Boy, I wonder if we should try to get up that hill?" I said.

"If we don't, we have to go all the way to Prairie du Chien," Thunderfoot said. "That's a lot longer road home."

We stopped in Lynxville to take a better look at the road. The route we were to travel went up the side of a huge Mississippi bluff. About three hundred yards up the steep incline, the road took a sharp turn to the left and continued up the backside of the bluff. That was the problem. To make the left turn, you had to slow way down and lose all of your upward momentum.

"Well, what do you guys think?" I asked.

Thunderfoot walked up the road a little ways and scraped his foot through the snow. "It's only six inches deep. We can make it."

"Okay. Let's go before it get any worse," I said.

We began the climb, and it was going quite well up to the turn. I didn't want to go too fast, but I had to keep moving upward. As I slowed down turning into the sharp curve, the wheels started to spin. "Uh, oh." The truck slid sideways and came to rest up against the left bank at a right angel to the boat.

"Oops. That didn't work too well," Thunderfoot said.

I applied the emergency brake, and we got out to look over the situation. It was not good.

"There's no way to keep going up," I said. "We'll have to unhook the boat, get the truck turned around and go back down."

The boys agreed. "Scott, you get in the truck. We'll unhook the boat and lead it down the hill. Then you turn the truck around and meet us at the bottom. We'll hook it up again and go home by way of Prairie du Chien."

Scott nodded okay. Thunderfoot and I went to the back of the truck, unhooked the lights and safety chains, and then I said to Thunderfoot, "Hang on tight when I take the hitch off the ball."

Thunderfoot nodded.

I opened the latch and we lifted the trailer tongue of the off the ball. The boat rolled backward and we walked with it, one of us on each side, holding onto the trailer tongue. "This isn't so bad," Thunderfoot said.

We had started at a brisk walk, and soon we were trotting behind the boat. "Hold back on it! It's going faster!" I was starting to pant.

Then our trot increased to a fair-paced run. "I'm holding as much as I can," Thunderfoot said. There was a little panic in his voice. "I can't keep it slow. It's gonna get away if we don't run with it."

We ran as fast as we could, doing our best to keep the boat from veering off the road and crashing over the side of the hill. Then, just when I thought it couldn't get any worse, it got worse. My pants began sliding down off my butt. "Oh, no! My pants are coming down!" I yelled. Then they slid a little farther, and then they dropped to my knees. I was running as fast as I could, taking one-foot-long steps because my pants were now around my ankles, acting like a prisoner's leg restraints.

Thunderfoot was panting and laughing as we ran, me with my pants flopping along on the roadway. "Say no to crack!" he managed to get out between laughs, glancing over his shoulder at my long underwear – that was now sliding down just as my pants had done.

We were both laughing, and we could hardly hold onto the boat, but we finally reached the bottom and stopped the trailer against a mailbox post. There I stood, snow blowing around me, snot running from my nose, steam rising off my bare butt, and my pants and underwear in the snow. Thunderfoot was lying on the road laughing so hard I thought he was going to have a coronary.

Just then Scott drove up behind us. He beeped the horn and rolled down his window. "Say no to crack!"

I brushed off some of the snow from my pants and long johns, and got them back to where they were supposed to be. We all sat and laughed until I thought I was going to be sick.

"It's good nobody else was coming up this road," I said.

"Yeah," Thunderfoot laughed. "They'd have probably driven right over the side if they saw you coming down the hill like that!"

We maneuvered the boat trailer around with the tongue pointing in the right direction, hooked it up to the truck again, and drove down into Lynxville. We stopped at one of the local restaurants for a bite to eat, and to hear the weather reports.

"The road's closed to Prairie," the owner said.

"Oh, great," I moaned. "We can't get up the hill, and the highway is closed. What do we do now?"

"The motel has a couple of rooms left. Want me to call?"

The owner called the motel and confirmed a room. We had our meal, and then there was nothing more to do but to sit out the storm until the next morning.

"I'll call my neighbor to take care of the dogs; you boys call your moms and let them know we're all right."

After we ate, we drove the short distance to the motel, packed our fish in snow, and went to our room. Thunderfoot and Scott shared one double bed, and I had one to myself.

When we were all snug in bed, I turned out the light. "Well, that was pretty fun," Thunderfoot said.

"Yeah. That was great," I replied.

"From where I was sitting, it wasn't very pretty," Scott added.

"Yeah," Thunderfoot said. "From what I saw, it was pretty terrifying, too. I'll probably have nightmares, so if I yell out during the night, you'll know I'm reliving it."

It was quiet for a few minutes and then Thunderfoot yelled, "Say no to crack!"

Wise guy.

Thanks, Thunderfoot.

Turkey Trouble

When you apply for a turkey permit, you have a choice of the area and the time periods that you wish to hunt. Thunderfoot and I usually filled out our applications so that we covered all six time periods. We picked our favorite area as our first zone choice, and the other side of the river as our second choice. This year, I had chosen the first, third and fifth periods, and Thunderfoot had chosen the second, fourth and sixth.

My permit arrived in the mail, and then I saw Thunderfoot trotting across the back yard carrying his envelope. "What did you get?" he asked as he came flying through the door.

"Third period," I said.

"Bummer. I got first and fourth."

"You got two? You lucky little cuss! I've gotten two only once in my life."

"You just gotta know how to fill out the form," he said grinning.

It was only a little over a week until the first season, so we started making plans. We always hunted together, and that was the reason we tried for different seasons, so we could hunt more times. It really didn't make any difference to me if I shot a turkey or not. I just loved being out in the woods at dawn, listening to the gobbling – the sounds of hens and toms talking back and forth. The idea of fooling a big tom into making him think I was a turkey was the real reason I liked the sport so much. Fooling any wild critter with a call, like a turkey or a duck, just made it the sport for me. It was always exciting just to see them coming in. Killing the bird or ducks wasn't so important – fooling them into thinking I was one of them was the fun part.

"I think we should go up on the hill and wait for some gobbles on the first day," I said. "Then we can work our way to which ever side they happen to be on."

"Yeah, that's a good idea. They like that hilltop for strutting in the early morning sun."

We had this turkey thing down quite well. Of course, we had been hunting the same area for six years, so we knew the turkeys and their habits.

We had everything prepared, and the night before opening day Thunderfoot stayed over at my house so we'd be ready for an early start – at least an hour before first light. The hilltop that we liked to hunt required climbing a long, steep logging road, and it took us – well, it took *me* – quite a while to get to the top without having a coronary. Thunderfoot, on the other hand, was barely breathing hard when we reached the hay field at the top.

We had a quick breakfast of cereal and toast, loaded his gun and our turkey vests into the back of the truck, and off we went through the darkness to our favorite hunting farm. We parked near the milk house. Our friend Ken, who owned the farm, knew we would be there this particular morning, so we just left the key in the truck and began sneaking up the hill on the logging road.

Thunderfoot was carrying his shotgun, and since I didn't have a permit for this season, I only had my calls and a decoy in the back of my vest.

To those non-turkey hunters, I should explain a turkey vest. It's a wonderful invention that allows a turkey hunter to carry all of the toys it takes to get a turkey close enough to shoot, keeping his hands free. Our turkey vests are made of camouflage material with about a dozen pockets of all sizes to hold calls, gloves, hand warmers, candy bars, water bottles, head nets, shells, and the big pouch on the back will carry a decoy or two. If the hunter gets a turkey, it will fit in the pouch and can be lugged out on the hunter's back rather than carrying it. The vests also have a seat cushion attached to the back with a strip of nylon. While you are walking, Velcro holds the cushion up inside the vest against your back. When you get to where you want to sit, you pull the seat free, and let it flop down so you can sit on it. What a great idea.

We had climbed about half way up the logging road when I felt a little backpressure in the nether region. "Oh, boy. I think I'm gonna have to visit Mother Nature," I whispered to Thunderfoot.

"What a surprise," he whispered. "How many times have we gone hunting when you *didn't* have to do that?"

"Well, I can't help it. When it's time, it's time."

He just shook his head. "Let me get up the road a ways before you start."

I stopped and took off my vest and found my handy dandy little roll of toilet paper in one of the handy dandy pockets in the vest. I always had a little roll of emergency paper with me. I spied a tree broken off about two feet from the bottom, but it was still attached to the stump, probably broken when logs were skidded down the road many years ago. It was about eight inches thick and looked sturdy enough for a perfect place to sit and ponder the mysteries of life.

The broken tree was right on the edge of the road, right above a steep bank, so everything would drop away from the road and not offend my sensitive hunting partner.

I unhooked my bib overalls, lowered my boxers and sat down on the log, sliding across it far enough to get my business done. I put my elbows on my knees and relaxed. I was in about mid-deposit when the tree made a slight cracking noise. I tried to hurry. I was just about to stand up when the log cracked again, and both the tree and I went over the bank backwards. I rolled over backward about three or four times before I came to rest at the bottom of the hill. The log rolled down, too, and stopped when it hit my shins.

I was sitting there on the bare ground trying to get my bearings when I heard Thunderfoot chuckling. He was peering down at me over the edge of the road, sitting there with my pants around my ankles. "You think you could make a little more noise?" he whispered. "There are a few turkeys over across the river that didn't hear you."

I ignored him, got myself up, and brushed off the dirt and leaves that covered me. Thankful that I had missed my deposits and that none of that stuck to me, I used my paper and situated my pants. Then I had to walk all the way back down to the end of the road and climb the hill again to where I had taken my fall. When I got there, Thunderfoot was leaning against the tree, just shaking his head. "I swear. I should get college credit for this."

"Oh, dry up," I said. "Let's go hunting."

"Let me go first," he said. "I don't want to take the chance of you tipping over and knocking me all the way down the hill."

I socked him in the arm.

We finally reached the edge of the field, sat down, and waited for some birds to begin tree gobbling. Tree gobbling is just what the words imply. The toms roost together in one or several trees that are close together, and the hens do the same, somewhere nearby. When there is just enough morning light, the toms gobble from the tree, to let the hens know where they are, hoping the hens will fly down from their roost to where the toms are waiting. The hens, too, make a yelping sound to let the toms know where they are. That's the sound a hunter makes, trying to convince a tom that he is a hen that can't find her mate, so he should come to find her. If it's done right, you fool the tom into coming to you, and you get your bird. It works sometimes, and sometimes it doesn't, but it's lots of fun trying to make the toms come to you.

We sat and listened. Soon we heard a soft yelp from a hen down in the valley below us. In just a short while, a tom gobbled on the ridge just behind us. Then, seconds later, another one gobbled from the same area. Soon there were half a dozen toms gobbling and several hens yelping. "Wow. They're hot today," Thunderfoot said.

The gobbling went on for about ten minutes, and then it got quiet again. "They're flying down," I whispered.

We listened some more, and we heard a gobbler again, but then he was part way down the side of the hill toward the calling hens. "Let's sneak over to that point," I whispered. "When the toms are finished with the hens, they'll come up here and strut in this field.

Thunderfoot nodded and we snuck toward the point of the hill. We had seen birds in the field at mid-morning many times, and we figured these would soon be there, too. Turkeys are birds of habit. They do much the same thing every day, so if you watch them enough, you can predict what they'll do, and when. Tom turkeys like to strut in an open field, where the hens can see how beautiful they are. They puff all up and walk around like they're saying, "Look at me! Look at me! See how big and strong I am."

When we got to the point, we heard a gobble down below us. "They're with the hens," I said. "Get down in that clump of brush, and I'll sit here behind this big log." Thunderfoot nodded, snuck down about ten yards from me, and sat down in a brush pile. I staked the hen decoy I had in my pouch about ten yards in front of Thunderfoot, snuck back up the hill, flipped my seat down, and sat comfortably next to a big log. I sounded a soft yelp every ten minutes, or so, and after about an hour, the gobbles from down the hill were getting closer. I wished I could have sat with Thunderfoot to make sure he was ready, but there wasn't enough room in the brush pile for two, so I had to hope he was watching in the right direction, and that he would see the birds when they came.

The gobbles gradually got louder, and then I could see a big tom, in full strut, coming right to us. I quit yelping and watched. The tom strutted up to the disinterested decoy, making his drumming noise, parading back and forth, working himself silly trying to impress it. Then two more toms came up and stood, watching the show. They were a little smaller and probably younger, and were not allowed to participate. The strutting tom was the dominant bird and they had to wait their turn in the pecking order. (The turkey world has its hierarchy, and both toms and hens have a boss and underlings.)

It *was* quite a show, and I almost forgot about Thunderfoot. "He must be enjoying the display, and waiting for his shot," I thought to myself.

The tom turkey kept working to get the hen to submit to him, but she ignored him. Finally, he let his feathers down and stood there, looking at her. One of the other toms raised his feathers about half way, and boss tom chased him off down the hill. Tom number three followed, and all was quiet.

It wasn't much of a surprise to find Thunderfoot snuggled down, sound asleep and snoring quietly in the brush pile. His gun was lying beside him, so I slowly and carefully pulled it out from the brush and slid the safety off. Then I aimed at a clump of weeds a short distance away and pulled the trigger.

Thunderfoot came awake quite abruptly, just about jumping out of his shoes. He scrambled around, searching for his gun, not even noticing me behind him.

"Looking for this?"

He spun around and glared at me. "What the heck are you trying to do? Give me a heart attack?"

I was laughing so hard I couldn't answer.

"Jeez! I almost wet my pants! Are you nuts? Shooting a gun like that when a person is... oh, no. I was asleep."

"Yes you were, Sleeping Beauty."

He shook his head. "Don't tell me. Did a turkey come?"

I nodded. "Three of them came."

He hung his head. "How far?"

"See the decoy? One was there, and the other two were just five feet to the left."

"I suppose you're gonna tell everybody that I fell asleep and missed a turkey."

I shrugged my shoulders. "Not unless I hear that you told someone about my backward summersault down the hill, sans pants."

"Deal," he said, offering his hand.

We shook and then collected up the decoy. By now, it was close to lunchtime, and we were both pretty hungry. "Let's go back for some lunch, and maybe a nap," I said.

"Lunch... good idea," he said. "But for some reason I'm not real tired, though." Big grin.

Well, we didn't want to get a bird the first day, anyway. What would we do the rest of the week.

Thanks, Thunderfoot.

A Howling Good Time

Thunderfoot and I had spent the five days of his turkey season working on a group of toms that just wouldn't cooperate with us. Maybe it was stubbornness, or just a lack of any new ideas, but we had tried just about everything – without success.

Now it was my turn. The two-day wait between seasons had made me think about options, and I decided to leave the old spot and try for some new turkeys, elsewhere. Early on my first morning of hunting, we trekked up a logging road to another field at the other end of our hunting farm.

"I don't know if this is such a good idea," Thunderfoot whispered when we stopped for a breather. "We *know* there are turkeys over on the other hill. What if there's nothing up here?"

"If we don't hear or see any, then we'll try someplace else tomorrow," I whispered. "I just want to let those other birds rest for a while. I think we pestered them enough last week."

He shrugged his shoulders, and again we started walking toward the top of the hill. A few minutes later, we stopped again, trying to decide where to place our decoys and get set up for dawn. It was dark – really dark. The moon and stars were completely blanketed by clouds. The eastern sky hadn't started to brighten yet, and dawn was at least a half hour away.

"Let's cross the field and sit on that point that comes down from the woods... where we sat one time last year," I whispered.

Thunderfoot nodded. We walked across the hay field as quietly as we could. We were about halfway across when a coyote began howling just down the hill from us. Then, two or three more began howling all around us. "Holy smokes. Those are close," Thunderfoot whispered. He moved a little closer to me.

The howling became louder, and then some of the coyotes started yipping and barking. Thunderfoot stood right against my side, looking all around us. "Did you want to hold hands?" I whispered.

He turned to me with a look on his face that I thought might suggest that he *did* want to hold my hand. "No. But I don't want to get too far away, either," he said.

"Those coyotes won't hurt us," I said. "They probably smell us, and when one howled, the whole pack started. I'm sure we're not in any danger."

But Thunderfoot wouldn't move. He stuck to me like a wood tick. He matched me step for step all the way as I walked to where I knew we would find a point of woods that protruded down into the other side of the field. The point was a good spot to sit and watch for turkeys.

As we got close to the point, I stopped to try to ponder our position. Thunderfoot plowed into my back. I turned and stared at him. "Would you like a piggyback ride?"

"No, I wouldn't like a piggyback ride. What do you expect? You stopped without warning me."

"Maybe I should get some brake lights for the back of my hunting coat."

"Oh, you're such a comedian. I'm just about sick from laughing."

I could just make out the point up ahead, and we walked to it. "I'll put the decoys out," I said. "You clear out all the branches and leaves so we can sit."

"I'll help you with the decoys, and then we can come back here."

"I don't need any help with the decoys. What's the matter? Are you still scared of the coyotes?"

"Shut up! Let's get the decoys out."

We put out three decoys, returned to the point, and made a makeshift blind. I stood my gun against a tree and sat down on my vest seat. Thunderfoot didn't have his gun since it was my season, so he flipped his seat down and sat right next to me.

"Would you like to sit on my lap?" I said.

He gave me a dirty look. "Kinda touchy this morning, aren't you?"

"Touchy?" I said. "You're the one who seems to be nervous. You still worried about a coyote carrying you off into the woods? The Dingo ate my Baybeee."

"Oh, dry up and watch for turkeys," he whispered.

"It's so dark I can't see the decoys. How do you expect me to see a turkey?"

No answer.

We sat side by side, and after several minutes the sky in the east turned to a dark blue from the pitch black it had been. Soon after that we could see the silhouette of the other ridge, and gradually the dark blue faded to gray as the sky brightened to daylight. And with the daylight came the yelping from a bunch of hens in their trees, and a couple of gobbles off in the distance.

"Well, there's a couple of toms up here," I whispered.

Thunderfoot nodded.

The initial gobbling was all that we heard. Everything was quiet – no turkey sounds – only birds chirping and squirrels chattering. I brought out my favorite call and made a series of yelps, and then settled back to wait.

"Look," Thunderfoot whispered. He nodded ever so slightly. "Over to the right."

I looked carefully, and instead of turkeys, two does were coming across the field toward our decoys. "Well, at least we have *something* to keep us entertained."

We watched the deer eating alfalfa, working their way across the field. Every so often they stopped, raised their heads, carefully listening and looking around to make sure they were safe. The does fed right among our fake turkeys as if they didn't mind them at all. As they came closer, Thunderfoot whispered, "Well, there goes that theory that turkeys have chased all the deer out of some places."

I nodded in agreement. "Yeah, these seem to be pretty happy feeding next to turkeys."

By then, Thunderfoot must have felt safe from the coyotes, because he had moved away from his position of nearly sitting in my lap. "Feel safe now? You're pretty far away. Don't you think a coyote might be lurking around here?"

"Oh, you're such a smart butt."

Just then, one of the deer raised her head and sorted. The other one looked in the same direction. Abruptly their tails went up, they took a couple of hops to the right, and ran across the field toward the woods.

"What the heck was that all about?" I whispered.

"I don't know. Something must have scared – look, look!" Thunderfoot said with excitement, nodding and pointing to the left end of the field.

Two coyotes came on a dead run, hugging the ground as low as they could, crossing the field in just a couple of seconds. When they reached the decoys, the closest one pounced on one of the plastic hens. Thunk! The decoy tipped over with the coyote right on top of it. But as soon as he had the decoy in his grasp, he turned it loose like it was on fire. The coyote jumped about three feet in the air and made an about face. The second coyote understood what his friend had conveyed, and they both raced off back to where they had come from.

We both started to laugh. "Holy cow! Did you see that coyote turn that decoy loose?" Thunderfoot said laughing. "He reminded me of Wiley Coyote with that look on his face like 'Oh No!'"

"Wow," I said. That was worth getting up early. You don't see that every day."

"No foolin! That was great!"

By now it was late morning, and it looked as if it were going to turn into a pretty nice day. "My butt's getting tired," I said. "Let's pick up the decoys, get something to eat, and then get out the boat and try for some Northerns and Bass."

"Hey, now that sounds like a good idea."

We picked up the decoys and hiked down the hill back to the truck. While we drove back toward town I said, "You were pretty spooked when those coyotes were howling, weren't you?"

"No... I was just fooling around," he said.

"Yeah, sure you were. Then you go up there tomorrow by yourself, and I'll hunt someplace else."

He stared at me. "Boy, you're such a funny guy. You just make me laugh all day... Not!"

Well, *I* thought it was kind of funny.

Thanks, Thunderfoot.

Woof, Woof

With our first two turkey hunting seasons a memory, it was a three-week wait until Thunderfoot and I could hunt again. Thunderfoot had received two permits, and his second one was for the very last season of the year. The late seasons took a little more luck than the first because most of the hens were nesting by then, and there were fewer toms still in the mood to look for them. Of course, when you did find a lovesick tom, he was pretty easy to lure with the decoys.

But, in the meantime, we had to find something to keep us busy.

"Let's check those old night crawlers in the shop refrigerator," Thunderfoot said.

"I doubt that they're still alive."

"Well, if they are, we can go down by the bridge and soak them for a while and see what's biting. It's better than sitting around doing nothing."

I had to agree with that. In the back of the refrigerator we found the bait bucket that we had stored away last fall. I opened it expecting a nasty smelling mess, but the dirt was still moist, and when I shook it a bit, a nice bunch of fat night crawlers came to the top. "Wow, they're in good shape," I said.

"Let's go see if we can catch something," Thunderfoot said, grabbing a couple of my fishing poles and heading for the truck. We stopped at his house to pick up a couple of his poles, and soon we were at the riverbank just above the bridge.

We carefully stepped down over the rocks and boulders that had been dumped on the shore to keep the riverbank from washing away. I was especially careful on those rocks – concerned not only about falling and breaking my neck, but also about the snakes that liked living among them.

"What? You scared a rattler is gonna grab you?" Thunderfoot teased with a big grin.

"It doesn't have to be a rattler. I see any snake and I'm outa here."

He laughed and called me a sissy, but I ignored him.

At the river's edge, we each found a nice flat rock to sit on, far enough apart that we had room to fish, but close enough to share the one container of night crawlers. We baited our hooks and tossed our lines out into the water. It didn't take but half a minute and I caught a small sheepshead.

"First soft water fish of the year," I said, swinging the fish past Thunderfoot so he could get a good look.

"You're not gonna count that little thing are you? You must really be desperate to win an ice cream to keep that little thing."

I just smiled, and a few minutes later, I caught a nice walleye. Thunderfoot was still waiting for his first bite. Then just as I released the walleye back into the river, he had a jolting strike on his pole. He set the hook, and the fish began pulling line off his spool. "Holy cow! It's a huge one!" he shouted.

His fish put up a good fight and it seemed to just dog down, staying on the bottom. "Are you sure it's a fish? Is it pulling?" I asked.

"It doesn't seem to be swimming, but I can feel it shaking its head and pulling. It's like he's hanging onto the bottom."

Finally, his line started to move. He pulled and tugged, and gradually gained some line. We could see it swirling just below the surface, but I couldn't figure out what kind of fish it was. It seemed long and skinny and dark colored, and it made me think it might be a flathead catfish. "Maybe it's a small flathead," I said.

"It's too early for them, isn't it?"

Just then the fish came to the top and Thunderfoot dragged it up on the rocks. "What the heck is that? Hey! My fish has legs!"

The fish wasn't a fish at all, but a salamander called a Mud Puppy. The twelve-inch-long creature had dark brown/black mottled coloration, four legs with very sharp-looking claws, a big mouth full of teeth, and it was very, very angry.

"That's a Mud Puppy!" I said.

"Jeez! It's an ugly critter. How am I gonna get if off my hook?" Thunderfoot said.

"Just grab it like you do a catfish and take it off," I said bravely.

"Oh, just like that," he said as the Mud Puppy hissed and crawled around on the rock, trying to get back into the water. "Here. If it's so easy, you do it," he said, and he swung the nasty little critter over at me.

The Mud Puppy landed right at my feet and immediately grabbed my right pant leg with its teeth. Once it had a good grip, it grabbed hold of my leg with its front feet and dug its claws into my jeans. Of course, meanwhile, I was trying to get up off the rock and make tracks away from the little monster.

"Holy cow! It's got me!" I shouted. I began kicking, trying to dislodge the critter, and the harder I kicked the harder it held on. Meanwhile, Thunderfoot was rolling on the rocks laughing.

The Mud Puppy let loose with its jaws and climbed a little farther up my leg, like it thought it was going to sit in my lap. That did it. I gave a mighty kick and off it went, right into the river... along with my right shoe.

Thunderfoot was laughing so hard that he couldn't sit up, and when my shoe flew off into the water, I thought he was having a stroke. The Mud Puppy's teeth must have sawed through Thunderfoot's line, because when it hit the water, the line went limp and Mr. Puppy was gone.

My shoe floated for a couple of minutes, and then sank below the surface. I sat with my head between my knees, hoping that The Big One wasn't going to hit just then.

When the excitement finally settled down, Thunderfoot was able to sit up. Tears still streamed down his face. "Holy smokes. That was the funniest thing I've ever seen. Your shoe flew halfway across the river."

My heart rate had slowed down, and I had to laugh, too. "Jeez, you little snot. Why'd you throw that ugly thing over here? I about had a heart attack."

"You said it was easy to take them off. I thought you wanted to show me," he said, laughing again.

"It's a good thing I went to the bathroom before we left home."

We both had another good laugh.

We caught several more fish, but thankfully, no more Mud Puppies, and after an hour, we climbed up over the rocks to go home – me with one bare foot. When we got to the grass on the bank above the rocks, I stopped, took off my left shoe, and threw it in the river.

Thunderfoot began laughing again. "You should have saved it, just in case you ever lose a leg."

I grinned at him. "That's a cheery thought. But with you around, it's probably just a matter of time till I do," I said. "With my luck, I'd lose the wrong leg, and the shoe wouldn't do me any good anyway."

"Hey! I've never even come close to making you lose a leg."

Just give him time, I thought.

Thanks, Thunderfoot.

Sneak Attack

We had been anxiously waiting for the final spring turkey season. Thunderfoot had a second permit, so with him as the gunner, we were off to the turkey woods again. It really didn't matter to me that I couldn't do any shooting. I loved the springtime, and I never got tired of trying to fool a turkey. But the later seasons required us to get up at an ungodly hour. It was light a few minutes earlier each day, and by the sixth week of turkey season, it seemed like we were getting up in the middle of the night to be ready by dawn.

In the month since our last turkey outing, I had made a major purchase and was anxious to try out my new hunting toy. For the past several years, turkey-hunting blinds were becoming quite popular. These were little houses made of camouflage fabric that would hide the hunters from the sharp eye of the turkeys, and could be set up and taken down in just a few minutes. They featured several windows that could be zipped open, and through which the hunters could shoot.

I had postponed buying one because the early models seemed a little complicated to set up, especially in the dark woods. It appeared to be more trouble than it was worth. The second reason keeping me from getting one was that I just couldn't believe that a turkey would come close to something the size of an outhouse that hadn't been there in the woods the previous day. I was quite certain they would steer clear of a blind, and I had a hard time accepting this new idea.

But, after dozens of conversations with hunters who used the blinds, I was finally convinced. "They'll walk right up to it and don't worry a bit," one of my friends told me. "They don't see it as a threat." Well, I decided to get one, and we would try it out on opening day of the last season.

"This'll give us a chance to move a little, and to get a good shot without being seen," I told Thunderfoot as we drove through the darkness toward our turkey hunting farm. "And a turkey coming in from behind won't see us moving, either."

"I think it sounds great," Thunderfoot said. "And if you get tired, you can lay down and have a nap, and if you move, you won't spook my turkey."

"He might hear me," I said.

"Not if I pinch your nose shut." Big grin.

We got out of the truck at the farm and closed the doors as quietly as possible. We put on our vests, Thunderfoot uncased his gun, and I slung the blind over my shoulder. It weighed only a few pounds, and folded up, it was the size of a golf bag with a similar strap that allowed me to haul it easily on my back, keeping my hands free to carry a gun, if I had been carrying one.

We hiked the path to the area that we liked to hunt. "We've got about a half-hour till light," I whispered. "Let's set up the blind here in the corner of the field."

Thunderfoot nodded.

I opened the drawstring on the end of the carrying bag and slid the blind out onto the grass. It looked kind of like a short, fat umbrella without a handle. A couple of pulls, and a tug here and there, and it popped up, ready to use. Its shape was a geodesic dome, and I had to tip my hat to whoever designed this neat little house. We zipped the door open and crawled inside. There was plenty of room for the two of us, and there could have been a third hunter. With twelve small windows spaced around it, we had our choice of shooting ports. Each window was covered with a screen of camouflage netting, and the idea was to shoot right through the netting. The turkey would never know we were inside the blind.

"This is just too cool," Thunderfoot said.

"It would be better if we had some chairs."

"How about those folding lawn chairs? Aren't they still behind the seat in the truck?" he said.

"Yeah! I forgot about them. They'd work great."

"I'll run back and get them," Thunderfoot said.

"No, you wait here. I'll go. You're the one with the permit. I'd hate to have a turkey come by while you were gone and not be able to shoot it," I said.

Thunderfoot nodded an okay.

I slipped through the door and looked at the sky. The east was beginning to brighten and the sky was turning blue. It wouldn't be long before it would be light enough for the turkeys to fly down from their roosts, and I wanted to be back inside the blind before they started moving around.

I hiked back to the truck. We had two of those new space age chairs that folded up into a small package, and opened to a real comfortable chair with a backrest. We used them a lot for fishing at the riverbank, and they would be perfect for the turkey blind.

I slung the chairs over my shoulder and started back to the blind. Daylight was here and I was surprised how fast dawn had turned to daytime. As I approached the rise in the field, about halfway between the truck and the blind, I slowed my pace, crouching down and kind of waddling, just in case there were any early turkeys in sight. I peeked up over the grass on the rise and sure enough, there was a tom turkey standing in the edge of the field about a hundred yards from Thunderfoot and the blind.

I lay down in the grass and watched, not able to move any closer without spooking the bird. And then I heard a "yelp, yelp, yelp." Thunderfoot had seen the bird and was calling from the blind.

The tom turned and looked at the blind but didn't move toward it. We hadn't had time to put out any decoys, so I guessed that the tom didn't see any girl turkeys that interested him. Then he puffed up and displayed his pretty feathers, strutting down the hill toward the ditch at the bottom of the field. Thunderfoot called again, but the tom now had his eye on something that did interest him, and he wasn't having anything to do with that invisible hen.

I looked toward where the tom was headed, expecting a hen to be waiting for him. But all I saw was a rusty old milk can lying partly buried in the edge of the field. The tom pranced around the milk can, displaying his feathers. I laughed to myself. That stupid tom must have thought the milk can was a hen. So much for detailed decoys.

Thunderfoot yelped again, but tom wasn't interested. I lay there watching the tom, and then I could have sworn that the blind had moved from where it had been originally. I must be seeing things.

I looked back at the tom, still strutting back and forth, trying to impress the rusty milk can, and in the corner of my eye I noticed the blind moving. It rose up about six inches off the ground, and then I could see Thunderfoot's feet moving under it, toward the tom. He was trying to sneak up on the turkey, staying inside the blind. I could hardly believe my eyes!

I kept watching. Every time the tom would turn and strut, Thunderfoot moved the blind five or six feet closer. With a couple more moves he would be in range.

Actually, he moved three more times. The blind was just about twenty yards from the tom when I saw the gun barrel slide out one of the windows. There was a puff of smoke, and then the sound of the blast reached me. The tom lay on his back, flapping his wings. The kill was complete. Then the blind moved rapidly across the remaining pasture, flipped over, and Thunderfoot emerged pick up his bird.

I could see his grin from a hundred yards away. He held up the bird and gave me thumbs up. I returned the gesture.

There didn't seem any use in carrying the chairs to the blind now, so I left them in the grass and walked across the field to Thunderfoot and his bird.

"You crazy little fool. I can't believe you got away with that!" I said laughing as I slapped him on the back.

He grinned. "There's more than one way to skin a turkey."

"I think that's a cat, but I get your idea."

We folded up the blind, slid it back into its carrying bag, and walked back to the truck. "That's a pretty cool new toy we've got," Thunderfoot said.

"Yeah, I guess so. I wonder if the guy who designed it ever thought it would be used for *sneaking up* on a turkey?"

"Probably not. But he doesn't know me," Thunderfoot said.

Obviously, he doesn't.

Thanks, Thunderfoot.

Just Plumb Foolishness

"The toilet won't go down!" Thunderfoot yelled from the bathroom.

"What did you do?" I asked.

"What do you think I did? That's kind of a stupid question."

"Jeez! Now's a great time for this. I'm gonna be late as it is."

"Hey, it's not like I did it on purpose. This isn't the first time it got plugged, I bet," he said defensively.

He was right. My toilet plugged about twice a year, right on schedule. It was because several years ago, I had cut a section out of the pipe running from the house to the septic tank so I could put in a drain from the spare room. At the time, I was using the spare room as a makeshift workshop for my business. Some time later, I moved to a larger shop and just cemented over the opening in the room, but left the T in the pipe. Now, at about six-month intervals, paper and other debris gathered in that T area, and eventually it plugged. In fact, I was so tired of going to the hardware store and renting a toilet snake, that I just bought one so I had it when I needed it. Of course, it always seemed to plug at the most inopportune times.

"Well, you'll just have to not use it till I get home," I said.

"I can fix it... I've seen you do it before."

I'd have rather waited until I returned home that evening, but I didn't have a lot of choices. I had to be at a meeting that would last most of the day, and Thunderfoot was dog sitting for me. He didn't have school, and he was usually at my house anyway, so it worked out nice for him to stay there with the dogs.

"Get the snake out of the shed," I told him.

While I prepared my papers and a few other things for the meeting, Thunderfoot trotted out to the boat shed and found the sewer snake and a big pair of heavy black rubber gloves that I wore when I was clearing out the sewer pipe. I went to the back of the house where he already had the clean-out access opened up.

"All I do is run this down the pipe and ram it back and forth till it clears up... right?"

"Yeah. Just go slow and don't wreck anything."

"No faith in me." He shook his head. "Just go... and don't worry about this. I'll take care of it."

"Ok," I said. "I'll see you later. " And off I went.

The meeting broke for lunch so I thought I'd call home to see how the plumbing job was coming along. The phone rang, and rang, and I was about to hang up when Thunderfoot finally answered, panting like he had been running.

"Hi. Where were you?" I asked.

"I... uh... I was out back."

"Doing what?"

"Just about to finish up with the plumbing."

"You're still doing that? What's the matter? Did you have trouble?"

"I've got it under control. What time are you gonna be home?"

"Maybe about six. Are you sure everything is all right?"

"Don't worry. I'm just about done. See ya later." He hung up.

For some reason, that call didn't reassure me, but it wouldn't help to call back, so I just went back to the rest of the meeting.

The meeting was finally over at almost five o'clock, and the drive home took over an hour. When I pulled into the driveway, I was surprised to see my brother's pickup parked there. I was also surprised to see the back yard lit up with floodlights!

My brother came walking around the house wearing an amused grin on his face. "Don't get excited," he said. "Thunderfoot had a little trouble with your sewer and he called me to give him a hand."

"A *little* trouble?"

"Yeah, well, you know that V-shaped handle on the sewer snake? The thing that you squeeze to grip the snake?"

"Yeah, I know. It slides up the snake as you go so you can use it to push easier," I said.

"Well," he went on, "Thunderfoot forgot about that, and he put the V-handle down the pipe. Of course, it went okay as long as it was going down, but when he tried to pull it back out, the V caught in the pipe and he couldn't get it out."

"Oh cripes! I thought he knew how to use it," I said.

"Well, the V got stuck in the pipe way out near the tank, so he called me and I came over. We decided that the only way to fix it was to dig up the pipe, cut if off, pull the sewer snake out from there, and then put in a new piece of pipe."

I just shook my head. Such a simple job... and now such a big one.

"It took a little longer than we figured, so I went home and got my floodlights," my brother said. "He's been pretty worried that you'd be mad, so go easy on him."

"Ok," I said. We walked around the house.

Well, when we reached the back yard, Thunderfoot was lying on the grass next to a trench about six feet long, by about a foot and a half wide – very much resembling a grave. His hands were folded across his chest, as if he were ready for burial.

Despite the mess in the yard and my being a little peeved that he hadn't listened to me, I had to laugh.

"Just roll me in when you're ready," he said with his eyes closed.

We all had a good laugh.

"If you'd been just another twenty minutes later," he said, "I'd have had it done."

"What did you think? That this *grave* wouldn't catch my attention?"

He shrugged. "I guess not. But I thought maybe you wouldn't come in the back yard till the grass grew back."

I cuffed him on the head. "I'm not that senile!"

They had the new piece of pipe and a couple of rubber couplers that would splice it into the old one, and in a short while, everything was fixed and we started filling in the hole. My brother stayed with his lights until we finished, and then he went home.

"Thanks for helping," Thunderfoot said as he left.

"No problem." He grinned as he pulled out of the driveway.

"Well," I said. "I suppose you're faminished."

"No foolin," he responded. "Plumbing is hard work."

"Go order a pizza and I'll pick it up... on my way to the hardware store to pay for the pipe and connectors."

"Okay," he said, and then he hesitated. "I hope you're not mad at me."

"No. I guess not. You did your best, and besides... now that T is gone. Maybe we won't have to do this again."

"Yeah, that was my plan," he said, grinning from ear to ear.

Sure it was.

Thanks, Thunderfoot.

Night Fishing

"A kid at school was telling me about fishing for bass at night up at Blackhawk Lake," Thunderfoot said as we drove down the road.

"At night?" I said. "Remember the time we went fishing at night and I ended up in the river?"

"Yeah, but that was a long time ago. And you do this from a boat, so you won't fall in so easy."

"Oh, sure. But if I fall in, I'm gonna be in lots deeper water. What did this kid tell you that makes you think we should do this?"

"Well, he said they go up to Blackhawk at night and use top water baits – Hula Poppers, and Buzz Baits, and Jitterbugs. Y'know, there's lots of bass there, and he says they catch some huge ones at night."

"Why would it make any difference? Why would the big ones bite better at night?" I asked.

"Well, he said the big ones just feed at night, and that's why they're big, 'cause nobody fishes much for them at night."

He was deadly serious. Then he got me with the clincher.

"He said they catch some big walleyes at night, too."

Now, as much as I like to fish, for any kind of fish, I like fishing for walleyes better than any other. All fish are fun to catch, but walleyes had always been my favorite. I think it goes back to when my dad took me walleye fishing when I was a little kid. For some reason, I was pretty good at it, and over the years, walleyes have become my fish of choice. Blackhawk Lake had a good population of big walleyes.

But it was hard for the fisherman to find them at Blackhawk because there was no normal walleye structure, as it was pretty much that way in most man-made lakes. They're like big featureless bowls of water with weed beds that extend out from the shore for thirty or forty feet, until the water gets too deep for them to grow. Walleyes that live in these lakes are usually weed-oriented fish. They lie in the weeds during the day, and then feed along the weed bed edges at night when the light is low. They're really hard to catch – almost impossible in the daytime.

"Walleyes, too?" I asked.

"Yup. Lots of them five or six pounds... and bigger. He says they are laying on the bottom stacked up like cordwood."

Hmm. Maybe this was worth a try, after all. "Well, the season opens Saturday. I guess we'd better try it Saturday night," I said. "That is, if you don't have a hot date."

"There's no date hot enough to keep me from fishing," he said grinning.

Good boy.

Living along the Wisconsin River as we did, we enjoyed open season on all fish, except Muskies, all year long. The Wisconsin and its sloughs didn't have a closed season like the rest of the inland lakes and rivers where it closed in the fall for bass, northern, and walleyes. That made it nice for us. For the rest of the State, the game fish season opened on the first Saturday in May, which was the upcoming weekend.

Saturday came and we got the boat ready for night fishing. We didn't want a lot of extra junk in the way when we stumbled around in the dark, so we put away everything that wouldn't be used. We each rigged up four rods and reels with top water baits on three for the bass, and deeper running crank bait on the others for casting along the weeds for walleyes.

We filled the lantern with fuel and put new batteries in our flashlights. Then we waited for it to get dark.

It was rather eerie to see an empty parking lot at such a popular lake. Most of the time it was full of cars and trucks, and someone was always waiting to put a boat into the water or to take one out. But now, when we backed the boat down to the water's edge, we had the entire lake to ourselves, and I didn't have to hunt for a place to park the truck. In just a little while we were motoring out across the water.

"Let's head over by the dam," Thunderfoot said. "My friend told me that's a good area to fish."

I used a spotlight to navigate along the shore, and up ahead, past the picnic area and the swimming beach, I could see the dam. I stopped the motor, shut off the spotlight, and lit the lantern that bathed the boat in bright light.

"Okay. Let's try for some bass first," Thunderfoot said. "I guess we just cast out and reel back. These baits make a lot of fuss on top of the water, so I guess that's how the fish find them."

"Well, we'll see," I said.

We began casting and it didn't take long to discover that our lantern was creating a problem. Within five minutes after lighting it, there were about ten thousand flying bugs in the boat, landing on us and crawling all over us. They were everywhere!

"Boy! That light has got to go!" I said.

Thunderfoot shut off the gas valve and the light slowly died out. After a few minutes, our eyes adjusted and we went back to fishing again.

"How we gonna know where we're casting?" Thunderfoot said.

"I guess we have to listen for a plop. If you don't hear the bait hit the water, you know it's on land."

After many casts, we were both getting weeds on our bait. I turned on the spotlight and saw that we had drifted into the weeds next to shore. "Back us up with the paddle. We're in the weeds."

Thunderfoot grabbed the paddle. Soon we were making plops in the water again. A few casts later, I was reeling back, listening to my bait gurgling on top of the water when there was a huge splash and I felt a tug on my line. I set the hook and missed, but my bait came sailing back through the darkness and hit me right in the throat. "Arrrgggghhh! I'm wounded!" I yelled.

Thunderfoot turned on his light and helped me get the bait untangled from my shirt. Luckily, the hooks hadn't stuck into my neck, but my line was a hopeless mess of tangles, so I retired that pole.

A few minutes later, Thunderfoot missed a fish, too, and his Moss Boss came back, hit the side of the boat, and broke in half. Now he had half a Boss on the end of his line. He, too, retired that pole.

In the next half hour, we each managed to get another pole hopelessly tangled, and we still didn't have any fish. I turned on the spotlight and pointed it down into the water. We happened to be right along the edge of the weeds, and sure enough, there were twenty or thirty walleyes lying in the sand, just at the edge of the weeds. I could see the glow of their translucent eyes. "Holy smokes! Look at those walleyes," I whispered.

"Why are you whispering? Do you think they can hear you?" Thunderfoot grabbed his deep running crank bait pole. "Shut that light off before you spook them. Let's try to cast right along this weed line and see if we can catch one of them." He was excited.

Well, casting along a weed line in the dark isn't as easy as it sounds. If we cast too far toward deep water, we were out of walleye range. If we cast too close to the weeds, we got our baits full of grass. It only took about ten minutes to figure out that this was more difficult than it seemed. And in another ten minutes, we had our deep running poles tangled up beyond repair, especially in the dark.

"Well, that worked good," I said. "I've got one pole left that isn't tangled."

"Me too. Let's try some other area for bass."

I started the motor and found our way to an area where we had once caught many smaller bass in the daytime. I shut off the motor and the light, and we started fishing. Thunderfoot had a fighting fish on his hook almost right away. When he just about had it to the boat, it got off. When it spit the hook out, the bait went flying through the air and wrapped around the end of his pole about fifty times. "Well, stick a fork in me. I'm done," he said.

I laughed. "Don't worry... I've been too lucky with this bait. I'll be tangled soon, and then we can go home."

Two casts later, I didn't hear a plop. "Did you hear that hit?"

"Nope. Not a plop," he answered. "How close are we to shore?"

I turned on the light. We were only a few feet away from the bank. "A little too close," I said.

I reeled up, and then I could tell that my bait was hooked on something on the shore. "Be a pal and climb out and get that bait for your daddy."

He laughed. "Yeah, right. I'll hold the boat while *YOU* go look in the woods for *YOUR* lure."

He pushed us up to the shore with the paddle and I jumped out onto the bank. I reeled and walked and followed my line up to the trees. Of course, my lure was about fifteen feet from the ground in a tree. "It's up in a tree," I said.

"And that's my problem... how?"

"You're littler. You can climb trees better. Come here and help me," I pleaded.

"Oh, jeez! I swear, I should get college credit for working with the handicapped," he grumbled.

I heard him jump onto the shore. He came to where I was, and then, in just a few seconds he was up the tree and had my bait free. "Now, can you reel it up? Or do I have to do that for you too?"

"Oh, don't be such a smart pants."

I reeled up and shined my spotlight so he could find his way back down. When we walked back toward the shore, I shined the light on the bank. No boat. "Where's the boat?"

"I left it right here on the bank," Thunderfoot said.

"Did you tie it up?"

"No. I just pulled it up to the bank."

I pointed the light out onto the water, and there was the boat, about twenty feet from shore.

"Oh boy. Now that's a dilemma," he said.

"Well, you're gonna have to go get it. You let it get away."

"I wouldn't have let it get away if you had been able to climb that tree and get your lure."

"Well, one of us has to go out to get it."

"Rock, paper, scissors," he said.

I hated rock, paper, scissors. I always lost. But we had to do something, so Thunderfoot counted to three and we both opened our hands to paper.

"Tie."

"One, two, three." I figured he'd go with paper again, so I went with scissors. He had rock.

"Rock breaks scissors. Have a nice swim."

"I don't suppose you'd like to go for two out of three," I said.

"Not a chance. Kindly fetch my conveyance, my good man."

I took off my clothes and piled them on the bank. To say the water was cold is an understatement – it was icy – and I was wading in thick weeds that harbored who knows what kind of slippery, slimy critters. When the water was up to my belly, I had to swim, but then I was free of the weeds and out in the open water – water that was full of big walleyes with big teeth. My imagination was running full tilt as I reached the boat. Of course, graceful as I am, I couldn't pull myself up over the side, so I had to tow the boat back to shore. Thunderfoot, helpful as he was, shined the spotlight on me as I plowed through the water.

I finally staggered up onto the shore, and I was about frozen.

Thunderfoot had all he could do to keep from busting out laughing. He must have felt a little sorry for me, though, because he took off his sweatshirt and dried off my back, and then gave it to me so I could dry off the rest of me.

When I was dressed again, we climbed into the boat. I started the motor and shined the spotlight out onto the water. Surprise, surprise! Fog had settled in during my little rescue mission, and now the entire lake was covered in thick, white mist. "Oh, boy! This just keeps getting better all the time," I said.

"There's a streetlight at the boat landing," Thunderfoot said. "I guess we gotta just cruise along the shore till we see that."

We motored slowly for over twenty minutes until we could just barely see a bright spot in the fog. Thankful that it was the light at the landing, we pulled up and Thunderfoot held the boat's rope while I backed the trailer down to the water. A few minutes later, the boat was loaded and tied down, and we were on our way home.

"Turn that heater up," Thunderfoot said.

"Oh? Cold are you? You should have been in that water if you think it's cold here."

"Well, you were the one in the water, so I'll have to take your word for it," he said grinning.

We drove on toward home. "Well, I think that's enough night fishing for me," I said.

Thunderfoot laughed. "Yeah, I think we'd better stick with daytime fishing from now on. We can get into enough trouble in the daylight, without stumbling around in the dark, too."

"One thing about it – I managed to get a bath both times," I said, thinking back to another night fishing trip when I fell into the river.

"Yeah, you have a thing for night time swimming. And from what I saw of you tonight, you'd better stick to that. If anyone saw you in the daylight, they'd run for their lives."

"Are you saying that I'm not swimsuit model material?"

"Not even close."

Thanks, Thunderfoot.

Thunderfoot Trump

It seems that every small town in America has something that makes it famous. There are "Capitals Of--" everywhere, and they range from Wild Turkeys; to Czechs; to Norwegians; to Mushrooms. Of all the things that a small town could lay claim to fame, our town chose the Morel Mushroom.

The Morel is a spring mushroom that is considered a delicacy by millions of people. They grow in many places around the world, but are particularly abundant in the area of the Wisconsin River valley where we live.

The reason they are so abundant is because of Dutch Elm disease. A few decades ago this tree disease spread through the mid-west and killed off the majority of the elm trees that grew along shady streets, in parks, and on the hillsides and in the valleys. There were thousands of dead elms in the woods, and a morel mushroom loves nothing better than one of these dead trees for a host.

As a morel pops out of the ground, it opens its porous skin and releases thousands of tiny spores into the air. These spores sail on the wind and eventually fall to the forest floor. If they are lucky, they fall near a dead elm, and then they feed for the next several months on the energy that is being released by the roots of the dead tree.

The following spring, if conditions are right, the spore has been transformed into a morel mushroom, all scrunched up in a little ball just under the surface of the ground. When the air warms enough, and there has been enough rain, the mushroom swells up and pops up out of the ground, releasing its spores, and continuing the cycle.

Somewhere, at some point in time, a person who was either really brave – or really hungry – picked a few of these ugly little fungi, took them home, and ate them. He found them to be quite tasty, and from then on, the Morel was considered a delicacy. Of course, with the large number of mushrooms that were found each spring around all those dead elm trees in the area, someone decided that it would be a good thing to have a celebration honoring the Morel. And thus, our town became the Morel Mushroom Capital of Wisconsin.

One of the things that happened when this festival began was a surprising rise in the value of a bag of Morels. For years, my friends and I had loved to pick Morels in the spring, for fun. It was a great time of year to get out into the woods after a long winter, and it was an activity that allowed us to get some exercise and enjoy nature. But after the first couple of years of the Morel Festival, the mushrooms suddenly became very pricey. Instead of *giving* them to your friends and neighbors, you now *sold* them to the tourists who came to the festival. I guess that's called American Capitalism.

Surprisingly, more people came and the Morel Festival became more popular, and soon the price of Morels was at a point that made you scratch your head in wonder. And that was on Thunderfoot's mind, too, as the upcoming Festival drew near.

"You got a scale that I can weigh mushrooms on?" he asked.

"Yeah, I've got that digital fish scale that's really accurate. Why? You don't have any mushrooms."

"But I will have by the weekend."

"They've been kind of scarce, so far," I said. "We need some rain to make them pop."

"I'm going out after school tomorrow, and then every day after that till Saturday when the Festival starts," he said.

"Well, I've seen you hunt mushrooms," I told him. Don't plan any purchases based on your earnings just yet. You haven't found any, so far."

He gave me one of those "Ye have little faith" looks. "Don't worry. I'm gonna scour every tree on Ken's farm. I'll be rich when this is over with."

I didn't get too excited about his enterprise, and by the next day I had forgotten about it completely. I was getting dinner ready when he came through the front door carrying a plastic grocery sack that looked pretty light.

"Well, Rockefeller? Make a million on Morels today?" I asked.

"Oh, dry up!" he whined. "I walked about ten miles and all I found was three little ones."

I peeked in the sack at the three little baby Morels at the bottom. "You should just take a sandwich bag. It would look fuller."

He gave me a look that had murder in it. "I just can't find these dang things," he said. "I don't know what I'm doing wrong."

"Are you looking for dead trees?"

"Yeah, I'm looking everywhere. I just walk and look at the ground, and I look at all the trees."

"You're wasting your time looking all over the place," I said. "You have to find *dead* trees. That's where they are."

He looked at me pitifully. "Will you come tomorrow and show me?"

"Yeah, you poor thing. I'll help you."

Big grin.

I picked him up after school the next day, and we headed for the hills. "You work down that hillside," I said pointing to the hill below us. "I'll drive out to the end of that field and work on the other side. Then we'll meet somewhere down there and see what we've found."

Off he went and I drove out across the field on the worn path that our farmer friend had made when he planted and harvested his crops. I parked, got out of my truck, and studied the hillside I was planning to hunt. Along the side of the hill I could see the branches of a dead tree sticking up through the green leaves of the other trees around it. I headed toward it.

When I got closer, the tree looked good. It had been dead for three or four years, as the bark was just beginning to peal off and hang. That was the perfect age for a mushroom tree. Too young and the wood was too hard, and no nutrients were leaking out into the soil. Too old and the tree was used up. This one looked to be just right.

I walked up to it and looked at the ground around it. It took a couple of minutes before I saw the first Morel, and then, as I carefully walked around the tree, I saw that there were Morels all over. I decided to wait for Thunderfoot so he could see what the right tree looked like.

I sat on a stump and after a few minutes I saw him sauntering through the woods. His mushroom sack was still sticking out of the back pocket of his jeans, so I knew he hadn't found any yet.

"Hey! Find any?" I yelled down to him.

"There ain't no mushrooms on this farm."

"Come on up here," I yelled.

He climbed up the hill grudgingly and soon he was standing in front of my stump.

"No luck?" I asked.

"I found one of those ones that grow on the side of a tree."

"Did you look at dead trees?"

"I didn't see any dead trees."

"See any dead trees around here?"

He looked around the area.

"Look closer," I said.

Then he saw the dead tree right behind me. "Oh, yeah. There's one right there."

He was standing there looking up at the branches of the tree, and his right foot was about ten inches from a nice Morel. "They aren't up in the tree," I said. "Look on the ground."

He began looking all over.

"If that was a rattlesnake, you'd be dead," I said, pointing to the ground at his feet.

Then he saw the Morel. "Holy smokes! I was almost standing on it."

He bent down to pick the mushroom when he saw another, a few feet from it. Then he saw two more sticking up from under a leaf. He was scurrying around like a chicken chasing a grasshopper, picking mushrooms like they were going to sprout legs and run from him.

"Come and help me. There's millions of them!"

I worked my way to the opposite side of the tree, and after about twenty minutes, we had found all the mushrooms that were there. "If you come back here in a couple of days, there'll probably be more, too, so keep this place in mind and check it again."

He nodded.

"So, now do you think you can find them?"

"Now I know what to look for. Jeez, I saw a tree like this back down there. I'm going back." And off he went.

"I'll meet you back at the truck at about six," I shouted to him.

He just waved over his shoulder.

I hunted for another hour and then walked back to the truck with a bag full of nice mushrooms. It felt good to sit and enjoy the sun as it dropped into the west. A short while later Thunderfoot came huffing and puffing up the hill with his nice bag of mushrooms. "Boy! I'm gonna come back tomorrow. I've only covered about a fifth of this woods."

"Well, tomorrow you can come alone and spend all the time you want."

We went home, put the mushrooms into the bottom vegetable compartment of my refrigerator, and covered them with a damp piece of cloth to keep them moist.

The next day he came through the door just as it was getting dark. "Look at these. Jeez! I'm gonna be rich."

He had a sack and a half of nice mushrooms that we added to the ones already in the refrigerator. This went on for the next three days, and my refrigerator was getting pretty full of mushrooms. Luckily, the first day of the Festival was the next day, so I hoped he'd have luck selling them, and give me back my fridge.

Thunderfoot came over early the next morning. We rigged up a basket that we could hang on my digital fish scale and weighed out the mushrooms into one-pound bags. There were nearly ten pounds.

"How much are they paying for them this year?" he asked.

"I've heard about $15 a pound so far."

"Holy smokes! That's... mmm... carry the four... that's $135 plus what I can get for the part of a pound." His grin was bigger than the trunk of an old elm tree.

"Why don't you set up a card table in front of the store and sit there and see what happens?" I said.

He made a little cardboard sign and sat down at the table with his bags of Morels. About an hour and a half later he came running into the store. "I'm out of mushrooms already! I'm going to the woods!"

He was gone all day, and that evening he came over with a little more than five pounds of mushrooms. "There's not one mushroom left on that whole farm," he said. "I must have walked fifty miles today."

I had to admire his energy. I helped him weigh them, and when he added the new ones to the leftovers from the last batch, he had six bags of mushrooms that each weighed a pound, plus a few extra. "Just put an extra one or two in each bag," I said. "After tomorrow all the tourists will be gone and nobody will pay for them, so you might as well give them a good deal."

He agreed, and added the bonus mushrooms to the bags.

The next day he set up his mushroom business and sold out before the crowd had even begun to gather for the big parade – the culmination of the Festival.

"Another $90," he said, proudly showing me a wad of bills.

"Jeez! You did good," I said.

"Not bad. Not bad at all," he replied.

"So, Mr. Trump... what are you going to do with all that money?"

"Well, I've decided to finance an expedition to the upper part of Lake Michigan over Memorial Day weekend," he said.

"Really? What kind of expedition will that be? You and your knot head buddies chasing those northern girls?"

"Nope. This money isn't going for girls. It's for a trip to remember for a pretty special guy and me."

I wasn't sure what he was talking about. "Trip to remember?"

"Yeah. Since I'm gonna graduate in a few weeks, I thought maybe me and my best buddy should take a good trip and try to catch some of those Lake Michigan walleyes like we did a couple years ago. This money will be for that... I'm buying this time."

I didn't know what to say. The thought of a trip to Lake Michigan for walleyes was a great idea, but the idea that it may be one of our last trips together made me choke up. My eyes got a little full.

He put his arm around my shoulder and gave me a squeeze. "Whatya say?"

"I'd say you're quite a kid."

"The feeling's mutual," he said.

Thanks, Thunderfoot.

Gullible

Thunderfoot and I were on the road again, headed to the upper peninsula of Michigan for a long weekend of fishing. It was the last weekend before his graduation from high school. For me, it was a bittersweet trip, as I knew things would change after that. But I put that in the back of my mind and concentrated on having a great time of fishing for walleyes on Lake Michigan.

We had been to this area a few years earlier, enticed by watching a TV show about the place called Little Bay de Noc. That time we had caught many beautiful walleyes, and I had even taken a dip – though not on purpose – in the big lake. It was such a fun trip that we had been talking for the past two years about doing it again, and now we were on our way.

Thunderfoot had amassed quite a nice little bankroll selling morel mushrooms a couple of weeks earlier, and he had decided to use the money for this trip. This was a completely new experience for me. I argued that I could pay like I usually did, or at least share the expenses, but he insisted. "Hey, this is free money," he had said. "America is a great place. You can go out in the woods and just pick up money, so I think we should use it for a fun time... not on something like clothes or books." I guess that made sense, but I still felt funny about him paying. It had always been my treat for the past six years, and it was hard to change that old habit.

Thunderfoot had called ahead to rent a little cabin at a resort that was right on the water. In fact, there was a dock right in front, so we could just tie up the boat each evening instead of loading it on the trailer.

He grinned as we pulled into town. "Any chance you'd like to stop for tacos?"

"No way, Jose!'" I said laughing. On the last trip to this place, he had talked me into tacos that upset my stomach, and the end result was me falling into the lake while attempting an emergency potty maneuver over the back of the boat. I wasn't taking any chances with tacos this time.

"How about Mac's? It's right up ahead," I said.

"Mac's, it is."

One thing about pulling an eighteen-foot boat was that the drive-through was out of the question, and regular parking spots were unusable, so we parked the boat in the back of the *McDonalds* lot. We brought our bag of burgers, fries, and cokes to eat out by the boat. On such a nice spring day we hated to be inside, and although I have never had any problems with anyone stealing from the boat, we felt better about keeping an eye on our gear that was just lying in the bottom. I hated to think of how much that would mess up our trip.

We were standing on either side of the boat, using the deck as a picnic table and chatting about fishing, when a gust of wind blew Thunderfoot's fries off the deck, scattering them across the parking lot. "Holy cow! My fries!" he shouted.

Just as he bent down to pick up the box, still containing a couple of fries, about twenty seagulls descended out of nowhere, squawking and fighting over the spilled fries. Thunderfoot put his arms up over his head and ran from the melee. "Holy smokes! They attacked me!"

I was laughing so hard I could hardly swallow the bite of hamburger in my mouth. The birds cleaned up every fry, and then one of them perched on the side of the boat, grabbed the half of the hamburger that Thunderfoot had left on the deck, and flew off. "Hey! Come back here you buzzard!" he shouted.

He saw me laughing, and then he began laughing, too. "Jeez! Those things came out of nowhere. I thought they were gonna eat me, too."

I finally managed to get my bite of burger down without choking. "It reminded me of an old Alfred Hitchcock movie, *The Birds*," I said.

"Alfred who?"

Generation gap.

"Well, I'm gonna go get some more lunch," he said. "I didn't get full on that one."

He came back with another bag of food in a few minutes, and it didn't take long for some gulls to start circling overhead, watching for another feast. Thunderfoot watched them for a while, and then he grinned, holding a French fry up in the air. Two gulls swooped down and hovered just above it, but neither one would take it from his hand. He tossed it into the air and one gull grabbed it in flight. The other tried to take it away, and then off they flew, squawking like crazy.

Well, that led to both of us tossing fries up and watching the gulls catch them, until we ran out of fries. "That is so cool," Thunderfoot said.

"Yeah, and a good way for us not to overeat."

We went to the cabin and launched the boat at the landing just a short ways down the lakeshore. Thunderfoot drove the truck and trailer back to the cabin, and I drove the boat to the dock in front. While I helped Thunderfoot unload our clothes and food, I said, "Think we should try to catch a few walleyes for supper?"

He put his arm behind his back. "Force me," he said.

I just barely touched his arm.

"Oh, okay. I give. I give. I'll go along," he said with a grin as big as Lake Michigan.

We fired up the boat and took off down the lake to fish some of the same places we had fished the last time we were at the Bay. We caught several smallish walleyes that would be just right for a meal. We motored back to the dock, tied up the boat for the night, and then cleaned the fish at the little fish-cleaning shack. The fresh walleye fillets made a wonderful supper with raw fried potatoes and baked beans – a feast fit for a king.

Thunderfoot decided to enjoy the view down at the lake while I finished cleaning up the kitchen. A few minutes later, he came back inside, went to the cupboard, and grabbed a handful of slices from the loaf of bread. "There's a bunch of mallards down there begging. I'm gonna give them some bread." He sprinted through the door. When I finished the cleaning, I walked down to the lake.

There was Thunderfoot standing by the shore with at least twenty-five mallard ducks surrounding him, quacking like crazy and gobbling up the pieces of bread he tossed to them. "Get more bread," he called out when he saw me coming. "These guys are really hungry."

I retrieved the rest of the loaf, and soon we were both feeding the ducks. Before long, a couple of seagulls noticed the free lunch, and they, too, were screeching and swooping down, trying to steal some of the ducks' bread. Within minutes there were two dozen more seagulls, and we were quickly running out of bread.

"I hope they get full," Thunderfoot said. "I'd hate to see them attack."

"I think we'll be okay," I said. "At least I will be. I doubt that they'll try to take something as big as me away to sea." He gave me a strange sort of stare, and then he decided I was kidding.

"That's it, guys," he said as he tossed the last scraps of bread. The birds searched the ground for another few minutes, and then the gulls soared off toward the lake and the ducks waddled back into the water, moving down the shoreline, looking for another duck lover.

We sat there and watched the sun go down, and although it wasn't very late, we decided to go to bed so we could get up early the next morning for a day of fishing.

Since we had given the ducks all the bread, we drove to a small diner just down the road and had a big breakfast of eggs, ham, fried potatoes, and a pancake on the side. We figured with all that food in us, we'd be able to last almost all day. It was a glorious morning and we set out onto the lake. We had decided that we'd just catch and release all the fish during the day, and keep a few toward late afternoon for supper. We didn't plan to take a bunch home. We were there just for the fun of catching them.

We used jigs and we were catching quite a few fish, but none that were very big. We noticed that several other boats fishing the area were trolling. Every once in a while we'd see one of them net a nice, big fish.

"Why don't we try trolling?" Thunderfoot said after we watched a ten-pound walleye come to the net.

"I hate to troll. You know that."

"Yeah, but they're getting those big fish, and all were getting are these little guys. Come on... trolling isn't so bad." He gave me one of his pitiful stares. "Wouldn't you like to see me catch a big one?"

He sat there looking like a poor little waif, so I said, "Okay. We'll try if for a while if you think we have to."

Big grin.

We each rigged up crank bait on a casting rod and reel, and let them out behind the boat about fifty feet. I drove the boat slowly down the lake... mindlessly trolling.

That's what I had always thought of trolling. It was mindless fishing. I just didn't see any skill in dragging bait behind a boat, hoping for a fish to bite on it. To me, casting a jig was the way to catch walleyes, and it always would be.

At any rate, we trolled, and then we trolled some more. As it was my usual luck when trolling, we caught nothing but weeds. Every so often our bait would drag through some weed beds, requiring reeling up and cleaning the junk off the lure. At least it gave us something to do to break the boredom.

Thunderfoot was about half asleep when I noticed his bait skipping across the surface. "Your bait is fouled with weeds," I called to him. "It's on top."

He looked back at his bait. "I thought that felt funny," he said as he began reeling it in. He had the bait about half way to the boat when I saw a seagull swooping down toward it. "Hurry up," I yelled. "There's a gull after it!"

Just as I said it, the bird hit the water, grabbed his bait, and began flying off. Thunderfoot's mouth dropped open. He held on for dear life and played the bird in the air, like he would a fish in the water. "Holy smokes! He's gonna take my rod!"

"Hang on tight!"

Right then I'd have given almost anything for a camera. There sat Thunderfoot with his feet braced against the front deck, reeling in a seagull, fifty feet above the boat, struggling like crazy to get away.

The fight went on for several minutes, and then we could see the bird was getting tired. "He's coming down easier now," Thunderfoot said.

"What are we gonna do with him when he gets here?"

"Grab him and take the hook out and let him go," Thunderfoot said as he reeled the bird closer.

As the gull got closer to the boat, I realized that it wasn't one of those little ones about the size of a pigeon. It was one of those giants that stand about two feet tall with a four-foot wingspan.

"That's one of those big ones," I yelled.

"Yeah, I noticed. But it's just a bird. How mean can he be?"

We'd soon find out. The bird was now only a few feet above the boat. I stood up and Thunderfoot led the flapping bird toward me. I grabbed its body and just as I did, it began slapping me in the head and face with its wings – it felt more like someone was slapping me with a couple of pine planks. I very quickly decided that this wasn't the way to subdue the bird, and I let go.

"You had him. Why did you let him go?" Thunderfoot yelled.

"He was beating me to death," I said. "I need something to throw over him to keep him from slapping me with those wings." I saw my jacket lying on the floor and picked it up. "Okay... bring him in again."

This time I wrapped the jacket around the bird's wings to keep him still. He struggled for a bit, but then he settled down. Thunderfoot's lure was in the bird's mouth and I was thankful that just one of the hooks was stuck in its beak. "Hold him tight and I'll take that hook out," I said as I handed the bird to Thunderfoot. He wrapped his arms around the bird and held him so he couldn't move.

Just as I took hold of the hook stuck in the bird's beak, he turned his head and clamped down on my index finger. "Yeouch! He's got me!" I yelled. Thunderfoot began laughing and almost lost his grip on the bird. I thought the gull was going to bite my finger off, but I pried with my other hand and finally got him to release my finger. "Jeez! He's got a bite like a snapping turtle."

I wasn't about to try that again. I found my needle nose pliers in my tackle box, got hold of the hook and popped it out of the bird's mouth. "Okay... let him go," I said.

Thunderfoot removed the jacket from the bird. It flapped its wings and flew off into the air.

"Wow! That was fun," Thunderfoot said.

Gull feathers were all over the boat, but it seemed the bird would be okay after his little encounter with us. Thunderfoot picked up my jacket from the floor of the boat and laughed. "The bird left you a little present," he said, opening the coat toward me. Sure enough, there was a big streak of gull poop decorating the lining.

"Looks like he wasn't very grateful for all my work getting that hook out," I said.

We had a good laugh, and then we decided that trolling was over for the day. We went back to our jig fishing and we soon had a mess of fish for supper. After we ate, we went down the road, bought a couple of loaves of bread for the ducks and gulls, and then had a good night's sleep.

The next day we fished until noon, and then it was time to get on the road for the long trip home. The highway runs right along the lake for many miles until it goes off to the west as it enters Wisconsin.

Thunderfoot looked out at the lake as we drove along. "Probably the last time we'll see that together for a while," he said.

"Maybe so," I replied. "But if it is, we'll have some fun times to remember about it."

"Well," he said, "I didn't get a ten pound walleye, but I'll bet that gull was at least ten pounds."

"Yeah, no fooling. You're the gull champeene of all times."

He punched my arm and grinned. That about summed up our many trips together. Nothing more needed to be said.

Thanks, Thunderfoot.

It'll Be Easy

Thunderfoot careened into the driveway and came to a sliding stop, throwing up a big cloud of dust. He got out of his car, waving the dust away and coughing. "Jeez! Why don't you get this driveway fixed? It's making my car all dusty."

"Why don't you drive a little more sensibly so you don't make so much dust? And at the same time, you might not destroy what's remaining of my seal coating," I retorted.

"You mean there's blacktop under all this pea gravel?"

"Not blacktop – seal coating. It's a layer of tar with pea gravel rolled down on top of it. It's lots cheaper than blacktop. But it doesn't last forever, and it looks like I'm going to have to get it done again soon."

"How much does it cost?"

"It was $500 the first time, but I think it costs about $300 for the second coat. They don't have to use as much oil the second time."

"Why don't you just put on some of that black stuff from the hardware store?" Thunderfoot said. "I've seen lots of driveways that are all nice and black and slick looking, and they don't make so much dust when you drive in."

I shrugged my shoulders. "I guess I've thought about it, but I just never got around to it."

His face lit up. "Sounds like a good project for us," he said, nodding his head up and down.

While I would have liked to have the driveway sealed, I wasn't sure if it was one of those jobs that Thunderfoot and I should attempt. I tried to be obvious in my lack of enthusiasm.

But he persisted. "Let's go take a look at that stuff at the hardware store and see what's involved." It was obvious that he thought this would be a fun job, and I knew he would pester me until I agreed, so off we went to the hardware store.

Thunderfoot squatted down and began reading the instructions on the five-gallon pails of driveway sealer. "How long is your driveway?" he asked.

"Oh, I guess maybe seventy feet," I answered.

"And wide?"

"Hmm. Part is wider than the rest... maybe twenty-five feet on the average," I said.

I could see him figuring and calculating in his head. "It should take about five of these five-gallon pails," he said. "And look! They're on sale, too!"

Sure enough, the sealer was advertised at only $8.99 per pail. Such a deal. "You really think we can do this?"

"Sure, and this will only cost you less than $50. Just think of the money you'll save. How hard can it be? We pour this stuff out and smear it all over the driveway, and presto! A nice, black, dry, dust free driveway." Thunderfoot had that look that told me his mind was made up, so I agreed. We loaded up five pails of the sealer on a cart. "We'll need some kind of brush or squeegee to put it on," he said, and went off in search of a clerk to show him what was available for applying the sealer. I pushed the cart up to the check out and waited. Thunderfoot came back carrying a long-handled brush with a squeegee on one side. "This is the gizmo we can use to squeegee it on or brush it on... and it's only $8.95," he said, gaily adding it to the cart.

"Is that all we need?" I asked.

"What about the pea gravel? Do you have a big broom to brush that off?"

I shook my head, and he trotted off toward the back of the store. In a little while he came back with a big, stiff push broom and laid it on the cart. It was $17.95.

"Is that it?" I asked.

He nodded yes, with a grin as wide as my driveway.

My *less than $50* investment had just risen to about $75.

I parked my truck on the grass and started to sweep all the loose pea gravel off the driveway with the big broom. It became quickly apparent that there was much more pea gravel than we had anticipated. I had only swept a few feet and there was already a big pile. "You better get the wheelbarrow and the scoop shovel," I said. "We'll have to haul this off."

Thunderfoot went to the garden shed, came back with the tools, and we scooped up the gravel. He wheeled it to the back yard, dumped it by the canoe rack, and by the time he returned, I had another pile ready for him. Two hours later, I was about ready for heart surgery; I had a huge blister on my right hand; and Thunderfoot was getting slower and slower on his trips to the back. "This is turning into one of those jobs from hell," I said.

"I didn't think there was so much pea gravel," he admitted.

"Well, we're gonna take a break," I said. "We'll have some lunch, and then I'm having a nap. This will wait a while." He followed me to the house and we made sandwiches.

It only took a minute for me to fall asleep in my recliner after all that hard work. I woke up about an hour later and saw Thunderfoot sweeping and loading more gravel. As much as I hated to, I went out to help.

It took all day to remove the pea gravel from the driveway, and when we were done, there was a pile that would fill a pickup truck.

"Who'd have thought there was so much?" Thunderfoot said.

It was too late in the day to spread the sealer, so we called it quits. We'd do it the next day. Thunderfoot went home, and I took a long, hot shower and sat down to rest. Every bone in my body ached.

Thunderfoot was bustling around in the kitchen before I was even up the next morning. The smell of frying bacon coaxed me to drag my aching muscles out of bed.

"Morning!" he said as I staggered into the kitchen.

"Morning," I mumbled. I gingerly sat down to eat. He was all smiles and chattered about how much fun spreading the sealer would be. I was still aching from the previous day and not nearly as chipper as him, but when we finished our breakfast, I drudgingly went with him to resume the work on the driveway.

"You know, there's a lot of dust and dirt on it," I said. "We'd better get that off or that stuff won't stick."

Thunderfoot nodded in agreement. Suddenly his eyes lit up and he trotted off to the garden shed. He came back with the leaf blower and a long extension cord. "Watch this," he said. He started the blower. Dirt and dust billowed and the whole yard was engulfed in fine dust from the pea gravel. He went back and forth for over an hour, and finally it seemed that the driveway was clean enough to spread the sealer.

When we opened the first bucket we could see that its contents had settled. After quite a bit of stirring with a stick, the black stuff seemed to be pretty well mixed, so I poured a puddle of the goop on the end of the driveway. Thunderfoot began spreading it out with the squeegee.

The instructions were to pour out a gallon, and that it should cover about ten square feet. Thunderfoot scraped and pushed and the gallon covered about three square feet. "Hmm. It doesn't go as far as it says it will," he said, looking down at the card table sized patch of glistening sealer.

"The driveway is too porous," I said. It soaks up a lot more. If it was newer seal coating, it probably would go farther."

"Well, let's use what we have and then see how much more we need."

By the time we had used up the five pails, both of us had sealer all over our feet and legs, and we were a long way from being finished – it had covered barely a third of the driveway.

"This is going to be a bit more of a job than we thought," Thunderfoot said scratching his head.

I just stared at him. I knew this had been a bad idea right from the start.

We went back to the hardware store and bought all the sealer they had in stock. They had more coming in a few days, so we took the six pails, raising my total investment to a little over $125. They covered the driveway to about the halfway point, and we were out of sealer again. "Well, we'll just have to finish next week when they have more at the store," Thunderfoot said.

We poured some paint thinner on an old tee shirt to scrub off the sealer from our hands and legs. It didn't come off very easy, leaving our skin quite red and sore. "Jeez, that stuff is tough," I said. "I hope it sticks on the driveway that well."

The hardware store clerk called the following Tuesday to let me know they had received more sealer. Thunderfoot and I drove up after school and I bought eight more pails. My total investment was now at about $200.

We unloaded the pails and Thunderfoot inspected the finished portion of the driveway. "That part we did really looks nice," he said.

"Yeah, it did turn out good," I said.

"Well, let's get these on and we're done."

"It's supposed to rain tomorrow, and the instructions say that it needs to cure for twenty four hours before a rain. Maybe we should wait till later in the week."

"Awe, hooey. It ain't gonna rain. Let's get it done."

Against my better judgment, I agreed, and we started pouring and spreading the sealer. It was almost dark by the time we finished and the air had become considerably cooler. "I hope it's warm enough for this stuff to dry tonight," I said.

"Oh, don't worry. It'll be fine," Thunderfoot said, surveying the finished job.

We put the equipment away for the night, and then scraped and rubbed ourselves raw again getting the sealer off our legs and hands.

I heard the first thunder about three in the morning. I lay there hoping against hope that the rain would hold off until the sealer had dried, but of course, it was raining a few minutes later, and it continued steadily all the rest of the night. That morning I went out to see how our newly laid sealer had faired.

I just about cried when I saw the driveway. The fresh sealer that had been applied the previous night had just melted away and was running off into puddles along the driveway and down the sidewalk. Now I knew why the stuff was so hard to get off our skin with paint thinner – it was water soluble, not oil based. The new half of the driveway was ruined.

I just stood there with rain running down the back of my neck when the phone rang.

"Did it get dry?" It was Thunderfoot.

"Nope," I said.

"Is it ok?"

"Nope."

"Oh, boy!"

A few minutes later he came through the front door shaking his head. "We shoulda waited, I guess."

I just nodded. "Want some breakfast?"

We were kind of quiet while we ate. Finally he said, "I'll pay for some of the new stuff to fix it."

"What?"

"I talked you into doing it last night. I'll buy the sealer to fix it."

As disappointed as I was that the job had been ruined, I had to smile at Thunderfoot's thoughtfulness. I put my arm on his shoulder. "I'll pay for it. It's not your fault."

"But – "

I shook my head. "Forget it. We'll let it dry out and then get some more sealer and do it again. It'll be all right."

Later that morning the rain stopped and we went out to look at the mess. Not only was the driveway a nasty looking mess, but now the sidewalk from the house to the driveway was covered with black tar, too. I was standing there staring at it when Thunderfoot suddenly got a look of inspiration on his face.

"Remember that building show where they put a new pathway over an old one? You know, they put sand down and then put those patio blocks on it, and it made such a nice sidewalk?"

"Remember the driveway project that was going to take five pails of sealer? And now we're going back for more and it will end up being about twenty pails instead of five?"

"Yeah, but that wasn't like this. We can measure... and find the right size blocks, and all it will take is a little sand, and we can get that off a sandbar down at the river for free, and then we can make this real nice sidewalk and..."

I turned away and went to the house for my checkbook. There was no reason to argue with him. I hadn't won an argument in over six years, so it was a waste of breath to even start.

When all was said and done, the job had required twenty-three pails of sealer, and I had just under $300 invested. But the driveway looked great. As for the new sidewalk, he hasn't mentioned it in a while, so I'm hoping he's forgotten about it.

One thing about him... he's never short on enthusiasm.

Thanks, Thunderfoot.

Remember That Time?

I had been thinking about this day for quite a while. On one hand I was happy for Thunderfoot, and on the other, I knew our friendship was going to undergo some changes. It was graduation day.

Thunderfoot had been working like crazy helping his mom get their house ready for the big party that would be held in his honor. But there was work to be done before the party, and poor Thunderfoot had been slaving all week to make everything perfect. His mom even made him paint the garage and the trim on the house. Of course, he tried his best to get me to help, but I wasn't about to let anyone sucker me into painting – especially him. I had cleaned up all of my lawn furniture and helped him haul it over to their yard to add to the tables and chairs that had been gathered from everyone in the neighborhood.

I saw him across the back yard on a ladder stringing those little clear Christmas lights through the trees so the party could go on into the evening. The yard looked great from where I stood, and I was sure his mom had made sure everything was just right.

The graduation ceremony was scheduled for two o'clock, so I tried to find something to keep myself occupied until it was time to go to the school. I had just started straightening up the boat shed when Thunderfoot walked across the back yard carrying a fishing pole and a coffee can that looked like it might contain fish worms.

"Whatcha doin'?" he asked as he walked into the shed.

"Just puttering. What are you up to?"

"I gotta get out of here for a while. I think mom's gonna drive me nuts."

"I thought by now everything would be clean and painted and ready."

"She keeps coming up with new stuff all the time," he said. "She even made me clean up my bedroom."

"Well, I've seen your bedroom, and it probably needed a cleaning... if I remember right."

"I like having my stuff out where I can see it," he grinned.

His bedroom was, well, I guess the best word would be a disaster area. He had a perfectly good chest of drawers, but instead of putting the stuff away when his mom washed it, he chose to pile all of his clothes on the floor. Jeans were folded and piled in one spot, shirts in another, underwear another, and so on. "That way I can find just what I want without looking all over the place," he always said when I teased him about his messy hovel.

"Did she make you put your clothes away?" I asked.

"Yeah, but I fooled her. I just slid them under the bed."

"So, what did you have in mind with that fishing pole?"

"Let's go down to the bridge and just sit in the sand... bottom fish for a couple hours. I've got plenty of time before I have to be at school, and I want to get away to someplace quiet."

It sounded like a good idea to me, too, so I grabbed a pole and a little tackle box with hooks and sinkers, and off we went. We didn't even take lunch, so I knew that this was an impromptu trip.

When we crawled down over the bank to the sandy shore and picked a good spot to sit, two forked sticks were already sticking in the sand. "Must be a good spot," Thunderfoot said. "Somebody left their pole holders."

We baited up with a big fat worms, tossed our lines out into the river, set the poles in the forked sticks, and settled down to watch for a bite. Several minutes passed and I finally said, "Big day today. Are you excited?"

He shrugged his shoulders. "I guess. I'm glad to be finished with high school, but... things are gonna change, and I'm not so happy about that."

I saw his eyes were filled with tears. I slid over a little closer and put my arm on his shoulder. "Hey. It's not going to be the end of it. We'll still see each other and do stuff."

He nodded.

Just then I got a bite. I jumped back to my spot, grabbed my rod and set the hook into a small river shiner that came right in without hardly any fight. "Oh, boy! A trophy," I said.

Thunderfoot laughed. "Pretty much what you're used to catching, isn't it?"

I unhooked the fish and threw it at him. It glanced off his shoulder and into the river where it swam out of sight.

"We've caught some pretty good ones in the past few years, haven't we?" he said.

"No foolin'," I replied. "I hate to admit it, but you've become a pretty darn good fisherman. Of course, not as good as me, but close."

"I've learned a lot since that first time we went squirrel hunting," he said. "How come you decided to take *me* hunting? Lots of kids came into your shop?"

I thought back to the first time I'd met him six years earlier. "I don't know for sure," I said. "You just seemed like a nice kid. You were real friendly, and when you bought that beef jerky and tore it in half and gave your brother the biggest half, I thought that was pretty cool."

"You remember that beef jerky?"

"Yeah. I guess it just struck me as something that a nice person would do, and I guess that's why I asked you to go hunting with me."

"Boy! Remember that?" he said, grinning. "You went down the hill backwards into that fence. Jeez! I almost peed myself laughing. Then I chased that stupid squirrel for about a mile, and when I came back you were standing in your underwear trying to get your pants out of the fence."

"It's a wonder that you didn't take off and never get near me again, seeing me there half naked," I said.

"Jeez, that was funny. Bloop! Right over backwards."

"Well, I'm glad it happened if it made you think I was a fun guy, because from then on, we sure did a lot of funny stuff."

"Remember the ten gauge?" he said. "Holy smokes. I thought that thing broke my shoulder."

I laughed, thinking back to that frozen day in a goose blind at the Horicon Marsh when Thunderfoot and I were waiting for a goose to fly close enough. We each had a twelve-gauge shotgun, and I had my single shot ten-gauge along, in case the geese were flying extra high. Thunderfoot had pestered me all morning long to shoot the ten-gauge, and I had finally given in. But that gun weighed over eleven pounds and was about as tall as he was. He was still pretty scrawny, and he could barely hold the thing up, let alone shoot it. But he insisted. Finally, I told him to shoot a lone goose coming right toward us. He followed it until it was right over the blind, about forty yards up. When Thunderfoot touched off the three and a half inch magnum, the recoil came right down on top of his shoulder and snapped his head back. His thumb, wrapped around the stock, hit him right on the end of his nose. His hat popped off and landed out of the blind in the pasture. He lowered the gun, his eyes filled with tears, and he looked kind of bewildered. "I think I broke my nose," he said as tears streamed down his face. I was laughing so hard that I slid right down the wall of the blind and landed on my butt in the pile of empty shells and pop cans littering the floor. It was one of the funniest things I'd ever seen while I was hunting.

"Yeah, that thing had quite a kick," he said grinning. "And now, thanks to my good buddy, I've got a ten-gauge of my own, and I'm big enough to handle it."

"That was funny… you have to admit," I said.

"Yeah, about as funny as when you found that big snake in my mushroom bag," he said laughing. "Jeez! You almost had a heart attack."

"You little snot. I'm still mad about that. You know I don't like snakes. That was a mean thing to do."

"Oh, poor baby. I'm so sorry," he said.

I was thankful that he must have learned that I am afraid of snakes, and that had been the only time he pulled a snake joke on me. It was during spring mushroom hunting season, and I was showing Thunderfoot what they looked like on his first time trying to find some morels. In doing so, I had run across a little grass snake that made me scream like a teen-aged girl, and he thought it was real funny. Later, when we met at the truck, he dumped a big black snake in my lap as I sat on the tailgate waiting for him. Needless to say, I caused quite a scene, and lucky for Thunderfoot he could run faster than me, or I'd probably still be in prison for murder.

"When you screamed, that note was almost up there where just dogs can hear," he said.

"Oh, sometimes you're so clever."

Just then he got a bite. He grabbed his pole and set the hook into a good, fighting fish. "At least it's not one of those little minnows you catch," he said as he reeled in a good-sized sheepshead. "Baaa, Baaa. A sheeper." He removed the hook and tossed the fish back into the water.

"Remember that time you caught that sheepshead and used it for bait?" I said. "…When you swung it to cast it out in the river and you hit that old lady in the head with it?"

"Oh, jeez! That was so funny," Thunderfoot said. "Her son got really mad at you."

"Yeah. You took off and he thought I did it. I thought I was going to get a good beating. He was huge."

We had been fishing in early spring for walleyes on the bank below the dam. Thunderfoot was using crawlers instead of minnows because he didn't want to get his hands cold in the minnow bucket. There was a family above us fishing, too, and besides the mom and dad and two kids, there was an old lady, all dressed up in her 'Sunday Go To Meetin' coat and a hat that looked like a turban. Thunderfoot caught a sheepshead, and just then the dad above us caught a big, northern pike. Thunderfoot decided to put on a big hook, use the sheepshead for bait, and try to catch a northern. He got his pole all rigged up and cast side arm toward the river. About halfway through the cast, the sheepshead came off the hook and flew fifty feet up the riverbank. It smacked the old lady right in the side of the head, knocking off her turban. I couldn't help laughing, and her son, about six and a half feet tall and built like a linebacker, thought I had been the one who hit his mother with the fish. Of course, Thunderfoot took off down the bank for safety, and there I was, trying to decide whether I preferred getting beaten to death, or drowning in the cold water. We finally worked it out, but it cost me all of the walleyes I had caught – a small price compared to the cost of plastic surgery to re-align my nose that would have surely been altered.

"I could stand there for the rest of my life casting a sheepshead and never hit that lady again," Thunderfoot laughed. "That was one in a million."

"No kidding. A classic," I said. "I was scared that her son was going to kill me with his bare hands. In fact, you've just about scared me to death quite a few times."

"Oh, bull. When?"

"How about when you nearly ran my brand new boat up on the back of that pontoon?"

"Oh, yeah. You about pooped that time didn't you?" Thunderfoot laughed.

I had just gotten my brand new dreamboat – shiny, not a scratch – and we were taking it on its maiden voyage. All day long I had run the big gas motor when we moved from one fishing spot to another, and all day long, Thunderfoot had pestered me to let him drive the boat. Finally, I gave in and let him get behind the wheel. He fired up the 150 horses and drove us upriver to a new fishing spot. He had done a good job, so I decided to let him drive some more, and not long afterward, we were going along the channel, and he gave the motor a bit more gas than I liked. But he was having such a good time that I decided to let him go. When you drive a boat on a river, you use the same rules as on a highway. You keep to the right of the channel, and if you want to pass another boat, you pull to the left and go around. Well, there was a pontoon boat ahead of us, going much slower than we were going, and Thunderfoot yelled to me over the noise of the motor, "Can I pass him?"

I nodded and motioned to go to the left. He nodded okay. He opened up the motor a little more, and we were rapidly getting close to the pontoon. A pontoon boat makes a horrendous wake since it's shaped like a back yard deck rather than a boat, and suddenly we were right behind the pontoon, caught inside his wake. The guy on the pontoon turned and saw this huge boat bearing down on him, and he waved us off, trying to get Thunderfoot to turn. The problem was that Thunderfoot was trying to turn, but couldn't get past the big wake. I yelled at him to turn sharp and give the boat more gas, and just in time, we jumped the wake and went around the pontoon.

I made a cutting motion at my throat. Thunderfoot cut the engine back and we slowed to a drift. The pontoon went past just then, and the guy looked like he was heading for the cardiac unit at the nearest hospital. I was about to bawl out Thunderfoot for his mistake, and then thought better of it and explained the correct and ethical way to pass another boat.

"That was pretty exciting," Thunderfoot said as he set the hook and missed the fish that was biting.

"Yeah. I came close to a heart attack that time," I said. "Just about as close as when I found that rattler at Bogus Bluff."

"Oh, holy cow! I thought we were gonna have to get a block and tackle to drag your carcass out of that little cave," he said laughing.

My fear of snakes had made a little cave-exploring trip into quite an exciting adventure. Thunderfoot had heard the legend about counterfeiters and buried gold in a cave on one of the river bluffs. He talked me into going with him in the cave. We had started walking down a long passageway that kept getting progressively smaller. Before long we were crawling, and a little later, we were shinnying along on our bellies with rock walls pressing against us on both sides and above. Being a little full figured, I was beginning to worry about getting stuck, but Thunderfoot kept pushing me onward. The trouble was that my flashlight died, and he wouldn't give me the good one. So, the only light was that shining past me from his light. We came to a corner in the tunnel, and in the low light I suddenly saw a rattlesnake's tail just ahead of us. I panicked and tried to scoot backwards to get out of the cave, and after a few minutes of terror and shouting, I had the good flashlight. In the better light the snake's tail turned out to be part of a corncob. Of course, Thunderfoot had a great laugh over that one. He still points out killer corncobs to me every chance he gets.

"I've always thought about how mad the guys from the Rescue Squad would have been, if I had dropped dead in that cave. Imagine the trouble they'd have had getting my body out."

"Maybe we'd have just filled in the opening and left you."

I had a huge bite and set the hook, only to catch another of those little river shiners. "Boy! You've got the touch for catching those little guys," Thunderfoot said.

"It takes special skill to catch the little ones."

"Which are you more scared of?" Thunderfoot asked. "Snakes or horses?"

"Oh, no question there," I replied. "Snakes. Horses I can see coming a lot farther away."

"Boy, that time the horse chased you was funny."

"Yeah, that was a barrel of laughs."

The incident happened when Thunderfoot and I were rabbit hunting on his grandpa's farm. There was a good rabbit ditch on the back forty where treetops and stumps had been dumped for years. It made good cover for bunnies, and we usually had some good shooting when we hunted there. On this particular day, we were headed toward the rabbit ditch when I noticed a horse standing at the end of a fenced field. The horse watched us as we neared the fence and he perked his ears forward like he was trying to hear what we said. "That horse looks mean," I said to Thunderfoot. He laughed at me and called me a sissy, and then he started across the field. The horse watched him, but didn't bother him. When he got to the other side, he climbed over the fence and stood there, looking at me, wondering if I was coming, or not. I was not really enamored by horses – ever since I was a little kid, when the one I was riding had decided to lie down and scratch its back. Of course, that traumatic experience scarred me for life, and since then I had always been really hesitant when it came to getting near horses. Thunderfoot was taunting me, so I decided I'd take the chance. Naturally, as soon as I got about halfway across the field, the horse started after me, and I ended up on my back in a brush pile after vaulting the fence, attempting to escape.

"That was about the fastest I'd ever seen you move," Thunderfoot chuckled.

"I can be a speedster if the jaws of death are behind me," I assured him.

Just then he got a bite and caught a carp. "At least it's not a minnow," he said.

"Yeah, yeah. Just you wait. Sometimes smart guys get their just deserts, too."

"Like when?"

"Oh, I remember a kid that was acting pretty smart and got a mouth full of cow pee."

We both began laughing over that memory. I had taken Thunderfoot and his friend, Dillon, to the State Fair for the day. We had seen lots of cool things and eaten just about every treat that existed. After a few rides on some contraptions that made my stomach feel like a blender, I suggested that we look at some of the animals. In the poultry barn, Thunderfoot had pilfered an egg from a crate that held chickens, and a short while later, in the dairy barn, he had slipped it into Dillon's pocket and smacked the pocket with his hand. Thinking he had pulled a great joke, he ran off down the aisle with his mouth wide open, laughing, when a cow tethered to the wall suddenly slapped him in the face with her tail – that had just been soaked with a load of hot, fresh cow pee. Thunderfoot stopped dead in his tracks. He turned toward us, as if his arms and legs were suddenly sticks. "Ohmygosh! I got hit by cow pee!" Dillon and I – and everyone else in the barn – had a gut splitting laugh at poor Thunderfoot, and after we all recovered, we hosed him off, and hosed the egg out of Dillon's pocket.

Thunderfoot was pretty upset with us for laughing, but we didn't care. We tormented him for the rest of the day. It was like Christmas for me, because I very seldom had a laugh on him – I was usually on the receiving end of the jokes.

"That was a pretty funny day," I said.

He shook his head. "Yeah, I guess it probably was. But, boy! That cow pee was nasty tasting stuff."

We chuckled at that for a while, and then he got a bite and caught another sheepshead.

"I wonder if your bowling ball is still out there," he said, nodding toward the middle of the river.

"I suppose it is," I said. "I guess it depends on how deep it went into the sand when it hit."

The bowling ball incident started out innocently enough when Thunderfoot was helping me with a bi-yearly cleaning of my junk closet on the porch. He found my old bowling ball. One thing led to another, and of course, he talked me into going bowling that evening. Needless to say, I was my usual, graceful self, and slid too far with my foot, doing the splits. I ripped the butt right out of my pants. Of course, this had to happen amidst a packed bowling alley, and my red plaid boxers now were in full sight. On the way home, I stopped in the middle of the bridge and unceremoniously dropped my bowling ball into the river. Poor Thunderfoot thought I had finally gone around the bend.

"You thought I'd lost it that day, didn't you?" I said.

"Close," he said. "I was glad there weren't any sharp objects in the car. By the way, speaking of things falling into the water, how about the time you did a back flip out of the boat into Lake Michigan?"

"Yeah, I remember that... and if I remember right, that was your fault."

He looked so innocent as he grinned at me.

Of course, he was referring to my famous Taco Bell incident, when we were at Little Bay de Noc on the Upper Peninsula of Michigan, fishing for walleyes. We had gone north to the big lake after watching a TV show about the good walleye fishing there, and during our stay, Thunderfoot had pestered me to stop at Taco Bell for lunch every time we drove past the restaurant. Finally, I gave in and filled my belly with tacos and other spicy food. That just about did me in. I spent a long night suffering from heartburn and frequent trips to the bathroom, and the next day when we were a long way from shore, I had an emergency call from Mother Nature. After arguing about going in to shore, I finally had decided to sit on the back of the boat and do my business over the side. It wasn't that I wanted to do it, but that I knew I'd never make it all the way to the shore. Of course, Thunderfoot couldn't let well enough alone, and just as I was baring my backside, he turned the back of the boat toward a bunch of other boats that were fishing in the area. In my haste to try to cover myself, I lost my grip on the motor and fell backward into the lake, with my pants around my ankles. Of course, he thought it was hilarious. The people in the other boats all had a good laugh, too. I guess it was a pretty good show.

"You just have no respect for your elders," I said.

"It's pretty hard to show respect for someone who is pooping over the end of a boat," Thunderfoot said, laughing.

He grabbed his pole and missed another bite. He baited the hook and tossed it out again. "That was the last crawler," he said.

"Well, I suppose we'd better get back soon, anyway. What time do you have to be at the school?"

"Graduation starts at two, so I have to be there at one-thirty."

We sat quietly for a while. I guess we were both thinking of the fun times we had shared, and how our relationship would change, now that he was finished with high school. The part time work at my shop wasn't enough for him to make a living, and he wanted to get out into the world and try new things. I understood how he felt, but it didn't make it any easier to think of him moving away.

"You know, we'll have to make plans for another trip up north," he said.

"Yeah. We should do that... maybe this fall, or next spring."

"We sure had a lot of fun those other times," he said. "That big moose trying to get in our boat... and the bears... and all of those good shore lunches... wow! That sure was fun."

I had to laugh when I thought about the funny things that had happened on some of the trips. The moose incident was pretty scary, but funny, too. Thunderfoot and I were fishing in Canada when he spotted a moose in a shallow bay, feeding on underwater weeds. We motored into the bay and then I oared us closer so Thunderfoot could get a picture. He was kneeling on the front seat and watching the moose through the camera viewfinder.

"Go closer," he whispered. I moved us closer. "Closer," he whispered again. We were getting quite close, but I pushed on the oars once more and we slid through the weeds, coming to a stop about ten feet from the moose. Just then Bullwinkle rose up from eating weeds, saw us right there in his face, and he let out a bellow and charged the boat. I was oaring backward as fast as I could, and Thunderfoot was crawling backward in the bottom of the boat shouting at me to "Go fast – back!" Well, we got away, but he harped about me trying to get him killed for the rest of the trip. I reminded him that it was he who wanted to get closer. His excuse was that the moose looked pretty small in the viewfinder, and he didn't realize that we were *that close.* So, obviously, it was my fault.

"I just about had one of those very rare teenager heart attacks," he said.

"I still think you wet your pants," I laughed.

I had a bite and caught yet another river shiner.

"Jeez! We should skip graduation and go Northern fishing," Thunderfoot said. "You've caught enough bait for a whole day of fishing."

"It takes a lot of skill to catch those little guys with the little mouths. Those big sheepshead just swallow it, and that's why you can catch them… no skill required."

He threw a clod of mud at me and then set the hook and reeled in another sheepshead. "Well, that's the end of our bait."

"I suppose we'd better get back. Your mom is probably worried that you'll be late for your graduation. And after all the work she's done to get the house and yard ready, she'd *really* be mad if we skipped it," I said.

"Yeah, I guess so. Let's just sit and watch the river for a few more minutes," he said.

We sat side-by-side in the sand and watched the river drift by. A nice breeze and the gurgling water made the day seem so peaceful. I saw Thunderfoot's eyes were full of tears again.

"I'm gonna miss stuff like this," he said.

"Me too."

Thanks, Thunderfoot.

Pomp and Circumstance

I left my house a half hour early so I'd get a good parking spot at the High School for Thunderfoot's graduation. As I neared the school, I realized that everyone else must have had the same idea, because the school parking lot was full and the streets were full for two blocks around the school. I finally found a spot, parked and hiked to the gym where the ceremony would be held.

It was one of those spring days that, with just a little push, the weather could have turned hot and muggy. As long as the sun stayed behind the clouds it was comfortable, but as soon as it peeked out, the humidity rose and the air quickly became rather sticky. Of course, by this time of year I was used to wearing a tee shirt and shorts, so a shirt and tie with long pants was a little stifling.

I arrived at the gym and showed my Guest ticket to one of the high school boys who were acting as ushers. This ticket allowed me to sit in the chairs that were lined up on the gym floor where the families of the graduates sat. The rest of the onlookers had to sit on the bleachers, which was akin to a Chinese water torture. I've always thought that if you wanted to get information or a confession from someone who you suspected of wrongdoing, just make him sit on the bleachers to listen to hours of boring speeches. He'd confess in no time.

There was a hum of conversation; teachers and school administration people were hurrying here and there getting everything ready for the ceremony to begin. I saw Thunderfoot's mom and his brother, Caleb, sitting in the Guest section. They motioned to me. "Why don't you sit with us?" Thunderfoot's mom said. I squeezed down the row and sat.

"Thanks," I said. "How are you doing, Caleb?"

"Good. Are you coming to the party later?"

"Sure. Wouldn't miss it," I said.

Just then the choir came in and took their places on the risers behind the stage. Then the band filtered in, and soon everything seemed to be ready. The time was getting near for the graduates to come in, and I was getting a lump in my throat, thinking about this as being the end of Thunderfoot's high school career. How had it come so fast? It seemed like only yesterday that I had met him as a young boy, and now he was all grown up and going off into the world.

I guess I'm an old softie – always have been. Thunderfoot often made fun of me when I cried at a movie. I've always been that way, I guess. I can remember when Lassie came home... my gosh, I cried like a twelve year old girl. I'm one of those guys who gets emotional when the flag passes in a parade, or when a particularly patriotic song plays. I can't help it. That's just the way I am.

Just then the School Board members and the principal took the stage, and the crowd began to quiet. The band director raised his arms, gave the downbeat, and the band started playing the mournful chords of Edward Elgar's *Pomp and Circumstance*. Everyone's eyes turned to the entrance as the first pair of graduates slowly marched in. Everyone stood, and my heart was in my throat as the sounds of the music filled the gym. About midway in the line of graduates, Thunderfoot walked with his friend, Scott, at his side. They had been friends for years, and now they were taking their final walk together as classmates. They came down the right side of the gym, turned at the back, and then paraded up the center aisle between the Guest sections. Parents and friends were stepping out into the aisle taking pictures and movies, as their graduate passed by.

When he saw me standing there watching, Thunderfoot gave me a little wink and a grin as he and Scott came down the aisle. Try as I might, I couldn't keep a tear from running down my cheek. They passed by and took their places with the rest of the graduates. Then the speeches began.

It seemed like everyone in the class made a speech, and every teacher, every school board member, and maybe even some members of the audience might have taken a turn. One good thing about all those speeches was that I had the opportunity to get my emotions controlled and settled down a little. Finally, the speeches were over and the graduates were called up, one at a time, to receive their diplomas. As his name was called, Thunderfoot strode across the stage, not a scrawny little boy any more, but a tall, handsome, confident young man. He received his diploma, turned to smile at his mom and me, and then he went back to his seat and waited while everyone in the entire class received their diplomas. The principal walked up to the microphone and presented the graduates. The entire class stood up and cheered and threw their hats into the air. Some had smuggled in confetti and stilly string, and there was utter chaos for a few minutes. When that part of the celebration had settled down, the kids picked up their hats while the band began playing *Pomp and Circumstance* again, and they all filed out of the gym.

Once the graduates were all out, the guests and the rest of the people in the gym began a slow procession into the cafeteria where the graduates had formed a line around the outside of the room. It was mass confusion trying to find anyone, but eventually I saw Thunderfoot and his friends, Scott and Jerry, all standing together, shaking hands with people who were wishing them well. I made my way to the boys and shook hands with Scott and Jerry.

And then I came to Thunderfoot. I didn't want to embarrass him, so I offered my hand. He stared at it a moment, and then he threw his arms around my neck and just about dislocated my head with a bone-crunching hug. "You get more than a handshake," he said into my ear.

"I'm real proud of you, you know," I said.

"Yeah, I know."

I hated to let him go, as if this were the last chance I'd ever have to hug him again, but I knew there were people coming down the line waiting for their turn to congratulate him, so I let him go and stepped back. He gave me a grin. "We'll talk later."

I stayed at the cafeteria for a while, talking with friends, and soon the room began to thin out as people left for parties that were starting all over town. I went home and changed into shorts and a golf shirt – I thought a plain tee shirt was a little *too* casual. Then I walked across the back yard to Thunderfoot's house to join his graduation party.

The yard and garage were full of well-wishers and relatives. I met many of Thunderfoot's relatives, and I talked with his grandparents for quite a while. People came and went all afternoon, while Thunderfoot greeted everyone and was the perfect host. By late afternoon things settled down a little, and he finally had a chance to sit with me at the picnic table and catch his breath. "Holy smokes! I didn't know I knew so many people."

"You're such a popular guy, no wonder," I said. "So, what's on for tonight?"

"Some of my friends and I are going to a party at one of the kid's house out in the country. They're having a band and all kinds of stuff. We're all staying over night, so no one will be driving."

"That's a good idea."

"I didn't tell you before... I guess I just didn't want to finally say it. But I'm gonna be working this summer, out of town," he said. "Jerry and Scott and I got an apartment, and we're gonna work at that place where they build those two piece houses up in Lancaster. I hope you're not mad."

"Mad? Why would I be mad?"

"Well, I guess I thought you might be mad that I wouldn't work for you again this summer."

"Hey, I know you can't make a living working for me. It was okay when you were in school, but now you need something that'll make you more money than I can pay you. I'm not mad at all. I'm glad you got a good job so quickly."

Just then a car pulled in, and Scott and Jerry jumped out, and then a girl I had never seen before stepped out behind them. She saw Thunderfoot and waved and smiled at him.

I looked at him. "And that would be...?"

He flushed beet red. "A girl I met a few weeks ago."

"I see. Does this girl have a name?"

"Yeah, she does."

I waited.

"Oh! You want to know her name?"

Just then the girl strolled up to the table. Thunderfoot jumped to his feet. She put her arms around him and gave him a kiss on his cheek. He was so flustered he didn't know what to say, but he finally turned and said, "Crystal, this is my friend, Dan, and Dan, this is Crystal."

I said "hi" and Crystal said, "I've been wanting to meet you. Jamie talks about you all the time."

"I hope it's not *all* bad," I said, laughing.

"No, not at all," she said. Then she leaned to my ear and whispered, "Jamie thinks you're about the best guy in the whole world. He said you've done a lot for him, and you'll always be very special to him."

I just hugged her and said, "thanks."

"Uh, we're gonna go to the party now, okay?" Thunderfoot said.

"Sure. Don't let me stop you. And have fun... you only graduate from high school once."

Thunderfoot turned to Crystal. "I'll meet you in the car."

She said goodbye and walked to the car where Scott and Jerry were waiting. She waved as she got in the back seat. Scott and Jerry waved, too.

"Well, I guess I'll go then," Thunderfoot said.

"Have fun... but be careful."

"Yes, Mom!"

"You know what I mean. Don't do anything stupid."

He grinned at me. "I probably won't have to worry about that, as long as you're not there. Most of the stupid things that I've done in my life have been with you."

So, we *had* done some dumb things together. But at least we'd had a lot of fun.

He threw his arms around my neck. "Thanks for everything. I'll never forget all our good times together."

I put my arms around him and hugged him; I felt like my heart would break. "I love ya, kiddo," I whispered.

"Me too."

He walked to the car and got in the back seat with his new girlfriend. As the car pulled out of the driveway I saw his hand come out of the window and wave goodbye.

I thanked his mom for the nice party, and then I sauntered slowly across the back yard toward home. I had an empty feeling inside. I had known for a long time that this day was coming, but now that it was here, it was hard to accept. It would be really quiet without Thunderfoot in my life every day, as he had been for the past six years. Oh, sure, we'd still get together once in a while, but it wouldn't be the same. He had a new life ahead of him, and it would take him to faraway places.

I flopped down in my recliner and began idly paging through the latest copy of the newspaper. A classified ad caught my eye:

Seventeen-year-old Norwegian Boy desperately seeking Host Family. Enjoys fishing, movies, and skiing. Loves dogs and animals. Call 1-800-***-****

Hmm. That sounded interesting. I'd always thought it would be fun to host an exchange student. Maybe tomorrow I'd call and see what this program involved. It just might be a lot of fun.

Then, just as soon as I had that thought, I felt guilty. How could I be thinking of replacing Thunderfoot so quickly? Of course, *no one* could ever replace Thunderfoot, but this might be a way to put some new adventure into my life. An image of his face popped into my mind, and he had that grin that I had seen so many times. "Give them a call," he said. "It's okay – really – we'll still be friends no matter what." I smiled and picked up the phone. One thing I had learned from Thunderfoot was that no matter how old you feel some days, you always get a new shot of life with a kid around the house, and you never know when a little trip to the river or the woods will turn into a great adventure.

Thanks, Thunderfoot... for everything.

Last Thoughts from Thunderfoot

I remember the first time I met Dan. We had just moved to Muscoda, and my little brother and I decided to check out the fishing store just down the street from our house. When we walked in the front door, Dan was sitting behind the counter, sorting out piles of bills and writing them into a ledger. Instead of ignoring us, he smiled and said "hello" and asked if he could help us find anything special. I said "no" but then I asked if it was all right if we just looked around. He told us to go ahead and left us to check out the stuff in the store.

A while later, I bought a beef jerky, and we got to know each other a little. He seemed like a pretty nice man. After we left, I told my brother that I thought I'd like to get to know him. For one thing, he had a lot of good stuff in his store, and for another thing, he was friendly.

A few days later I took my dog over to meet him, and he asked me to go squirrel hunting with him, and that was it. From then on, we became good friends and, well, you know the rest.

Dan had a little mishap that first day of squirrel hunting. He ended up hanging backwards over a fence on the side of the hill. Instead of getting all mad and stuff, he laughed about it and apologized for having to cut the hunting trip short. Of course, his pants didn't have any back in them any more, and he had a bunch of cuts and scrapes that were bleeding pretty badly.

That day taught me that Dan had a good sense of humor and didn't take himself too seriously. And he treated me like an equal – not like some kid who didn't know anything. Of course, I *didn't* know anything much about hunting and fishing, but I soon learned, and boy, what fun I had learning.

I shot my first deer with Dan. I shot my first turkey with Dan. I shot my first duck, and my first goose with Dan. I caught my first of many kinds of fish. I went to Canada where I just about shared a boat with a huge moose. I went up north and almost was dinner for a bear. I saw Mt. Rushmore. I flew in an airplane and landed on the water. I helped Dan bury and mourn over three of his dogs that got old and left us.

We had so many laughs that I can't begin to remember them all. There were countless times when something I did ended up with Dan in the water, or rolling down a hill, or stuck in the mud. There were so many times when we started out right on track and ended up with a hilarious adventure. I was the cause of some of them, but Dan did his share of foolishness, too. He's just a big kid, really.

He got me back on some of my mischief, too. Like the time at the State Fair when I got hit in the face with a cow pee tail. He thought that was real funny, but then he bought me a new tee shirt. He got me almost every time we went fishing, and I had to buy ice cream because he caught the first fish of the day. Of course, I usually didn't take any money along, just because of that.

We shared a lot of funny, exciting adventures. But we shared a lot of quality time together, too. We sat in the duck blind watching sunsets turn to dusk and then night. We gazed out at a million stars and watched the Northern Lights from a dock on a Canadian lake. We felt the pride and majesty of Mt. Rushmore. We shared countless hours just sitting and watching nature, enjoying everything from the call of a turkey to a chickadee landing on our gun barrel.

Dan taught me a lot about hunting, fishing, and life. But he did it in a way that it wasn't like preaching. It was like learning by example. I learned that hunting is more than killing something – the hunt is much more important than the kill, and is much more memorable. I learned about hunting ethics, and the fact that a fair chase is more important than a full game bag. There were countless times when we could have shot a limit of ducks by just waiting until ten minutes after closing time, but instead of shooting late, we watched them land on the pond in front of the blind with our guns unloaded. There were many times when we could have shot a turkey from its roost as we snuck into the turkey woods. But what honor would there have been in that? How could we be proud of a trophy that we took unethically? The answer was, of course, we *couldn't* be proud of it, and so we didn't do it.

Before I met Dan, I thought that any fish I managed to get to the shore was going home with me. Then I watched as Dan returned a fish back into the water, and smiled as he watched it disappear. He never told me that I should let any fish go, but after watching him release many big, trophy fish, I tried it, and found it to be a real good feeling. Now I keep some smaller ones for eating, and let the big ones go back, to fight another day and to give someone else the thrill of catching them. And, it's a good thing.

A hunting trip or a fishing trip can be memorable without a full limit of ducks or a big stringer of fish. Time spent with a good friend is just as rewarding as a trophy for the wall. The trophy that you save from these quality hunts and fishing trips will be in your memory forever.

Now things will change. Tomorrow my friends and I will move into our apartment and begin our new jobs. Tomorrow evening when I get home, I won't be able to run over to Dan's and see what he's got planned. I'll be too far away, but I'll think about him and I'll wonder what he's up to. I think he'll probably do the same, worrying that I'm okay and wondering if everything is going all right for me. It'll be strange not seeing each other every day, but we'll eventually get used to it.

We'll still see each other on weekends, and I'm sure we'll still have a few fishing and hunting trips together, but it won't be like it used to be. I guess this happens to everyone. Your situation changes, you move on, and life goes ahead. But no matter where I am or what I'm doing in the future, I know we'll still be friends.

When Dan first began writing down these stories many years ago, I thought he was wasting his time. Who would want to read about such simple things that we did? Who would see anything funny or exciting in them? They were just stories about a couple of guys who did things that most people do when they spend time in the outdoors. Well, I guess I was wrong. And I'm glad that I was. We've met a lot of great people and have made a lot of new friends through these stories. I hope you have enjoyed our adventures and have had a smile or a laugh or maybe a tear from them. We had lots of laughs and tears over the years, and we have made memories that will last us a lifetime.

I'm glad I got to know all of you, and I hope each and every one of you finds someone special to share your time with that will bring you such fun and enjoyment as we had. Till we meet again... I'll just say thanks.

Thunderfoot.

ABOUT THE AUTHOR

Dan Bomkamp has made his home in the Wisconsin River valley all his life with the exception of his college years in La Crosse. He has been an avid hunter and fisherman his whole life. For many years he was in the sporting goods industry and began writing in the 80s for outdoor magazines. He is active in the Foreign Exchange Student program having hosted 33 boys from 13 countries over the years. Golden Retrievers have also been a big part of his life. He had at least one Golden sharing his home for 33 years. He lives in Muscoda with his cat, Tigger and his Boston Terrier, Buster.

E-mail: Danbomkamp@live.com
Website: www.Danbomkamp.com

Other books by Dan Bomkamp

The Gosey
Big Edna
Voyageur
Lost Flight
Tag
Whiteout
Spirit
The Lost Treasure of Bogus Bluff
November Gales
Bringing Ethan Home
The Boy Who Fell From the Sky

Non-Fiction
River of Mystery